THE DEVIL'S RIFLE

THE DEVIL'S RIFLE

KEITH MUELLER

ISBN 978-0-9961189-4-1

DEDICATION

I would like to dedicate this book to those fighting to stop human trafficking and child prostitution. And to those who come after—those who work to lead the abused back into the Light.

Acknowledgements

I would first like to thank my wife; though she's now gone from me, she taught me a great deal about 'drive' and self-starting. I also want to thank my English teachers, both in high school and college, who taught me grammar, spelling, and the attention to detail needed to write. Also, I want to thank friends Sherry Folb, Holly Chapman, and Lisa Raymond who have worked very hard to help me with my stories. And finally, I want to thank that inscrutable power which has placed so many people and events in my path to teach me empathy, and expand my awareness of the human condition.

PROLOGUE

*T*he sun hung motionless, close to the horizon in the morning sky. It looked too big, and seemed to have a strange, reddish glow that imparted its color over the land. The air was extremely clear, Curt thought—much clearer than the air in Erieuxta, only a short distance away at the bottom of this mountain. Curt shifted his gaze to the low, rocky plateau upon which this compound had been built—it seemed a forbidding place. Short scrub grass struggled up in places between rocks and boulders. He drew in a deep breath, turning his face once more toward the sky. The chilled morning air rushed into his lungs. Curt felt the cold bite deeply into his chest. He realized the altitude was very high—the air just didn't seem to fill him as he'd expected.

He looked away from the translucent blue dome of the sky. He had to find out where the hell he was! He glanced around nervously, suddenly acutely aware of his exposed position. He was crouching on a reddish tile roof almost twenty feet above the ground. How had he gotten here? Furthermore, where was here?

He looked out from his position and saw the flat roofs of a number of similar dwellings across a narrow, unpaved street. Below him, he studied the structures. They appeared to be made of adobe and they reminded him of the pueblos of the American Southwest. The walls that faced him were a warm, red-orange color, sloping in slightly toward the rooftops. They were windowless. A few rose in tiers to as high as three stories. Only three doors were visible—all were closed and appeared to be a heavy, dark metal inscribed with geometric figures.

Curt's gaze wandered slowly up the narrow roadway that stretched ahead into the compound. No vehicles were visible, but then, these people wouldn't have electric conveyances—though Curt had no idea why he'd know such a thing. A light breeze stirred the dust into small eddies that whirled and danced around the foundations of the dwellings. His eyes followed them until they were swallowed up in a shadow.

The boy raised his eyes and gasped in amazement. In the center of the small town, casting the shadow that had swallowed the swirling dust, was a pyramid. The stepped sides rose into the air at least sixty feet. Farther on, he could see other dwellings, and then a high wall.

Curt had just made the decision to try to get down from the roof and go into the compound when he heard chanting. He listened intently. The words were muffled and unclear. He crept to the slightly raised parapet at edge of the roof, listening intently. He heard a group speak and then a much larger group respond. He guessed they were somewhere inside the large pyramid performing *a religious rite—but it wasn't the religion of Eribus.*

He heard himself say, "How do I know that?"

Suddenly he found himself on the street, unaware of how he'd gotten there. Once again he felt uneasy. He rubbed his hand over the back of his neck and realized he was sweating...his heart was beating too fast. He could hear himself breathing, and was surprised to find he was gasping for air. He felt as though he'd just completed a long run. His head hurt, and his vision was darkening—narrowing into a grey tunnel. He realized he was about to pass out.

The part of him that seemed to be floating just above his body noticed that the chanting had stopped. Distantly, through the encroaching numbness, he felt a vibration in the air and in the ground. He glanced at the sky; it was darkening. He could even see a few stars overhead. "Impossible," he whispered, "The sun's only just risen."

The vibration became a sound—a sound Curt didn't hear, but felt. A bass note that seemed to shake the very ground on which he lay. In the distance, he heard screaming. As the preternatural twilight deepened, he saw a shadow, then two more. In just a moment he would see the people who cast these strange shadows...God! The shadows!

He stared as the first being appeared. It looked vaguely like a man. It had a large chest, but inhumanly long, spindly legs. Its skin was the color of parchment, blood vessels tracing a roadmap across the surface. It waved its hairless, monkey-like arms in the air, turning toward the boy. It emitted a strange, guttural sound that Curt somehow knew were words.

He looked into its eyes—all six of them, and saw desperation, pain, and fear. The feeling of numb terror left him. It was replaced by a sorrow so great that he felt he might die of it. A deep sob wracked his chest. He gasped, but there was no more air to breathe.

Slowly, numbly Curt raised his gaze. A small, triangular-shaped blue light was rising rapidly from the pyramid complex. Then something happened to it, and a word entered Curt's mind—'origami'—but that was absurd. The thing winked out, leaving only a morning sky that was black—a blackness that was as deep as death...

1

Sarah Wells arrived home from school at three forty-five. She had only two blocks to walk after she got off the school bus. It was still hot this early in October, and Sarah was glad she didn't have any farther to go. She hurried up the front walk and let herself into the house. The air conditioning was a welcome relief from the ninety-degree weather outside. Still, she walked into the hall and lowered the setting on the thermostat from eighty, where her dad always insisted it stay, to sixty-five degrees.

Much better, she thought with a satisfied smile as she heard the compressor on the roof begin its rumbling. The fan started immediately, and Sarah stood for several minutes under one of the ducts in the living room. She'd have to be sure to listen for her mom coming home so she could raise it back up before her mother could see where it was set. She sighed; at least it was the weekend. She hoped to make it over to the Old Pueblo Mall tomorrow morning to meet up with some of her friends—if her parents let her, that is!

After cooling off a little bit, she walked to her room, dropping her books on the small desk that stood against the wall near the window. She walked back out into the hall, and down to the bathroom to throw some cold water over her face. Afterward, she blotted her face with the light purple hand towel hanging from the rack. She snorted in derision. Her mother had insisted the color was mauve. She slung the towel back over the bar.

Sarah glanced into the mirror, studying her reflection. As usual, she was somewhat frustrated by what she saw. Her hair was cut in a mild 'punk' style— it was as far as her parents would let her go. She sighed again; parents were always so unreasonable about everything, it seemed. By the time she'd hit the seventh grade, she'd hoped to gain a little control over her life. But her father had put his foot down when she told him she was considering dying her hair. He didn't think bright blue hair would be 'becoming.' "What a stupid word," she mumbled, remembering…

She smiled as she recalled how the table lamp had fallen on her father as he sat down in his easy chair that night. The shade struck his head and knocked his glasses off. When he picked up his glasses amid the shards of the lamp, much to his irritation, he discovered the frame had bent, and when the bulb exploded, well…that was just icing on the cake! She chuckled—it couldn't have worked out better if she'd planned it. One of these days she'd show them. One of these days she'd show all of them.

Wouldn't Mom just go postal if she knew about Richie! Mom would just die if she knew that Richie's my new boyfriend. She laughed again at the thought. It seemed her mother didn't like any of the boys she liked. She laughed at that, thinking of Richie's torn jeans and almost uniformly black tee shirts advertising various heavy metal rock bands.

But she stopped laughing when she thought about what her father would have to say about that, and what he might decide to do. Sarah turned out the light and went back into her room. She turned on her stereo, cranking it up…way up. She liked music louder than her parents did. Bobby liked loud music as well.

Bobby had finally left. He'd just turned sixteen the week before he disappeared. He'd told her of his plans to…evaporate, as he liked to put it, and he had promised he'd write to her just as soon as he was settled in. He confided he was going to live in a hippie commune up north somewhere. He hadn't known exactly where it was, but he'd obviously found it, or he'd have come back home. He'd heard about it from a couple of kids at school. One of them had given him a telephone number. Sarah had been surprised initially; she hadn't known there were still such things as hippies, or communes. She'd expressed her doubt, but Bobby had been adamant, insisting the place really was there. And then he'd grinned at her.

There, he'd explained, nobody owned anything—and there'd be lots of drugs, too! Bobby had said that with a smile. Sarah smoked pot now and then, when she could get away with it, but Bobby had done acid once or twice as well as some other things. In Sarah's opinion, Bobby really knew what he was doing! Sarah ambled into the living room, walking out the front door and down the sidewalk to the street. She opened the mailbox, reaching in to take out the small bundle of envelopes. She sifted through the mail rapidly, hopefully. She was disappointed, once again, to find no letter from her brother. He'd been gone two months now, and she was beginning to worry about him. She went back into the house, tossing the mail on the dining room table, and back to her room.

Sarah heard her mother's car pull into the driveway about thirty minutes later. Well, now the games would begin. She ran to her desk to turn down her stereo, and then out into the hall to turn the thermostat back up to the required setting of eighty. She knew her mother probably wouldn't check it, but why take the chance.

"Hi, Mom," Sarah said as she opened the door for her mother.

"Hi, Sarah. How was school today?"

"It was okay, I guess," Sarah responded as she walked back out to the car with her mother to help her bring in the groceries. Sarah stared into the trunk. Mom bought as though they were still four…

"Some of my friends are going over to the mall tomorrow…is it okay if I go?" She waited for a response.

"If you finish your homework tonight, you can go to the mall tomorrow," Lydia Wells said as she put the milk into the refrigerator. Sarah breathed a sigh of relief. She didn't have any homework…well, not much anyway. She took the paper towels to the linen closet, stashing the rolls on the top shelf. She went back into the kitchen, but almost everything else was put away by then, so she went to her room.

"I'll start my homework now," she called as she closed the door. She sat at her desk, looking at a photograph of Bobby.

"I hope you're having a good time," she whispered.

By the time Bob Wells Sr. drove up at five o'clock, most of Sarah's English homework was done. It was easy enough to do—she was almost finished reading Hemingway's *The Old Man and the Sea*, or TOMATS as Sarah had come to call it. But next week the hard part would start; she'd have to begin an essay on the meaning of the fisherman's long struggle with the fish. She'd just closed the book when she heard her father come in. She could hear her parents muffled voices—there were several short exchanges, and then silence. *Probably hugging.* She waited another minute.

"Hi, Dad," she called as she opened her door.

Bob Wells was already sitting in his easy chair, the lamp table a little farther away from the arm these days. He glanced at Sarah over his newspaper.

"Hi, honey. How was school?" *Same damn question every night—as if he cared.*

"Alright, I guess," she answered noncommittally, "but I'm glad the weekend's here."

"Yeah…me too," he said, and that was all.

Sarah went back to her room, listening. She couldn't hear her mother in the kitchen, and she couldn't smell any food cooking. They were probably going out to dinner. If she was having any luck at all, they'd allow her to stay home. *Well, there's no time like the present to find out.*

Sarah noticed her dad's sports jacket. They were going out, all right. He always wore a damn jacket, even in the summer. Her mother was dressed nicely in a conservative blue pants suit. Sarah knew she didn't want to be seen in public with them. Her dad always insisted she 'dress up' when they went out together…

"Why don't you get dressed, honey? We'll all go out to eat."

Sarah was ready for him. "I've got some homework to do," she pleaded, "Mom said if I got it done tonight I could go to the mall tomorrow."

"That damn mall. Isn't there some better way you can spend your time than hanging around shopping malls like some kind of street freak?"

"Dad," Sarah said with disgust, "why can't I, like, do what I want?"

Lydia intervened—she could see where this conversation was going, and she wanted to head it off right now, before the evening would be ruined.

"Oh, Bob. She's been doing her schoolwork all afternoon. She's reading Earnest Hemingway, you know."

"Yes," Sarah said hopefully. "TOMA…I mean, *The Old Man and the Sea*." She could see that her dad wasn't especially impressed.

"Kids're supposed to do schoolwork," Bob said, scowling. "She's going to have to learn some sense of responsibility before she grows up."

"Bob, she's just fourteen. She has all of high school before her yet," Lydia responded matter-of-factly.

"Just like Bobby?" There was a brief, tense silence. "Oh, alright," Bob finally relented, "you can stay home tonight and do your schoolwork, if you want to—but nobody comes over, okay? No visitors while you're here alone, got it?"

"Okay, Dad," Sarah responded. "Thank you." She was pleased.

Her parents went out the front door, and Sarah watched them through the window as they passed the two ocotillo cactuses and disappeared from sight. Moments later, Sarah saw her mother's Volvo backing down the gravel drive, her father behind the wheel. Sarah didn't even try to speculate as to where they might be going. They were gone and she had the house to herself for three or four hours.

She went to the refrigerator and made herself a sandwich of cold cuts and lettuce. She started back toward the sofa, realized she'd forgotten something, and turned back into the kitchen. She opened the refrigerator and grabbed a can of soda. She didn't even look at the label—she liked them all.

She decided to call Linda before she finished her homework. She lifted the phone from the glass-topped end table and set it on the floor in front of the sofa. She sat down in front of the sofa on the carpet, picked up the receiver, and dialed Linda's number.

"Hello," the masculine voice said. *The ever-present parent.*

"Hello, Mr. Brock, this is Sarah. Is Linda home?"

"Hold on a minute, Sarah, I'll go get her," Mr. Brock replied.

"Hi, Sarah. What's up?" Linda sounded cheerful.

"I thought I'd call to see what time you're going to the mall tomorrow."

"Come over about nine. My mom says she'll drive us."

"Okay, see you at nine." Sarah wasn't looking forward to the bike ride to Linda's house. How she wished she had a boyfriend with a car! Oh well, Tucson's weather was starting to cool off, and it wouldn't be too hot early in the morning. "I was thinking maybe we can, like, sneak into an R-rated picture if we go to one of the early shows," Sarah suggested.

Linda giggled. "Yeah! That would be neat." Linda added that she'd see what was showing.

Sarah and Linda talked for about an hour, then hung up after Linda's dad yelled at her about being on the phone too long. Sarah put the dish in the sink, grabbed another soda from the refrigerator, and went into her bedroom and back to her homework. But first, she turned on the stereo. Loud rock and roll always helped her study.

It was about nine o'clock when she looked up at the clock. *The Old Man and the Sea* was finally done. Sarah had finished her math homework, too. The phone rang once…twice…Sarah jumped to her feet, racing back into the living room. She almost tripped in her eagerness. Maybe it was Richie! Sarah knew she loved him. She snatched the receiver to her ear. "Hi," she said.

"Uh…hi," a strange voice answered. The voice was male, but older than Richie. "Is…uh…Sandy there?"

"Nobody named Sandy here," Sarah said brightly, "I'm Sarah."

"Then I must have the wrong number." The voice sounded like it belonged to a guy who might've been sixteen or seventeen.

"Maybe that's, like, too bad for Sandy," Sarah said in her most grown-up voice. *I might be able to have some fun with this guy.*

"Well, uh, Sarah, you're pretty sure of yourself, aren't you?" The voice sounded friendly.

Sarah asked, "What's your name?"

There was only a second's pause. "I'm Paul."

Sarah demanded, "And who is this…Sandy?" *This is fun!*

"Sandy's my girlfriend." There was a pause. "I was thinking of going over to see her if she's home."

"At nine at night?" Sarah could hardly believe it! Even for sixteen-year-olds, nine was awfully late to start a date.

Paul said, "I don't have to work tomorrow, so I'm not worried."

"What about Sandy's parents? Like, don't they have any say in this?" *This was getting good…*

"Well, Sandy lives in her own apartment," Paul responded. "Whatever we do and when is our business."

Sarah was intrigued now. This was getting even better than she'd originally thought. "Were you going to…stay all night?" She fully expected to be told it was none of her business. Still, it was exciting to think about.

Paul responded casually. "Why not? Some of the most interesting things happen at night, if you're awake to see them."

Sarah paused. *Just what did he mean by that?*

Paul asked, "Don't you ever stay up to see what's going on?"

The girl snorted. "Nothing interesting ever happens around here," Sarah responded with conviction. "It's really boring around here. Believe me when I say that's the total facts of the case."

Paul laughed. "How do you know if you've never looked?"

Sarah was starting to feel a little uncomfortable with this conversation. She said, "Paul, I gotta go finish my homework, and you should call Sandy."

Paul laughed. "Sandy'll be up most of the night anyway."

They said their good-byes, and Sarah was relieved. "Wow," she said softly, "that was really getting weird." She drank another soda and finished her history assignment. It was almost ten o'clock. She figured her parents probably went someplace for a drink before coming home. Wasn't that a laugh? Mr. and Mrs. 'Business-man' could drink as much as they liked, but she and Bobby couldn't smoke pot!

2

Sarah sat there on the floor in the living room, watching an episode of a science fiction series that was called 'Beyond Reality.' She found the show to be moderately interesting. It involved a couple of university parapsychologists who investigate occult and supernatural phenomena. Sarah liked these spooky shows. In this particular episode, called 'Sins of the Father,' a little girl has dreams implicating her father in a murder. The show always intrigued Sarah; sometimes she wished she could just shift into some alternate reality like the characters in the show did from time to time. Yeah, she really liked that idea for sure!

Maybe she could just disappear one day like Bobby had disappeared. Maybe he would finally send her a letter telling her where he was so she could leave too. This particular episode, however, brought back other thoughts she'd had from time to time since her brother had vanished; these were darker thoughts, 'what-if' kinds of thoughts, that sometimes involved her father, and sometimes even her mother. She didn't like thinking these kinds of thoughts because, if true, they meant that she wasn't safe living in this house. *What if?*

As the closing credits for the show began running across the television screen, Sarah found herself thinking about the time Bobby got caught with a joint in the second floor boy's bathroom at school by the school's custodian. The janitor had marched him unceremoniously straight to the principal's office, where he'd had to sit in the outer office enduring the cold, fish-like, alert scrutiny of Mr. Danielson's secretary. Miss Richards was an old bat, Sarah thought, and not for the first time, with her grey hair all bundled tightly up on top of her head, and her glasses halfway down her nose, kept from falling by a silly looking nylon cord. She had a way of looking at someone that could make a person feel like they were invisible.

It was almost fifteen minutes before Mr. Danielson would finally see him. Bobby had confided to Sarah later that night that he'd been really scared then; not of what Mr. Danielson might do, of course, but of what their father would say or do when he found out what had happened. And to make matters even worse, Mr. Danielson had made Bobby open up his locker and surrender the small baggie of pot he'd brought with him to school that day. It was the last of what he had.

If the principal had wanted to, he could've called the cops and had Bobby arrested. He could also have suspended him. Instead, he'd called Mom and Dad. Mom had come down to the school as soon as she'd gotten the call from

Mr. Danielson to pick Bobby up and take him home. It was class change time right then, and Mom had escorted Bobby through the crowds of students milling around the halls on their way to their next classes. It had been so horribly humiliating to be paraded down the hall by his mother like some second-grader, and in front of all those other kids. Bobby said the principal was smiling when Mom came into the office to take him home. After that, she'd done her best to avoid the principal.

And as it turned out, Sarah had correctly guessed, Bobby might've been better off in the hands of the police. Mom and Dad had been furious. Sarah took a long drink from the soda can, hardly tasting it at all, as she recalled her father, red-faced and shaking with anger. Mom had called him at his work before she'd left to pick Bobby up, and he'd actually come home early.

Sarah happened to be home that day, recovering from the flu. She almost wished she'd been at school that afternoon. Sarah knew right away that this was going to be really bad; Dad never left work early. It was like he had something to prove to everyone. He'd stormed through the door, almost slamming it off its hinges behind him. The thunderclap of the door slamming made Sarah, who was in her room, jump in fright.

Sarah recalled opening her door, and coming down the hall toward the living room. Dad was raging, screaming for Bobby to come out of his room before he had to go in after him. From the entrance of the hallway, she saw what was happening. As soon as Bobby was within reach, Dad had grabbed Bobby by the shoulders, and begun shaking him violently.

"You little…! I oughta' beat the hell out of you; that's what you really deserve, you ungrateful wretch! Here your mother and I try to give you a nice home to live in, and good food on the table, but that's not good enough for the great Bobby Wells, is it? No, of course not! You have to do drugs, don't you? I'm not getting paid for the time I had to take off to come home, you little criminal. Did you think about that?"

Sarah saw Bobby flinch back from their father's rage; neither of them had ever seen him like this. But Robert Wells Sr. wasn't finished just yet. He'd paused for a breath, and continued shouting with no lowering of the decibel level. "You're taking food off of our table, clothing off your mother's and sister's backs. You ever think about them? What your actions might mean to them?" Her father was backlit by the afternoon sun shining through the front window, and she could see flecks of spittle flying in tiny, silvered drops from her father's lips.

"You have absolutely no gratitude at all, eh? Nothing's more important than what you want, right? Am I right?" As Robert Wells spoke, his voice continued

to get louder and louder, his face darkening alarmingly. Sarah had lunged forward, grabbing at his arm, afraid of what the clenched fist might do. Bob Wells
shook her off with a violent jerk of his arm, but he finally released his son,
shoving him roughly away from him. "Okay you ungrateful little monster, you
wanna act like a criminal? Do you? Well, we can treat you that way, you know."
He paused, taking a breath, thinking out his next thought. "Yeah, Bobby, we can
treat you just like the criminal you're turning out to be."

Sarah had looked at her mother in fright and desperation. Sarah could see
that Lydia was pale and scared, but Sarah couldn't miss the anger that was also
blazing in her eyes. Lydia finally spoke, her voice low and filled with an icy
quality that Sarah found just as disturbing as her father's red-faced ranting. "I
hope you didn't bring any of that…that poison into this house, young man."

Bob senior glanced at his wife approvingly. He smiled, nodded, and said,
"I've got an idea, Lydia." He returned his attention to his now cowering son. "I
think we'll have to search your room, just to make sure you haven't brought any
of that stuff in here. What do you say to that? You think that's reasonable under
the circumstances? I do, and so, I'm sure, does your mother."

Bobby turned his wild, frightened eyes toward his mother. He said in a
low voice, "I don't have any weed in the house, Ma, and that's the truth. Mr.
Danielson took all that I had, honest!"

"Honest? You dare to use that word? Dope addicts don't know the meaning
of the word 'truth,'" she responded.

Bobby was almost crying now. "I'm not a dope addict, Ma," he pleaded.
"So I smoke a little grass once in a while to relax, so what? You guys drink all
the time to get high. I don't see any difference."

That was when Bob senior whirled with an inarticulate roar, and slapped
his son across the face—hard. The boy staggered back beneath the blow. "You
show a little respect for your mother, you rotten…" But he didn't have time to
finish what he was about to say.

Sarah screamed and ran to Bobby. The blow had caught him off-guard and
he'd lost his balance, stumbling back against the arm of the sofa. He'd been
surprised, but he'd managed to dodge the blow somewhat, and he wasn't really
hurt beyond the red weal growing along the right side of his face.

Robert Wells had then turned his attention to Sarah. He grinned at her, then
turned to Lydia and said, "We better search Sarah's room as well. Who knows?
She might be using the stuff too; gotta make sure."

"That's not fair, Daddy," she shouted. "I didn't do anything."

Bob smiled grimly. "I guess we'll find out, won't we?" And that was the
end of the conversation. Robert Wells had closed the subject by shoving past

Bobby, and walking in long strides down the hallway to Bobby's bedroom. He flung open the door, and stalked in.

Mom and Dad had searched both of their rooms that afternoon. And in Sarah's opinion, they'd not been gentle about it either. Sarah hadn't even been involved, but her parents wouldn't take her word for it; they were just assuming because she was Bobby's sister, that she must have pot in the house. Now, she sat on the living room rug, fists clenched, recalling how her father had pried the lock from her diary when she'd refused to open it for him. He even read some of the entries! That was her private stuff; her innermost thoughts about things, and nobody, not even her father, had the right to do such a thing. There were even laws that protected a person's privacy; she'd read about that in school. But now a slight smile crossed her lips, as the tears of rage and frustration ran down her cheeks. *He didn't find the good ones, thank God,* she recalled. *What if he'd seen all that stuff about Richie?* In the end, the search had been futile—it'd turned up nothing but hostilities.

And a little later that night the fluorescent bulb above the mirror in the bathroom exploded. It wasn't real late yet, and Sarah had been lying on her bed, thinking about the events that had transpired that evening. It just wasn't fair. She'd done nothing to be treated like that by her father.

Then she heard the distinct, hollow 'pop' of the fluorescent tube. Her father let out a startled yelp, and she heard her mother anxiously inquiring what had happened. Sarah grinned in the darkness of her bedroom. It was kind of funny, really, almost like she knew what happened right then, though of course she couldn't have. Some of the flying glass cut her father, but it wasn't serious. Mom had put some antibiotic ointment on the cut under his eye, and then a Band-Aid.

By the time Sarah had crept down the hall to peer into the living room, her father was already back in his easy chair, looking at a magazine. Sarah had gone back to her room, not daring to let either of her parents know she was still awake. But sleep hadn't come easily that night. Sarah kept hearing the light bulb explode, and her dad's shout. She found it oddly satisfying; feeling like he'd deserved it after what had happened earlier.

The search of that evening hadn't turned out to be an isolated incident, as Sarah had initially hoped. The search procedures became a periodic event that was repeated randomly every couple of days. Sometimes they'd just search her room, sometimes just her brother's, and sometimes both. She'd quietly bought another diary, which she kept at home, never locked. Her mother and father frequently perused her entries, which now were nothing more incriminating than stuff about school, and vague comments about other students and teachers. Her old diary she now kept in her locker at school.

It was obvious, though, that neither she nor her brother would have any privacy any more. At random times, both she and her brother found their parents snooping around their rooms. Of course this was after a full two-week grounding for both of them, just another unfair part of their lives. Mom and Dad were sneaky about it, even when they weren't at home. She wondered how many times they'd been in her room when she'd been at school and never even knew about it. Bobby left home for the commune less than a month after 'the searches,' as they'd come to call them, had been instituted.

Sarah sighed, all the anger gone now, only hollow loneliness remained, as she thought about all of this. Her dad had called the police once they'd realized that Bobby was gone, but with no leads of any kind to go on, the search quickly went cold. Though the police had questioned her, Sarah had feigned ignorance as to her brother's plans. She didn't lie to the detective who'd questioned her, she'd rationalized; she really didn't know where her brother was… not exactly, anyway. All he'd said was that he was going to a hippie commune up north somewhere. All she'd heard was a mention of Prescott, and another, even smaller place called Hobbs a little to the north of Prescott. But that didn't mean that's where Bobby was; most likely, it was just a place where someone would pick him up. *Heck, he could be anywhere by now.* Pretty soon she'd leave too, once Bobby contacted her and told her where he was. She'd be gone so fast it'd make her parents' heads swim.

But there was that thought, brought on by the television show she'd watched. *What if Bobby didn't get the chance to leave? What if Dad accidentally beat him to death?* She shook her head, dismissing the thought as it passed through her mind. If her father would have done such a thing, it would've been that night when he was at his most angry. Once the searches had been initiated, Dad had seemed a lot calmer. She guessed it was because he wasn't finding anything to be mad about.

She pushed herself to her feet, slouched into her room, and got ready for bed. When her parents got home, they'd probably watch something stupid on the television like the news or 'The Tonight Show' for the rest of the night. She took a long shower, trying to wash off the dredged up memories. It didn't work. As she dried herself, she glanced at her reflection in the mirror. She thought she was pretty cute. She dried her hair, put on the extra large tee shirt that was now a nightgown, and climbed into bed.

It was about eleven-thirty when her parents finally came home. Sarah heard the murmur of the Volvo's engine as it pulled into the drive—the gravel crunching under the wheels. This was followed immediately by the very faint rumbling of the garage door as it opened. She heard the door slide down again a moment later. In a minute they were inside. There was a slight jangle and clatter as Bob dropped his keys onto the ceramic tile of the kitchen floor, followed by a soft curse.

"Shh…you'll wake Sarah, then you'll be sorry," Lydia whispered. Sarah pushed herself up in bed, listening. She knew they'd been drinking when she heard her mother giggle—that was about the only time she giggled and laughed like that and seemed to have fun. She heard her mother giggle again, but it was short lived. There was a moment's silence. *Kissing,* Sarah surmised. Then she heard her parents' bedroom door close softly, and there was an even deeper silence.

Sarah closed her eyes, but sleep eluded her, and she lay awake in her bed. She was having difficulty falling asleep. She heard a slight sound. *What was that?* She quietly got out of bed and tiptoed down the hall to her parents' room. Her mouth was dry. She was trembling. The door wasn't closed all the way; apparently the latch had stopped it when Dad had pulled it shut. She felt lightheaded and nervous as she leaned to her left, and cautiously peeked into the room.

One table lamp was still turned on, and the faint pink light shone dully on the white-painted walls. She heard more than she saw, but she knew her parents were standing by the bed, close together, alternately drinking and kissing. She could just see her mother from her vantage point. She still had her shoes on; she was really loaded tonight. She put one hand over her mouth to stifle a laugh. She was spying on her parents!

"…*some of the most interesting things happen at night, if you're awake to see them…*"

Sarah caught her breath. *I shouldn't be doing this! How did Paul know?* Sarah had just pulled back from the slightly ajar door, when she heard someone walk to the night table. "Well…I've had enough for tonight," her mother said, in a slurred whisper. Her father mumbled something she couldn't make out, and her mother giggled again. Sarah heard the wine glass 'tink' as it bumped into the bottle as one of them set it on the night table. She crept slowly and silently back to her room where she quietly shut her door, feeling alternately elated that she'd actually spied on her parents, and ashamed for the same action. She was perspiring, and didn't feel hot. Why was that?

She'd deliberately spied on her parents. She felt ashamed—and a little excited, too. She lay in bed, her thoughts in turmoil. *Why did I do that? My own parents, for God's sake! Still, they spy on me, and they spied on Bobby.* Now she was feeling the anger again. *They deserved it.* She closed her eyes, her thoughts and emotions turning in her mind. No one saw the heavy glass ashtray on the living room table spinning crazily…

3

The bell. *Well, that's it for another week.* Curtis Paxton looked at the drawing he'd been working on in art class, his last class of the day. It was competent, he supposed, but it didn't really convey the strangeness of the place or the terrible feeling of watching morning become night. No, he hadn't just watched it; he'd felt it—actually experiencing the sudden lack of air, and the suffocating feeling that had accompanied it. *How can that be,* he wondered, *how can dreams be so…realistic, and yet so peculiar at the same time?* He stood, picked up his drawing pencils and art pad, and put all of it under his arm as he left the room.

He walked a short distance down the hall to his locker and put his art materials inside. He liked art, but he liked weekends better! He grabbed his math book, almost forgetting he had some homework in that subject, and headed for the exit. As he walked, he thought again about his dream. It'd been years since he'd had that dream. In fact, he'd almost convinced himself that he'd never really had it at all; that instead it had been the plot of some science fiction television show he'd seen as a child. The intensity of it was frightening. *What could it mean?*

"Hey, Curt! You wanna work on the car tomorrow?" Tommy Driscoll interrupted Curt's reverie in his usual loud fashion. Tommy was with a guy Curt recognized, but didn't peronally didn't know beyond the weird poems he sometimes contributed to the school paper. He was surprised to see him with Tommy.

"I dunno," he responded, rapidly scrutinizing Tommy's buddy. "When?"

"Tomorrow morning's what we had in mind; the earlier the better. We got a lot of work to do if we're gonna get that beast running. Oh, by the way, Curt, this is Carl Larsen; you guys know each other?" Tommy glanced from one to the other expectantly.

Carl shook his head, smiled at Curt, and said in a quiet voice, "Uh…hey, Curt…what's happening?"

Curt nodded, returning Carl's smile, trying his best to size him up. He replied with a vague, "Not much, I guess."

"Carl's gonna help us work on the car, man. He knows stuff." Curt acknowledged Tommy's eager comment reluctantly, but after all, the car was Tommy's. Curt didn't like or trust some of Tommy's friends. Tommy was a great guy to pal around with, Curt thought, but he had terrible judgment when it came to some of the kids he liked to hang around with. Carl Larsen was probably going to be another one of those kinds of friends.

Curt had recognized Carl, and knew that Carl was the police chief's son, and running with the police seemed distinctly uncool to Curt. If someone so much as lit a joint, everyone might get busted. But that wasn't the only thing about Carl that Curt didn't care for. Because of his interest in art, Curt worked on the school newspaper, and Carl was always submitting weird poems for publishing. The faculty advisor for the paper was a personal friend of the chief, so Carl's poems were always published, no matter how off-center they seemed. Mrs. Blackwell had told him once that really good poetry was written to make the reader think. On occasion, as in dreams, the images might disturb, but that it's always done to make a point. Curt couldn't argue with that; Carl's poems did stand out, that's for sure!

And what business was it of his, anyway? He looked at Tommy, and said, "Yeah, I'll get over just as soon as I can." Then he turned to Carl, and said, "Nice to finally meet you, Carl."

The other boy was still smiling. "Uh…nice to meet you too, Curt. See ya' in the morning." Curt nodded, turned, and walked down the hall.

As he walked toward the journalism classroom, he was once again lost in thought. He tried to remember Carl's last contribution to the paper. Curt couldn't remember the words, but it was a bizarre poem. That one made him think Carl might actually be insane. Fortunately, Curt was an illustrator for the paper, so he was able to avoid any confrontations of an editorial nature. He grinned as he thought of the row that would happen if he actually got to choose what was published in the paper.

When he arrived at the journalism classroom, it was a madhouse. Everyone was busy trying to get the last-minute details finished before the weekend, so the paper could be distributed on Monday. Curt was always impressed by the diligence of the students who worked on this job; they'd still be here an hour after everyone else's weekends had already begun. Curt walked to the front of the room, and put his illustrations for the school Halloween party on Mrs. Blackwell's desk. Halloween illustrations were always the really fun ones, he thought. He picked up his math book again, and turned to go. He paused when he saw Carl's latest contribution lying on the desk next to where he'd laid his drawings. The poem was untitled.

Cold glass image.
The writhing black twists
Of midnight's coiled shadow.
Furnace eye.
Icefire gaze held fast.

Pressed tightly
To shivered sanity.

Curt shivered in spite of himself when he read it. He supposed it was a good one for the Halloween edition. But all of Carl's poems seemed to be Halloween nightmares. What had the last one said? He remembered it'd been quite long. Not able to recall it from memory, he went to the file drawer, picking out last week's edition. He turned to the arts page and read. This poem didn't have a title either; none of them did as he recalled. Then again, some of his drawings and paintings didn't have titles either, and he didn't think that meant there was something wrong with him. He shrugged, and read the poem one more time.

Secrets hidden,
Fears unsolved,
Forever within
The churning vortex of regret
That sucks one within one's self
Until the one is none,
And Charybdis is all.

Then self-deceit and blame to others,
Raise the mighty Scylla
From the rocks of despair,
And reaches out
Till nothing exists
Between the dragon heights,
And the whirlpool depths.

Curt didn't need to read it again. He knew Carl was demented—he had to be to write this stuff, didn't he? Then Curt thought of Gahan Wilson, the cartoon-ist who made a living with his odd cartoons. He'd seen a few examples in his dad's old Playboy magazines from time to time. He smiled ruefully, realizing the subject of Carl's sanity would have to wait, pending further investigation.

He returned the back issue of the paper to its proper place in the file. Mrs. Blackwell, who'd been on the other side of the room helping a student with the sports page layout, was now back at her desk. She smiled at him. "Hello, Curt. Drawings delivered on time again, I see?"

Curt nodded, saying, "I put the illustrations you wanted on your desk, Mrs. Blackwell."

"Yes…I saw them. I'm certain they'll be perfect, Curt. By the way, did you see Carl's latest poem?"

Curt grinned, admitting he had. "Yes, Mrs. Blackwell, I read it. Just as spooky as all his other poems."

Mrs. Blackwell laughed at that. "We'll be running it in a few weeks, and I'd like you to do a drawing to go with it."

"Okay, I'll work on it a little this weekend."

"Don't you want a copy of the poem?"

"Naw, I read it," Curt responded.

"I happen to have a photocopy of it right here, Curt. You might as well take it for reference, don't you think?"

"Alright, Mrs. Blackwell," Curt answered reluctantly, "I'll take it along. I'll show you what I come up with on Monday."

"That will be splendid," she replied. Curt smiled, took the proffered poem, and turned to go. Mrs. Blackwell watched him as he walked out of the room. She stared after him for a moment, even after the door had closed behind him.

Curt walked out into the cool October air. A light breeze was blowing in from the north, and it was feeling a little chilly. He pulled on his old denim jacket, looking up. The sky was clear today, almost dazzling in its clear, cloudless cerulean brilliance. It reminded him of the sky in his dream. *Erieuxta.* He shuddered. The weather was cooling off. *Maybe winter would finally come to Hobbs, Arizona…*

"Hey, see you tomorrow," Tommy shouted from the street, once again interrupting Curt's thoughts. Curt waved to him. Tommy shouted again as he climbed into the school bus. "Make it about eight-thirty or so, okay? We got a lot to do if we want that thing running before the end of the year."

Curt shouted back, "Got it, Tommy. Eight-thirty." He shot his friend a thumbs-up gesture, as the dark interior of the bus swallowed Tommy's next shouted comment. Curt grinned; he didn't think Tommy even knew how to speak in a normal tone of voice. But he had that car, and Curt had found he was anxious and interested in getting the thing running too. Saturday morning was okay, Curt thought. But Saturday night he had a date, and nothing was better than that—not even building a hotrod.

Curt walked slowly to the bicycle racks in front of the school and unchained his bike. The black painted metal pipes of the rack were still warm to the touch from the sun, but not blistering as they'd been only a couple of weeks earlier. He knew that if anyone still wanted any more hundred-degree weather this year, they'd just have to go over to Interstate 17 and head south a couple hours to Phoenix. *Seems like it's always a hundred degrees in Phoenix.*

He wrapped his chain around the metal frame of the bike under the seat, secured it with his lock, jumped on his bike, and pedaled down the street. As the cool breeze clutched at his hair and tugged at his jacket, he thought about his family's move to Hobbs from Phoenix in 1987. It'd been a time of adventure and tragedy. He recalled the excitement of the move. They'd vacationed in Hobbs several summers prior to their move and found they'd liked it up here; the lifestyle was slower, and the weather more accommodating to human survival. Then Kent Paxton had heard about the new Speedy-Serv franchise opening soon in Hobbs. He'd qualified for a managerial position, and it was good-bye Phoenix!

They'd only been in Hobbs six months, just enough time to make a down payment on a house so they could move out of the rental, when the drunk in the big brown Lincoln Continental tried to pass on a curve. The road into Hobbs was a winding, two-lane strip of asphalt that was hemmed in by big trees and rock formations. There was, of course, a posted speed limit of fifty. Most people drove faster than that, but that particular day there was a motorhome traveling on the road, laboriously rumbling down the road from Hobbs toward Prescott.

The Continental pulled out from behind the lumbering motorhome with Minnesota plates, accelerator floored. The driver almost made it; he saw the oncoming VW Microbus, but he must have thought he had the room to get back in his right lane. He didn't. The Highway Patrol said he'd apparently tried to swerve back in, and the driver of the motorhome had slammed on his brakes when he'd seen what was about to happen. None of it did any good. The big Lincoln struck Susan Paxton's old Volkswagen bus head on at an estimated eighty-five miles per hour. A microsecond after the impact, the bus was half its original length, and Susan Paxton was dead.

The only person to blame was the drunk who, it was said, drowned in his own blood with the Lincoln's steering column punched through his throat. It'd been a rough time for Curt and his dad, but they were finally through it now. Business was good at the Speedy-Serv auto repair shop, and getting better all the time. Both Curt and his dad had begun dating.

Curt leaned hard into the turn, the wind whipping his hair as he shot his way from Hennessy onto Avalon Street. The daydreams of Cheryl had just begun when he found himself in front of his house. He wheeled his bike into the garage, leaning it against the east wall and well out of the way. It wasn't even four o'clock yet. His father was still at work, of course; the night manager would not come on duty until six, so he had about two and a half hours to himself.

He walked to his room and tossed his books on the desk. He had some homework, *math*, but it'd keep—he was getting a 'B' so far anyway, and that was good enough for college admission. He had some weekend chores to do, so he decided to start now. He didn't want anything to keep him out of the car tomorrow night. Cheryl was going to the movies with him. He'd been dating Cheryl Hanson for about ten weeks now. Curt remembered telling Tommy Driscoll.

"Cheryl's the girl of my dreams," his friend had said—then added with a leer, "my dirty dreams." But that was just how Tommy talked, and he hadn't said it again after he found out Curt and Cheryl were dating steadily. Occasionally Tommy would ask him how things were going between them, fishing for lurid details. He didn't mind; he liked dating a girl other guys were hot for...but business before pleasure. He went outside again and pulled the mower from the garage.

4

Sarah woke at eight o'clock Saturday morning. As she dressed, she went over the previous night's events in her mind. *Whew...what a wrong number THAT turned out to be!* As she shook her head in disbelief, she pulled on her miniskirt, and tugged the zipper. It wasn't as short as the black leather one she'd wanted to buy, but the colors were bright. She walked back to her closet and stood there a moment, deciding what top to wear. Finally she reached in, and grabbed one at random. It turned out to be a good choice. She put on the white blouse she'd cut short right after she'd bought it, so her bare stomach showed.

She walked into the kitchen, and with hardly a glance at her mother, she opened the cabinet and removed a box of cereal from the shelf. She didn't care what it was this morning; she just wanted to be done and out of the house. She wanted to be away from her mother's eyes. She walked back to the table, cereal box and bowl in hand. She poured the cereal, it turned out to be raisin bran, poured on some milk, and ate her breakfast in silence, avoiding direct eye contact with her mother.

She was relieved that her parents were not paying much attention to her this morning. But Sarah was afraid her mother might see in her eyes, somehow, what she'd done the previous night. She wondered if her mother could somehow tell that she'd spied on them. She found herself blushing, and became angry with herself. *Stop it right now, idiot! You wanna give yourself up?*

Her father was reading the morning paper as always, and that was a relief. His face had not appeared from behind the business section, even when her mother had stood to bring him more coffee. She finished her cereal, and jumped up to leave. For the first time she thought about her short skirt, and the fact her father could see her thighs. Self-consciously she pulled at the hem.

"Bye, Mom. Bye, Dad," she called back over her shoulder as she hurried out the door, and into relative freedom. This was definitely no time for lectures, and she believed implicitly that one would be coming if she dallied too long. She'd learned not to wait for lectures. *Out of sight, out of mind, they say,* she thought with a superior smile. She jumped on her bike, and pedaled away from the house just as fast as she could. She glanced up at the sky—it was brilliant and cloudless. The sun had bleached the blue to whiteness where it burned in the morning sky. She stopped at the light at Pima—there was already a lot of traffic.

Linda lived in one of those houses with a flat gravel roof. Sarah occasionally wondered why the roof didn't turn to mud in the summer rains and just flow away, letting the house flood. She jumped off her bike, and rolled it to the side of the garage, where she leaned it against an oleander bush that grew there. She didn't bother to lock it; nobody around this neighborhood would steal it, even if they saw it half hidden by the big oleander.

She walked around to the side door that led into the kitchen, and knocked. Mrs. Brock opened the door with her usual smile. "Hello, Sarah," Mrs. Brock greeted her as she entered the house, "you look nice today."

Sarah smiled back. Mrs. Brock was an adult, but she wasn't like her parents. She looked at the woman and said, "I'm ready for a hard day of shopping at the mall." Mrs. Brock laughed. *Too bad my parents aren't as cool as Linda's.*

Linda came in from the living room when she heard her mother talking with Sarah and said, "I hope you're ready to go, 'cause we're just on the way out the door." Sarah nodded, and they all walked out to the garage. Linda used the automatic opener that her mother handed her, and the door rose by itself, almost like magic, Sarah thought. When the door stopped moving, they all walked into the cool interior, and climbed into Mrs. Brock's white Aerostar minivan.

The Old Pueblo Mall was a fairly new structure, only three years old, built on Prince Road near Campbell Avenue. It was a nice neighborhood. It'd quickly become the place to hang out. This Saturday morning was no exception. The parking lot was already half full, and the mall had just opened. Mrs. Brock pulled up to the curbing in front of the JC Penney store, and the two girls jumped out, sliding the side door of the minivan shut behind them.

"I'll be back at five, girls," she called after them, "make sure you're here in front at five." The girls waved their understanding, pushed open the wide glass doors that led into the store, and were swallowed up.

It was almost eleven when the girls had tired of shopping for the time being, and had made their way to the theater. Ahead of them, Sarah could see two boys who were leaning against the wall between the Sears store, and the movie theater. One stood with a skateboard under one foot, leaning on it and casually making it roll forward and back…forward and back. As they walked past, Sarah deliberately kicked the skateboard. The boy, not expecting the sudden, sideways movement of the board, almost fell into the trash container beside him as he struggled to maintain his balance. His friend had to grab his shoulder to help him right himself again. They glared after the girls, surprised that a girl would do something like that.

"Oh, I'm sorry," Sarah said, turning to look back at the two boys. She was hoping the innocence and sincerity she was trying to put into the words sounded right. She looked coyly at the boy she'd almost tripped.

"That's okay," the boy smiled shyly. He looked as though he'd like to say more, but Sarah turned her back to him again and was walking away.

She turned toward Linda, and whispered loudly, "He's kinda cute, isn't he?" Linda just stared at her. Sarah continued, speaking in a stage whisper she was certain the boy could hear. "He's got, like, enough zits for the whole city…I wonder who turned his face inside out?" As Sarah laughed, Linda glanced back, and saw the boy blushing, and staring at the floor. She felt sorry for him; acne wasn't his fault, and certainly nothing to make fun of. She glanced over at her friend who was still snickering. Sarah had been getting mean lately. She wanted to say something to Sarah, maybe ask why she was being so mean. But before she could decide what to say, suddenly there was a loud noise. A dozen heads turned along with Linda's and Sarah's.

"Richie!" Sarah laughed delightedly. Nobody on the planet could burp as loud as Richie. In just one small instant, he'd grossed out at least a dozen people! The boy was grinning as he walked over to where the girls were standing near the ticket windows for the theater. Sarah put an arm around Richie's waist, snuggling up against him and touching his long blonde hair with her other hand. There were two boys with Richie. They watched for just a second, and then turned to go without so much as a word. Sarah watched them as they slouched off down the mall in the opposite direction.

Both were about fifteen, she guessed. They dressed much like Richie, in old, faded jeans with holes torn into the knees and almost clean, faded black tee shirts portraying heavy metal rock bands. One wore Nikes with the laces untied and dragging on the floor. She looked back at Richie and smiled. Richie was cool! He'd cut slits in the sides of his shirt—they looked like gills.

Richie pulled Sarah tightly against his hip, and grinned down at her. "Have you heard from Bobby yet?"

"Naw," Sarah responded with a slight wave of her hand. "And the cops don't even know which way he went." That pleased her immensely. She thought, *cops aren't too bright.* "Cops aren't too bright," she said, repeating her thought for Richie's benefit. She knew he agreed with that sentiment.

Richie put his right arm around Sarah, and his left arm around Linda. Linda pulled away, turning to Sarah. "I didn't know you were meeting Richie today."

"I didn't either," she responded, "but as long as we're all here, we might as well go to the movies together."

Richie said, "I like walking with two girls at the same time…it makes me feel like a pimp." He laughed, and Sarah noticed that Linda looked a little shocked by that comment—and a little red in the face. She was actually blushing! *It's so cool how the things he says cause such a reaction in people,* she thought.

She grinned up at Richie. "Show me your Cadillac, Mr. Pimp, and I'll let you take me for a long ride in the country." She laughed, seeing Linda blush once again.

The glass ticket cage confined a bored young man with a wimpy goatee who sold Richie the R-rated tickets he'd asked for without question. Sarah squeezed his waist again. Richie was just so awesome, and she was so lucky to snag him as her boyfriend! The three of them passed into the darkened theater. Richie took the lead, of course, and parked himself in the center of the last row, right under the projection booth windows. Sarah stepped around him, pulling down the seat on his other side.

"Park it," he grinned.

The aisle lights dimmed. The theater had no curtain to raise; nowadays that took too much time. Curtains violated the most basic tenant of modern movie-going entertainment—take as much money as you can, pack them in tightly, and keep them no longer than absolutely necessary. Then spew them out to make room for the next herd. Richie wasn't thinking about aesthetics, however. He leaned back in his seat, putting his arms around both of 'his' girls. He slipped his hand down behind Sarah's back. She leaned forward a little bit, and then back against his shoulder. Sarah felt his hand moving on her side.

Linda watched the movie as it began, trying to ignore what Sarah and Richie were doing. Suddenly she felt Richie's other hand snaking down her back as well. She froze—she hadn't expected this; startled, she sat frozen for a long moment, hoping he'd just stop. Hoping that this was just another one of Richie's crude jokes. She was wrong about that, however. Richie was trying to force his hand around behind her while he was making time with Sarah! She wondered briefly what she should do. If she made him stop, Sarah would know what was happening. That could screw up everyone's relationships. She felt like crying. She hated Richie for this.

But she refused to be a part of this ugly game. Richie made a grab for her just as she stood to leave.

Sarah hissed, "What the hell are you doing?"

Richie whispered back, "I was just trying for a double play, baby." He grinned, but Sarah was far from mollified. Richie seemed oblivious to the situation, and for a while turned his eyes up to the movie screen to watch the film. Though she said nothing more, Sarah was seething.

Since Linda wasn't about to go back into the theater, she waited for Sarah in the lobby. Suddenly she heard a commotion inside the theater, and the sound of shouting and running feet. She was surprised to see Sarah and Richie and the rest of the audience pouring out of the theater no more than twenty minutes after she herself had left.

Sarah laughed. "The projector lamp exploded and started the film on fire. You shoulda' seen the smoke in there!"

"Yeah," Richie agreed, "the guy up there in the booth was swearing almost as good as me." Sarah, her brief, bright anger now past, squeezed his waist.

"And that takes some doing," Sarah added as an afterthought.

"We better get outta here, though," Richie said. "We don't want anyone to ask about our tickets and why we were in that R-rated movie."

Linda made certain she walked next to Sarah the rest of the afternoon. Sarah didn't seem to notice, and Richie said nothing. Linda felt relief when her Timex was closing in on five o'clock. "We gotta go, Sarah," she said, "my mom's gonna be outside any time now."

"Yeah, I know," Sarah responded. Sarah kissed Richie goodbye. Linda saw their tongues touching. She glanced away. Richie was such a pig—a beast. Yet hidden within Linda's inner turmoil of anger and shame was a tingle of excitement when she'd seen them touching and being touched. She noticed now, though, that when they walked from the theater, there was a little distance separating them.

She breathed a sigh of relief when Richie had finally swaggered away toward the game arcade near the food court at the other end of the mall. Sarah, in spite of her anger at Richie's behavior with Linda, giggled proudly when Richie exploded with a belch that must've shaken the plate glass windows of the shops. There was a word for boys like Richie. And Sarah knew what that word was—that word was 'awesome'! Linda wondered briefly if he was going to meet another girl. She shook her head in disgust. What on earth did Sarah see in him? Maybe she'd have to reconsider her friendship with Sarah if this kind of behavior continued. She knew she didn't want to be pulled into the scummy kind of relationships that Richie and Sarah seemed to like.

Later, Sarah didn't linger at Linda's house. She said her goodbyes and hurriedly pedaled home. She was excited. She thought about Richie holding her in the theater, and damn if the projector's arc lamp didn't explode just when they'd had that argument about Linda! *What a coincidence that was,* she thought as she turned her bicycle onto her street; still, it had been exciting in its own way, hadn't it? Sarah stowed her bike in the garage next to her mother's Volvo.

"Hi, honey," Lydia called cheerfully from the kitchen. Mom was cooking dinner—that meant they weren't going out. *Damn!*

"Sarah, would you take out the trash for me?"

"Sure, Mom," she replied.

The sun was low on the western horizon, bleeding an arterial spray into the deepening blue of the sky. Sarah didn't notice; she was thinking about Richie... and her mother and father. *Some of the most interesting things happen at night, if you're awake to see them...*

She let the screen door slam behind her as she re-entered the house. That always got to Dad; too bad he wasn't home.

"By the way, there's some mail for you in the living room, honey," Lydia said in an offhand manner.

Sarah tried to move casually into the living room. She dug through the mail. At the very top was one of those 'Have You Seen Me?' lost child flyers. *Pretty soon Bobby'll be on one of these.* She believed that many of those children simply didn't want to be found. They were free.

She glanced through the rest of the mail quickly. There were food ads, an electric bill, something from an insurance company. *Damn!* The only thing addressed to her was an ad for a mail order music company. She walked into her room and tossed the envelope on the bed. There was a knock on her door.

"Yes, Mother..."

"Sarah, honey? Please don't use the credit card to buy your records. Remember what happened the last time," Lydia admonished. "Your father was furious, if you recall. You can buy them at the store with your allowance money."

"I won't," she answered in a disgusted tone. She recalled her father spanking her...spanking her! That was just too much, way too much. Being spanked at thirteen was demeaning—*abuse*. Lydia shut the door. Sarah turned on her stereo, slipping on earphones. She wanted *loud* rock and roll.

She belly-flopped onto her bed, picking up the envelope. It wasn't sealed right, and fell open in her hand. As Van Halen exploded in her head, she withdrew the advertisement from the envelope. *A couple of new CDs would be a nice change.* She suddenly realized she hadn't bought any new music in almost a month.

A piece of paper fell from the envelope, butterflying down to the bed spread beside her elbow. She noticed immediately that it was hand written. Sarah no longer heard the music. She recognized the handwriting and caught her breath. The note was from Bobby.

5

Saturday morning had turned out to be even cooler than Friday had been. The sky was overcast with a thin veil of pale grey clouds that were almost invisible. The wind carried a chill that promised even cooler days ahead. But Curt wasn't complaining; he loved this kind of weather. He started out from his house about seven-thirty, after scrambling a couple of eggs and frying three strips of bacon. His dad had already left for work; there was some problem that needed sorting out regarding inventory, so this Saturday he'd had to go in, leaving Curt to his own devices. Now, with breakfast done, and both his and his father's dishes carefully washed and placed in the drying rack, he was ready for the day. Almost as an afterthought, he went to the refrigerator, took out a can of Coke, and shoved it into his jacket pocket to drink on the way. He knew it'd take him almost an hour to get to Tommy Driscoll's 'ranch.' These days, in the parlance of Arizona realtors, a 'ranch' was any kind of house, regardless of size, just as long as it sat on at least a half-acre of land.

The Driscoll ranch was located just outside the main part of town, on about three-quarters of an acre. The house was a split-level built in the sixties. Back then, it'd been outside the Hobbs city limits—but now it was just about a mile inside the town.

Hobbs was a small, but growing community, though nowadays most of the new residents were middle- to high-income retirees.

Curt took his time, arriving almost exactly at eight-thirty. Riding a bike on Highway 86 wasn't as dangerous as it might sound, at least along this section of the road. A number of traffic lights and boulevard stop signs had turned it into more of a suburban street rather than a highway. Nevertheless, since the accident that had claimed his mother, Curt always rode carefully, and with constant awareness of the traffic around him.

He turned off the highway onto a crushed gravel path marked only by a metal mailbox perched atop an ornate, rust red antique plow that now served as the box's support post. Riding up the long circular drive, he heard the voices of two boys coming from behind the house. He couldn't quite make out what they were saying as yet, but he recognized one of the voices as that of his friend Tommy—so that meant the conversation HAD to be about one of two things, or perhaps both. The subjects in question would be cars…and girls, not necessarily in that order.

There was a lull in the conversation, and Curt heard the crunch of the gravel under the wheels of his bike. He put some muscle into it, standing up on the pedals to increase his speed. He rounded the corner of the garage, going fast now and leaning hard to the right. He hit the brakes, and skidded sideways to a halt, spraying a cloud of dust and gravel over both Tommy and Carl. Both boys were sitting on the Chevy's back seat, which was currently leaning against a huge cottonwood tree, and they were taken completely by surprise. They both flinched back from the patter of the gravel as it fell around them. Carl jumped up, startled. His cigarette, which had been hanging from the corner of his mouth, spun through the air, leaving a smoking contrail that reminded Curt of the Japanese Zero John Wayne had shot down on television the night before.

Curt grinned at Carl. "You always that clumsy?" Curt tested the police chief's son, watching for his response. Would he take the joke, or would he explode in anger?

"Nah," Carl said with a laugh, dusting himself off as he spoke, "I…uh… was done smoking it anyway." All three laughed. "Besides, I got more right here." He patted his breast pocket, and a little cloud of dust rose up, luminous in the bright sunlight. Tommy looked up from dusting himself off as well, and that was when Curt saw the bruise, an angry yellow and blue smear, spreading over his left cheek, darkening when it reached his eye.

"What happened to your face?"

"Aw, the damn jack handle slipped. Hacked me a good one too. I thought it was going to knock me out for a couple minutes. That was last night after I got home from school."

"You're too clumsy, Tommy," Curt said, being serious now. You bashed your face about two weeks ago, too, as I recall." He eyed his friend, watching his face. Tommy laughed nervously, reached between his feet, and opened the small blue plastic cooler. He pulled out a beer, tossing it to Curt. "Catch," he shouted, allowing the can to arc high up into the air before heading back down toward the other boy.

Curt grabbed at it, almost dropping it. "Geez, Tommy! Now it's gonna explode when I open it."

Tommy laughed, rapidly returning to his seat. "Can't get any on the Chevy's upholstery, or you'll ruin it."

Carl, immediately taking the hint, sat down quickly beside Tommy, with a smug look on his face, recognizing the auto's seat as safe territory, insuring that Curt's beer wouldn't 'accidentally' explode in his direction. "Yeah," Carl taunted, "go explode your beer in the weeds; you're probably good at that anyway, considering how you caught that thing."

Curt laughed. Perhaps Carl wasn't so strange after all. He popped the top of his beer, carefully pointing it away from the other two boys. A liquid white gush of foam burst between his fingers. He leaned the can away from himself as the foam fountained out like a geyser. Even so, his hand was soaked to the wrist, and some of the beer was soaking into the cuff of his shirt. He jockeyed the beer into his right hand, shaking some of the wetness from his left.

"Crap, man…you musta lost over half the can!" Carl snickered. "You need to learn to catch better." Once again they all laughed.

The work on the car progressed smoothly throughout the rest of the morning. The rebuilt 427 V-8 was finally back under the hood, or would've been, had there been a hood. By noon they were finished; all the hoses were properly attached, all the sparkplug wires inserted in their proper firing order. Hopefully, with just a few minor adjustments and a little gas, they'd know if it would run… or not. Tommy stood beside his dream car, wiping his hands on an oily rag. He was satisfied with the morning's work. But, there were priorities, and lunch was number one right at the moment. The gas would have to wait anyway until Tommy's dad got home, so Tommy could steal a little out of his tank.

Tommy's mother had come home from shopping at eleven-thirty, and had already started some hamburgers. The boys smelled the burgers frying as they cleaned their hands under the outside spigot beside the garage.

Curt looked up from scrubbing his nails, and his gaze rested on the 'Stack.' That was what he and everyone else called the lone chimney towering above the scrub trees, a black silhouette against the bright blue sky. It was so big it looked as though it might be right in Tommy's back yard—but in reality, it was almost a mile away.

Curt, impelled by a sudden idea, said, "Hey, guys, after we eat let's go over there and look at the Stack." He gestured toward the thing.

Tommy made a face, and shook his head. "Even little kids don't bother looking at a dumb thing like that. It's just a big tube pointing up into the sky as far as I can make out. Why would you want to waste time looking at an old chimney, Curt?"

Carl added, "Besides, Curt, there's a ten-foot fence around it with barbed wire at the top. My dad says that the city council voted to replace the barbed wire with that razor stuff."

"All the more reason to go now," Curt persisted. "This might be our last chance. Who cares what little kids like or don't like. Aren't you guys interested even a little bit?" He sounded impatient. He turned to Tommy. "Do you know anybody who's seen it up close? I know I don't."

"No," Tommy said, "but a kid was killed there just after World War II—

that's when the fence went up."

Curt was staring at the Stack, almost mesmerized, though he had no idea why. "I just think we should go while we have the chance. It'd be a real kick in the butt to actually stand inside the thing, don't you think? Maybe we can climb the fence. If they think barbed wire is too easy to get over, maybe it is." Curt turned to where Tommy had been standing—he'd disappeared.

A muffled voice drifted out from the garage, and Tommy stepped back into the open. He was carrying large bolt-cutter. He hefted it with a wide grin on his face. "Or maybe we can just cut off the lock. If there's a fence, there's gonna be a gate and lock, right?" He spoke matter-of-factly, as though this were a daily occurrence. Now he stared from one boy to the other.

"Imagine," Curt almost whispered, "actually standing inside the Stack. Standing inside that mystery, standing inside that history. That'd sure impress the guys when you tell them about it, and probably all the girls at school too." The thought of impressing the girls sealed the deal, as Curt had thought it would. The covenant was silently made. Tommy stood the bolt cutter against the back wall of the garage, and the three boys went into the house for lunch.

The wind blew coldly across their hands and faces as the boys shot down Arizona 86 from Tommy's house. Lunch had been rapidly devoured, and the adventure of the Stack had begun.

Carl shouted into the wind. "We'll have to be careful walking around in there…could be a cave-in."

Tommy laughed and shouted back, "It's broad daylight, for chrissake. Just watch where you step, and you'll be all right. Just don't set off an M80 inside or anything; now, that might just make the whole damn thing come crashing down." He leaned into one of the blind turns on 86 with the surety of a boy unfamiliar with words such as 'mortality.'

Still, the boys stayed near the shoulder—they knew about the driving habits of adults. Only one vehicle passed them that chilly afternoon—a beat-up '63 Falcon, its formerly red paint now a dull salmon pink and its engine chattering like an old typewriter. The Falcon traveled slowly, so nobody had to swerve or ditch his bike as sometimes occurred.

Coming out of the blind curve, they headed down a gentle slope. Coasting down the hill, Curt realized that even though the Stack was technically in town, access to it was so limited it might as well have not existed.

"Well, there it is," Carl announced, pointing. "We're almost on it now."

Tommy shifted the big bolt cutter he was holding across the handlebars of his bike. It made steering a bit more difficult. "This is as close as I've been on my bike," he admitted. "I've passed it with my parents when we go to Phoenix." Curt said nothing, but his eyes stayed fixed to the sinister grey cylinder that rose up into the skies above Hobbs.

Not many people thought there was anything to see there anymore, especially after the cleanup and fencing in 1946. That was a week after the tragic death of ten-year-old Larry Haggard. The bulldozers flattened and demolished everything still standing from the old sawmill but the chimney, and that, they hoped, would be the end of it. Big trucks had hauled away the rubble to discourage further explorations. The Stack though, still stood now as it had stood since the late nineteenth century when the sawmill had mysteriously exploded.

Trees had been plentiful back in the nineteenth century, and the mill prospered. Perhaps it had prospered too well, for the logging boom was not to last. Only sixteen years later, the really big trees were nearly gone from the region, and the mill did little work. In fact, only the owner and his wife were there on the day of the explosion. The detonation had been terrific, and had leveled most of the mill's structures. The owner and his wife were, of course, presumed dead. Who could survive such a cataclysm? Their bodies were never recovered, but that wasn't all that surprising really, considering the extent of the damage.

Most of the wood and adobe structures had been blown away from the chimney four hundred yards in all directions. The blast, of undetermined origin, oddly enough, had started no fires directly. It seemed almost miraculous that the chimney had stood up to that fearsome detonation.

A U.S. marshal all the way from Tulsa, Oklahoma, had come to view the destruction and try to find out what had happened, who had died, and who had survived. Authorities speculated that old Zachary Louben must've been storing explosives, though no real evidence for that theory was ever put forward—nor was there any motivation for him to store that much dynamite.

The story circulated for years that old Zachary had deliberately blown his mill for the insurance money, considering it had become a money-losing business. It seemed a logical possibility; the mill had been operating in the red for a number of years before the explosion, and had been steadily laying off workers. But if this story were true, why would Zachary blow himself and his wife up with the mill? A couple of newspaper reporters dug into that story a little deeper and discovered that nobody had ever claimed the insurance payout. Eventually, all of the stories, both logical and not so logical, died down to mere whispers and were ultimately relegated to documents archived in the town's historical society.

Even before the explosion, back when the mill was still in operation, some of the townspeople had occasionally referred to the chimney as 'the Devil's

Rifle,' although no one could say why. Perhaps it was simply because it had looked like a giant, smoking rifle barrel when it had been in operation. Perhaps there was another reason. Either way, the name lingered. Even now, the older inhabitants of Hobbs still referred to the chimney with that odd moniker, the Devil's Rifle.

The Stack stood atop a substantial hill that was densely overgrown with scrub oak and weeds. The boys slowed, surveying the fence for a point of access.

"Let's get off the road," Carl suggested. "You can see the no-trespassing sign."

Tommy was in the lead. He pulled off the road and into the scrub. The bolt-cutter still lay heavily across his handlebars. From here on, they'd have to walk. They hid their bikes carefully in the dense brush so they couldn't be seen from the highway. Curt studied the sign on the fence. The faded red and white paint was marred by several dark starbursts where bullets had struck it long ago.

"Hey! Here's a gate."

6

Tommy's yell broke through Curt's reverie; Tommy had a way of doing that. Several crows rose with raucous protests, black shadows against the brilliant sky. *Tommy's loud mouth even scares the birds,* he thought, and uttered a bark of laughter. Curt looked around for the others, but he couldn't see them; they were somewhere ahead of him, hidden by the brush. He pushed his way through the brush, collecting a couple of small scratches on the backs of his hands in the process. He just missed a cactus that had grown inside a Bird of Paradise bush. He found Tommy and Carl standing close together before the forbidding chain link fence that ran up almost as tall as a house.

Curt stared up at the top of it, seeing the sun glitter on the jagged points of the barbed wire hooks that ran all the way along the top as far as he could see. It didn't look to him like that wire would be all that easy to crawl over. He shook his head, wondering why adults always seemed to be worrying about stuff that probably wasn't ever going to happen.

Curt heard a dull clunk as Tommy tugged on the padlock, hoping that perhaps it was unlocked, and would simply open for him. It didn't. Curt returned his attention to his friends just as Tommy began examining the old lock more carefully, squatting down on his haunches. He rolled the lock in the hasp to better examine it. Curt moved closer, listening to the conversation.

"This is a Master lock," Tommy said, squinting up at his friends. They crowded closer to have a look.

"So what," Carl stated. "We're not here for a lecture on locks, Tommy boy. Cut that thing and let's get this over with."

Curt couldn't help but laugh. "I'm surprised you can even tell what the brand is, considering how long it's been rusting there." The lock was old, and was covered with a patina of ancient, blackened rust with an occasional patch of reddish brown. It had the appearance of having been there since the age of the dinosaurs.

Carl bent over for a closer look, taking hold of the lock, and giving it a hard tug. "The shank's rusted solid into the body of the lock," he commented. "Even if any of us knew how to pick locks, this one's unpickable."

"Do any of us know how to pick locks?"

Carl turned to Curt, and said, "Maybe…"

They turned their attention back to the lock. Curt whistled. "Boy, that has been there a long time."

"It might've been there a long time, but it won't be for much longer," Tommy said with a grin. Tommy hefted the bolt cutter. They all glanced guiltily toward the road at the sound of an approaching truck, ducking down instinctively. They saw only the top third of the large trailer as the eighteen-wheeler roared past them toward town.

"At least nobody can see us," Tommy commented. He stood once more, and returned to the gate. "Now, as I was saying before I was so rudely interrupted…" He lifted the bolt cutter and set the jaws around the shank of the lock. His muscles bulged as he squeezed the long, red, steel handles together. There was a squeal of indignant protest from the lock as the shank burst in two. Curt picked up the lock. They'd have to try to reposition it so it looked like it was still locked, at least upon casual inspection. They shoved the gate open, its rusty hinges squealing, and filed in single file, closing the gate behind them.

They climbed the steep embankment for five minutes. Their path wound back and forth past dense brush and cactus. Finally reaching the crest of the hill, they stood together, surveying their surroundings. There was nothing much to see…only the Stack; but in reality, that was plenty. The three boys stared at it silently. The thing reached an accusing finger into the air, pointing mutely toward something unseen in the blinding, brilliant, hazy blue sky, like the finger of a mute prophet raised to make a long forgotten but important point. The shadow of the chimney, black and hard-edged, stalked across the land, a slowly moving indicator of the passing of time.

Carl nudged Curt, bringing his attention once more to the here and now. In his hand he held a lighted joint. Curt took it from him. Here he'd been worried about Carl and the fact that he was the police chief's son, and now it turned out that he was the one who remembered to bring the dope!

"Thanks, man," Curt said. He took a toke, again looking up, studying the Stack. He passed the joint to Tommy. There was a loud sucking noise.

Carl laughed, and Curt explained that Tommy did everything noisily, and smoking reefer was no exception. Carl looked around nervously now, as Tommy laughed, coughed, and passed the joint back to Carl.

Tommy waved a dismissive hand. "Nobody'll hear or see us here, man," he said with complete confidence. "We may as well be on Mars," he added, and then struck out boldly for the Stack.

As they approached, the size of the thing became even more apparent. It stood well over a hundred feet tall, and was sixteen feet in diameter. The three boys walked slowly around its perimeter. The blocks that made up its outer surface were large and well fitted to one another. For its time, Curt thought, it was an engineering marvel. The shadow side felt cold, but it was that time of year.

Tommy was in the lead, walking slowly, running his fingertips along the surface of the thing. Curt took another hit on the proffered joint. It was short now, scorching his lips. Tommy found the opening. It was on the side facing away from the highway. It was about twice the size of an ordinary door.

The walls of the Stack were three feet thick at the base, and appeared to be made of some dark stone, precisely cut and closely set. The boys were amazed; how had this been built here in 1881? It seemed impossible, especially here and that long ago. How could something like this even be here?

"So," Curt said quietly, staring into the dark interior, "are either of you sorry we came to look at it?"

Carl just shook his head, and Tommy didn't even appear to have heard Curt's question.

Tommy walked cautiously into the cool interior. He whistled softly as he looked up the Stack, his whistle echoing strangely off the blackened interior walls that seemed to form a tunnel leading straight up into the sky, which was now just a bright disk overhead. The others entered behind Tommy, though Carl stayed close to the entrance, watching the other two boys. Awed silence followed.

Tommy shuffled his feet. "This is pretty cool, but it really could collapse," he whispered. "Maybe we'd better go."

"Just be careful, and you'll be alright," Carl said in a whisper. He was still just inside the entrance, though the others didn't really notice.

Curt walked across the sand and ash covered floor and was examining the far side of the chimney, his eyes moving aimlessly over the bricks. Carl watched him in a half-interested fashion. A small clod of dirt fell from somewhere up above, thumping heavily into the sand beside Tommy. He turned around, and with all pretense of bravery forgotten, ran toward the opening he'd just passed through.

In his panicky haste to leave the confines of the Stack, Tommy bumped into Carl. Carl stumbled, and almost fell. He managed to lurch back to his feet, and sprayed sand over Curt, who'd also stumbled and lay now in the dirt. He pushed himself back to his feet, slapping his shirt and jeans in a vain attempt to dust himself off. But once he was back on his feet, he didn't leave with the others. He stood, staring up, seemingly drawn to the curved wall of the stack.

"Come on out," Tommy urged from outside the Stack. But Curt didn't seem to hear him; something else had caught his attention. Curt took a quick step to his left, and brushed away the dust from a brick that jutted from the wall at an odd angle. The brick looked loose. Why would it be loose? He ran his index finger carefully along the brick; its placement didn't have the engineered look of the others, but more like it had been hastily replaced after it had been removed.

"Curt! Come on!" Tommy called, more urgently this time, dancing from foot to foot in excitement. Curt, oblivious to Tommy's urging, was still staring at the oddly placed brick. He dug at the old mortar with his fingertips, carving out a groove around the brick. When he finally had removed enough of it, he grabbed the edges of the brick, and tugged.

Old mortar fell in dusty cascades, and the brick finally came loose in the boy's hand. There was a soft grating sound as the brick slid out of its ancient opening. But it was what glinted faintly in the exposed opening that now attracted Curt's attention. A small pyramid about three inches at its base was nestled inside an opening that had been hidden by the brick. He reached in and grabbed it, dropping the brick to the sandy floor. He stared at the odd pyramid for a second more, and then he ran outside.

The air and the sun felt warm compared to the chill inside the Stack. Curt coughed out some dust, and held out his open hand, showing the others the peculiar crystalline stone, for that's what it now showed itself to be. Incised into the flat surfaces of the strange stone were vaguely geometric designs or glyphs of some sort. They meant nothing to the three boys.

Clouds were moving in quickly, and it would be raining soon. Curt stashed the mysterious crystal inside his shirt. "What could it be, do you suppose?" he wondered aloud. Tommy just looked puzzled.

"Damned if I know," Carl responded. "Why would someone hide that thing way out here, anyway?"

"It must've been here a long time," Curt speculated.

"Maybe it was part of a sign or something else from the mill." Carl didn't sound at all sure.

"Yeah, mutant mind," Curt retorted with a smile, "a sign written in a language nobody can read, and so small, nobody can see it, and then stashed behind a brick inside a chimney—that's not good for business, Carl, even if you're looking for those customers inside a blasted out lumber mill's chimney." Carl shrugged.

Tommy said, "Maybe someone just put it there as some kind of joke or something."

"That doesn't make sense either, Tommy," Curt said with a shake of his head. "What's the point of making some elaborate joke that nobody will ever see? And what fun is it if you're not there when the joke's discovered?"

"Yeah," Tommy replied. "I see what you mean."

"Well, whatever it is, I think we should head for home," Carl offered. "We can figure it out later."

The downhill trek was easier than the uphill, but just as they were approaching the clump of stunted trees where they'd stashed their bikes, Carl stumbled, falling heavily against Curt's right shoulder. Carl almost fell, but managed to regain his footing. Curt wasn't so lucky. With a yelp, he went sprawling face first into the rocky ground, missing an outcrop of black granite by mere inches.

"Goddamn, Carl," Curt said, after catching his breath, and rolling onto his side, "watch where you're going." Curt sat up, brushing the dirt from his hair and shirt. Carl watched him, but as yet had said nothing.

Tommy was snickering quietly. "Have a nice trip?"

Curt laughed in spite of himself. He knew he'd have some bruises by tomorrow, but he wasn't hurt beyond that, and after all, it was pretty funny. "Maybe Carl should take some walking lessons."

Carl looked innocently at Curt. "Maybe, uh…you should take flying lessons." All three laughed at that.

"Or at least landing lessons," Tommy added.

"Oh, I think I'm pretty good at the landing part," Curt said.

Curt was back on his feet by the time the other two had stopped laughing. He reached into his shirt and retrieved the crystal. "This damn thing nearly skewered me," he said. "It's got sharp points." He rubbed his side where the stone pyramid had poked him. *That'll leave a bruise too,* he thought. He looked at the small crystal again, and tucked it back in his shirt—this time on the other side of his body.

Tommy was at the gate, which was now closed once more. He was carefully rubbing the lock and the gate with a rag he'd been carrying in his hip pocket. "There," he said, shoving the rag back into his pocket, "that should take care of any fingerprints we might've left on it." He was quite pleased with himself.

Carl replied, a half-smile crossing fleetingly over his face, "You can't get fingerprints from something that rusty. The surface isn't smooth enough for a clear impression, and the surface is too dusty in any case too."

"Yeah?" Tommy looked at Carl speculatively. "And how would you know something like that…television?"

"No, dummy," Carl responded, "are you forgetting my dad's the police chief? I learn things from him." Tommy could make no reply to that.

Curt said, "Let's make like the Good Shepherd and get the flock outta' here!" The boys laughed once more as they rolled their bikes back to the road. No one saw them re-enter the highway. They sped toward home. Tommy dropped out first. Then Curt cut right on Avalon. "See ya' Monday, maybe," he shouted to Carl as he made his departure. He thought Carl was pretty cool, after all—even if he was a little clumsy. He laughed out loud, and an older man watering his front lawn stared after him.

7

Sarah was feeling dizzy. She lay on her bed a moment, the rock and roll blasting from her headphones like boiling lead now forgotten. She re-read Bobby's letter.

> *Sis,*
>
> *First, tear this up and flush it after you read it. It's really cool up here. If you still want to come, you have to make sure you're not being followed. Ride your bike to the U of A Sunday. Ditch it in a bike rack. It'll be a long time before anyone notices it. Don't chain it. Maybe someone will steal it. Catch a ride to the bus station, and take a bus to Phoenix. Hitch to Cordes Junction. There's a McDonalds just off of Cordes Lakes Road. Use the phone and call the Junction Paradise Motel. Ask for room 34. Someone will come and pick you up. Be careful and be cool.*
>
> *Bobby*

Sarah sat up. She just realized she'd have to call Richie! Surely he'd want to go to this commune with her. She grinned up at the ceiling, as Blue Oyster Cult's oldie 'Don't Fear the Reaper' burned through her ears and into her brain. She sang along, slightly changing the lyric, "….here, but now I'm gone…"

She jumped up suddenly, the earphones falling from her head, the song, only a whisper now, drifted up from Sarah's pillow. "…Romeo and Juliet are together in eternity…" This was going to be a real adventure! She leaped to her feet, ran to the door and flung it open. "Mom, can I use the phone, please?"

"Okay, honey, but only for a few minutes. Your Dad's due home any time."

Sarah grabbed the phone and went back into her room, closing the door behind her. She dropped to the floor, with her back against the door. Her hand was trembling with excitement as she dialed Richie's number. She got it right the second time.

A man answered on the fourth ring. "Hello?"

"Is Richie home, Mr. Owens? I need to ask him about the English assignment," she rapidly improvised.

Richie's dad laughed. He tried to imagine anyone asking his son anything about school—he couldn't. "Richie's not home yet, I think he's still at the mall," Laurence finally replied. "He told me he was meeting someone there to play some games at the arcade." Sarah said nothing. "I'll give him a message, if you'd like. Are you Sophie?" his dad asked helpfully, "Why don't you gimme your telephone number, and I'll have him call you when he gets home. I'm not sure what time that might be, though."

Sophie? Who the hell's Sophie? He must've heard my name wrong, she concluded. She replied, "You got my name wrong, Mr. Owens; it's Sarah."

There was a pause. "Oh…okay…Sarah, um…let me have the number and I'll see he gets the message." Sarah repeated her number twice, to make sure Mr. Owens got that piece of information correct at least, and then she hung up. *Damn,* she thought. *When he calls back, my dad'll probably be home and answer the phone.* She knew he'd be really pissed if he knew about Richie.

It was six when Robert Wells finally pulled into the drive. He slammed on the brake, and shoved the shifter roughly into park. He yanked the key from the ignition, and stepped out into the cool evening air. He slammed the car door, and it made a very satisfying bang. He dropped his keys into his trouser pocket. He stalked to the rear of the car, and cursed to himself when he had to take the keys from his pocket once more to open the trunk.

He shoved the trunk lid up roughly and leaned over, picking up his golf bag and clubs. The garage door was going up; Lydia had seen him come in. *Too damn bad,* he thought sullenly, *she's a day late and a dollar short with that one. I'm damn sure not going to start the car again.* When the door was barely high enough to clear his head, he walked in, tossing his clubs off into the corner by his workbench.

Robert Wells had had a very bad day, and bad days seemed to be coming more and more frequently these days. He swore under his breath, as he met Lydia by the door that led into the house.

Lydia looked worried. "Hi, Bob," she said, trying to keep things light, "how was the game?" But the look on his face gave her the answer. She followed her husband into the kitchen.

Bob sat at the dining room table, shoulders slumped, head lowered. His eyes were closed. All that morning his golf game had been just a little bit off, and the new executive the firm had hired just last week had beaten him—HIM! It was unfathomable! Until today, the Trent Computer Consulting Firm's unofficial golf tourneys had always gone to Bob Wells—oh, occasionally he'd let old man Trent win a couple. You have to keep the boss happy, after all.

This new guy, though, he didn't really belong in the firm at all. He was young and brash and his hair was way too long. *It's not the 1960s anymore, damn it,* Bob raged in his mind, *this guy's giving our company a bad image and a bad name. If the company has problems, I damn sure know where the blame'll fall.*

Old man Trent had hired this…interloper, over Bob's protestations; the old man thought the guy had good ideas, though, and had hired him anyway. For Bob, that was like a slap in the face. Bob didn't think the new guy's winning the tourney was a good idea at all, not one little bit. And then, to add insult to injury, Bob had lost the baseball pool too. His favorite team had lost a key game. Any game Bob bet on was a key game in his mind.

Not only had he lost another two hundred dollars, he'd had to pay that god-damn hippie! Robert Wells knew that here, at least, he was king of his castle.

And so, at the dinner table, as her dad ranted about the game, the new guy, and the new guy's hair, Sarah's heart sank as her mind wandered. *Why is Richie still at the mall?* Probably he'd gone to the arcade to be with his friends—but they'd certainly be looking for girls, and Richie already had a girlfriend…didn't he? *Sophie.* The name flashed briefly through her mind, and she immediately dismissed it as a mistake on the part of Richie's dad. She didn't know anybody named Sophie at school, and Richie had never mentioned the name either.

Dinner didn't inspire her, but she forced herself to eat. *Who knows? It might be a day or so before I'll be able to sit down and eat again.*

After dinner her dad seemed to be in a better mood, but Sarah still volun-teered to do the dishes. It sounded like she was being dutifully helpful, but in reality it would position her close to the phone. Bob and Lydia were in the liv-ing room watching an episode of 'Cops' on television. Sarah was determined to be the first to the phone when it rang. It didn't. Finally, with the dishes washed, dried, and stacked back in the cabinet, she went to her room, frustrated, con-fused, and not just a little angry with Richie. She looked at her reflection in the mirror. Her face stared glumly back at her. *Well, too bad for Richie,* she thought, *he should've called…he had his chance. I guess I'll leave tomorrow and just send him a note like Bobby sent me.* And at that very moment, the phone rang.

Sarah's heart leapt as she jerked open the bedroom door, and ran down the hallway. But she was too late. She could see her dad holding the phone to his ear. *Damn!* She heard his voice, angry and loud. "No, you listen to me young man. Nine is way too late to call Sarah. You got that?" Bob's face was red. He might be losing it at work, but by God, he'd not lose it at home as well!

"My Sarah's only thirteen, you little punk, so if you don't leave her alone, I'll call the police and have you charged with child molesting—and don't think for a minute I can't do that!" His voice was rising. "Don't you ever call here again. You got that? My Sarah's not interested in you; but I am, you got that? This is your one and only warning, young man. One and only!"

Sarah's eyes brimmed with tears. Through her tears she saw the refracted image of her father as he suddenly jerked the phone from his ear, his face turning an alarming shade of purple. He wore a look of utter contempt and disgust. He slammed down the receiver, and now Sarah smiled. Richie must've given her dad one of his trademark 'thunder belches,' as he liked to call them. He was clearly still her boyfriend, despite what he'd done with Linda.

Sophie…

Sarah watched her dad get out of his chair, his television show forgotten. She shut her door quietly.

Her dad didn't even knock; he just walked right in. "Who's this little snot Richie?"

"Why?" She feigned ignorance as to what had happened—she thought it would be safer that way.

"The little bastard's an uncouth pig, that's why!"

Sarah spread her arms, a look of what she hoped was confusion on her face. "Daddy, he's just a kid in one of my classes. Why are you so uptight?"

"Don't you talk to your father that way unless you want trouble, young lady."

Sarah bit back her next remark, and said nothing. Bob's voice was low and menacing. "Why did that boy call here?"

Sarah thought fast. "He wasn't in class Friday; maybe he wanted to ask me what the assignment was for the weekend." She smiled inwardly.

Her dad let out a loud breath, and his facial color was returning to normal. He'd bought her story! He turned without another word and stalked from the room. Sarah shut her door once more. Imagine the nerve! *He just walked right in…what if I'd been…*but she forced the thought to stop there. The rest of it was just too creepy to think about.

Sarah decided she'd have to get away quickly. Everything was going to be all right. She sat on her bed, making her plans. She couldn't carry much on her bike. She'd have to pack carefully. She thought for a moment. She'd need her jacket and her sweater and some underwear for sure. She pulled a brown paper grocery bag from the trashcan in her room, dumping the contents in an open dresser drawer, which she then pushed shut with her foot. She stuffed her clothes into the bag. There might be room for a sandwich, but she'd have to make it in the morning.

After her shower, she lay in bed awake, too excited for sleep to be able to creep up on her. She was thinking about what she might need to take with her. Was she forgetting anything? After she left in the morning, there'd be no coming back. She thought of money. "Damn," she said softly, "I gotta get some cash for tomorrow. I may have to pay a cab or something."

She rose quietly, opening her door a crack. Her parents were already in their bedroom. She padded into the living room on bare feet. The drawer on the end table contained only eighty-five cents. She quickly scooped it up—it was better than nothing. The only other source of money she knew of would be her dad's wallet. She hoped her parents would be asleep by now.

She stealthily approached their door, and listened, ear to the panel. There was no sound. Well, she'd just have to risk it. She knew her dad would've thrown his wallet atop the bureau near the door. If they were asleep, it'd be easy to take. Silently she turned the knob, nudging the door. It swung about eight inches before stopping. She waited. They hadn't heard her.

Sarah stole a quick glance into the room. They were both quite occupied at the moment, silently kissing. She reached into the room, feeling along the top of the bureau with her left hand. *Please let it be there,* she silently begged. Her fingers touched leather. She had it! She wrapped her hand around the wallet, withdrawing quietly. She rifled through the wallet, taking all the cash, and then replaced the wallet back where she'd found it. She felt her anger rise as she counted the bills in her hand. Forty dollars? That was all he had in his wallet? *Why doesn't he carry more cash? And how come I don't get any money even though Daddy makes a bunch?*

She lay on her bed. Her sudden and not quite understood rage had passed, and the plate glass picture window in the living room stopped vibrating. Some caulking had worked itself loose and now lay like small, whitish worms on the carpet. The excitement of the impending adventure returned, stronger now that she was actually prepared. She was glad she was finally on her way. She felt a deep sense of satisfaction. She'd seen her parents at their angry moments, and at the few happy ones—she knew there was nothing more she could learn from them now. She glanced under her desk. She could just see the vague outline of the brown paper bag that held her future.

8

The Ford Escort Curt's dad drove wasn't exactly the greatest car around, but it was new, and it was Saturday night. Curt grinned as he backed out of his driveway. He slid the shifter into drive, and as he began accelerating, he turned up the radio, allowing the rock music from the local FM station to fill the car. They were playing an oldie by Big Brother and the Holding Company. Curt liked the rough sound of Janis Joplin's voice.

He glanced at his watch. He'd told Cheryl he'd pick her up at seven—he'd have plenty of time. They were going to the drive-in movie. Though the rain that had seemed imminent only a short time ago had passed them by, the air held a deeper, damper chill than on previous nights. This'd probably be the last movie of the drive-in season, maybe even forever. The Hobbs Motor Theater was probably the last theater of its kind still showing films in Arizona.

Curt wore his jeans and an old denim shirt under his jacket. One of the reasons he liked the drive-in was that he wasn't expected to dress up. The second reason, at least for Curt, was already waiting by her front door when Curt turned the corner, and drove slowly through the twilight. He turned on his headlights; it was already getting dark thanks, to some extent, to the clouds still hanging in the western sky.

Cheryl was seventeen, closing in on eighteen, and Curt would turn eighteen very soon as well. Sometimes she liked to point out that she was older and therefore wiser than he. She was a grade behind Curt due to a long illness in the second grade. Curt admired her short blonde hair and her tight jeans as she ran lightly to his car as he swung in toward the curb, slowing as he approached her house. She jerked open the Ford's door, not waiting for Curt to get out and open it for her in a more chivalrous display. She was inside the vehicle almost before Curt had managed to bring the auto to a complete stop.

She smiled at Curt. "Let's roll, baby," she purred. "We don't wanna be late for the last movie of the year, do we?" Then she shifted her eyes ahead expectantly, as though there was nothing more to be said on the subject. She seemed very self-assured—and with her looks, Curt could understand why. He gunned the engine, and the Escort roared off…as well as a Ford Escort is capable of roaring.

Cheryl glanced over at him. "So, what did you do today?"

Curt smiled, and said, "Tommy, Carl, 'n me went down to the Stack this afternoon. Tommy brought a bolt cutter, and he cut the lock off the gate. We actually went inside the Stack!"

"Really?" Cheryl sounded intrigued. "Well, tell me what it was like," she said eagerly, "I wanna go too."

"Wait a sec, Cher, that thing almost fell on us today. Some stuff fell on our heads while we were running out."

Cheryl liked excitement, but she didn't have a death wish. *Still,* she thought, *it'd be a great place to make out!* "Take me there sometime," she said aloud. "I'd at least like to see the outside of it close up. It's pretty big, isn't it?"

"That's what all the girls tell me anyway," he said, grinning.

Cheryl playfully struck his shoulder. "I was referring to the Stack, silly boy."

Curt grinned at her. He was glad she was interested in the Stack. Perhaps, if the conversation stayed on that subject, they could avoid the almost inevitable discussion about what would happen next year… "It's big, alright. It looks like it's a hundred feet tall, maybe even taller. Its got a really big door, and all three of us could fit inside at one time."

"Ah, ah," Cheryl admonished with a wag of her finger, "three's a crowd."

Curt turned on his signal, checked his mirrors, and changed lanes. For a second he thought of his dad. Katie Higgins had probably already picked him up. His dad and Katie were using her car tonight so Curt could use the Escort. He wondered where they might be right now. "Oomph!" Curt was taken by surprise; Cheryl had lightly punched his shoulder.

"You're gonna pass the drive-in if you keep daydreaming like that. Something like that could make a girl jealous you know." She looked amused. She was convinced Curt was really thinking about her.

"Okay, okay, I can handle it," Curt responded with mock seriousness. He hit the brakes, sliding into the left turn lane. The light had just turned yellow. He didn't think he could stop in time, so he gripped the wheel, pressed the accelerator, and cut a sharp turn into the dark entrance to the theater, a mere second before the light turned red.

"Whew…that was close," he said.

Cheryl put her hand over his on the gearshift. "Well, we don't want to be late and miss anything, do we?" She giggled.

As the line wound slowly past the hedgerow of thick oleanders that ringed the parking area of the theater toward the ticket booth, Curt told Cheryl about the odd crystal he'd found behind the loose stone in the old chimney earlier that day. She seemed interested, so he told her he'd stashed it in the glove box. She popped the box open, reached in, and withdrew a terrycloth bundle. She could feel the hard, triangular surfaces of the crystal even though it was wrapped in an old towel. As she examined it, he paid for the movie.

The woman in the brightly lit ticket booth was looking at Cheryl through the Ford's windshield. Curt glanced in the direction of her stare, and saw Cheryl leaning forward in the seat, head lowered, staring at the crystal in the wan light of the ticket booth. She was holding it almost reverentially in both hands.

Curt was beginning to become uncomfortable with the scrutiny, and he could hear the engine of the car waiting behind them revving impatiently. "She makes really weird cookies, doesn't she?" The woman in the booth looked startled. Cheryl heard the exchange, and after the woman had given Curt both the ticket and his change, he drove off into the deepening night. From the corner of his vision, Curt saw Cheryl lift the object to her lips, pretending to take a bite of the crystal. Curt laughed.

An old green Mercury Grand Marquis with dark tinted windows pulled up to the ticket booth. The driver rolled down his window about a foot, and reached out with his money. He paid for all three occupants, and then rolled the dark glass back up. All he'd said was, "Three." The woman in the booth watched as the big Merc rumbled slowly into the darkness.

Cheryl and Curt were laughing at a joke she'd heard in school on Friday as he searched for a parking spot. The lot was only half full, and there was no shortage of parking spaces. As Curt pulled into the spot he'd chosen, the high beams of the car a few spaces behind them flashed blindingly in his mirror. Dazzled, Curt squinted into the mirror, trying to see the vehicle. The offending lights were extinguished. Curt was surprised he couldn't see the car in the purple twilight—it seemed to have simply vanished into the night. Curt figured it was probably painted some dark color, like blue…or green.

The film began, filling the huge screen before them with the flashing images of coming attractions.

Cheryl looked puzzled. She was still holding the odd crystal in her lap on the hand towel, staring at it. "What do you think this thing is?"

"I dunno," Curt responded with a shake of his head and a shrug, "it was hidden behind a loose brick inside the Stack."

"Why would someone hide it out there? It looks like it took a lot of work to make. Carving rock can't be easy."

Curt ventured, "It looks like something you might see in a Dungeons and Dragons game—maybe it's magic!"

Cheryl laughed, setting the pyramid on the seat between them. "I think it's from Mars, and the squiggles on it say, "I want to kiss you." She slid closer to Curt, finally putting the crystal back in the glove box. Now only the shifter was between them. Curt glanced into the back seat; it was full of notebooks and papers—stuff belonging to his dad.

Cheryl took Curt's hand, and the ritual began—the ritual that was the third reason Curt liked the drive-in. He'd been dating Cheryl all semester, and except for the bit about next year, it'd been a smooth relationship. The movie faded into the background. The sound, blaring from a low-grade speaker hanging from the rolled down window, went almost unheard. Curt's entire attention was focused on what Cheryl was doing to his right ear with her tongue. He turned, intending to kiss her, but instead, his groin met the floor-mounted shifter. He collapsed into his seat, clutching at his crotch.

Cheryl giggled as she looked on in surprise. "I...um...think I'll go get some popcorn while you get ahold of yourself," she said in mock seriousness.

By this time, Curt had regained some of his composure, and he laughed with her. She snatched his wallet from the dashboard, and opened her door, and stepped out into the darkness. He could hear her laughter drifting back to him on the night air as she walked off toward the snack bar. He took the hand towel that Cheryl had neglected to put around the crystal, and wiped the fog from the windshield, and watched the film; it took him a few minutes to remember what had been going on.

As she moved through the darkness, Cheryl saw the film reflected backwards in the dark, wide windshield of the car two rows behind them. The glass shone in the reflected light, and Cheryl could see no one inside the car. She shivered. It felt spooky to her as she walked past it. There were maybe a dozen people at the snack bar when she got there. When it was her turn, she bought a large tub of popcorn, and two Cokes that looked to Cheryl to be mostly ice.

Against the huge, bright screen in front of her, Cheryl could see only dark silhouettes. As she passed the old car with the Cinemascope windshield, she heard its door softly close. She glanced nervously at the car as she passed. It was dark green and long—something from an earlier time. The windows were so dark the car still appeared to be empty. She shivered.

But by the time she was back with Curt in his Escort, her anxiety had passed. She looked at him with mock concern. "You okay?"

"Yeah, I'm just fine," Curt responded. They sat for a time, eating popcorn and drinking melted ice cubes that tasted vaguely like soda.

"Mrs. Blackwell told me on Friday that she wants me to illustrate one of Carl Larsen's poems."

Cheryl made a face. "His stuff's interesting, I suppose, but I think he's a real mental defective."

Curt laughed. "Well, this next one's as strange as the others," he said. "He writes weird stuff, but I think he's okay in person."

Cheryl wrinkled her nose, and Curt smiled. "Carl's the one who brought the pot when we went to the Stack," he explained. "He doesn't act at all like a police chief's son, I'll tell you that."

"Yeah, well, I've heard some of the girls talking about him, Curt. They don't seem to like him very much."

"Well, actually, this was the first time I met him," Curt offered, "He's really Tommy's friend, I suppose."

Cheryl smiled faintly. "In that case, I won't hold it against you."

"Well then, just what exactly will you hold against me?"

"You'll find out," she responded cryptically…but with promise.

The second feature began. Cheryl took Curt's hand and began systematically kissing his fingers. He gently kissed her willing lips. Their tongues touched, Curt remained watchful of the shifter, and the second feature wound its way backwards across the Cinemascope windshield of the big, green Mercury.

By the time the film ended, the windshield of the little Ford had to be cleared of fog once more. They drove slowly out of the theater, with Cheryl leaning her head against Curt's shoulder. "Maybe we should've tried to use the back seat," she offered in retrospect.

"Yeah, probably, but all my dad's business stuff's back there. It would've been damn near impossible to move all that stuff into the front seat and not get it all screwed up. I want to be able to borrow his car next weekend too."

Cheryl laughed. "That might've been what happened with us if we'd been back there instead of up here."

Curt laughed as well. For some reason he felt relieved. He'd wanted to go all the way with Cheryl, but now he wasn't so sure. There was an awful lot of future in front of both of them, and an accidental child wouldn't make that future any easier for either of them. But, Cheryl hadn't asked him about college even once—so that was something, anyway. The light change caught Curt by surprise. He floored it, hitting the intersection with the yellow. It was a good thing it was still yellow, because as he shot forward he noticed that there was a police car in the other lane. And now, sitting beside the patrol car at the red light, was an old green Mercury Grand Marquis, its engine rumbling beneath its long, green hood.

By the time the light had changed again, the Ford Escort was long gone. The Mercury left the light slowly, allowing the police car to pull out ahead of it. The car cruised down the street slowly, the streetlight's reflections crawling across the dark green paint and the tinted glass. Now, the driver's side window was open, and rock and roll music drifted out, blending with the low, almost animal-like engine sound.

Curt pulled smoothly to the curb in front of Cheryl's house. Cheryl kissed Curt slowly, lovingly. Then her parents turned on the porch light, and the moment had passed. She whispered, "There'll be more chances, lover. Lots more." She smiled at him as she opened her door, again not giving him time to get out and do it for her. Curt watched her as she walked to the door. The curtains covering the picture window of the living room shifted back into place, and the door opened. Cheryl walked in, and her mom shut the door behind them.

Curt didn't sleep well that night. He was surprised; he'd been really tired when he'd finished his shower and climbed between the sheets. He'd figured he'd be out like a light ten seconds after his head hit the pillow, which he was—but he didn't sleep well, despite how tired he was and how quickly he'd drifted off.

Curt opened his eyes. He was sitting in the easy chair in the living room. He had only one light on, a table lamp just to his right. He was reading; study-ing for a physics exam, based on the book he was holding. At first everything seemed normal.

Gradually, Curt became aware of something outside the house. He didn't hear anything, nor see anything—he just knew. He glanced nervously around the room. All of the drapes were pulled tightly shut—all except the one by the bookcase. The edge was caught on the crank, and the night stared blackly into the room. The opening was only an inch wide, but Curt was convinced that who-ever, or whatever, was out there could find that opening and stare into the room.

Suddenly he felt a blind panic—sweat stood out on his brow, and it crawled down his spine like some kind of insect. He lurched to his feet, dropping his physics book. He stumbled toward the bookcase—it seemed a far greater dis-tance than he remembered. He resisted the sudden, mad impulse to just fling the drapes wide. Instead, he jerked it closed with an almost spasmodic motion. He sat down slowly on the floor. The mad dash had chilled him; he was shivering. He exhaled sharply, only now aware that he'd been holding his breath.

The other windows! There were other windows! That thought renewed the panic. He scrambled to his feet and ran to the kitchen, then to the bedrooms, but all the drapes were fully closed. He'd almost sat down again in the chair when another wave of panic struck him. He whimpered; it was more of a stifled scream. He suddenly realized that no matter how tightly the drapes were closed, small gaps were always present somewhere up the center seam—drapes could never really be closed, could they? Perspiration ran down Curt's face dripping from his chin. His shirt was wet; it clung to him like some panicky animal. He was shaking uncontrollably now.

A thought.

There was something that could be shut. It wasn't drapes, it was something else. Doors! Curt ran into the short central hallway and slammed the living room door. Sweat trickled down his back. It felt like some kind of insect was crawling along his spine. Lurching like a drunk, he slammed first the bathroom door, then the two bedroom doors. He sank to his knees. He was crying, shivering.

The panic!

Curt looked up, and through tear-filled eyes he saw the window he'd forgotten. He saw the window he couldn't cover. The skylight. Curt stared into the threatening night and saw the moon and a bright red star.

The skylight.

What if it got up on the roof? It could see in! Could it open windows? Could it take it? Could it take it? What was it he should let it take?

Curt awoke with a start. He felt as though he'd been dropped onto his bed from a great height. He jerked up. He was sweating, even in the chill night air. He took two hitching breaths and began to regain his composure. He glanced at his window. The drapes were wide, and the glimmer of the porch light across the street shone on an empty yard—and an equally empty sidewalk. He exhaled slowly, grinning, now feeling foolish. *Heck. We don't even have a skylight!* Curt thought he could hear an automobile in the distance. He slept fitfully the rest of the night. The dream didn't repeat itself, but his mind kept telling him that somehow, somewhere, he'd left a drape open...or was it a door?

9

Sunday morning. It was time. In her excited state, Sarah had hardly slept a wink; but she didn't care. This was going to be the adventure of a lifetime, and a little lack of sleep wasn't going to dampen her enthusiasm. She rose quietly, and padded down the hall to the bathroom to take a shower. She took a very quick shower, and toweled herself dry. She slipped into her robe, and returned to her bedroom. *Not mine any more,* she thought. She felt both elated and somehow sad at the same time, but sadness and doubt could wait. Now it was time to move.

Sarah shut the door behind her and dressed rapidly, squirming into her jeans and buttoning up her long sleeved blouse. She glanced into the big mirror mounted over her dresser, and picked up her hairbrush and ran it several times through her hair. She bounced the brush in her hand, wondering if she should take it with her. It was small and it didn't weigh much, so she decided the brush would travel with her into the unknown.

She slipped into her faded denim jacket, glancing anxiously around the room. She realized she was leaving a lot of stuff behind. Richie. She quickly ripped his number out of her address book. For just a second, she glanced at the little brown Teddy bear she'd had since she was a child.

That's all done and over with, she thought. *The bear's part of the past; I'm heading off into the future,* she suddenly realized. She folded the paper with Richie's telephone number, and shoved it deeply into the pocket of her blouse under her jacket. She glanced again into the mirror. She looked…completely normal. She grinned. This was the first time in a long time she'd wanted to look the way most people consider 'normal.' But, she was going to be on the road, hitching rides most likely, and thought she'd be more likely to get a ride if she looked like everyone else.

"School's out," she said softly, shoving her textbooks to the far back corner of her desk. Then she stood a moment, motionless. Recalling Bobby's instruction, she finally tore up his note, and walked once more to the bathroom, where she flushed the scraps. On her way back to her bedroom for the very last time, she could hear the quiet conversation of her parents in the dining room. *They don't even have a clue,* she thought, and almost laughed. She stepped into her bedroom, not bothering to shut the door behind her this time. Why should she? This wasn't her room any longer. She stooped, retrieving her bag from its hiding place beneath her desk. She pushed her hairbrush down between the folds of clothing, and stood once more. She rolled the top of the bag tightly—her plans were made, and it was time.

She took a deep breath and stepped out of her bedroom. She walked down the short hallway, into the living room. Through the door into the dining room, she could see her dad where he sat at the dining room table, finishing a cup of coffee. He was obviously going golfing again; he was wearing those stupid golfing clothes. She thought he looked ridiculous in those long, dark blue shorts. But even worse, was the damn hat he always wore. Herringbone plaid he called it, and whatever that meant, it translated into 'ugly' in Sarah's mind. But today was different. Today she'd say nothing, and let him just go his merry, stupid way. *Good,* she thought, *playing golf'll get him out of the house early, and out of my way.* She smiled at him when he looked over at her from the top of the newspaper he'd lowered for a moment.

"Gotta take out the trash," Sarah said casually. He smiled back at her, and the wall of paper once more ascended. It was a wall as hard to scale as any stone wall or battlement of any fairytale castle. Sarah thought that was probably the real reason he read it every morning, so he wouldn't have to talk to her. Secretly she was hoping the 'office hippie' would kick his ass at golf again today. She opened the back screen door, and stepped out into the yard, being careful not to let the door slam shut on its spring hinges. There was nothing to be gained by picking a fight with her father today.

She walked to the far back of the yard where the block wall stood. The wooden gate was closed, but not locked, she noticed. That was important today. She lifted the galvanized steel lid of the can that stood next to the gate, but she put her bag behind it, rather than inside of it. Then she crashed the lid back in place, wanting them to hear their good girl taking out the trash. Sarah was determined to not say anything that might rile her father today.

She thought she'd put on a very good performance. Even if they were watching her, which would be unlikely, they'd never suspect anything. She looked toward the north. There were some wispy clouds hanging over the Catalina Mountains, but the rest of the sky was a beautiful, unmarred, pale blue. She turned and walked back to the house at a leisurely pace—no point in seeming excited at this stage of the game. She was doing everything the right way. Bobby would be so proud of her if he were watching her Academy Award winning performance.

She was suddenly aware that she was smiling. That smile faded when she opened the screen door. She was briefly tempted to let it slam, but then thought better of it once more. What she was about to do would change her life forever. Her dad was gone from her life, she realized suddenly—like her bedroom, like her Teddy bear. All a thing of the past now; none of it belonging in the future she was running toward. She looked at her parents.

Bob Wells was kissing Lydia. "I'll be home about three-thirty," he announced. His wife smiled at him.

"Have a good time, dear—and remember, honey, it's only a game, alright? It's only a game." Lydia knew, though, that it was anything but 'only a game.' It saddened her to see her husband so compulsively bound to win that the game he'd loved for most of his life was now just another job to him.

Bob Wells glanced at Sarah. "See ya, kid."

"See ya, Dad," she said with a smile painted on her face. "I hope you win, Daddy," she said sweetly. "Are you playing that jerk from work again?"

"Oh yeah," her father replied. "Today his butt's gonna be mine. Today he's gonna be the one handing over the hundreds."

"Hundreds?" That got Lydia's attention as well as Sarah's. "You're betting hundreds of dollars?"

But Bob Wells just shrugged. "When you're making a point, it needs to be made in such a way that nobody misses the message you're delivering."

"What's the message, Daddy?"

Bob looked at his daughter for a moment, then at his wife for a much shorter length of time. He lowered his eyes guiltily, seeing the disapproval in Lydia's expression. "I gotta get going, ladies. It wouldn't look very good for me to be late for the rematch, would it?" Sarah nodded eagerly in agreement, but Lydia just stared at him. *Not any problem of mine,* Sarah thought, *this is all the past; it doesn't even exist anymore.*

Bob shut the door behind him, and Sarah said, not realizing she was speaking aloud, "Well, that'll get him out of the picture for a while."

"What, honey?" Her mother had shifted her attention from the closed door to her, and Sarah thought that probably wasn't a good thing.

"I said I got to, like, finish some research for my English paper, Mom." The improvised lie came easily to the young girl. "I'm going to have to go to the library for a bit, is that alright, Mom?"

"What's the assignment, honey, maybe I can help you."

She glanced at her mother. Lydia was looking right at her. "Um, well, we have to go through the fiction section and find a book we think we'd like to read. And then we have to read it, and check up on the things the author says to see if he knew what he was talking about, or if he was just making it all up."

"Sounds…complicated," Lydia said, trying to understand that kind of research assignment set before a fourteen-year-old.

"It's not really," Sarah lied, "my teacher says we only have to check on five facts and write a report on it."

"Well then, that's fine, dear. I guess an assignment is an assignment. Just don't forget your key, okay?"

"I already got it, Mom." Sarah thought about the key. It was in the trash in the kitchen—she'd never need it again.

Lydia turned to her daughter and said, "I'm going shopping this morning. I should be home about one-thirty. You think you'll be home by then? You know your father doesn't like you gallivanting around for hours and hours."

"Mom, c'mon. I'm gonna be at the library doing this stupid assignment. I want to get it done and over with so it'll be part of the past and I won't have to think about it anymore. It's school work, Mom." She stood, hands on hips, looking at her mother.

"Okay," Lydia conceded. "But you absolutely positively have to be home before dark, do I make myself clear?"

"Yes, Mom." Sarah smirked as she turned to go. Her mother didn't even know that the library wouldn't be open at seven-thirty on Sunday morning.

Sarah wheeled her bike from the garage, which was still standing open from when her father had left. As she rode around the block, she felt exhilaration flooding through her—and just a little anxiety. All of this had been so sudden. It was exciting, but it was oddly frightening as well. She turned off the street, and rode up the alley, where she leaned her bike against the wall and opened the back gate silently. She snatched the bag from behind the garbage can, and silently closed the gate, letting the latch fall into place with barely a 'click.' She strapped the bag to the rear fender of her bike with a heavy elastic cord and swung her leg over the seat; she was ready. She stood on the pedals, and as her speed increased, so did her sense of freedom. There was no more fear, no more hesitation. Her family was gone. Her entire life was gone. *Burning bridges,* a half-heard warning briefly surfacing in her mind, *burning bridges...*

As she headed into central Tucson, making for the University, she rode at a leisurely pace. She didn't want to wear herself out early on. The turn arrow at Speedway was green, so Sarah stood, leaning into the turn. She hardly glanced at the storefronts as she rode past. Her reflection rippled across the plate glass like a passing dream. The air moved momentarily to let her pass, and then it closed silently behind her, as though she didn't exist.

Lydia decided to get the trash out of the kitchen before she dressed to go shopping. She was glad that Bob was going to be home before dark...maybe he'd mow the front yard without having to be asked. *Please, God...let him win today.* She lifted the green plastic bag from the pail in the kitchen, gave it a practiced twirl, and wrapped the wire tie around the twisted portion to keep it closed. She walked out into the cool morning air. She followed the back sidewalk to the garbage can. She lifted the lid. Inside she saw two more green plastic bags, just like the one she was holding in her hand, bulging with trash. *Didn't I see Sarah carrying out the brown paper bag from her room this morning? Oh well.* She had to get dressed. She dropped the bag on top of the others and put the lid back on. Inside, in the darkness, a lone key shifted slightly from an orange peel to a greasy paper towel.

At Country Club Road, a police car stopped next to Sarah at the traffic light. She looked steadily ahead, watching from the corner of her eye. The cop hardly noticed her, only glancing for an instant in her direction. He didn't appear to be even remotely interested in what she might be doing. Then the light was green, and the police cruiser was gone, quickly out-pacing her.

Sarah laughed. "I'm gone too." She was glad she was leaving Tucson. She figured that since the police hadn't been able to find Bobby, they wouldn't be able to find her either. She laughed, throwing back her head in glee. Her parents actually still thought Bobby had been kidnapped! The cops proposed a number of theories, early on. One was the theory that he might've run away, but Sarah's mom and dad dismissed that idea immediately. Bob and Lydia knew they had everything to offer him—a nice house, nice cars, and a college fund that already exceeded six grand, and he was only sixteen! No, Bobby hadn't run away, they were convinced.

Two days after his disappearance, Bobby's bike had been discovered in a dumpster in South Tucson. That clinched it for Sarah's parents—and even the police were convinced Bobby's disappearance was foul play. Still, two weeks later they'd turned up nothing more than the bike. There were no clues; it seemed nobody had seen a thing. There'd been no ransom note, and no body had been found either. Lydia cried, and Bob had sworn and looked grim. Sarah thought their mourning was rather short lived, but at least they were finally letting her out of the house by herself again. She recalled the previous month of total confinement, and made a disgusted sound.

She'd thought she'd go insane, being held a virtual prisoner in her own house, for God's sake. If her mother couldn't be there for some reason, Sarah had been driven to and from school by a neighbor, and was never allowed anywhere on her own. After a couple weeks of 'supervised' existence, Sarah thought that if she never saw another adult as long as she lived, it would be far too soon. She realized on some level that her parents really hoped that Bobby would be found alive and well, though she was at a loss to understand why. Bobby had been constantly harassed by their dad about everything—he didn't dress right, talk right, or even study right. She shook her head in disgust. She wondered from time to time if, on some very deep subconscious level, they might know, or at least suspect that some stranger had not kidnapped Bobby but that he'd run away. She grinned. She'd find him, she thought with complete confidence, and then they'd both be gone.

10

Sarah had been pedaling her bike at a rapid pace most of the way from her home to the University. And though it wasn't very hot yet this early in the morning, she was damp with perspiration from the effort. But she chose to ignore her discomfort, opting instead for speed. In fact, though, her speed was probably endangering her more than assisting her at this point in time. There'd been a couple of close calls at intersections when she'd just barely skimmed past the front or rear bumper of an auto making a right or left hand turn. Twice she'd coming very close to dumping the bike. Another time a delivery truck being driven by an equally careless driver had almost sideswiped her.

Each time she'd come close to dying that morning, she promised herself she'd be more careful, but then the urgency would come back, the fear of being caught. Each time that possibility entered her mind, she'd find herself pushing her luck, once again traveling at a dangerous speed, hardly aware of the risks she was taking. When she finally reached Speedway Boulevard, she was forced to slow due to the heavy traffic. She crossed Speedway in a crosswalk, with the green walk sign, just east of the University, and continued on, now using the sidewalk as her bike path.

She had to move even more slowly, due to the pedestrians and other bicycles that shared the sidewalk with her. She inhaled deeply, and instead of feeling impatience, she found herself relaxing, grinning for all the world to see. But she was invisible; nobody she passed paid any attention to the young girl on the bike. She was feeling more exhilaration now than ever, her fearful thoughts of being stopped and taken back home diminishing as she approached her destination. In just a couple more minutes, she'd be on the campus. She'd dump her bike and disappear just as surely as Bobby had.

Sarah slowed even more now, and finally entered the University of Arizona campus off of Speedway. At Mountain Avenue she turned south, and rode toward the center of the campus, staying close to the curb.

Sarah had been on campus a few times in the past with her family. They'd been to the museum and once they'd gone to see a play put on by the drama department. Because of these trips, she somewhat knew her way around. She watched two joggers in yellow sweats run past her. They never even glanced in her direction. She took a moment to feel the bicycle beneath her; feeling the tires as they bumped over the expansion cracks in the sidewalk. It was a comforting and familiar feeling. She regretted having to leave her bike, but she knew it was the only way.

Where she was going, she knew she'd need no bicycle; and even if she happened to, she could probably just borrow one. From her very limited knowledge of the hippies and communes of the 1960s, things heard only second and third hand, any bicycles would probably belong to the group and just be sitting there for anyone to use.

She decided to park her bike near the Student Union building, figuring it would be a very high traffic area. The more people who passed it, she reasoned, the more likely it would be stolen, and that was important, she knew. She dismounted, and rolled her bike along the sidewalk to a series of bicycle racks. She put the front wheel into the slot, but didn't use the chain or lock, which she left rolled conspicuously around the base of the saddle.

She snatched up her paper grocery sack, turned, and walked away briskly without so much as a backward glance. Like her former life, her bicycle was now just a ghost of a very forgettable past. A University police car cruised past her once; that had given her a start, but the car just kept on its slow patrol. In a moment, it turned a corner and was gone from sight. A jogger crossed her path a moment later, practically running her over. She thought it was amusing. *All these people running nowhere...*

Sarah had walked almost all the way back to Speedway before a driver slowed to take a look at the hitchhiking girl. The car pulled to the curb and stopped for her. As it turned out, she got a ride from a student on her way to her job off campus.

"Where you headed?" the young woman behind the wheel asked.

"The bus station," Sarah responded. "My...grandmother is sick in, ah... Pennsylvania, and she wanted to see me before she died."

"Oh," the girl responded. "I'm sorry about your grandmother." After that exchange, their conversation ceased entirely. The girl was lost in her own thoughts and didn't seem interested enough to ask Sarah any more questions. That was fine with Sarah; she realized she'd almost blown it with the lie about her grandmother. She sat silently in the battered Volkswagen bug, looking out the window as the little automobile chattered and grumbled its way down the street, thinking of what she would say once she got to the bus terminal. The best lies, she realized, were well prepared lies.

She stared with only mild interest at the storefronts along Stone Avenue as they drifted in and out of her view. A few blocks from the University, she saw a man in torn and dirty jeans and a torn sweater glance up from foraging in a dumpster in the alley next to a Rexall drug store. He stared blankly as they passed, mouth hanging slightly open in what Sarah took to be a confused expression. A cigarette dangled precariously from his lower lip. In a heartbeat, he was lost behind them.

Sarah turned back to the front, watching as the city where she'd been born faded gradually from her memory as it passed through the smudged windshield of the old Volkswagen. Tucson wasn't real anymore, she thought. Not like it had always seemed, anyway. It was like a 'once upon a time' story; maybe fun while it lasted, but not intended to last forever. She felt like a dreamer beginning to awaken as the last flashes of some odd dream passed through her mind.

When Sarah and the nameless red-haired girl in the primer-gray Volkswagen finally parted company, Sarah had only four blocks to walk to the bus station.

"Be careful," the girl in the car said as Sarah picked up her bag of belongings from the torn rubber mat between her feet.

"I will," Sarah said, and right then she actually meant it. The driver waved one final time, and the Volkswagen pulled from the curb in a cloud of blue smoke and rattling valves. Sarah watched the car until it disappeared from view. She began walking. She laughed softly when she caught herself nervously glancing down each alley she crossed. "No time to chicken out now," she whispered reassuringly to herself, "the only thing that can scare me now is having to go back home. At that unpleasant thought, she picked up her pace, smiling again. She didn't look down the other alleys she passed on her way to the bus terminal. She knew she'd most likely be in Phoenix before anyone even missed her.

Sarah walked into the bus station, and walked to the window. She looked at departure times and destinations. "May I help you," the ticket seller said to her.

"Ah…yes," Sarah responded. "I'd like to buy a ticket to Phoenix, please. The soonest one, if there's a seat left."

The woman consulted her schedule and papers, and looked back up at Sarah and smiled. "You're in luck, young lady. There's a bus leaving in twenty minutes; you have plenty of time."

"Thank you," Sarah said with what she hoped was a sincere smile. "My grandfather's sick, you see, and I'm going up to see him." She handed some cash to the cashier, who counted it briskly, and gave the girl her change.

"The bus is that one over there," the woman said, pointing. Sarah looked in the direction she was pointing and nodded in understanding. She clutched the paper sack to her breast as she headed over with her ticket in hand.

About ten minutes before departure, Sarah was in her seat on the Greyhound, sitting near the back, next to the aisle. Beside her was a man in a three-piece suit. He was about her dad's age. He was studying some papers on top of his leather briefcase, and had made no comment whatsoever when she'd sat down beside him. *Good,* Sarah thought, *just keep doing your paperwork.* Only now, Sarah regretted not bringing her Walkman—some loud rock and roll was clearly in order. Then the doors closed, and the big diesel engine roared to life. Sarah heard the gears clash, and then engage.

She relaxed a little, realizing now that she'd been harboring a vague fear of being found out and taken back to her parents. But now that fear was a thing of the past, something to be forgotten just like the entire, miserable city of Tucson. Finally, they were moving. She watched eagerly as the bus lumbered out of the deep shadow of the station and into the sunshine. It grumbled once more, and began moving ponderously toward the freeway, which Sarah knew was only a short distance away. Then she saw the sign; it read 'Interstate 10 North.' Now she was really on the road!

The desert lay flat and monotonous along both sides of the highway. The brush and grasses were green from the recent rain. In the distance, the mountains rose up, cutting a jagged horizon against the brilliant blue of the sky. Sarah gazed at them for several very long moments. Her mind whispered the question, *Are we even moving?* That was a disturbing thought. The mountains seemed always the same impossible distance away, forever on the horizon.

She dropped her eyes quickly back at the highway. The creosote bushes and palo verde shot past, blending in a vague, olive green smudge. Closer still, the edges of the asphalt flashed by in a bluish-grey blur. Looking at the road she got a better feel for the speed they were traveling—that was much better than staring at the eternal horizon of mountains that made her feel as though she was standing motionless. The man in the suit had not raised his head the entire time from his rows and columns of figures since they'd left the bus station.

Sarah took a few minutes to look around the interior of the bus. It was filled with people; it didn't appear that there was a single vacant seat. Across the aisle, a fat lady with two small children dozed, her head slumped forward on her ample bosom. Sarah wondered idly why any man would want to get close enough to someone who looked like that…close enough to get her pregnant… twice. She snorted at the thought, and the man in the suit glanced over at her inquiringly. When she didn't respond to his gaze, he went back to his work. She was feeling a little drowsy now, with the anxiety of her escape dwindling as the bus rumbled on. The sound of the engine was soothing and steady. Sarah closed her eyes and napped.

When she opened her eyes again, she discovered it was raining. She looked silently out what had been dust-smudged glass when she'd drifted off. Now the rain made muddy runnels down the window. She watched the raindrops, as they slid along the glass, pulled by the wind created by the speed of the bus. The suit in the seat next to her had apparently finished sorting his papers. The briefcase was closed in his lap, and both hands were folded tensely on the lid. He didn't appear to be very happy about the rain, and sat, scowling out the window.

The low, constant roar of the big diesel engine filled the interior of the bus, a constant, thrumming background under the voices of the passengers. The two children across the aisle were fussing now. The boy hit his sister on top of her head with a rolled up paper. She wailed. Fat Momma looked over disinterestedly, searching her voluminous purse, producing two small bags of potato chips. Then she pulled out two more for herself. Sarah watched, fascinated as the children both tore into their bags. The girl, tugging a bit too eagerly at the top of the bag, sent a few chips flying. But she still had enough to fill her mouth, so she didn't complain. It seemed as though the woman had a grocery store inside her purse! The two children were already exhibiting signs of the bulges and rolls their mother had perfected. Sarah shook her head; she knew those two kids would almost certainly be real outcasts by the time they reached junior-high.

Sarah shifted her attention back out the window. Traffic was picking up now, and she felt some of her original exhilaration returning. The mountains she'd thought to be forever before her were now part of her vanished past. Along with the increase in traffic, came intersecting roads. The names were unfamiliar, but she recognized Chandler, the name of the city adjacent to Phoenix. More traffic and more roads meant they were finally getting closer to Phoenix. The trip had taken way too long, but now it was almost over. Fat Momma was saying something to her son in a loud whisper. She belted him across the back of his head with her open hand, and he began wailing. She shook him violently, but he continued to cry.

The bus was slowing now as it found its exit and left the Interstate. The drizzling rain had stopped. She wouldn't have to walk in the rain after all; that had to be a good omen, she figured. The suit was gathering his things together. He checked the contents of his briefcase another time as Sarah wondered where he thought his stuff might've gone. The six-year-old boy across the aisle was only sniffling, and the little girl was staring out the window. Fat Momma was eating a bag of corn chips.

11

The heavy odor of diesel exhaust again filled the bus as it entered the Phoenix Greyhound terminal. She glanced at her Timex watch; it was a little past noon. Sarah heard the air brakes squeal as the bus slid smoothly to a stop, and all at once she was really there! Passengers were pushing themselves to their feet, gathering their things as they did so. The suit beside her closed the lid of his briefcase and snapped the latches.

She rose, and bent to pick up the paper sack that had been between her feet the entire trip. The suit gave the bag a suspicious glance, but she was already moving away from him. In just an instant, the man was far behind her as they all made their way down the narrow aisle to the doors. Sarah followed Fat Momma and her two children down the aisle, and out of the bus, finally walking into the daylight. She looked up, squinting. The rain squall the man in the suit had been so worried about had passed quickly, long before they'd arrived at the terminal. *Adults worry way too much,* Sarah thought, *and most of the time about the wrong things.* She smiled smugly; she knew a lot more than her parents realized, and she wasn't afraid to use that knowledge. The clouds were now high in the sky and seemed almost colorless.

To the west was a long row of featureless red brick structures. They looked old, and were covered with soot and graffiti. Sarah stared at the closest message. 'Beware. The night is coming for you.' Sarah shivered, and for a brief second, thought the message a personal warning. But she quickly cast that thought aside.

Sarah turned north, and started to walk. She guessed that the freeway was about a mile away. She hefted her paper sack, and felt a slight give in the paper. She could walk if she had to. She pulled off her jacket and wrapped the bag securely up inside of it. She tied the sleeves together, and started walking, carrying the coat like a large purse.

She'd just started walking up First Street with her thumb out when an old, off-white El Camino pulled to the curb just ahead of her. Sarah approached the vehicle carefully. She bent at the waist, and looked inside, staying about a foot from the window. Sarah glanced through the dark tinted window. She could barely see through the glass. The man inside reached over and cranked the passenger side window down almost all the way into the door. He looked to be about forty, and was wearing a denim work shirt with the sleeves rolled up above his elbows. He was deeply tanned, and she figured he worked outside.

The driver of the El Camino gave the girl as careful a look as she'd given him. Apparently satisfied, he asked, "Where you headed, girl?" Sarah saw him glance at her bundled up jacket for a second, but then he looked back up at her face.

"I gotta get to the freeway. Can I get a lift?"

"Sure. Hop in." He leaned over once again, and popped the latch on the passenger side door. She climbed in and he put the transmission in gear as he glanced in the mirror and pulled out onto the roadway.

"Best put your seatbelt on, miss," the man said. "Traffic can be mighty iffy right here in the downtown area." He glanced over to make sure the girl had complied. Satisfied, he continued, "My name's Mike. What's yours?"

"Name's Mary," Sarah lied. "I'm going to Flagstaff to see my brother." She smiled at him, and he seemed to want more information. *Adults!* "My brother's a ski instructor at a resort a little north of Flag," she improvised.

"The Snowbowl?" Sarah nodded quickly, not really knowing the name.

Mike rubbed his chin thoughtfully. "Snowbowl doesn't open until November or so. There's no snow there this time of year."

Sarah was almost on the edge of panic. Why did adults always have to be so snoopy? She thought about asking the man to just stop and let her out, but that would be even more suspicious. Instead she said, "Oh, we're not going to ski." She laughed as though Mike's comment had been a joke. "He's going to teach me the basics and all that before it actually snows." Sarah shifted her eyes toward Mike, but he was looking ahead through the windshield. Mike nodded, and grunted, and for the time, at least, there was silence inside the old truck.

They were sitting at a red light, watching the crossing traffic, waiting for the light to change. Mike glanced over at Sarah once more. "I think it's supposed to be raining up north," the man said helpfully. "Got a raincoat in there?"

"No, no raincoat, but I'm sure I'll get a ride. My brother knows I'm coming in this evening, and he'll be waiting for me at…a McDonalds." Sarah was glad now that she hadn't done anything as stupid as telling this stranger her real name. He was getting way too snoopy for her. She turned her attention to the windshield, watching the city pass as they headed west on Van Buren to Seventh Avenue, then north once more. Billboards crowded the sky with offers of new cars at great rates, hotels everyone wanted to stay in, and restaurants that served the best food in town.

A jetliner roared overhead on its final approach to Sky Harbor Airport to the east. The noise startled Sarah, and Mike laughed, pulling finally to the curb. "Well, Mary, this is where you want to get off. Just ahead is I-10, a bit further west, it splits and continues to Los Angeles, or turns north on I-17. Make sure that whoever gives you a ride is goin' north. Good luck, Mary…and be careful, alright?" She nodded, and Mike waved as she shut the door. Mike rolled the window back up, and shoved the El Camino into gear, pulling away from the curb, leaving Sarah standing by herself once more.

Sarah glanced at her watch. It was already eleven-fifteen. It would be hours yet before anyone would start to wonder where she was. Sarah figured that at least another three hours would pass before her father came home. She hoped he'd gotten beaten at golf again. With any luck at all, they'd not even be slightly concerned until it got to be around five o'clock and called the library. She laughed, knowing the library close to their home wasn't even open on Sunday. She felt incredibly clever, almost like a spy in a movie. A piece of corrugated cardboard blew past, and on impulse, she grabbed it. She'd make a sign! She fumbled a moment in her bag, and found the felt-tip marking pen she'd brought along, not knowing why at the time. She carefully wrote the big, black letters. FLAG.

She looked up the entrance ramp. Above her she could see cars and trucks as they shot down the asphalt in both directions. She hefted her jacket once more, making sure her bag was securely held, and trudged up the entrance ramp. She knew she'd probably have to wait for a ride. She also knew that if she walked on the Interstate proper, the cops would stop her, and she didn't need that hassle right now. As she reached the top, she saw a steady stream of traffic, feeling the artificial wind they made as they shot by, only a few yards ahead of her. If she got lucky, she'd get a ride right away.

The red Ford Taurus pulled back onto the access road. Sarah found herself sharing the rather well worn back seat with a couple of equally well used suitcases. She watched the two girls in the front seat carefully. After the interrogation she'd received from Mike, she decided she needed to be more on guard.

The driver glanced into her rearview mirror and looked at Sarah. "I'm Toni," she said, amiably enough, "and this is Carla." Carla put her hand in the air in a 'hello' gesture. Toni continued, "So, what's your name, and where are you headed today?"

"My name's Ann," Sarah lied again. She'd decided to use a different name than she'd used with Mike—just like a real spy would. "I'm, like, goin' to Cordes Junction."

Toni looked surprised, glancing nervously at her companion. "Cordes Junction? Really?" She shot a quick look into the mirror again.

Carla said, "That's a fair distance from here, Ann. Are you running away?"

Sarah was startled. It was like this stranger was reading her mind. "No," she answered casually, "my brother lives in Prescott and I'm going up to see him." The two girls in the front seat looked at each other. Sarah felt they didn't believe her, but the Taurus continued along at an even sixty miles an hour, so apparently they weren't going to dump her.

Interstate 17 wound its way north. Sarah listened intently to what the two older girls were saying to each other. She learned from the girls' conversation that they were students at NAU, and they were heading back to Flagstaff after a long weekend in Phoenix with friends. They talked on and on about the parties and the boys. Sarah was pleased. She'd be in Cordes Junction in about ninety minutes, and the girls would vanish to the north and be far from any search or questioning should anyone come looking for her. It was almost twelve forty-five by this time. *Still lots of time to disappear,* Sarah thought as she slouched down in the back seat, trying to make herself invisible from passing autos like a spy might do.

Toni was an aggressive driver, swerving recklessly around slower vehicles as though she owned the road. Sarah noticed with some relief that the two girls had all but forgotten her in their animated discussions about teachers, classes, and boyfriends. Judging by the conversation, Sarah thought that Toni really liked to party. Carla seemed a little on the shy side, and didn't like discussing her boyfriend's romantic side with Toni. Toni didn't seem to notice, and the miles drifted past under the wheels of the red Taurus. Sarah thought about Bobby, and wondered what the commune might be like. She hoped they had good food; she knew she'd be really hungry by the time she got all the way there…wherever 'there' actually was. She also thought of Richie. She was certain that Bobby and Richie would be good friends, since they seemed to like the same video games and films. She'd definitely have to call him as soon as she was settled.

The desert gave way to green shrubs and tall grasses. They were climbing now, heading into the mountains. Toni stayed in the fast lane almost the whole way, swerving into the right lane only when it expedited her passing a slower car in the left lane. She wasn't about to get behind some truck lumbering along at thirty up these steep hills. At one forty-five that afternoon, Toni finally slowed her manic pace and pulled off the highway. She drove to the McDonalds east of the freeway as Sarah directed. "Well, this is it," she announced to Sarah. "Where's your ride?"

"I've gotta call," Sarah responded. "Got the number right here," she said, flashing the bit of paper she'd scrawled it on. Thanks for the ride." Sarah opened the back door and, maneuvering her bundle past the girls' suitcases, stepped out into the cool breeze. She shivered, though the sun was warm. She wished she was wearing the jacket. But the breeze subsided, and the warmth of the sun was a welcome change.

The girls waved goodbye, and headed back toward the Interstate. Sarah went to the outside payphone. She looked around, but there was nobody nearby. She opened the yellow pages, scanning the motel listings. She found what she was looking for. She withdrew some change from her purse, counted it out carefully on the metal shelf below the telephone, and then pushed the coins into the appropriate slots, and dialed the number of the Junction Paradise Hotel.

"Junction Paradise Hotel," a businesslike and very bored voice said.

Sarah smiled. *Some paradise.* "Hi. I was wondering if you could ring a number for me?"

The man sighed loudly. "What's the room number, miss?"

"Please connect me with room thirty-four."

"Just a moment." Sarah heard the phone ringing.

"Uh...hello?" The voice of room 34. Sarah guessed the voice belonged to a boy maybe three or four years older than her.

"Hi," she said brightly. "This is Sarah. You know...from Tucson? I was, like, told to call you?" She spoke carefully, not wanting to make any mistakes now.

"Well, Sarah," the voice of room 34 said, "I'm really glad you made it. Your brother's been real anxious to see you again. Was gettin' away hard?"

"No big deal. I just walked out."

"Did you follow the instructions? And I mean all of them?" The voice was suspicious now, testing.

"Yep," Sarah answered confidently. "My parents don't even know I'm gone yet. My dad's probably still losing at his golf game, and my mom thinks I'm at the library." She laughed. "They can't possibly even be wondering yet."

"Very good, Sarah, very good." The voice was friendlier now. "You wait right there near the phone, alright? I'm only gonna drive by once. If you've gone inside for a hamburger or something, I'll just leave you there. Sorry to be so...uh...harsh, but we have security issues. Stay right there. I'll be down in just a couple of minutes. I'm close by. Boy, is Bobby gonna be glad to see you." There was a click, and Sarah was holding a silent phone. She hung up, glancing around the parking lot. A large motor home had just pulled in. The occupants were much older, and very preoccupied. They never even glanced at the young girl standing by the phone. Sarah unwrapped her grocery bag, and put on her jacket. She carefully picked up her bag—suddenly it seemed very small. She sighed, tucking it carefully under her left arm. *This is all I own now.*

It was exciting thinking about Bobby and Richie, but she felt a little sad, though she couldn't have said why. Then she heard the muffled throbbing of an auto's engine. She turned around, and saw that the car was slowing. Her eyes ran down its shining dark green length. The windows were dark as well, affording her no view of the interior. The driver's window rolled down, and behind the wheel Sarah saw a boy of about seventeen. He had light brown hair and clear blue eyes. He put his elbow on the edge of the door, and leaning out, he smiled. "Uh…are you Sarah?"

"Yes… yes! Thanks for coming." The boy smiled broadly at her. He leaned over and opened the passenger door. She ran around the wide hood, and practically leaped into the seat. She sat back, looking appraisingly at her escort. He was wearing jeans and a grey sweatshirt. He smiled again.

"Hi. I'm Moondog."

Sarah stared at him and giggled. Moondog laughed too as the big Mercury swung around the parking lot and floated up the entry ramp to Interstate 17.

"We all pick new names for ourselves," Moondog explained. "Makes it harder for the cops to identify you without your name."

Sarah was delighted. This was a good idea, and fun too! "I'll need a new name too, won't I?"

Moondog laughed again. "Let's get you moved in first, okay?"

Sarah nodded. "Do you, like, get hassled by the cops a lot? I mean, I read that cops don't like communes very much." It was warm enough to roll down the windows. Sarah was about to reach for the window crank, but Moondog seemed to guess her thoughts. "Uh…we need to keep your arrival a secret until you've settled in. Best keep the windows up for now, alright?"

Once more, Sarah agreed. The car moved smoothly along the asphalt.

12

"Did you tell anyone you were coming?"

Sarah smiled at Moondog. "No. I wanted to invite my boyfriend along but my dad wouldn't let me talk to him. My father doesn't like any of my boyfriends. I don't know what he's so afraid of; a lot of the girls in my class have boyfriends."

Moondog glanced sharply at Sarah. The Mercury slowed. "Did you tell him you were running away?"

"Well…I told him a while ago that Bobby'd run away and that he'd let me know where he went."

Moondog was quiet for a moment, then recommenced his interrogation. "Uh…does he know where you are now? You didn't share the message we sent you, did you? This is really important, Sarah."

"No," the girl responded, a little frightened now, "he only knows Bobby went up north somewhere to live in a commune, and that I wanted to join him as soon as he let me know where he was."

"Do you think he'll tell anyone what you told him?" The big automobile slowed even more, and Sarah thought that Moondog might just dump her right there on the road. "I mean besides your boyfriend…did you speak to any of your girlfriends about this? I know how girls can talk."

"Ha!" she said defensively, "The biggest blabbermouths I know are boys, always talking about girls and football and stuff like that." But Sarah knew that wasn't what he wanted to hear, so she answered his question. "Nope," she answered with a firm shake of her head, "Richie's cool, Moondog; really cool, like Bobby. He won't talk to anyone, especially my dad or the cops. Besides, the last time we talked about it, which was a couple of weeks ago now, we were wondering if the commune might be up in Canada or something. Neither of us thought it would be this close."

Moondog smiled. "What's Richie's last name?"

"Owens. Why?"

Moondog could tell Sarah was getting antsy, starting to rebel against the questioning. He smiled at her, and gently pushed the accelerator. The Mercury was once again picking up speed. Moondog continued in a calm and neutral voice. "Well, once you're…uh, settled in you can contact him." He added with a friendly smile, "We can get him up here the same way we got you…secretly. I'm sorry about all the questions, Sarah, but we need to be safe; you know how it is. If the cops find our place, they would arrest all of us, saying we kidnapped you. And once you see the place, you'll see that it's not a prison." He laughed disarmingly. Sarah relaxed a little.

Moondog turned on the stereo. Loud rock and roll blared from the surrounding speakers in true stereo. Moondog glanced at Sarah, the pride evident on his face. He grinned, turning up the volume a little more. He had to shout to be heard above the music. "The Mercury's sound system had been vastly improved from the standard car radio," he shouted, "I actually did most of the work on this car myself."

Sarah approved, shouting back, "I love this song!"

The Mercury shot down the blacktop, traveling at a steady seventy miles per hour. Sarah saw a sign flash past her window that said that Junction 86 was ten miles ahead. The sign meant nothing to Sarah, who'd never been here before. She was content for the time being, watching the landscape flash past the window. The terrain was becoming hilly and there were a lot more scrub oak and other small trees.

Sarah gradually became aware of a low, sour smell. She supposed it had been there all along, but she hadn't noticed it until now. She wondered what it was; it really stank. She sniffed twice, and wrinkled her nose. Moondog noticed her reaction and turned down the stereo.

"What's the icky smell?" Sarah turned in her seat to face Moondog.

Moondog laughed easily, explaining, "Some of us were partying in here last night," he explained. "We drank quite a lot of wine. I'm sorry for the smell. I'm…uh, afraid I kicked an open bottle under the seat, and we didn't get it all mopped up, I guess. Kinda' rank, huh?"

Sarah smiled back at him. She was beginning to like Moondog, despite only knowing him this very short time. She felt she could trust him. She wasn't upset anymore, for after Moondog's apology, she realized his questions were important if the commune was to continue being a safe place.

Moondog reached between his legs, and picked up a small, yellow, plastic box. "Here," he said, offering her the box, "uh…this'll help make up for the smell; besides we're almost there."

Sarah pulled off the plastic lid, and gave a small sound of delight. Inside lay a neatly rolled joint. She glanced approvingly at Moondog. He grinned. "Go ahead, Sarah, we got lots of good dope."

He reached forward and pushed the cigarette lighter into its socket as Sarah retrieved the joint. The sweet, fragrant resin smell reached her nostrils instantly. Sarah wasn't a heavy doper, but she could tell this was really good shit! She looked expectantly at Moondog, waiting for a light. The lighter didn't pop out of its socket. Moondog reddened, his hands clenching the steering wheel very tightly.

"Goddamn!"

Sarah jumped in her seat as Moondog slammed the lighter with his fist, and uttered the loud epithet. She looked at him warily, as he glanced in her direction. He saw the worried look on her face, and his frown changed instantly into a smile.

"How about matches instead," he said quietly, "I've got matches here somewhere." He slid open the metal ashtray, and groped around inside of it, retrieving a book of matches. Sarah fired up the joint, and took a deep hit. She handed it to Moondog, holding her breath as long as she was able. Moondog accepted the joint, but he didn't take a hit; he just held it for Sarah until she was ready to go for another hit. Sarah accepted the joint, and took another drag, handing it once more to Moondog, who carefully laid it in the ashtray.

"We'll do the rest of it when we get home, alright?" Sarah nodded, but she hardly heard what her companion had said. Moondog turned the steering wheel, and the big Mercury glided smoothly off the main highway, its twin exhausts making a deep rumble that was felt more than heard under the music blaring from the car's radio. The exit ramp cut under Interstate 17 and became State Route 86.

Sarah's head expanded. A fine numbness spread from her temples, slowly engulfing her entire head. It almost felt like a spider's web being woven around her head. It took a minute for this to sink in—she realized she was *very* high. "Whew…I'm like, really stoned." It seemed to Sarah that someone else had spoken. She looked at Moondog, who seemed to be much farther away from her than the auto would allow. She laughed, living in the moment.

Moondog reached for the joint, now burned quite short, and finally took a deep hit himself, and then extinguished the joint in the automobile's ashtray. "Uh…we got bangin' dope, babe," he smiled knowingly. "You ain't seen nothin' yet."

Sarah found herself deep in thought. She wanted to ask Moondog something…but what was it? She felt it was something important. "Hey, Moondog, have I ever, like, met you before? I mean before today, you know? There's just something about you that seems very familiar…"

The boy laughed. "I never did get to talk to Sandy."

Sarah went suddenly numb, the weed making it difficult to think. An image. Her father and mother. She blushed. "Paul."

Moondog smiled knowingly, and nodded his head. "After your brother told us about you, I had to check up on you. You don't mind, do you? I hope I didn't scare you that night." He watched her closely. She blushed once more, and Moondog looked back at the road. Now Sarah became aware of the narrow road and the tight turns.

"You did scare me, you know…"

Moondog apologized once more. "Look, I'm sorry about all that, Sarah. I, uh…had to talk to you to see if you were serious about coming up here. We gotta know a little bit about anybody we let in."

"But you didn't ask me anything about coming up here." The whole conversation was strange, and Sarah attributed it to the drug.

Moondog pointed ahead. "Look up there," he said excitedly, "see that?" Ahead of them stood a tall, grey object. "That's the Stack," Moondog explained. "It's an old incinerator from a lumber mill. It hasn't been used in a hundred years, and now the kids all just call it the Stack."

Sarah stared in wide-eyed wonder at the cyclopean stone finger pointing accusingly into the slate sky. Sarah tried, but she couldn't see what it was pointing at. The Mercury made a wide turn, and Sarah watched the Stack as they passed. It brooded over the town silently, almost watchfully, like some dark sentinel serving even darker masters. She shuddered, looking ahead once more. Over the hill, she saw the first house. Out behind the garage was an old Chevy. It looked like a hot-rod. Moondog noticed the direction of her stare.

"They wouldn't stand a chance," he commented. He was smiling, but not in a friendly way at all. "Nobody can beat this car."

"This is kinda big for a hot-rod," Sarah said in wonder.

Moondog laughed again, slapping the steering wheel. "Honey, this car's supercharged, and nothing in these parts is as fast as this machine. Of that I can absolutely assure you."

Sarah smiled at him. At least he had a hot car. She found herself liking Moondog more and more as the time passed.

The Mercury, traveling now at a more leisurely pace, completed the turn onto Hennessy. Sarah looked with interest at the old buildings that lined both sides of the street. Most of the older ones were made of stone or brick, while the obviously newer houses of more modern design, were frame and stucco construction. It seemed odd to Sarah that there weren't more wooden homes; but then, Sarah didn't know the history of Hobbs and the things that happened there at the end of the 19th century. There were quite a few cars on the road this time of day. Hobbs didn't carry a heavy tourist load like Prescott, but it got its share, and many of the tourists decide to stay once they experience the comparatively mild winters compared to Minnesota or Wisconsin.

Moondog turned onto Avalon. "We'll avoid the downtown area and most of the heavy traffic by coming this way," he explained. Sarah saw that this was primarily a residential area with neat wooden houses with picket fences, tall trees, and green lawns. She saw little kids riding tricycles, and older kids on skateboards, shouting to each other as they shot down the sidewalk. To Sarah, this town didn't even look real; it was like the old photographs she'd sometimes see in schoolbooks showing buildings and street scenes from the 1950s or even earlier. She considered it pretty, but also pretty boring.

Ahead of them, the traffic light shifted from yellow to red. Moondog slid the big Mercury up to the crosswalk, and held the brake pedal down. This one was a long red light, and occasionally the police staked it out to bring the town a little more revenue from impatient drivers. Avalon widened into four lanes a block ahead, but right here it was a narrow mess, and with the recent rain, it was even worse than usual. Sarah heard a muffled sound, and looked past Moondog.

The boy glanced once in the direction of the rumbling engine. "That's an old 1970s Dodge Challenger," he offered.

Sarah listened to the loud pipes and looked at the black hood-scoops on the yellow hood. The sunlight glinted off the posts that penetrated the hood near the headlamps on both sides. Through each post, a small chrome padlock glimmered. The driver glanced over at them. Sarah thought he looked to be about thirty-five.

"He can't see us." Moondog's voice startled Sarah.

"Can you take him?"

"Of course I could," he said confidently, "I'd leave him in the dust."

She laughed. "Go for it!"

"Naw, I can't," was Moondog's rather confusing, if somewhat reluctant, response. Sarah said nothing, and Moondog continued looking straight ahead. "Maybe some day, but not this day," he mumbled under his breath. It seemed to Sarah that he was almost speaking to himself. He didn't even glance at the Challenger beyond that first look. The light turned green, and the Dodge pulled rapidly ahead of them.

Sarah was clearly disappointed. "I thought you said you could blow his doors off, Moondog. Why didn't you?"

Moondog didn't smile as he explained. "You can't outrun Motorola, Sarah...that's a cop. He's a detective."

"Oh."

"We'll...uh, be there soon," Moondog said to break the long silence as they drove past the hospital. Sarah saw the Challenger in the parking lot. The Mercury turned right, climbing into the hills. Now the houses were farther apart, and occasionally there was a pine tree among the oak and the brush. Moondog cranked down his window. He motioned for Sarah to do the same, and she complied. It was good to feel the cool, fresh air.

"It's okay to have the windows down now that we're out of the downtown area, nobody'll see us." He was smiling again.

Sarah liked the wind in her face. It made her feel like she was getting somewhere. Moondog handed her the matches. She had to roll up her window to keep the match lit. He handed her another joint. She sucked in the smoke. It was very hot, and she began coughing.

Moondog laughed. "You're a real lightweight, aren't you?"

The spasm had passed. She laughed, choked a little, and wheezed. "Jeez! That's smooth!" Moondog laughed with her, and once again, Sarah felt the numbness spreading. Her body seemed light as air, and twice its normal size. She rolled down the window and looked out once again. The green of the trees was intense; she blinked. Houses were few in this part of Hobbs.

At the bottom of a steep hill, she saw an old stone house. The lawn was wide and well cared for. The color was a dazzling yellow-green next to the deeper color of the forest behind it. A man stood on the front porch. He seemed a little heavy in the middle, not quite paunchy. Sarah looked at his face. It was too far for Sarah to know his eye color, but she could see he was sporting a crew cut. She thought only military people still wore such an outdated style. There was a police car parked right in front of the closed garage door.

The man looked out from the shade of his porch, watching the Mercury cruise up the hill. Sarah looked back at him. He watched them until the car crested the hill and was lost from sight. She shivered. He'd been like that chimney in a way. He'd just...stood there watching...

13

"That's our, uh…destination up there." Moondog gestured with his right hand. Just over the bare, black rock, Sarah saw the red shingles topping a round stone tower. The cupola was steeply peaked, and reminded Sarah of something she'd expect to see on a European castle. The Mercury flowed around a wide bend in the road, its engine grumbling. Now they were passing the black rocks on Sarah's side. In some places, the rough-cut rocks jutted menacingly out over the shoulder of the road. To Sarah, they could almost have been dangerous animals waiting, muscles tensed, to pounce on unwatchful travelers. She shivered, and then they were past the outcrop.

She shifted her gaze to the other side of the road. There stood the house, silent and half hidden in greenery. Sarah gasped—it was beautiful! The old Victorian structure crouched atop the hill, the deep brown of the ancient stonework contrasting sharply with the freshly painted white trim that surrounded windows and doors. The front porch had a shallow peaked roof that was supported by brilliant white pillars. There were three chimneys. The large windows reflected the Mercury as it rounded the house.

The garage, built to the north of the house, was a rectangular box; a strictly utilitarian cement block affair, much newer than the house—and it seemed very much out of place. The structure had been painted dark brown with white trim in a vain attempt to make it match the house. There were stalls for three automobiles, if the three roll-up doors were any indication. Only the door on the left was open. It swallowed the Mercury in one mouthful, the big steel door thudding into the cement floor behind it.

Moondog said, "Wait here a minute," and opened the door and stepped out into the blackness. Sarah heard the soft crunch of his shoes on cement as he walked away. The sudden darkness exploded into light as he flipped a switch on the back wall of the garage. Sarah winced; she was still stoned. Shielding her eyes with her left hand, she opened her door and stepped out. Moondog crossed to her side, closing the big Mercury's door for her. He looked down at her, gently placing his hand on her shoulder.

"Are you okay?"

Sarah did her best to smile as her eyes became accustomed to the fluorescent glare. She said, "I'm fine, Moondog…just still stoned, you know?"

"Oh yeah," he replied, "I know."

Sarah looked up at Moondog. He was taller than Richie, and older. She was pleased, but she didn't know why. *I, like, got a boyfriend.*

"Well," Moondog said, "here we are."

Sarah clutched her tattered brown bag. "Can I see Bobby?" She was anxious to see her brother; it showed in the hopeful softness of the request.

Moondog grinned down at her. "We…uh, need to get out of the garage first." Sarah laughed at his joke, and Moondog put a hand on her shoulder again, guiding her toward the door at the back of the garage. Sarah walked with him through the door, and found herself in a long, bare cement corridor lighted with hanging bulbs. Moondog led her along the hall, and stopped at an open door. "This is your room, Sarah. Get settled first, and then you can meet everyone else." Sarah opened her mouth to speak, but Moondog spoke before she could. "And yes, you'll be able to see your brother. He can hardly wait himself, you know."

Sarah walked in, and Moondog shut the door behind her. She tossed her bag onto the neatly made bed. Beside it was a small metal chest of drawers. There was no mirror. She looked around, and thought the room strange. She wondered why there were no windows—the pale green, painted, cement block walls stared blankly back at her, with no answer of their own. She heard the lock snap behind her, and whirled. A thought fluttered briefly through her mind like a frightened little bird. *Why did they lock me in? Still, they let me keep my bag, so it can't be a prison, can it?*

But the remains of her high distracted her from that line of thought. She examined her surroundings once again. There was only one other door, and that led to a small bathroom. She noticed that there were no windows in the bathroom either. There was a new bar of soap, still wrapped, and a clean white towel and facecloth. Both were precisely placed on the towel bar, with not one corner out of place. Sarah returned to the small bedroom and sat on the one straight-backed wooden chair in the room next to the dresser. Her eyes were drawn to a reflection near the floor under the dresser. Bolts. The dresser was bolted to the concrete floor. She registered the thought, but then allowed it to slip down into her unconscious mind.

She was tired and let her head rest against the wall behind the chair. *I wonder how long I'll have to sit here before someone comes to get me?* She wasn't sure how long she'd been sitting there, she'd been dozing when she heard a key go into the lock and the lock turn. She awoke with a start, and stood. The door swung slowly outward, and a heavy-set woman dressed as a nurse came in.

"Hello, my name's Mary," the nurse said with a warm smile. She walked toward Sarah, her white hospital shoes making a soft susurration as she moved along the concrete floor. Mary set the stainless steel tray she'd brought in with her on the small dresser beside Sarah. "Now don't be afraid," she consoled in a motherly fashion, gently placing her hand on the girl's shoulder. "I'm going to tell you exactly what's going on around here. You want to know, don't you?" She smiled again, and Sarah managed to smile in return.

Mary put her arm around the girl, drawing her gently toward her. "Every new person who comes here goes through the same thing. First, for the rest of today you'll stay here in this room." Sarah tried to protest, but Mary held up her hand. "I know you have questions, but you must understand, so do we. The reason the room is completely barren is that we don't want anything to distract you from your first meditation." Sarah started to speak, but fell silent when she couldn't recall what she'd wanted to say.

"Your first meditation, Sarah, my dear, will be the following—I want you to ask your internal mind if you really want to be here." Mary paused long enough to let that sink into Sarah's still drug-clouded mind. "That's what I want you to think about, Sarah. Do you understand this request?" Mary droned on. "If, in the morning, you've decided you've made a mistake, we'll get you safely home with your promise that this place remains a secret." She paused again. "Even if you decide not to stay, the others here want to. It's very important to think of the group." She stared at Sarah silently.

Sarah turned her eyes self-consciously from that stare. "I take tonight to see if I, like, really want to stay?"

"That's right, dear." Mary patted the girl on her shoulder.

"But I'm sure I want to be here right now."

Mary laughed. "You need to learn patience, my dear; we nurses always have a lot of patients." She laughed at her own joke, but Sarah hadn't understood. Mary continued without hesitation. "Anyway, here's your dinner for the evening." She pointed to the tray she'd carried in with her. She turned, heading toward the door.

She paused at the door. "I'll see you again after you eat," she called back over her shoulder. She walked out, her shoes making that strange, disturbingly snake-like hissing. Mary shut the door behind her, and Sarah heard the door latch snick into place—no sound of a key. *It locks automatically.*

Sarah lifted the white linen napkin covering the stainless steel tray. She sighed. It appeared her 'dinner' would consist of only a small salad; she'd been hoping for a Big Mac. She picked up the tray and walked to the bed, placing the tray on the seat of the chair beside her. She picked up the fork and tasted the salad. She had to admit that for a salad, it wasn't all that bad. And it wasn't exactly like she'd never eaten a salad before. She thought briefly of home, and just as quickly banished the thought. She'd forgotten just how hungry she was. She wolfed the salad in just a few minutes, and the small glass of water—served, strangely, in a stemmed wine glass. She wiped her lips with the linen cloth that had covered the tray, and placed the now empty tray, with its utensils atop the bureau, realizing it hadn't been enough food. She sat again in the uncomfortable chair. She was still hungry. She thought for a moment.

Suddenly, she sat up straight. She just remembered! A sly grin crossed her features. She'd remembered that she had a candy bar somewhere among her belongings. She'd remembered buying it from a vending machine and putting it in her bag at the bus station in Tucson just before boarding the big Greyhound. She leapt from the chair, and dug through her bag, which was still sitting on the bed.

The Snickers bar was there. Ripping the end of the wrapper, she ate the bar ravenously. The sweetness dulled her appetite, and she felt she was finally coming down from the dope she'd smoked with Moondog in the car on her way up to…wherever exactly she was. She placed the candy wrapper on the dinner tray, smiling and wondering what the nurse's reaction would be. Then she lay back on the bed, staring at the ceiling. She thought she heard thunder, far away and muffled. *Do I want to be here? When will they let me see Bobby?* She closed her eyes; she was suddenly very tired.

The lock turned, and Sarah jumped, suddenly awake and wide-eyed. She realized she'd dozed off. She wondered how long she'd been sleeping. She looked at her Timex and was disappointed to see that it wasn't running. She shook it. Nothing happened; the time was frozen at three-twelve. She shook it once more, vainly. *Damn battery must've given out.* She glanced up as Mary entered, carrying a stainless steel pitcher. "My watch quit," she announced. "Do you know what time it is?"

Mary walked to the bureau to retrieve the tray, saw the candy wrapper and smiled. "We don't keep time here," she explained quietly, "time is an artificial creation of mankind, and we find it…confining." Sarah just nodded, not comprehending what Mary had said. She was still sleepy, after all, and not in the mood for philosophy, even if she'd known that was the word she was looking for. "The dinner was very good." She saw the corner of Mary's mouth turn up.

"Even the dessert, right?"

Sarah laughed. It looked like Mary the nurse just might be okay after all. Mary used the stainless steel pitcher she'd come in with to refill Sarah's 'wine' glass with more water. There was no ice.

"Will I get to see Bobby tomorrow?"

"Oh, I don't see why not," Mary said in a conciliatory way. "You know, he's just as anxious to see you as you are to see him. He's been asking about you constantly." Mary picked up the dinner tray, and the pitcher. She stared at the glass for only a second, and then said, "I'm going now. Why don't you take a nice shower, sweetie, and go to bed. You must be very tired from your adventures today. I'll come and wake you in the morning."

The door latched behind her. Sarah sighed. Getting slowly to her feet, she ambled into the bathroom and took a nice hot shower. Mary was right; it had been a very long day. After the shower, she dressed in an old tee shirt and cotton panties. She sipped some of the water in the wine glass. She turned off the table lamp upon the bureau; it was the only source of light in the room. She climbed into the bed.

14

Curt slept late Sunday morning. When he awoke, he was quite surprised to find it was already almost ten. He swung his legs out of bed and sat up, placing his feet on the cool tile of the floor. He sat there for a few minutes, looking out his window. The rain that Saturday's sky had promised was drizzling down in what Curt knew would probably be only a cold, isolated shower, passing in a couple of hours. He rose, wandered into his bathroom, and took a long hot shower. As the water washed over him, and a warm cloud of steam enveloped him, he forgot the terror of the night before, allowing the frightening dream to go down the drain with the night-sweat and soapy water. Now, as he was toweling off, he thought about his date with Cheryl.

"Whew…that was some date," he said softly. Then he half-laughed as he recalled his embarrassing encounter with the shifter of his dad's Escort. He slung the towel over the bar, and padded back to his bedroom. He dressed swiftly, figuring he'd wait to call Cheryl until about twelve o'clock or thereabouts. This early on Sunday, Curt knew she'd most likely be in church with her parents. He pulled on a plain grey tee shirt and a worn pair of jeans, still thinking about Cheryl. He just wasn't sure what he should do. If he was going to apply for admission to Arizona State University, he'd have to get his ass in gear. He toyed with the idea of discussing it with his dad, but they'd had that conversation, and Curt knew he'd promised to fill out the applications. Once he was accepted, he'd shoot for some kind of scholarship. He was certain his grades would be good enough to warrant their approval; almost all straight A's the whole semester.

He sat down on the edge of his bed once more, thinking about Cheryl. Cheryl wanted him to stay in Hobbs. She reasoned that after graduation he could get a job right here in Hobbs or maybe even down in Prescott as a graphic artist in one of the quick-print places, but he really didn't want to spend his life making business cards and resumes for other people—there had to be more to life than that.

Cheryl had been working on him since the second time they'd gone out together. He visualized Cheryl in church. *She's an evangelist just like the ones on television,* he thought to himself. *She's trying to save me for herself.* He wondered briefly if that meant she didn't trust him to remain faithful to her while he was in Phoenix going to school.

His thoughts drifted back to the night before, and the steamy interior of his dad's car. She'd tried to talk him into having sex with her, right there in his dad's car at the drive-in. She'd been pretty persuasive too, as he remembered the incident now. She'd done a little more than talk about it, he recalled. He knew what people meant by the word *protection*, of course. It was a subject that had been covered in school only last year. But Cheryl had been very insistent; almost, Curt thought, demanding. The incident with the shifter was the only thing that had prevented him from going along with her plan right there and then. Now, the morning after that night, he was glad he hadn't given in. And he now had to wonder...was Cheryl *trying* to get pregnant? Was that why she'd been so oddly aggressive all of a sudden? Was she planning on maybe using that as a tool to convince him to stay here?

The thought frightened Curt—that would certainly hold him here in Hobbs, alright! He knew he'd never be able to just walk away from such an obligation, even if it was only as far as Phoenix. And he knew that Cheryl knew that about him as well. He marveled at how clearly he could think about all of this in the cold light of morning, yet only the night before, had the shifter not intervened, it wouldn't have mattered to him very much; in fact, he realized now, he hadn't even thought about the ramifications of what they'd been about to do. That thought scared him too; that he had allowed himself to be so short sighted. Cheryl made him feel so good that all other thoughts and possibilities seemed secondary. Secondary? Hell! All of the thoughts—*afterthoughts,* he corrected himself—that he was thinking now, had been entirely nonexistent last night.

He tied his sneakers, and left his bedroom, closing the door without thinking about it. This was something he'd never done before. *I might've left something open...was it a door?* The thought barely registered in his conscious mind, and then fell back into shadow. He headed down the hallway. He suddenly realized he was hungry. He was in better spirits by the time he'd reached the kitchen of their small home. He grabbed the box of Kellogg's corn flakes from the kitchen shelf over the dishwasher, and walked into the dining room.

He froze in the doorway, staring. There, in his place at the table, lay a piece of towel and a pyramid shaped crystal that dully reflected the light coming in through the dining room window. The thing almost seemed to glow softly with its own odd, internal light. There was also a remnant of a joint lying on the towel beside the pyramid.

Kent Paxton looked evenly at his son from across the table. "I give up," he said amiably enough, "what is this thing?"

Kent spoke casually. He was thirty-eight years old, but he wasn't yet too old to remember being seventeen. He suspected that his son smoked dope occasionally, even though he'd advised against it. But Curt's grades were very good and besides, he'd used it himself on rare occasions once upon a time in his more wild youth.

He'd been a child of the sixties. But he was now a reasonably success-ful businessman in the community. He and his son had had discussions on the matter. Kent had advised his son to, at the very least, avoid speed, coke, and hallucinogens. He was confident his son was only an occasional user, and that he never indulged at school.

Kent smiled. There'd been some rough patches in their relationship to be sure, but they'd become closer this last year, he and Curt. Susan's sudden death three years ago had almost split them apart. Curt had stayed away for days at a time, and when he was home, he'd hardly spoken. Those times behind them. Still, with everything looking up now, this very strange discovery worried Kent. At the moment, the odd stone was what was on his mind.

Curt quickly responded to his father's question, but he surprised himself. He didn't lie to his dad very often because he didn't feel the need to. Up to now, they'd always had a very open relationship. But now it just came flood-ing out, with no thought beforehand. "I found it on the way to the snack bar at the drive-in last night…in the dirt. I thought it was a cool looking thing, and I picked it up. I don't know what it is, though," he concluded lamely.

Kent looked at his son for a moment, and then his gaze returned to the pyra-midal stone. "It looks like some kind of rock crystal to me, with inscriptions. It might be a talisman." Kent looked back up at his son, studying his face. The boy seemed genuinely surprised by that thought, and Kent breathed a mental sigh of relief, relaxing a little bit in his seat. At least he knew Curt wasn't involved in devil worshipping or some other cult thing. Kent distrusted Satanists just as much as he distrusted Baptists or Catholics. Organized religion in any form was not high on Kent's list of favorite things. He stared evenly at Curt. "Be careful with that," Kent admonished. "Its owners may want it back."

Curt looked up from his corn flakes, and stopped chewing for a moment. The realization that it probably belonged to someone else hadn't really entered his mind; he'd simply assumed it was so old it was a long forgotten artifact, and therefore anybody's property. And the idea that someone might come looking for it hadn't occurred to him either. Kent went on to suggest, "You know, Curt, I think you should just get rid of it." Kent was very serious now, and Curt knew it. "Some of the people who're into this kind of thing can be…unpredictable. They tend to take these things very, very seriously, and they can be violent."

"Aw, if it was all that important to someone, why'd they drop it at the drive-in?" Curt remembered how he'd found it carefully hidden behind a loose brick inside the Stack. There was an uncomfortable silence for a moment.

"Yeah," Kent conceded finally, looking back down at his toast, "you're probably right. I still think you should ditch it, though, just to be on the safe side." He watched his son intently as he wrapped the stone in the towel. He'd ignored the roach completely, and walked into the living room.

By eleven, the rain had stopped. Curt tried to call Cheryl at noon, but there was no answer. He tried once more at one o'clock with the same results. Her parents had probably decided to drive down to Phoenix for the day to visit relatives, or maybe do some shopping. So he and his dad sat on the sofa side by side for almost an hour, in comfortable silence. Kent was reading a book while Curt was working on some sketches for the illustration he needed to do for Carl's poem.

He sketched rapidly; the very soft, very black lead pencil was really getting a workout. Kent, having finished a chapter in his book, glanced over to see what his son was so diligently working on. The drawing was of something alive, but deep enough in the surrounding darkness that its shape was vague; more to be guessed at than actually seen. All Kent could really make out were what appeared to be tentacles—or perhaps they were very long, spidery arms. Deep in the darkness, six red eyes burned. The image on the paper made him think of one of his favorite science fiction, horror story authors—Howard Phillips Lovecraft.

Kent felt a chill. "What's this?"

Curt laughed easily, handing the sketchpad to his father for closer examination. "Oh, I'm supposed to do an illustration for the school paper. This one's for the Halloween edition coming up later this month. It's an illustration for another one of Carl Larsen's lighthearted poems." His dad snorted a laugh, having read the last one. Still, it had been oddly frightening, as though the boy's mind actually saw into the strange, dark realms of his poetry.

Curt laughed once more. "It's pretty creepy, isn't it?" Kent nodded, without further comment, and Curt continued. "I had that dream again Thursday night. You know, the one I used to have years ago, before Mom died?" Kent nodded again. "The dream seemed to fit the poem, or maybe the poem fits the dream, and brought it on. Either way, I thought I'd try to combine the two. I figure, if I'm gonna have the stupid dream anyway, I might as well make use of it."

"Well, it looks like a natural combination to me," Kent replied with a chuckle. "Carl's poems and nightmares." Kent returned the drawing pad to his son.

"Yeah," Curt responded, "Carl's poems might be a little weird, but he seems to be okay in person. I finally met him; Tommy introduced us after class last week." Kent said nothing. Curt got up and turned on the television. A football game was coming on in just a couple of minutes, and they both enjoyed watching these games together. It was almost a ritual between them. At two that afternoon, during a commercial break in the game, Curt tried again to reach Cheryl. There was still no answer—*Phoenix, alright! Damn!* He'd no sooner put the receiver back in its cradle when it rang. He was disappointed when he discovered it was Tommy on the other end. Curt told Tommy he'd meet him at the mall after the game.

Tommy was playing video games in the arcade when Curt arrived a little after three-thirty. His friend was just about to fire the winning shot at an extra-terrestrial monster when Curt, who'd managed to sneak up behind his concentrating friend, suddenly slapped his shoulder.

"Damn!" Tommy's shot went wild and the extraterrestrial monster proceeded to have him for lunch.

Curt laughed. "I hope that was a girl monster, Tommy. I'd hate to think you'd let boy monsters get that close to you."

Tommy laughed and released his grip on the rocket launcher. Curt dropped in a coin and tried his luck, but he fared no better than his friend had. They both played several games in concentrated silence.

As Tommy was playing his last game, Curt asked, "Are you okay? How much have you had to drink this morning?"

Tommy paused, but didn't look over at his friend. "Aw, get off it, Curt. It's Sunday, you know. Everybody takes a drink on Sunday." He threw Curt a nervous smile. "I figured out that I could steal the booze from my old man when he's not around, just as long as I don't take too much at any one time. I just refill his bottles with a little water. He usually can't tell."

"Usually?"

Tommy released his hands on the video game controls, and turned to his friend. "Well, now you know the real reason I got this black eye." Tommy smiled, and then laughed as though there was nothing wrong with his father beating him. Curt thought back to the other bruises he'd seen on Tommy's neck two weeks earlier, and ones he'd seen even before that, but he said nothing further about it. He changed the subject. "Hey, I got an idea…let's get something to eat."

Tommy brightened. "Let's get a pizza. I feel like pizza this afternoon; it reminds me of the aliens' faces in this damn game we're playing." Curt laughed along with Tommy. They turned from the game, and wound their way through the adults and other kids meandering around the mall that Sunday afternoon.

The two boys ate a pepperoni and mushroom pie at the pizza place in the food court of the mall. Later, as they walked out to their bikes, Tommy paused, and glanced around nervously. Curt only partly registered what was going on, but then Tommy took a folded photograph from his shirt pocket. He opened it, glancing around another time, and handed it to Curt without comment. It was glossy stock, a color eight by ten photograph.

Curt saw the flesh, and thought at first of his dad's Playboy magazines, suspecting initially that Tommy was showing him a 'skin picture,' as he referred to them. But this was no Playboy centerfold! Curt stared, mesmerized. This wasn't a page torn from some magazine. This was an actual color photograph. In the photo a cute young girl with short blonde hair lay on her back on what looked to be a tiger skin rug. The photograph was dimly lit, giving it an oddly sinister appearance. The pose she struck in the image left little to the imagination. She seemed to stare blankly at Curt from the photograph with a face that looked like it had been recently cut with a razor in several places along her left cheek.

"Neat, huh?" Tommy's comment interrupted Curt's thoughts. With that short blonde hair, she reminded him of Cheryl. "Carl got it for me. He said the police confiscated some of this stuff from a guy caught selling it to high school students. He says some of it's a whole lot better than this one. Some of it shows people being tortured." Tommy grinned. "Carl's dad brought some of it home. He said I can't say anything about it, because his dad doesn't know he took this and he doesn't want to get in trouble."

"Why on earth did you take this? It's police property. It's probably evidence in the case against the guy the cops busted." Curt pointed to a number that was written in ballpoint in the upper left margin.

Tommy ignored the comment, and went on with his own thoughts. "Isn't that a laugh? Our fearless police chief is protecting us from smut so he can have it all to himself."

"Did you just hear what I said? This is police evidence. Taking it's a crime."

Tommy's face was blank for just a second. "I don't really know…"

Curt laughed at that, and said, "That's too weird for me, Tommy. Better watch out or you'll end up in jail for stealing court evidence." He handed the picture back to Tommy.

Again Tommy's face was blank for a second, and then he responded, "I never thought of that."

"Just give it back to Carl, Tommy, or better still, tear it up and throw it away. It's got our fingerprints on it now, you know."

Tommy thought about that for a moment; he'd not considered what Curt had just told him, but it surely made sense. He crumpled up the picture, and dropped it into the trash barrel standing beside one of the pillars that marked the front entrance of the mall. He seemed vaguely unsure of himself to Curt. Twice it appeared he was about to say something, and then changed his mind.

15

Tommy stared at the trash receptacle for a long moment, and then shoved his hands into his jacket pockets. "Know what, Curt? I'm gonna have a girlfriend like that one of these days."

Curt snorted. "I don't think there're any girls like her in Hobbs."

"Well, then," Tommy replied with complete certainty, "I'll just have to find a girl somewhere else, I guess. He grinned lecherously at Curt. "Carl says you'd be surprised what goes on around this town. He says his dad tells him all kinds of interesting stories about the people that the cops arrest."

"So you're telling me you want to find a girl who's a criminal? That sounds like a really good idea, Tommy, you can take her home and show her where the silver and jewels are stored so she can come back at night with her real boyfriend and steal all your stuff."

Tommy paused, that oddly vacant look returning for just the flash of a second. "I never said I wanted her to be a con, Curt. All I meant was I'll find a cute girlfriend like the girl in the picture. I'm not gonna hang around with criminals; I'm smarter than that."

"I hope so," Curt said with a grin, "there are a lot of girls at school, Tommy. Can't you find someone in one of your classes you'd like to go out with?"

"Oh, I do go out with girls," Tommy said defensively, "almost every weekend." Then he grinned. "But I want a girl who won't refuse to go out with me on a second date," he said with a laugh. "Carl says girls who like to fool around are out there, Curt. And right here in Hobbs too!"

"I'm sure Carl has all the answers," Curt responded sarcastically. "So how come he doesn't have a girlfriend of his own?"

"Oh, he does," Tommy said with a confident nod. "He says she's already out of school, though. He told me once that his girlfriend works in the police station as a file clerk, and that she's already twenty years old."

"Yeah, sure…tell me another." They laughed together, and then parted company. Curt stared after his friend whom he'd known since his family moved to Hobbs. Something bad was happening to him, but Curt just couldn't figure out what it was…beyond his strange and rather sudden friendship with Carl Larsen. Perhaps, he considered, he should re-evaluate his friendship with Carl too.

Curt got home about four o'clock and tried again to call Cheryl. *Still no answer.* He headed off to his room to finish his homework. He tackled math first, because it was the subject he disliked the most. His dad had told him once, or maybe twice, even back in elementary school, "Do the subjects you hate first. Then the ones you like will be like dessert after you've eaten your broccoli." Now Curt laughed. That had been very good advice. He turned the page in the math book, and began figuring the last answer he needed for the next class.

Kent arrived home after doing some shopping about an hour later. It was now five in the evening. He unlocked the front door, and carried the groceries into the house. He dropped his car keys onto the dining room table, and set down the three bags he'd carried in. He listened. The house was silent. He smiled, thinking, *must be math.* He laughed softly, and opened the smaller bag. Tonight they were having cheeseburgers and onion rings, compliments of Ronald McDonald. He set the table, and called for Curt.

"Hi, Dad," Curt said as he emerged from his room, again unconsciously shutting the door. "What's for supper?"

"Wash up and I'll tell you."

Curt grinned. "Beat'cha to it."

"In that case, we're having hamburgers. Pull up a chair and let's eat before everything gets cold."

For a time they ate in silence. Then Kent asked, "So, tell me Curt, what did you decide about that stone you found at the ah…drive-in."

"Oh. I almost forgot to tell you. When I went to the mall to meet Tommy this afternoon, I took it with me. I tossed it into the trash can at the mall."

"Why not just throw it away here?"

"I was thinking about what you said about maybe people looking for it. I thought it would be safer to throw it away at the mall; that way, even if it was found, nobody'd be able to say who threw it in there, or when."

Kurt nodded approvingly. "You'll either be a good cop one day, or a good criminal." He laughed. "Anyway, I'm really glad you got rid of that thing."

"Me too, Dad," Curt said, smiling. *Why am I lying about this? Gotta think about this…*

After eating, Curt offered to do the dishes, which his dad readily agreed to. Kent went into the living room and sat in his spot on the sofa, and turned on the television. He kept the volume fairly low and picked up the newspaper, removing the rubber band. In the kitchen, Curt marveled at how his dad could read the paper and watch the news on television, and keep it all straight. But he had other things he needed to think about; important things like why he started lying to his father again. This was something he hadn't done since right after his mother died.

What is it about that stone? Why can't I let it go? It's just a stupid rock, after all. It's important, his subconscious whispered to him. *It's important. I can't let it get away until I at least try to find out what it is.* Curt placed the two plates into the drying rack beside the sink, and turned his attention to the stainless steel flatware they'd used. *Why would anybody stuff that stupid thing behind a brick in an old chimney? I wonder how long it was really there? Could someone really be looking for it?*

While the mortar had been easily removed along the sides of the brick, who could say how weak the rest of the mortar in there might be? For all Curt knew, it might all be soft and dusty. He shook his head. He just couldn't bring himself to believe that the rock had been put there recently. *I bet that thing's been in there a hundred years. Still, I better find a good place to hide it. I'd hate for my dad to stumble across it now that I've told him I threw it away.* And as Curt finished the dishes, he thought no more about the strange pyramid currently hidden under his tee shirts in his dresser drawer.

With the dishes done, he walked into the living room. "I'm gonna go finish my homework, Dad."

"Fine. We can watch a movie a little later when you're finished up."

"Cool."

Curt walked down the hall, and stared for just a second at his bedroom door. He didn't remember shutting it when he'd come out for dinner. He shrugged, opened the door, and went in. He almost closed it behind himself, but then he didn't. He walked back to his desk, and sat down. His math was already done, so he turned to his history assignment; a short essay on the reasons behind World War II. It took him about twenty minutes to knock that out, and then he looked at the sketch he'd almost completed for the school paper.

That thing staring out at him with many eyes should have been frightening, but it wasn't. Curt recalled the intense fear and pain that same creature had felt in his dream of Erieuxta, wherever that place was supposed to be. *Just a dream, dummy,* he reminded himself as he'd done when he'd been eight. He closed the pad. His schoolwork was done. He'd suddenly decided to leave the drawing just as it was; deliberately not quite finished. *That's how this creature's life would have been,* he thought, *done but not quite finished.* The thought saddened him. He went into the living room and sat beside his father. This time he made a conscious decision not to shut his door.

Kent looked up. "I rented a movie for us tonight."

"Cool, Dad, what's the title?"

"It's called *The Terror Within*. It's a Roger Corman film. Could be corny and stupid, but probably fun to watch."

"I can go for stupid and funny," Curt agreed. "Even if it's scary, it won't match any of Carl Larsen's poems."

Kent grunted and smiled as he rose to push the tape into the player. "I can vouch for that one, Curt," he said.

They watched the movie together, eating popcorn, and critiquing the make-up of the monsters and the dialogue of the characters. In all, they had a very good time. When the film ended, Curt went to the telephone and picked up the receiver. There was no dial tone; the line was dead. "Stupid phone's not working," he called out to his father.

"Most likely the rain," his dad commented. There was a sudden clap of thunder. "Or," Kent continued, "lightning may have struck a pole somewhere. But don't worry, I'm sure Cheryl will be willing to wait until tomorrow to talk with you."

Curt laughed. "Sometimes I think you can read minds, Dad."

Kent made a face, raised his hands in mock threat and uttered a 'Woooooo' ululation. "After that movie, who can say what I may or may not be able to do?"

"Well," Curt commented dryly, "I already did the dishes so you won't have to do that at least. Though I can't imagine a mutant doing the dishes."

"Naw," Kent said, "I think they'd just lick them clean and put them away like that."

"Huh…matching set of green dishes," Curt countered, "sounds alright to me." They both laughed.

At ten, the phone was still dead. Curt stared out his bedroom window. It was dark, the moon was entirely hidden by the clouds. The porch light across the street and the streetlight at the intersection provided the only illumination. The wind was still blowing, but it seemed that the storm had finally passed over them. Curt showered, tried the phone one more time, and then went to bed. He lay back and relaxed. He took a deep breath as he felt the coolness of the pillow against his neck…

There was a noise.

Curt looked quickly at the window. Fortunately, the drape was closed…that was a relief.

A doorknob turned.

Curt sat up in bed, looking toward the bathroom door. It was opening. The light was dim, but Curt could not have mistaken what he saw. It was Cheryl!

He opened his mouth as if to speak and Cheryl giggled. "Shh! Your old man'll hear you." Curt stared. Cheryl was wearing the clothing she'd worn on their last date; except instead of ordinary fabric, her clothing seemed to glow faintly, accentuating her figure. The clothes also fit tighter than Curt remembered from that last date. There was a wide metal band across her forehead; probably incised copper. The designs were odd, geometric figures Curt felt he should recognize for some reason.

She was barbaric.

She was beautiful.

She walked slowly toward Curt. She crawled sensually across the bed, grabbing Curt's hair, jerking his head back. She kissed him. She caught her breath. Cheryl whispered something in his ear. Curt didn't quite catch it. She lay beside him a moment, saying nothing. Then she laughed, throwing her head back. She was whispering again. "I know what you want...do you know what I want?" She bent over him, kissing him again. Curt was paralyzed. She was kissing him, holding his head gently between her two cool hands. She pulled back, still smiling down at him.

"I know what you want..." But that was impossible! A person can't whisper without moving her lips. She was speaking again, low and almost inaudible. Curt had to strain to hear the words.

"Do you know what I want?"

Curt's hands were in Cheryl's hair now as she lowered her head to kiss him very slowly. For some reason, her hair seemed coarser than he'd remembered. She looked up into his eyes. Curt thought Cheryl's eyes were blue, not yellow... how could he have made a mistake like that?

She bent to kiss him once again. He touched her shoulder. It felt warm—and furry! Curt could only stare as she raised her head slowly. Her face was like a cat's; velvet-soft fur striped black and yellow; that odd copper band was still across her brow. She licked her lips. Cheryl's tongue couldn't be THAT big!

Curt heard her whisper, a rumbling, purring sound like an idling engine. "Give it back."

He heard himself say, "What?" His mouth was dry. He felt numb, barely able to form the words. All he seemed able to do was stare up at her; his arms and legs wouldn't move. He was paralyzed.

"Return the crystal." The thought was clear now. She looked at him imploringly from that terrifying cat's face.

"I can't, for chrissakes! I can't get back to the Stack now."

The words rumbled in her throat like the muted sound of an almost-muffled hot-rod. "Return it...give it back...you can do it!"

She bent over him again, only instead of a kiss, he felt that tongue move over his face; felt the startling roughness of its inhuman texture. He felt her divided upper lip. Cheryl the cat looked back at him. Her pupils were vertical slits in luminous yellow eyes. Slowly she dragged her lips up and away from him. He gasped.

The rumbling purr—soft yet now menacing. "Give it! Give it! I know what you want...do you know what I want?"

Curt could smell an animal scent now, pungent and strong, like the smell of the zoo. He could see how her lips were drawn back.

"My what big teeth you have!" A remembered line from childhood.

"The better to eat you with, my dear." The rumble that was barely audible. The thing that wasn't exactly a tiger, and wasn't exactly Cheryl lowered her head to Curt's neck. He felt the hot exhalation of her breath as her lips closed on both sides of his neck; he felt the points of very large teeth pressing. The animal scent was very strong now. But he couldn't move! He couldn't move; he couldn't pull away from the terror! The tiger that had been Cheryl closed its jaws. Curt heard teeth clash together...

He sat up in bed with a jerk. He was shaking, shivering. He glanced first at the bathroom door. It was shut. Then, more cautiously, he touched his neck and throat. He was still whole, unbitten and not bleeding.

"It was a dream," he whispered, more to reassure himself than to explain the facts. He laughed nervously, taking a deep breath. He rose, turned on the light and checked his neck in the bureau mirror just to make sure. Everything was still intact; but it had been so real! Outside, in the darkness, Curt heard a car engine somewhere nearby. The sound of the un-muffled engine purred and rumbled; it reminded him of...something.

16

The bell and the general confusion of a hundred kids milling about the school hallways tended to put Curt at ease. The crowds made him a part of the real world. He needed that this morning, especially after the frightening dream of the night before. He'd tried to see Cheryl this morning, but she'd just left her locker a minute before he got there, or so Sally Gibson had told him, and she should know—her locker was right next to Cheryl's. He moved up the hall with the other students to his homeroom class, walked in, and took his seat. He slept dreamlessly through homeroom, awakening only when the bell sounded once more to signal the end of that class, and the beginning of the rush to the next one. He got up, ran his hands over his head to get all of his hair flat once more, and headed toward his first period class, History.

Curt often found this class interesting, and only occasionally not. Curt generally liked history. This morning he was highly interested—today's class was about the history of Hobbs…and the Stack. Curt had already heard many of the stories, and he was curious to learn if they were truth or mythology. Captivated, he sat, pen poised over paper, as the teacher began the discussion.

Mr. Jenson looked at the class over his reading glasses, and cleared his throat. He was about sixty, with grey, thinning hair that might have been considered a bit too long. He looked around the class, waiting until he had everyone's attention, and then he began the day's lesson. "Hobbs was founded in 1877," he began. "It is believed by our modern historians that the name of the town comes from the word Hob or perhaps Hobgoblin. Hob being an obsolete name for the Devil, and of course then a Hobgoblin would be a goblin of the Devil; begging the question, would there be another kind?" The class laughed at his joke, and he continued, "Further, this reference may account for another name we'll be hearing about shortly." He looked around, smiling thinly at Curt. Mr. Jenson liked Curt; he was one of only a handful of his students who would give their full attention to the lessons.

"Compared to other mining camps and towns like Tombstone," he began once more, "Hobbs would've been considered tame in its day." He raised his index finger to make a point. "Now that's not to say there were no barroom brawls or side street killings—there were, make no mistake about it. One or two were actually famous, if indeed only locally. But local or not, the blood was real. And like the shootings in Tombstone and other towns of the era, they seldom resembled the 'showdowns' that Hollywood has managed to pass off as history.

"If a gunman behaved like any of the actors you've seen in films or television programs, they would all of them have most certainly died in their very first gun battle.

"For instance, the concept of shooting the gun out of someone's hand would have been impossible, even if one took careful aim. We have to keep in mind that firearms and ammunition in the days of the Old West were vastly less accurate than their modern equivalent, and the firearms had almost nonexistent sights, which made fine aiming impossible. Fanning a sixgun as we see in the cinema, that is holding the gun at waist level and slapping the hammer with the left hand to make the gun shoot very fast, or even simply shooting from the hip are among the greatest myths of the movie cowboy.

"Most of the killings of this time period were actually more like ambushes, or angry exchanges of lethal lead from the muzzles of drunken men's guns in saloons and dancehalls. Even so, Hobbs never had any famous gun-fighting marshals or sheriffs—or bad men either, as a matter of fact. The population was tough, but most people were basically honest. The women of Hobbs, at least in the early days, were dancehall girls and were seldom fought over.

"If there was going to be a problem, it would be on a Friday or Saturday night. That's when the miners and lumbermen were all in town to drink, gamble, and tell tall tales, and try to impress their friends and the women who frequented the taverns. Needless to say, the bartenders understood these men very well, and it wasn't at all uncommon to see a Remington or Mortimer double-barrel shotgun prominently displayed behind the bar. Back then, many shotguns were imported from England and Belgium to meet a demand the American gun makers of the time could not. Again, contrary to what Hollywood may have taught us, most of the shotguns were kept in their original, long-barreled configuration. But some were shortened dramatically, turning them into what we now call 'coach guns' or the ubiquitous 'sawed-off shotgun.' A ten-gauge shotgun spoke with authority, and no matter how drunk or rowdy a man might become, very few would challenge that authority.

"Every so often, a couple of drunken revelers would exchange shots in the street. The usual outcome would be two empty revolvers, a cloud of smoke, and two men in jail the next morning with hangovers almost as painful as a .44 wound." Again, most of the students laughed at the joke. "No," Jenson continued, "Hobbs just wasn't the kind of town Hollywood would be fantasizing over about eighty years hence. Are there any questions? No? Well then we'll move on.

"It was about this time that Hobbs's one 'mystery man' appeared on the scene. Zachary Louben opened his lumber mill in 1881. He came in quietly, and hardly anyone really noticed him, until he began the construction of the incinerator for his mill. The townsfolk wondered why the mill needed an incinerator of such huge proportions. It wasn't long after its completion that it got its moniker, 'The Devil's Rifle.' This is the reference I made before about the name of the town being Hobbs. Zachary Louben and his wife employed forty-three local men at the mill, and he paid well. That was a lot of people with jobs considering the time and place, so people ignored the differences between themselves and the Loubens.

"It seemed as though Zachary Louben neither drank nor gambled. As a matter of fact, he apparently would only come into Hobbs to buy supplies once a month. Interestingly, no one ever saw Mrs. Louben—not even the mill hands who worked for them. In fact, the only evidence on record for her existence were the sparse words of Zachary himself—and the occasional mail-order packages from back east that were addressed to Mrs. Louben.

"Some of the townsfolk, it seems, had concluded they were religious fanatics—perhaps some splinter group of the Mormon faith come down from Utah. But there was absolutely no evidence to back up those speculations, as they apparently never came into town for religious services on Sundays or even on the various holidays such as Easter and Christmas. It was also rumored they had a substantial amount of gold, or something else of value, somewhere on their property. The rumor hinted at a secret, hidden basement under their house. Stories such as this are frequently bandied about regarding the odd members of any given society. And though, after the events we're about to discuss happened, people later looked for this supposed treasure, they never found any evidence of that either.

"It was in October of 1887 when the first child disappeared—a girl of twelve had simply vanished. The population had grown considerably in the ten years since the town's founding, and by 1887 it had begun to take on a veneer of respectability. There was even a school by then, in almost the same spot as this one, which was built in 1900. The town marshal found no clues or evidence, and after the appropriate mourning, life went on.

"It happened again in 1889 and once more in 1891. The town was up in arms by this time, and meetings were held to discuss the problem. Zachary Louben attended some of the meetings, if the transcripts of those meetings are accurate. And then in November of 1891 the marshal arrested the minister's son. His father had discovered some girl's clothing in his son's room and had turned him in to the authorities. The mother of the most recently missing girl, a ten-year-old named Adeline Harrison, immediately identified the clothes as belonging to her daughter. Further, she said, they were the clothes she'd been wearing the day she vanished.

"The trial was short; the circuit judge came up from Prescott for the hearing. 'God's will was done,' he said, and seventeen year old Thomas Harper was 'hanged by the neck until dead,' his last words proclaiming his innocence. His father, the preacher, hung himself three days later; it was the day before Christmas.

"Hobbs was calm for the next four years. By this time the lumber trade in the region was dying out. Most of the big trees were gone already, and the remaining ones were so far away that the lumbermen gradually moved out, heading west and north where there was still work for them. Hobbs was in what we would now call a recession. The times were very hard, and people came together as a community to help one another; everyone except the Loubens, it seems.

"In October of 1895 a ten-year-old boy named Harper Johansson disappeared while out hunting for food for his family. People talked nervously, wondering if the child disappearances were being repeated. The new town marshal wasted no time and quickly organized a search party. Two days after the search commenced, the boy was found—or part of him, anyway. Scavengers such as vultures, crows, and coyotes had taken most of him by the time they'd found him. In spite of this loss, everyone breathed a sigh of relief. It would seem the boy had died in the hills while out hunting.

"In 1896 another child vanished. Thirteen-year-old Suzy was the daughter of one of the local 'women of the night,' so there wasn't much interest. As a matter of fact, it doesn't even appear that her last name was ever even reported or recorded, so now we only know her as Suzy. People just assumed she'd moved away to start a business of her own like her mother's, perhaps in Prescott. No search party was even sent out to look for the girl.

"A hunting party found the partial skeleton of a child in the hills in the summer of 1897. At that time and place there was no such thing as DNA evidence, so there was no way to identify the bones, and the pitiful remains were laid to rest in the town cemetery under an unmarked stone.

"The winter of 1897 was harsh in Hobbs, and the snow was deep in October. That was the month the marshal's daughter went missing. As in the past, a search party was organized. And as before, nothing turned up. It was, unfortunately, a difficult time to be looking for someone; the snow was said to have been three to four feet deep in some of the drifts. Marshal Thompson questioned everyone in the town; he was a man obsessed, stalking the streets day and night, asking questions, and then questioning the answers he was given. He spent a lot of time seeking the truths behind alibis, looking for lies. Days passed, then weeks. Thompson patrolled the streets with his brand new Winchester pump shotgun. He was hunting, and the population knew it, and it made them nervous. Furthermore, he was ignoring his duties as they related to the rest of his job. He neglected to arrest drunks and brawlers, and people were becoming upset with his actions.

"They called another meeting. This meeting would decide if the marshal should be allowed to keep his job and his badge. Jake Thompson was late for the meeting, which certainly didn't sit well with the town fathers. It was almost the 20th century, for God's sake! Shotguns in the streets were no longer acceptable, as far as the mayor and the city council were concerned. Those present had just come to that conclusion when the marshal showed up, shotgun in hand. He ignored the hostile stares, walked straight to the front of the church, and interrupted the gathering by roughly shoving the mayor, who had the floor, from behind the pulpit.

"After he'd stared down those who were angry with his behavior, and silence again reigned, he told the assemblage that a witness had seen old man Louben lurking around the marshal's house two nights before the girl's disappearance. He wanted to raise a posse, he announced, to go out to the lumber mill to question the fellow and his wife and any employees still working for him. There was a moment of silence, and then all hell broke loose.

"The detonation was deafening in Hobbs. Houses close to the Louben mill were actually knocked off their foundations; some of them completely collapsed, trapping women and children inside. Lanterns fell, kerosene spilled. The fires spread unabated all that day, and most of the next, fanned by high winds coming in from the west. For a while, it looked like all of Hobbs would go up in flames. As it was, most of the business district burned to the ground. The buildings that later replaced them were all built of stone and brick.

"It was four days before Marshal Thompson and his posse were able to reach the mill. They sat on horseback together, in silence, and stared. Only the incinerator's chimney and a partial wall of what had once been the Louben residence remained standing. But oddly, there was no scorching of fire—no soot, no ash at all. Once more there was an investigation, and in the end, nothing came of the disappearance of the marshal's daughter. All of the possible suspects, it appeared, were blown into oblivion along with the lumber mill. No bodies were recovered.

"Jake Thompson retired and moved away, a broken man. His wife stayed in Hobbs. The divorce was finalized in 1899. Former Marshal Jake Thompson died in an automobile accident in central Phoenix in the year 1921. He was quite drunk at the time, and it had been surmised that he'd not even seen the lamppost…or, as some suggest, perhaps he had.

"Things moved on in Hobbs. Copper mining caused a brief boom in the early part of this century, but that too faded within a very short period of time. Every once in a while, people would show up, searching for the 'Louben Treasure,' but all that remained was 'The Devil's Rifle.' Even famous treasure hunters of the era finally gave up the search, and that was the end of the Louben legend."

The bell jerked Curt back into the present. He'd been absolutely mesmerized by the story that Mr. Jenson had told them. At least he now had an understanding as to why the Stack was sometimes referred to as the Devil's Rifle! He shuffled his papers together and stood. He walked out the door and down the hall. By the time he arrived at the gym, he was almost late. He dressed out quickly; everyone else was already on the basketball court doing warm-up exercises. The coach scowled at Curt, but he didn't say anything. Tommy Driscoll was standing there, doing jumping jacks, and grinning at him.

Curt felt more like taking a nap than running around chasing a ball, but there was no slacking in Coach Johnson's class. So Curt spent the period dutifully running around in circles. He even got his hands on the ball one time, only to lose it almost as quickly when Tommy ran by him, and slapped it from his hands. He didn't care. He much preferred to watch professional basketball on television than play it in some small, smelly high-school gymnasium. Later, at their lockers, Tommy told Curt that Carl told his dad they'd been to the Stack.

Curt was shocked. "Why'd he do a dumb thing like that?"

"Dunno," Tommy responded with a shrug as he twisted the top from his thermos. "He said he told him Saturday night…and he told him about the stone pyramid you found too."

Though Curt was still looking at Tommy with his eyes, his mind flashed back to the odd dream of Cheryl. He almost laughed; how could there be any connection? *Give it back.* The very thought was ridiculous. Tommy glanced rapidly in both directions to see if anyone else was near them, and took a quick swig from his thermos, recapping it. Curt caught the unmistakable aroma of whiskey. He was about to make a comment when Tommy interrupted him. "Carl says his dad and the mayor are really pissed off. He said it's dangerous around the Stack and kids have no business playing there."

Curt snickered. "I don't remember playing, actually—and imagine! Mister 'Porn King' telling us what to do? That's a real laugh. And the pyramid thing is mine. I found it fair and square; I'm keeping it."

They both laughed as they tied their shoes. Curt would be eighteen next month; he certainly wasn't a kid anymore—and as far as he was concerned, that excluded him from the chief's remarks.

Tommy went on. "Carl says his dad told him you should turn the pyramid over to him. It's city property, and should be in the museum…or something. He's really angry that you got that thing, and as soon as he can get the paper-work together, he's gonna come and take it from you."

Curt was angry now. "Bullshit! I found it, and I'm keeping it. My dad said it might be a talisman; you know, witchcraft stuff."

Tommy responded, "Maybe there was some kinda crime up there involving witchcraft—you know, like those cattle mutilations?"

Curt snorted. "Uh, uh. It looked to me like it had been there for a long time—can't be any statute of limitations long enough to cover from the 19th century. Chief Larsen's blowing smoke, and we both know it. He just likes to throw his weight around." But Curt thought briefly of the missing children of Hobbs; had they been killed by some kind of witchcraft or devil worshipping cult all those years ago? He supposed it was possible, but it probably didn't matter anyway, as all the people involved in all of that were long dead by this time.

There was a loud *POP* from the direction of the showers, then another. Voices shouted and echoed against the tile walls. *Towel fight,* Curt thought. *Somebody's gonna have a sore butt third period!* Curt and Tommy left immediately. The boys were glad to trade the steamy air and musty odors for the cool October air.

Curt thought again about Cheryl…and a dream he now only vaguely remembered. It'd been sexy though, and it'd involved Cheryl. He remembered that in the dream she'd asked him to do something, but he couldn't quite remember what. He thought about it, but it seemed the concept was just out of reach right now. The boys parted company. Curt watched as Tommy sauntered off, swinging his small thermos by the handle.

Cheryl was in Curt's English class fifth period, and when the bell rang, he waited outside the room for her. As soon as he saw her, he resolved not to tell her he'd mailed his college applications this morning—at least not yet. He rationalized that this wasn't a lie, as he was saying nothing at all, and besides, he should wait for the right time to tell her. In the hall outside of class in front of everyone wasn't the place for that information to be shared. Cheryl bounced up to him, flashing a big smile and taking his hand. "Hi," she said simply.

Now he felt nervous, self-conscious. He cleared his throat, and looked around. There was nobody near enough to hear what he was going to say. "I had a very weird dream about you last night."

She paused, tipping her head. "And who gave you permission to dream about me?"

"Oh, I always dream about you," he responded, "only this dream was different...but I can't remember it now."

Cheryl was disappointed. "It's not fair to tell me this and then just say you can't remember it. If you happen to remember, you'd better tell me, okay?" She leaned over, kissing him on the cheek. Then she turned and entered the classroom.

The bell.

Curt was right behind her, and quickly found his seat. Fifth period always seemed long to Curt; he'd much rather be in art class. And, as usual, English passed slowly. The only thing keeping him awake was watching Cheryl, sitting two seats in front of him in the next aisle. And then, suddenly, wonderfully, it was over. Cheryl rose, saying something over her shoulder to Curt about her next class. Curt missed what she said. He'd been doing that a lot lately with Cheryl, and it was bothering him.

But Curt always forgot the things that were bothering him in his last class of the day. Art class was an excellent way to end the school day, he thought. The drawing he was doing to illustrate Carl's poem was finished; he'd looked at it two more times, and still thought it fitting to leave it a little unfinished in memorial for those dead...whatever they were. He applied a light coat of fixative to the drawing, and put it in a folder. He laughed now, as he realized he was speaking of his dream as though it had actually happened, and that those multi-eyed creatures had actually lived.

It was amazing! He'd done the illustration with no more than a cursory reading of the poem. He hoped that didn't mean he was starting to think like Carl. Well, in any case, he'd show the drawing to Mrs. Blackwell for her opinion. He walked next door to where the school paper was produced.

Mrs. Blackwell stared at the drawing for a long time. The scrawny, pleading arms and hands clawing at the air, the darkness—and in that darkness, multiple eyes! That alone should've been scary, but Curt's drawing had put into the eyes a pleading, helpless look that summoned sorrow instead of dread in her mind. Finally, she looked up at Curt. "Where did this image come from?"

Curt responded, "Oh, when I was about six or so, I'd dream about this creature. It was a very persistent dream, but it stopped when I was twelve. I had it again the other night." Mrs. Blackwell said nothing. "It seems to fit the poem, somehow," he concluded.

Curt was worried that she didn't like the drawing. Then she smiled, and said that it was a fine drawing, and that they'd use it. Curt was relieved. He rose to leave, and Mrs. Blackwell spoke. "Where do you suppose this is? Some other planet?"

Curt grinned. "It was a very realistic dream, Mrs. Blackwell, but I suspect it only existed in my mind."

Mrs. Blackwell responded, "Of course it did."

"I gotta go, Mrs. Blackwell. I gotta get to the library."

"Term paper?"

"Yeah…term paper." It was the best he could do at the moment.

17

But Curt didn't go to the library, not the school library anyway. He rode his bike down Yavapai Street toward downtown. He was going to the city library. At his destination, he jumped off his bike and locked it in the rack. He walked through the old brass framed glass doors. The building was of post-fire stone construction, and was a minor landmark in Hobbs.

Curt heard his shoes echo faintly off the tile floor. He figured that since he didn't have a lot of time, he'd ask the librarian for help. He thought the librarian might be 'original issue' with the library. Still, Mrs. Prutzman was always nice to kids as long as they behaved themselves, and didn't make a lot of noise. Generally, the rowdies spent little time in the public library—and even less time reading.

Now he was following Mrs. Prutzman down an aisle into the stacks, where the filtered sunlight cast a warm glow over the bindings of the neatly shelved books. Her black, high-heeled shoes made a sharp *click, click* as she walked ahead of Curt, scanning the markings on the shelves.

"We don't have too much on magic," she apologized, "but there's the *Man, Myth, and Magic* encyclopedia in the reference room. It has a fair amount of information on the subject as it was approached by different cultures around the world. Whatever we find here, I think you should look at that resource as well." She stopped suddenly, and turned to face the shelves. Her eyes gave a quick, practiced scan, and then stopped.

She stood on her tiptoes to reach the shelf she wanted, and Curt opened his mouth to offer assistance, but she quickly pulled several books from the shelf and handed them to Curt. Two shelves down, she found another book, and also handed that one to Curt. She smiled. "This should keep you busy for a little while, young man."

They walked out of the stacks, and Muriel guided him to an empty work-table. There he sat, and opened the first book, slowly leafing through it. It contained a number of illustrated pentagrams, and other 'sigils,' as the book called them. None of them looked like the small stone pyramid held safely in his backpack. Curt thanked Mrs. Prutzman, and she walked back to her desk at the front of the room. Curt turned back to the books, and was quickly absorbed in his research. There were pentagrams in all three of the books as well, but none looked like the five pointed designs he'd seen on the strange crystal. And further, the only illustrations of pyramids of any kind at all were of the large variety—those of Egypt, Central America, and the Ziggurats of Sumer, the most ancient of all.

Muriel Prutzman watched Curt from her desk at the front of the large room as he studied the books she'd found for him—and she saw an odd object he'd retrieved from his backpack after she'd left him. There were only three other people in the library at the moment, and that included old Mr. Farnsworth, sleeping with the newspapers. She walked over to where the boy was hunched over the table and his books. She enjoyed helping kids, and was always pleased when a member of the younger generation came into the library.

"Is there anything I can do to help you?"

Curt glanced up, smiling. "I found this thing a few days ago, and I'm trying to figure out what it is."

Mrs. Prutzman picked up the crystal, examining it. She turned it this way and that, examining the odd, geometric designs carved into its surface. The only part of the design she recognized was the five-ray star carved on one of the stone's facets. But that meant little; the tiny marks carved into each of the five rays of the star were unfamiliar to her. She set it carefully back on the table. "I've never seen anything like it before," she commented, "some of the symbols do resemble some of the ones in the books, but they're not exactly the same, so I don't know what to say." She looked at Curt. "Where did you find this?"

Curt answered truthfully this time. "I found it in the Stack."

"The stack? Do you mean that chimney out on Highway 86? The old remnants of the Louben mill?" She sounded worried more than any thing else, which encouraged Curt, so he continued his explanation.

"Yeah," he admitted. "It was inside, behind a loose brick."

Mrs. Prutzman sat down next to him, and picked up the crystal one more time. "As far as I know," she said in a low voice, "nobody's been up there since 1947 when that little boy died in there—that's a little before my time here, but I don't think it's too safe; you should stay away from there. If something fell on you and trapped you, you'd probably never be found."

He laughed in response. "I don't think I'm going back there, Mrs. Prutzman, we pretty much saw what there was to see, which really wasn't much. I just happened to see a brick that looked out of place, and yanked it out. This was in a hole behind the brick. I bet it's been there pretty much forever, don't you?"

"Probably, yes," she responded. "But even so, promise you won't do that again. I don't want to find out you got hurt or worse in there."

"I'm not going back," he said, and that seemed to satisfy the woman. He smiled, thinking of the librarian's words. *1947. So Mrs. Prutzman isn't original issue, after all.*

Muriel was still looking at the small pyramid. "Maybe," she said thoughtfully, "if you took a picture or two, I could send them to someone I know who might be able to help you figure it out."

"That's a great idea, Mrs. Prutzman," Curt enthused. "Who're you going to send them to?"

Just then someone came into the library. Mrs. Prutzman's sharp ears heard the soft sound of the door opening and closing again. She turned to see who had come in. A rather disheveled looking man was standing by the card file, but not looking in it. *Transient*, Muriel thought, and turned back to Curt. "I know a retired professor of comparative religion who lives in Prescott. He used to teach at a university back east somewhere; he made a lifetime of studying things like this."

Curt was overjoyed. "I'll bring a close-up Polaroid over tomorrow after school," he promised.

"That'll be fine," Muriel said. She glanced over to the card file. The derelict was gone.

Curt thanked Mrs. Prutzman again, and turned to leave the library, his backpack swinging from his left hand. He swung the library doors open and stepped out into the sun. The library was set back from the street, and Curt liked the grassy buffer zone with its small trees and picnic-style tables. A breeze ruffled his hair as he walked to his bike and undid the lock. As he wrapped the chain around the base of the seat and fastened it, he heard a car door shut. Curt put his backpack in the carrier on the back of his bike, fastening it there with an elastic strap, and pushed the bike down the neat gravel path to the street. He mounted the bike and began pedaling toward home. His mind was still dwelling on the pyramid, and the fact that the books he'd been examining offered not even the slightest hint as to what it might really be.

And because he was distracted with those other thoughts, he hadn't noticed the old green car pulling slowly from the curb a little more than half a block behind him. For a short period of time, the car kept its distance. He'd gone about a block when he became aware of the deep rumbling of its engine. He glanced quickly over his shoulder. A big car was closing on him rapidly.

The front passenger's window was being rolled down. The big Merc pulled up alongside him. The car was very close now, the engine both a sound and vibration with its proximity. Curt caught a glimpse of the man inside. He was old, perhaps fifty, and he looked awful. He was skinny—emaciated would likely be a better word. Curt glanced to the right to gauge how much maneuvering room he had between the green car and the curbing. When he looked back at the green Mercury, it had slid even closer to him! Curt was about to yell something when the man in the car suddenly leaned out of the window. His eyes were red, rheumy.

"Do you know what I want?"

A chill fell over Curt. He opened his mouth, but nothing came out. The strange man in the Mercury made a sudden lunge at him. He was out the window now almost up to his waist. Curt thought for a moment that he would come tumbling out onto the street. One scrawny, scabby hand closed over the shoulder strap of the knapsack in the luggage rack. Curt found his voice, "NO!"

The man tightened his grip, and pulled. He was so close now that Curt could smell the stale wine on his clothing, and on his breath. Curt leaned hard to his right and reaching back with his right hand, he yanked on the heavy nylon flap of the backpack. The strap held captive in the drunken man's hand broke.

Curt felt the bike suddenly heeling over hard to his right. Instinctively he swerved to the left in an attempt to regain his balance. His front wheel hit the Mercury's fender, dragging along the metal for less than a second. But that was all it took; Curt's balance was gone, and he fell to the street. The torn shoulder strap slid through the hand of the wino until the buckle bit into flesh. The man yelped out an obscenity, and let go. Curt hit the grassy area between the curb and the sidewalk, rolling twice. He was still clutching the knapsack.

The big Mercury's engine came suddenly to life. It thundered. The wide rear tires disappeared in a boiling cloud of white smoke and burning rubber. As Curt pushed himself up onto his knees, the acrid smell of burning tires stung his eyes and nostrils. He coughed. He saw the license plate of the offending auto, but he couldn't make out the numbers. Judging by the color, the license was an old Arizona plate.

The Mercury squealed around the next corner, leaning hard to the left, still burning rubber, and was gone. Curt heard the big engine fading away. *That car was really moving!* He got slowly to his feet, brushing himself off, and checking for any injuries. He was shaky and grass-stained, the right knee was out on his jeans, but he was still in one piece. He'd scraped the knee pretty good on the curb, and it was bleeding a little, but it wasn't serious. He felt very lucky, remembering the warning words of his father. *"Be careful with that," his father had admonished. "Its owners may want it back."*

As Curt stood, still coughing on the bitter taste that would've been more familiar on a dragstrip than on a city street in sleepy little Hobbs, a woman who'd just exited the library came bustling up, shouting that she'd called the police. A kid of about ten was jumping up and down excitedly on the lowest step at the front of the library, shouting, "I saw the car! I saw the car!"

Curt sat down on the bus bench, his bike leaning against his knees. He knew he'd have to take off before the cops arrived. They'd probably want to keep the backpack for evidence and would almost certainly confiscate it. Then they'd go through the contents and find the engraved crystal. The chief himself wanted it, though to what end, Curt couldn't guess. But it really wouldn't matter by then—he'd no longer have it, and though he'd get his backpack returned in a few days, it would be without the pyramid. Or, his mind suggested, maybe he'd not get anything back. They'd surely find the two joints inside that he'd purchased that day at school, and the chief would have the stone and Curt in one stroke.

He rose and wheeled his bike out of the gathering crowd, head carefully lowered against identifying eyes. So far, he'd not been seen by anyone who knew him, but that might not last either. If someone suddenly showed up who actually knew who he was, it would be all over. He needed time to think, time to talk with his father about the events of this afternoon.

The bike's tires were still inflated, and though the paint was scratched a little, the frame wasn't bent, and it was still rideable. He mounted the bike over the objections of the woman who'd called the police.

"You should wait, young man," she said with concern in her voice, "the police need to talk with you, and it might not hurt to let an ambulance attendant examine you before you leave."

He shouted to her as he pedaled away, "I'll call the police when I get home. I'm late and my dad'll worry."

Curt was cautious on the way home, making no stops, and looking frequently over his shoulder. At one point, the deep-throated roar of an auto's engine caused him to flinch and almost fall again. As the candy-apple red Camaro growled its way past him, he heard the stereo inside. It was turned up very loudly—it was playing something appropriate for the time and circumstance—something sinister—something dangerous. Though he didn't recognize the song, he recognized the group singing it—Jefferson Airplane. He shivered.

Curt arrived home at five-thirty. His dad would be home in half an hour; he'd call the cops then. He set his knapsack on his desk, and carefully removed the crystal. He unwrapped it.

Do you know what I want?

The thought echoed oddly in his mind. He'd heard it twice—one time this afternoon from the snaggle-toothed mouth of the man in the green Mercury, but where else had he heard it? The memory was almost there, right on the metaphoric tip of his metaphoric tongue. But there it stayed.

Curt looked at the crystal, and then at the torn backpack. Why did everyone want that damn thing? *That damn Carl Larsen, he steals porno from his dad to sell to the kids at school, smokes dope with us, and then tells his dad about our trip to the Stack and all about this pyramid. God damn it! Maybe I should just put the damn thing back in the Stack and forget the whole thing.*

Curt heard the Escort pull into the driveway. He knew he'd have to tell his dad about the man and the attack. Kent Paxton walked through the front door. He was carrying a pizza—a big one. Over dinner, Curt told his dad the story of the old Mercury and the library. Kent listened with interest and concern. What had his son gotten into? As they talked, the pizza disappeared quickly. When they'd finished eating, Kent called the police.

The officer who showed up at their door was sitting on their sofa now, carefully filling out the report on his clipboard. Curt described the Mercury in as much detail as he could. "It was a '66 or maybe a '67 model," he said, "with a high-powered, souped-up engine." His description of the man was sketchy— he'd only had a second's glance at him, and at the time he was thinking more about keeping his bicycle standing on its wheels. *Do you know what I want?* Curt went on to say that perhaps they'd thought he had money in his back- pack—or maybe some drugs.

"May I see the pack?"

Curt was prepared for Officer…Grant, the nametag on his starched, dark blue uniform shirt read. He went to his room and picked up the torn back- pack. The crystal now safely resided under his mattress along with his stash. He limped as he walked back into the living room. His left leg ached, and what he really wanted to do was soak in a nice hot bath for, oh, maybe an hour or so.

Officer Grant scrutinized the pack through narrowed, suspicious eyes. He removed Curt's schoolbooks, one at a time, flipping through them. A folded piece of notebook paper fell from his math book, and Officer Grant leaned over, snatching it from the floor before Curt could get to it. The policeman glanced at it and replaced it in the book. It was nothing more than this coming week's homework assignments.

He glanced at Curt, then returned his attention to the damaged backpack. He turned the backpack inside out, shaking it roughly. Curt smiled inwardly. He could tell the cop was suspicious of him, as they were always suspicious of the victims of crime. After all, it was always easier if something could be found or inferred about the victim that would make searching diligently for the perpetra- tor of the crime unnecessary. If the victim was guilty of something, they already had their man. What a joke! He'd been very close to dying that afternoon and the cop was sure it was, at least partly, his fault somehow.

"Did you take anything out of here since the...incident?" Officer Grant was staring at Curt.

"No, sir," the boy responded politely, "I left everything as it was...I thought it would maybe be important as evidence or something. It looks like there's some blood on the buckle here where he grabbed it." He pointed to the rusty-looking mark on the chrome-plated teeth of the buckle.

Officer Grant grunted, looking at the stains more carefully. "Do you think this might be your blood?"

Curt recalled the man's yelp of pain as he'd released his hold on the backpack. "No, sir. I'm sure he cut himself with it. It's why he let go."

"Alright," Officer Grant said finally, closing his notebook. "A detective will be here in about an hour. He'll need to impound your bike and backpack for a few days. We'll have to take it down to Phoenix; that's the closest lab. They'll check the blood type and check for possible paint residue from the hit and run vehicle. You should have your bike back in two or three days at the most."

Kent and Curt thanked Officer Grant as he left. He handed Kent his card, and turned to Curt. "If you remember anything else, anything at all, let me know, alright?" He actually smiled. Curt told him he would call right away if anything else occurred to him, and with that, Officer Grant departed.

At nine that night, a white Chevy van pulled up in their driveway. This was the forensics team. Immediately behind them, an unmarked, white Ford sedan pulled to the curb. Curt dutifully surrendered his bike and backpack in exchange for a receipt. He was assured he'd have his bike back in a week at the most. Curt nodded silently, and the men got back in the van and drove away. The detective stayed only a short time as well—just long enough to confirm that Curt had nothing else to add to the report Officer Grant had taken.

Curt went back to his room to finish his schoolwork, once more annoyed with himself for closing the door. He was still limping, but it had improved over the last two hours. His leg still hurt, of course, but he knew he'd be okay. He'd give himself that promised soak in the tub after his homework was done— it was a distinct motivator. He worked on his physics paper for an hour, and then shut the book. He went to his bed, reaching under the mattress. His hand touched the crystal. He'd promised Mrs. Prutzman he'd photograph it for her friend in Prescott. *Well, no time like the present,* he thought. Curt opened his window, sat on the sill, and enjoyed the cool breeze for a couple of minutes. He was feeling very tired, he realized, and he'd not get this done if he waited much longer...*where is the camera?* He sat for another short moment, trying to remember what he'd done with the thing. He hadn't used it in a while. He suddenly snapped his fingers, and grinned. He stood, walking to the closet, and pulled several boxes from the top shelf. Naturally, the camera was behind the very last one.

He opened the cheap vinyl case, and lifted out the old camera. He clipped the close-up lens onto the camera, and checked to make sure it was on tight. Next he put a dark blue towel on the bed for contrast, and the pyramid on the towel. When he was satisfied, he raised the camera to his eye and focused it. Then he remembered the flash. He grunted softly, and set the camera back on the bed. He looked in the camera case and discovered he only had two bulbs left. Hopefully, they still worked. He clipped one into the flash reflector, and raised the camera. Once more he focused the camera, and took the shot. The flash was bright, and Curt was convinced that it had been good flashbulb. He took a second photo, just to be sure. *Now if the film's still good...*

He peeled back the covering paper from the first Polaroid picture. He studied the image, waiting a few seconds for the other image to self-develop. Since he wasn't looking out his window right at that moment, he didn't see the dark green Mercury idling at the curb a little less than a block away. The car slid out into the street, like some monstrous cat. Somewhere in the back of his mind, Curt heard the engine as the car rumbled past his house. It was almost...purring.

Both of the photos turned out perfectly, so Curt put them carefully with his schoolbooks, and then slid the pyramid back under his mattress. He thought about taking that long, promised soak in the bathtub, but by this time he was now lying on his bed. The pain in his leg was almost gone, and the bathroom door was closed. *Best leave it.* He wondered briefly at that thought. He lay on his back, hands behind his head. He was still dressed, but he no longer cared about such trivial matters. And as he drifted off into sleep, he had one more thought. *Cheryl took something in there...* but that was ridiculous, of course. Cheryl had never been in his house at all. *Had she?*

18

The man sitting in the large, leather bound chair spoke quietly to his wife. He leaned forward slightly as he spoke, and the wan light of the dying fire flickered over his features. The old, supple leather creaked softly with his movements. The fire crackled and popped inside the containment of the stone-mantled fireplace. The room was large, the drawing room of a bygone century. No artificial light dimmed the shadows that danced and flickered across the walls and black walnut bookcases. Though it was still early afternoon, he picked up his crystal wine glass from the table, taking a sip. He'd bought this wine longer ago than he cared to remember—but it was excellent wine, and worth the cost.

"Time grows short."

There was a long pause. A log in the fireplace cracked open with a loud pop, briefly filling the room with the renewed light of fresh burning wood. The heavy woman, sitting in an identical leather chair across a small round dark wood table with dragon claws as feet, finally spoke. "I know, dear," she said in a soft and conciliatory voice, "but as long as that crystal eludes us, we have only one course of action open to us. I am fearful of that method; we barely got away with it the last time. I would not want to take such a chance again; who can say what tempting fate might bring a second time?"

The man sat back in his chair and sighed heavily. "I too realize the danger in that path. Still, what other avenue is open to us now?"

Again there was a pause as the woman considered the problem. "Maybe the girl can be brought to heel. We're being pursued. Can you not feel it?"

"Perhaps…"

The man turned back to the heavy volume lying in his lap, slowly going through the old book. The few words present on the old, brittle parchment pages were in Latin. He was very familiar with the language, and readily understood the large, finely hand drawn letters. But the words were not what he thought useful this day. He was spending most of the time looking at the illustrations. These consisted of meticulous, hand drawn, red and black diagrams; mostly they were of geometric shapes like pyramids, with directions on how to properly construct them and the materials that may be used—the latter being of most interest to him.

The Latin inscriptions were done in pen and ink—for though the ancient civilizations of both the Chinese and Koreans had movable type two hundred years before the time this book was written, the European printing press was still eighty years hence, and no Catholic Church dominated society would have tolerated the printing of a book such as this in any case.

The man looked up from his reading. "Don and Cal missed today. Don called a few minutes ago from a pay phone while you were downstairs checking on the new girl," he said as he carefully turned one of the vellum pages. "They're taking the long way home."

The woman smiled thinly. "I know, Vic. I saw. We'll just have to try again. There is surely a way to retrieve our property."

The man slammed the old book closed in anger, not caring should he damage the binding. "Damn! That boy is not going to interfere with this operation!"

The woman smiled. "The girl has promise, Vic. I can feel her power. We just need a way to tap into it."

Vic replied grimly. "Look, I know what her brother told you about the bulbs and mirrors and all of the other things. How do you know she can still do it? How do you know she can do anything else?"

The woman just shook her head, saying, "She's unconsciously found a way to suppress her power, and that's good. When it does finally break through, I wouldn't want to be the target." She laughed a mirthless laugh. "But still, I believe I can get her to direct it in any way we need."

Vic smiled. He knew what the next target would be—the mind of that Paxton boy for interfering. The last attempt had worked, he had to admit, but the results they'd wanted were not forthcoming. That boy still had the crystal, and they needed it badly. If Mary could gain control of the girl's power, and link it to hers, the boy would obey. Vic knew the headaches were weakening his wife's abilities.

He sat in silent frustration. In the end, though, he realized now, it was probably a good thing the Paxton boy was the one who'd found it. He knew nothing of what he possessed; he'd never be able to figure out its secret or to use it himself. No, it was safe enough where it was, but time was short; there was no denying that. And Mary had reminded him of that now familiar feeling of being hunted.

Retrieving the crystal should've been easy, but Mary's dream interference hadn't taken, and that wasn't a good sign. Her headaches were inhibiting her powers of concentration—that dream should've been dynamite! The Paxton boy should've given over the crystal by this time, either by accident or design. Yet he went about his business with an annoying casualness as though he didn't remember the dream, or maybe didn't care. It was truly maddening!

And now they'd just learned from Cal and Don that the boy was beginning to do some research on his own. Vic wasn't worried that the boy would—or could—learn anything useful, but if he kept dragging it around showing it to people, that other meddler might get wind of it, and that would surely be a disaster. He had to be stopped, and soon. As long as the pyramid remained in his hands, the thing was undoable, and it was only a matter of days now until the time had come. They could no longer risk waiting until the next cycle. Instinctively, Vic knew that this would be now or never.

That librarian would have to be watched as well. If that girl, Sarah, couldn't do the job soon, he might have to hire outside help…again. He didn't like that idea. There were too many outsiders involved already. Across the table from him, Mary sat silently, looking into the fire as though she expected some kind of sudden salvation to come from the flames. If indeed salvation was coming, they'd have to see to it themselves, just like the last time—just like all the last times. Vic returned the book to the shelf, this time removing a geology text.

Cal Johnson sat on his cot under the dim incandescent light that hung from the ceiling of his quarters. He held his left hand gingerly in his right, examining the wounds he'd suffered in that attempted theft of the boy's backpack. That damn steel buckle had pulled out a fair-sized piece of meat, just when he'd been so close. Why, he wondered, was life always dealing him a bad hand? He cursed softly under his breath, and pressed the sleeve of a dirty tee shirt over the still bleeding wound.

"Cal, you in there?" Cal glanced at the door. He recognized the voice of his friend Don Bristow. "Come on in, Don," he shouted, "door's unlocked."

Don Bristow pushed open the door, and strode into the room. He didn't look at all like Cal. His skin was deeply tanned from time spent in the sun. After spending ten years in prison, it was nice to feel the warm sun once again. Unlike his disheveled partner, his clothes, while not expensive, were always neat and clean. He was freshly showered, and noticed with some disgust that Cal was still sweaty from his encounter earlier in the day.

Don liked his job as the gardener around the estate, and he was quite determined that nothing would interfere with that, certainly not this idiot sitting in front of him. He didn't have to do too much real work; he just piddled around the grounds, pulling up weeds and mowing lawns, making a show of being legitimately employed. And the best part of the whole thing was that he was paid handsomely in cash for his services; well enough that he could afford to let the businessmen of Hobbs keep their money…at least for now. And he'd get to do some of those…other jobs that Vic or Mary needed done. He grinned. He was always the driver, and Cal had to do the dangerous stuff like hanging out a car window trying to steal a backpack from some dumb high school kid! He laughed, and Cal looked up at him, but he ignored the other man for the time being. He was reminiscing about some of those other jobs. But now he got to stay home; well, this was as close as he'd ever come to that concept, and he was smart enough to know it.

Sure, several months ago he'd made a few trips around the country buying children for Mary and Vic, but he'd been told they had enough now; originally there'd been eleven in all. He glowed in the praise he'd been given by Vic when he'd explained upon his return how careful he'd been. No more than two children were purchased at a time from any one...purveyor.

He'd shopped widely, crisscrossing the country twice, following information and leads. A few had been dead ends, and one had quoted an unreasonable fee, so Don had killed him and took three of his stable in one haul. Vic had paid him an extra thousand dollars for his ingenuity and his discretion. Don was smart enough to know that discretion was always worth a little extra cash.

Don looked at Cal and smiled. He was filled with loathing for this slug of a man—this waste of skin. But Vic wanted them to work together, so Don smiled.

"Have a seat, Don," Cal wheezed around the butt of his unfiltered cigarette, "I can use the company."

Don grinned. He knew that Cal needed a whole lot more than just some company; he needed a very thorough killing.

Don grinned at that thought, and inquired cheerily, "So, how's the hand? Looks pretty painful from here." He grinned again, hoping that observation was the truth.

"It hurts like hell, if you want to know the truth," Cal replied. "Boy. I was so close..."

"Close only counts when you're using hand grenades, Cal." Cal laughed because he thought it was a joke. Don laughed because he knew it wasn't.

"Even the old lady failed this time," Don said, worry finally creeping into his voice. "She's a weird bitch, isn't she?"

Cal hacked around his cigarette, his face wreathed in the tobacco fume of his coughing. "I'll tell ya, Don, my friend, she's even got me havin' bad dreams." Cal uncorked the almost empty wine bottle that had been standing on the small side table, offering it to Don. Don grimaced at the thought of that greasy bottle touching his lips. Cal, entirely misreading Don's facial expression, smiled back at him.

Don said, "Sunday night was really something, wasn't it? You ever see anything like that before, Cal?"

Cal recalled last Sunday night, and took another swig from the bottle. Don had driven that night; Don always got to drive, now that Cal thought about it.

He wondered why he was never allowed to drive. He'd have to bring that up with Vic the next time they had to go out. It wasn't fair that Don got to do all the driving; it just wasn't fair. He remembered that night... Mary was sitting in the back seat, and Cal was supposed to be the lookout. Cal didn't know what was going to happen; this was his first time. Don had seen it once before, but it still gave him the chills.

Don had parked the Mercury in front of a house on Avalon Street. Cal knew who lived there, of course—that Paxton boy. It was very quiet that night, with only the faint chittering of crickets to keep them company. Mary was relaxing in the back seat. The only sound inside the Mercury was her heavy, rhythmic breathing. Gradually, the breaths became shallower, longer, and quieter. Don recognized the early stages of her trance. Cal was busy with his task, watching the street for any sign of approaching traffic. There was none. When Mary spoke, Cal jumped. He didn't really hear what she'd said, but the sudden distraction roused him. Don smiled to himself—Cal was so easy to scare. In another place and time, he could really have fun with this moron!

Mary was muttering to herself. The men could barely hear her. The words were unfamiliar and indistinct, guttural and sinister sounding. "Ardif...Bordf... ohl.." Something like that, anyway, Cal recalled. Cal had glanced into the back seat with the sudden distraction, and froze, staring with his mouth hanging open. Mary was staring directly at Cal, but even he could tell she wasn't seeing him. Her eyes were vacant, expressionless.

She rose to her hands and knees in the back seat, her ample rump pushing up into the air. Cal was just about to think this was funny...Then she began those movements; the odd purring and whispering. Cal and Don both stared, mesmerized. She was behaving as though she was some kind of animal lapping up a saucer of milk! The parody was grotesque. Even Cal felt no desire for this woman. Now she was leaning toward Cal, eyes blank and unseeing. She was doing that purring thing again, with her lips slightly parted, the tip of her tongue protruding. Then she spoke again.

"I know what you want, do you know what I want?" She was still looking at Cal. Her eyes were filled with questioning—and something else ... Cal went cold as she made a loud animal noise.

"Car comin'."

Cal whirled back to face the front, grateful to have his eyes taken from the spectacle in the back seat. He felt ill—like he'd drunk either too much wine, or much more likely, not nearly enough. Cal stared from the windshield and saw the headlights of the approaching vehicle.

"Must be a cop," he'd said, almost hysterically.

Don glanced in the mirror. He could see Mary and what she was doing. He smiled coldly, bringing his eyes back to the windshield of the Mercury.

The car was still approaching, lights getting steadily brighter. It was time for action. Don fumbled with the ignition a moment, finally finding the key and turning it. The big engine roared for a second, and both men thought they heard Mary roar as well. Then the motor settled into its rumbling growl. Mary cried out as the Mercury lurched forward, away from the curb and into the dark street.

Cal glanced into the back. Mary was half sitting, half laying on the floor where she'd fallen. She looked up then, finally seeing this world once again. She stared stupidly at Cal. Cal didn't think this was funny anymore...

"Well," Cal said, coming back to the present, "I hope we don't have to do that again any time soon."

Don laughed, slapping Cal roughly on his shoulder. "Well, I told you that you were the lookout, you big dummy. If you'd've been doing your job instead of gettin' your jollies watchin' the old lady, you'd not have had to see any of that."

Cal nodded soberly. Which was hard for him, given his present total lack of sobriety. He tipped up the wine bottle once again, this time draining it. "Amen to that, brother. From now on, I'm just doin' what I'm told to do."

"Sage advice," Don said with a laugh.

19

Sarah awoke when she heard the key turn in the lock. Her quarters were so quiet, the latch sounded loud to her sleeping ears, loud enough to awaken her. She sat up, rubbing the sleep from her eyes. The door swung open on silent hinges, and Sarah saw that nurse, Mary, enter the room. Mary's eyes lingered on the girl for an uncomfortably long moment before she spoke. "Hurry up and get dressed, dear. Then we'll go see Bobby. You two can eat breakfast together and get reacquainted. He so wants to see you, my dear, it's all he's talked about for the last few days." Sarah fairly leapt from the bed. She used the bathroom and washed her face quickly, brushing her teeth next, and finally making a haphazard attempt to brush her hair. That she gave up on almost immediately. There were far more important things on her mind right at the moment.

Mary stayed in the room, near the door, waiting for Sarah to emerge from the bathroom. When the young girl emerged a scant seven minutes later, she smiled again. Sarah walked back to the bed, and picked out something to wear from her meager collection of clothes. Mary turned her back while the girl dressed.

Sarah was beside herself with excitement. This was the day she'd been waiting for, for what seemed like a very long time. Now that the time had actually arrived, her time apart from her brother felt like an eternity. She spoke to Mary's back as she pulled on her blouse. "We're going to see Bobby right away?"

Mary was momentarily distracted. "Huh? Oh, yes. Of course, dear. Just as soon as you're presentable, we'll go up to the dining room." She watched as Sarah buttoned the final button on her blouse. "We're all going to have breakfast together. But first, what is the answer to the question?"

Sarah paused, sitting there on the bed with one shoe tied, the laces of the other held in her immobile fingers. *What question?* Oh, yes, now she remembered. "I want to stay."

"Excellent," Mary said with a warm smile. "In that case, my dear, you're going to have a very busy day."

Mary walked to the door as Sarah finished tying her shoe. When the girl was ready to leave, Mary held the heavy door open for Sarah. They proceeded side by side down the short, narrow hallway. At the end of the corridor, Mary used her key once more and opened another door. She gestured for Sarah to walk in front of her. The girl complied. The narrow red brick stairway on the other side of that door opened into a small room on the first floor of the mansion. Sarah followed Mary into the parlor, looking around in wonder at the furnishings, lamps, and artwork. She turned her eyes to the long dining room table, and squealed with delight. Breakfast was waiting for them as Mary had promised, and so was Bobby.

"Bobby!" Sarah practically shrieked. Sarah ran to the table to hug her brother. Bobby looked up at her, but said nothing. Sarah hugged him fiercely, a hug that was not returned except in a most desultory, almost automatic way. Sarah pulled back a little, concern evident on her features. She stared down at her brother. "What's the matter, Bobby? Don't you recognize your own sister?" She leaned over her brother and hugged him fiercely. "I'm so glad you sent for me. I really missed you." She kissed Bobby, and finally, he gave her a second, very short hug. Tears were welling up in Sarah's eyes, tears of joy and frustration. What was wrong with her brother? Why on earth was he acting so strange, so…uninterested?

Mary intervened then, and insisted they sit and eat while breakfast was still hot. Mary pulled back the chair beside her brother, and Sarah sat, keeping her eyes on Bobby's strangely bland expression.

"Well, eat up," Mary coaxed. Sarah watched as the toast was passed, and the scrambled eggs and bacon were served up. The servant, a dour woman of perhaps fifty, wearing a black uniform with a short, white, lace-trimmed apron around her ample stomach, said nothing as she set the plates on the table, filling the glasses with milk from a large sterling silver pitcher. After the last glass was filled, she left, still without a word.

As they ate, Bobby became somewhat more communicative, telling his sister about his new life in the commune—he explained that it was referred to by everyone living there simply as 'The House.'

"Mary's guiding me in the search for my soul," he explained calmly. "It's very important work, and not as easy as one might think." He smiled at his sister, and took a drink of milk before returning to his eggs and toast. Sarah looked at Mary, seeking some kind of real explanation. The woman nodded, smiling. Bobby continued, "We're using a lot of acid, Sarah." Now he was grinning, excited for the first time that morning. "You absolutely wouldn't believe the places I've seen, the times I've traveled through, or the things I've become."

Sarah said nothing, for she didn't know what to say. Bobby seemed so utterly strange to her—not the loud, rebellious, fun to be around teenager she remembered. She wondered how such a profound change could occur so rapidly, and the question frightened her. She watched as her brother took another long drink of milk, and she saw the milk dribble unnoticed from the corner of her brother's mouth as he drank. She glanced at Mary, who sat watching her intently.

Bobby spoke in a subdued and very unemotional way. "I told Mary and Vic about how you can break things with your mind."

Sarah's eyes widened. "What? What are you talking about?"

Bobby waved one hand, and replied, "You remember the light bulb blowing up in Dad's face, don't you? That was really cool!" He laughed. "When I told Mary and Vic, they got all excited and asked me to write to you so you could come up here to The House with me."

"Of course I remember the bulb thing, silly, but I didn't do that! That was just something that sorta' happened, you know?"

Mary interrupted. "We, that would be Victor and I, think it's possible you did do it with a kind of extra sensory mental projection that's called psycho-kinesis. Another word for it is telekinesis—making things move or react with your mind without having to actually use your hands."

"Yeah," added the boy, grinning again, now obviously quite proud of his little sister, "Mary says it's called PK for short."

At first, Sarah had been confused. She'd never really considered the possibility that those strange occurrences could be connected with herself in any way, much less the later ones that Bobby didn't even know about. She recalled the projection booth fire. People could only do that kind of stuff in horror movies on late-night television. It wasn't real, and everyone knew it, even little kids.

Mary looked up suddenly, almost as if she'd seen Sarah's thought. She smiled. *This news should please Victor.* She watched the two youngsters as they finished up their breakfast and talked. Sarah looked around expectantly for the serving woman, hoping for seconds, but it soon became obvious that no more food would be forthcoming immediately.

Bobby suddenly rose. "I have to go back to my work." He turned his back and, without another comment, or even a glance over his shoulder, he walked away toward another door at the opposite end of the parlor. He swung the door open, passed through, and was gone.

"Bye," Sarah said weakly to the door as it finished closing. She was think-ing about the thin dribble of milk he'd still not wiped off his chin. She was concerned for Bobby—he seemed so...docile.

Now Mary was talking again. Sarah turned to listen. "Today, my dear, you will begin your first work for us." As she spoke, she reached into her pocket. Sarah was about to say something when a bright flash of light caught her attention, and distracted her. She momentarily forgot her question. She stared at the brightness, trying to ascertain exactly what it was that Mary held in her hand...

The silver chain twisted slowly in Mary's fingers. The faceted crystal at the end rotated with the chain, turning slowly in the light. The early morning sunlight, coming now through the open window, reflected itself into Sarah's eyes from the facets of the crystal ball. Mary smiled. *This child will be so easy.*

"That's it, dear," she crooned, "I want you to look at the light...isn't it pretty? Look into it, my dear."

Sarah stared at the crystal as Mary spoke; it almost seemed as though she no longer had a choice.

"Just relax, Sarah, and watch the pretty light. Slowly. Slowly...slowly. You are becoming more and more relaxed. Your eyelids are becoming heavy now, you are getting very, very sleepy." Yes, she did feel sleepy, just like Mary was suggesting. And yes, her eyes were getting very heavy...

Mary glanced up into Sarah's eyes. She was delighted. The girl was already in a light hypnotic trance, and they'd only just begun! "You are becoming more and more tired..."

Mary's voice droned on. It filled Sarah's consciousness and then spilled over into her unconscious mind. Now there was nothing but that voice telling her to close her eyes. Mary paused. The girl was under.

Mary told Sarah how things were. She told the girl that her psychic talents would be developed and used for the greater good, and not hidden and repressed out of fear or ignorance. She told Sarah that only she, Mary, could call forth the power residing within the girl's mind upon request. Sarah's telekinetic powers would only work when Mary wanted them to work.

Sarah understood all that Mary told her, though she really didn't remember very much about it after Mary told her to awaken some twenty minutes later. Mary was standing now, looking down on the girl. She was speaking, but Sarah couldn't quite understand what she was saying. She tipped her head, listening more closely this time. Then, understanding came. Mary was asking her to break a wine glass by only thinking about doing it.

Sarah looked up at the woman, the doubt evident in her features. "But I can't, like, think a thing to break," she advised Mary, "I'm afraid I don't understand what you want me to do."

Mary was prepared to be patient, at least for now. This kind of thing would take a little time, she realized. She calmly said, "Look at the glass." Sarah obeyed. "Now I want you to imagine that there's a vibration in the glass, like a plate window vibrates when a jet flies over."

Sarah tried to visualize the vibration. She imagined she could hear a jet coming over, low and fast. She imagined the glass shaking, vibrating...

Mary was watching the glass as well, and quickly noticed that nothing was happening. *Damn it!* Time was running out. There had to be a way to get past this stupid little girl's silly mental blocks. She knew that Sarah was capable, she just needed to find the trigger—the thing that would put the girl's special gifts in motion. Then there was a thought that came to her, unbidden. The words were those of the girl sitting before her. Something about a movie theater and her friends…Something happened in that theater, but what was it?

Mary allowed her mind to wander. She tried to pick up any thoughts that might be 'out there' for her to read.

"Sarah, dear…what was it that happened just before the projector bulb exploded?" She saw she'd distracted the girl. Now, maybe, she'd get to the truth of the matter. She saw Sarah blush momentarily, but what could that mean?

"Nothing happened," Sarah lied. "We were just watching the film when it blew up."

Mary sensed the lie, and sensed also another presence—a boy's face flashed briefly through her thoughts, and that of another girl, both unknown to her. She caught one part of a name; Ri…but she couldn't tell if it was the girl's name, or the boy's. She smiled gently at Sarah, successfully hiding her knowledge of the lie. "Alright then," she said calmly, "I would like you stay in this room for a little while longer, dear, and try to break the glass. You must work on this for an hour. I want you to concentrate very hard; you have no idea what's at stake here. We have very important life and death work for you to do."

"Life and death?"

"Yes, dear," Mary responded with another smile.

Sarah gave the woman a nod. "Okay, I'll try." Sarah could think of no reason for the woman to lie about something like that, so she decided that, for whatever reason, this was indeed important work, and she'd try very hard to give Mary what she wanted. She looked back at the wine glass.

Mary stood silently for just a moment, and then she said, "I'll be back in an hour, dear." Sarah only nodded. Mary quietly locked the parlor door behind her, leaving Sarah in guaranteed solitude. Sarah was far enough from the door, and in deep enough concentration she didn't hear the lock snick into place. Mary turned, and walked toward the library. She needed to do some research.

Inside, she went to the shelves that contained the books on psychic phenomena, and ancient magical grimoires—some many centuries old. She was seeking very specific information regarding what is called poltergeist phenomena, and all things related. She knew much of this already, and the book she now held explained the rest. She'd already known that psychokenesis was the scientific explanation for manifestations that had once been labeled 'poltergeist'—noisy ghost. Though neither she nor her husband believed in *magic*, per se, they could see the misinterpreted facts behind the mumbo-jumbo.

She knew all about hurled ashtrays and broken windows, she knew about the so-called 'rains of stone.' What she didn't know, until now that is, is that the triggering mechanism frequently revolved around the hormone balances, and their strong awakenings during puberty. It was a very potent force that could be retained through life if fully and consciously developed while the glands of the body made war with themselves.

She suddenly understood the meaning of Sarah's fleeting blush. It was clear as a bell. That Richie Owens boy—that was the name she'd pulled from the aether—had done something. The book mentioned sex and anger as frequent triggers. In this case, it might be either—except for the image of the other girl she didn't know. *Richie Owens...and that girl! That's it! The trigger that precipitated the events in that movie theater is anger; anger at Richie!* It fit with what the book was saying—puberty, raging hormones, and a strong feeling of anger. And furthermore, she knew full well from personal experience, that no feeling was stronger or cleaner than anger. Once she'd used the girl's power, she'd have it under her control forever.

She smiled. Now, finally, she'd found the key to the kingdom. She had the trigger mechanism for the psychic bomb she knew Sarah to be. She thought about how pleased Victor would be.

20

The next morning, as the sun shone cheerily through Curt's half-closed drapes, he grumbled something, slapped the alarm clock into silence, and thought about burying his head under his pillow and just forgetting to rise today. But finally he sighed, and pushed himself from his warm bed. He looked toward the window squinting into the light. *Well,* he thought, *at least I didn't have any more weird dreams.* He laughed as he padded to the bathroom to take his morning shower. The hot water felt good that morning, and Curt indulged himself, staying a bit longer than usual. Outside, he heard his dad's Escort backing out of the driveway, his dad on his way to work. He thought about that.

He'd been more than a little tempted this morning to just shut off the alarm, go back to sleep and ditch school today. After all, who would know? He could call in sick in a couple hours when he woke up again. He could fake a cough or a sneeze well enough to be convincing, at least over the phone. He could do it, and probably his dad would never find out. But then he heard his dad's car. His father, he realized, would get up every day, no matter what, and head to his job so they would both have food and shelter. Going to school, he realized, was his job—his obligation and responsibility to this family—to his father. That thought had gotten him going this morning.

Curt dressed, and walked to the kitchen. He yawned. He didn't really feel like breakfast, but he decided to eat anyway—a bowl of cereal and a couple of slices of buttered toast were easy enough to make. And if things went the way they usually did when he felt like this in the morning, he knew he'd probably be starving by lunchtime, and hating himself for not eating in the morning. It wouldn't be the first time. So he poured himself a large bowl of corn flakes, suddenly feeling hungry as the flakes rustled from the box into his bowl. He poured milk over the top, and sat down. As he ate his corn flakes, he noticed the morning newspaper that had been casually tossed onto the table in front of his father's chair. Idly, Curt picked up the paper.

He scanned the front page, and, between mouthfuls of corn flakes, he read the important news, and turned the page. Nothing in particular caught his attention, and he almost tossed the paper aside. But something attracted his attention at the last moment. It was the name Louben.

Now he looked more carefully. A small article toward the bottom of the second page caught his attention. It was a local news item, apparently of only mild interest, since it had been relegated to page two, and was near the bottom of the page with a small banner saying what the story was about. But it was important to Curt. It informed readers that the razor wire was going to be installed around the old Louben incinerator chimney on Wednesday of this week instead of next year.

An alarm system was also being installed, the article reported, that would notify the police department directly if trespassers tried to get over or around the fence. The article said it would be a state of the art alarm that nobody could bypass. Curt was doubtful about that, but he knew it would be impenetrable to him or his friends. He snorted a laugh, almost choking on a mouthful of corn flakes and milk.

The article went on to say that there'd been reports of teenagers seen in the area and a city-owned lock had been found with its shackle cut. The mayor, police chief, and city council had met and unanimously agreed to these measures, calling the cutting of the lock an act of vandalism. The police chief vowed, it was said, to catch the trespassers and bring them to justice. Curt finished his cereal, took his bowl to the sink, washed it, and put it in the drying rack. He went back to his room to collect his schoolbooks.

Curt carried his old backpack that he'd carried a year ago before finding the newer one that the police now were holding as evidence. He went into the garage, and strapped the backpack to the package holder behind the seat on his old bike. He pushed the bike out, shut the garage, and headed to school.

As he pedaled down Avalon, heading toward Hennessy Street, he was glad he hadn't sold the bike when he'd gotten the new red one last Christmas. In reality, he recalled, it had been his father's wise suggestion for him to keep both of the bicycles, saying that having an extra bike as a back-up could possibly be more important than the money he'd get for it if he sold it. Those words, he realized now, were virtually prophetic. He grinned. His father was a smart man.

This bike wasn't as fast as his new one, and it squeaked a little going downhill sometimes, but it was still good, reliable transport. The tires were good, and the frame unbent. The brakes still worked too. It would do until he got the other one back from the police. They'd said he'd have it back in a few days to maybe a week. He could wait that long. And who knows? They might even find the people who tried to run him down and rob him.

The Polaroid photos of the crystal pyramid Curt had taken the night before were securely stashed inside his English book. He planned to drop them off to Mrs. Prutzman at the library right after his last class was over for the day. He was hoping that the retired professor she was going to show them to knew what he was doing. For some reason, the longer Curt kept the stone in his possession, the more important it seemed to become. He also needed to speak to Carl; there was something important he had to tell him.

The wind cut through Curt's open jacket; it was colder this morning than the previous few days, but it felt good, too. The light at Hennessy was green as he approached it, and Curt didn't slow down. He stood up on the pedals, leaning precariously into the turn and flew down Hennessy, his chain squeaking and chirping merrily as he rushed toward Yavapai. There, he had to wait at the red light. He looked around nervously. There were a number of cars on the road with him at seven-thirty that morning, but Curt didn't see a single Mercury.

When he pulled up to the school, he saw Tommy leaning against the chain link fence that surrounded the school's parking lot—the real parking lot, as Curt thought of it, where actual cars were parked, not bicycles. Using the hand brake carefully, he came to a smooth stop. He dropped his foot to the asphalt, and dismounted.

Maybe, Curt thought, *I'll be parking on the other side of the fence in a few months.* He was certain his dad would let him use the car at least occasionally. It'd be cool to be able to drive to school, at least once in a while, instead of riding a bike. Curt rolled his bike around the fenced lot, and through the open gate that faced the front of the school. As he walked toward the bicycle rack, he could hear Tommy's rapid footsteps as he tried to catch up.

"Hey, Curt," Tommy shouted finally, "wait up."

Curt slowed his pace, letting his friend come up beside him. As Curt chained his bike to the welded pipes of the rack, Tommy spoke.

"How's things?"

Well, thought Curt, *here goes nothin'. If I tell one of 'em, gotta tell 'em all the same story.* He turned, smiling at his friend. "I took the crystal back to the Stack yesterday. After everything that's happened, I didn't think I should keep it. It ain't worth my life, you know what I mean?"

Tommy looked at him, his face set in a hurt expression. "Why didn't you stop by my house? I'd've gone with you."

"I know, Tommy, but I was in a hurry," Curt explained. "Did you by any chance see the papers this morning?"

Tommy just shook his head, grinning. "I don't believe in 'em myself, Curt. I figure that if there's something important goin' down somewhere, you or Carl or somebody else'll tell me all about it before school lets out for the day. And if it's not that important, I probably don't care anyway, and reading about it would just be a big waste of my time." He nodded smugly.

Curt said, "Well, here's one of those interesting things, Tommy. They're putting up the razor wire tomorrow instead of waiting for next year."

Tommy looked dumbfounded. "Really? Why? The last I heard, they had to wait until next year to get it in the budget."

"They're also gonna put in an alarm. The article said that 'somebody' saw some kids there, and that the police found the cut off lock. I wonder who that somebody might have been?"

Curt saw the light of comprehension in Tommy's eyes, and they both said, "Carl," simultaneously. Then they laughed.

"Speaking of Carl, by the way, he has a new ring," Tommy said. "In fact, he just showed it to me on his way inside just before you rode up; it's a great big gold thing with his initials on it. Says he got it from his dad. Must've been a reward for ratting us out."

Curt chuckled. "That wouldn't surprise me. I'm thinking that hanging with Carl is a pretty stupid thing for us to be doing." Tommy didn't respond to that statement, and they walked in silence for a moment. Curt decided to tell Tommy about the Mercury. Since he didn't read, he wouldn't know about it, and for all Curt knew, they might go after the others who'd gone into the Stack with him.

As they walked up the flagstone sidewalk toward the main building, Curt told Tommy about the attempted theft of his backpack, and about the evil smelling man in the hot-rod Mercury. As they parted company Curt said, "Good ol' Carl isn't in any of my classes. Would you tell him I told you I put the thing back? Maybe his dad'll give him another ring for his other hand."

Tommy laughed. "I'll bet that'll piss off his old man."

Curt laughed again. "Yeah. Let 'em put up their stupid razor wire and alarms. It's too late now, for Chief Larsen. I figure he'll know I've been in there twice before he, the mayor, the city council, and his whole damn department could get around to putting up the razor wire and the alarm. And, with the thing back where it came from, he can't exactly claim it for himself. The Stack's an official city monument now, according the article. The city council decided that one too yesterday. And make sure you keep watch, Tommy. If those guys came after me, they might come after you or Carl too. If they're not the police, and I can't see why they would be, they're somebody else who wants that thing real bad. Got it, Tommy?" Tommy nodded in affirmation, and promised to tell Carl third hour.

As they went their separate ways, Curt breathed a sigh of relief. At least that would get the police chief off his back for a little while. They now had no proof whatsoever that he'd actually taken anything. If they all thought he'd put the thing back in the Stack, there was no evidence. No evidence, no crime. Curt had seen enough television shows to know that much anyway. He smiled as he visualized the many and varied expressions that might pass over Carl's dad's face when he heard the news. He walked up the steps, and into the main hallway. He heard shouting and locker doors slamming—it was school bedlam, as usual.

He turned to his left, walking rapidly toward Cheryl's locker. He wanted to catch her before first hour to tell her his 'news' about the pyramid as well. He figured it'd be safer if everyone heard the same lie, and they all thought he'd put the crystal back where he'd found it. That would be the best for everybody.

Cheryl was standing by her locker talking with Sally Gibson. She looked over Sally's shoulder and saw Curt approaching. She waved to him. Sally turned also. He noticed that Cheryl had an amused look on her face, and Curt felt they'd been talking about him. He glanced at Sally. She looked away as soon as his eyes met hers.

Curt smiled, put his arm around Cheryl, and she returned the gesture. He liked the way Cheryl felt against him—the gentle swell of her breast and hip.

Sally said, "I'll catch you later, Cher. I better get going; I don't want to be late for class again." She looked briefly at Curt and said goodbye to him as well. He nodded to her. As Sally walked away, Cheryl reached down and squeezed Curt's butt. He jumped, and Cheryl laughed. "You know," Cheryl whispered, grinning, "Sally's really hot for your bod." She looked up at him coyly. "It's so sad to see someone so young and so frustrated. Sally's going out with Tommy Driscoll, you know. She just told me about it. I hope he's nice."

Curt was surprised that Tommy hadn't mentioned this turn of events to him. "Yeah? For how long?"

"Tonight's their first date. She said that he's taking her to see a movie at the mall."

Curt walked Cheryl to her first class. As they walked, he told her that he'd put the strange artifact back in the Stack. She seemed surprised, but the bell cut any possible comment to the quick. Reluctantly, he turned her loose, and ran toward his homeroom class. He was going to be late.

21

Though he was late, he arrived in time for the announcements of the day. It seemed that the police chief was going to speak to the senior class in the auditorium fourth period. Curt smiled. Though he wasn't psychic, he thought he knew the purpose of said assembly.

The rest of the morning seemed to drag on interminably. Curt was starting to actually feel nervous about the upcoming assembly. With the gradual passing of time, his mind formulated various potential problems. Had someone other than the chief's son seen them up there? Was it possible he'd been identified, or maybe the chief would bring the witness to the auditorium and let him or her look over the senior class, to see if the culprits the chief was seeking were there? Was he going to be arrested? His mind raced with all kinds of possibilities.

Hank Larsen stood at the microphone. Curt grinned up at him. Chief Larsen was of average height, and sported a crew cut that was so short it would've made a Marine drill sergeant envious. His dark brown eyes scanned the senior class slowly, almost as though he'd been the one to see Curt and his friends up at the Stack that day. His thin lips tightened imperceptibly when he spotted Curt in the third row. Then he spoke. The microphone made a whistling howl, and as the principal showed Larsen how to hold it, the assembled students snickered.

His monologue turned out to be the usual adult-authority speech Curt had expected. The chief droned on and on about how important it was to respect other people's personal property and the somber legal ramifications of trespassing and theft. His eyes were locked on Curt's.

Chief Larsen scowled. He looked back toward Curt once more. "Anyone with no regard for the sanctity of personal property is the enemy of the established order, that being the order of the law," he shouted. "That kind of person is also the enemy of every decent, honest citizen, and will stop at nothing as he compromises the community that gives him sustenance and education."

The students looked at each other in bewilderment. They still didn't understand the reason for the assembly, and the chief didn't seem to be making it any clearer.

"This type of...individual," here the chief made the word 'individual' sound as though he might be speaking of a bug, "is capable of almost anything. There's no telling what other, more heinous crimes he might be willing to perpetrate—or has already..."

Curt had quit smiling. The threat was coming through loud and clear.

"Criminals need to be removed from the society of decent, law-abiding citizens. This scofflaw individual might be a marijuana addict; he might be responsible for many, if not all the thefts in Hobbs over the last few years. He may even have resorted to murder. Who can say?"

Curt felt and heard the students around him shifting in their seats, some with heads together whispering, some openly snickering. The chief was losing them. Some of them used pot, and had turned off as soon as the chief had attacked them personally. Most of the others were simply responding to an authority accusing them of something they didn't even understand. In many of their minds, even the majority who didn't use any drugs, this was just another 'say no to drugs' line, and everyone knew it. Curt made a mental note to not smoke with Carl again—at least for a while until things calmed down a little bit.

By this time, even Hank Larsen himself realized he'd blown it; the kids were snickering, talking to one another, and some were even reading. He ended quickly, with one final, menacing glance at Curt, and strode from the stage, the spotlight glinting off his badge. He handed the microphone roughly to the principal, who almost dropped it. The assembly quieted as the principal made his closing statements and instructed the seniors to proceed to lunch immediately. Then he too strode off the stage. Curt thought the Chief's remarks had embarrassed him. The seniors left the assembly, a couple of them making hooting sounds in imitation of the microphone's apparent protest against Chief Larsen's words.

"Hey, Curt!" It was Carl. Curt slackened his pace so that Carl could catch up to him. He was interested in what the other boy might say, considering the fiasco of the assembly they'd all just left.

"Hey, Carl. What's up?"

"Tommy told me you put the thing back," the other boy responded.

Curt nodded. "Yeah…too many people trying to take it away from me. I thought it was a cool thing, you know? But yesterday, some guys tried to kill me for it."

Carl glanced away. "Uh…I guess I shouldn't have told my dad, huh?" Curt said nothing, and Carl continued. "My dad says he saw the police report you filed." Curt explained that it no longer mattered, as he no longer had possession of the crystal. Just then he spotted Cheryl.

"I …uh…hope you don't think my dad had anything to do with those guys who jumped you yesterday. They weren't cops, you know."

"I never said I thought they were, Carl, but they found out about it from somebody, and that's for sure. Look, man, I gotta go; I'm gonna sit with Cheryl for lunch. I'll see you later, okay?"

"Sure, that's cool, man." He looked slyly at Curt. "Cheryl's in my second period class. She's a real fox. You're a lucky bastard. Frankly, I don't know what she sees in you."

Curt laughed, and they parted company. *Boy! Today everything sounds like a threat,* Curt thought. He was beginning to worry that he might be getting paranoid.

He hurried to the cafeteria; his conversation with Carl had allowed Cheryl to get ahead of him, and just now he saw her turn into the lunchroom. He grabbed a tray, and worked his way through the line. Cheryl saw him when she was paying at the cash register at the end of the line. She waved, and gave him a big smile. That made everything else that had happened that day recede into the shadows.

He paid for his lunch, and wound his way between tables and wandering students until he reached Cheryl's table. He pulled out the chair beside the girl and sat down.

"Hi," she said simply. "What's going on in your life?"

"I don't know if you'll believe all of this," Curt began, and then he told her of his adventures over the last day. By the time they'd finished their lunch, Curt had filled her in on the story of the incident with the Mercury.

She clutched his arm, whispering, "I think I saw that car!" Curt looked up in surprise. "It was at the drive-in theater, I think," she continued. "It was parked about two spaces behind us. Remember the bright headlights? I think that was the same car you saw yesterday. I mean, it was big and it looked green to me in the lights." Curt recalled the headlights. "It gave me the creeps when I walked past it," she said. "When I was coming back from the snack bar, I heard the door close right next to me."

"Well, if they want the pyramid now, they can go to the Stack and take it themselves," he said with conviction. "I can't see why anybody would bother us again about it."

Cheryl and Curt put their trays back in the stack by the wall and headed out of the cafeteria, down the hall toward their fifth period English class. Though the class seemed to last way too long, Curt sort of got to share that time with Cheryl. She sat in the next row over, one seat up from his. He would look at her when he was beginning to lose his focus, and seeing her there, pen to paper diligently writing, would bring him back to this world as well. It made the homework assignment, given in the last moments of class, worth it.

Even sixth period art class seemed to drag today. Curt was anxious to get to the library and deliver the photographs to Mrs. Prutzman. The sooner they were out of his possession the better. And maybe, just maybe, she really did know someone who could make sense of all of this sudden drama in his life. After class, Tommy met him by his locker.

"Hey, Curt," his friend said, "what's happenin'?"

Curt swung the gray louvered door of his locker open. "I've been meaning to ask you if you had a chance to try the motor in your Chevy yet?" Tommy looked at him blankly. "You know," Curt urged, "your '55?"

"Oh, yeah," Tommy responded in sudden comprehension. "The Chevy!" He laughed nervously. "It runs alright. Once I get the brakes in and the front end aligned, it'll be ready for a test spin."

Curt thought about the car. It would be fast; just about everything that could be done to an automobile to increase its horsepower had been done to that almost magical 1955 Chevrolet. Even the exhaust was only one step above straight pipes—it would be loud. He wondered idly if Chief Larsen would scowl when he heard it. The thought made him smile. He turned to face Tommy, and said, "Hey, Tommy, I hear you're taking Sally Gibson out tonight."

Tommy grinned lecherously. "She's one of the hottest girls I've ever seen. God I hope she puts out."

Curt shook his head. Tommy was incorrigible. "Don't her parents mind her going out on a date on a school night?"

"Naw. Besides, we're not gonna be out late."

"I thought you were going to the movies?"

Tommy leaned in, and whispered conspiratorially. "We're really going up Hobbs Hill Road. There's a make-out spot up there near the mayor's house."

"Isn't that where that girl was assaulted?"

Tommy grinned. "I'm gonna use that story to encourage her to get close to me. I can hardly wait." He grinned again.

"Does Sally know? I mean about your side trip up Hobbs Hill Road? You ought to tell her, you know. What if she doesn't want to go?"

"She'll figure it out once we get up there, she's not a dumb girl, I don't think." He laughed again. "Well, I hope she's a little dumb. I don't like girls that think too long about making out and stuff. Well, I gotta go. I got a hot date tonight."

Curt watched Tommy saunter away, his ever-present small thermos dangling from his hand. He shook his head in dismay. Tommy was going to end up in trouble, he was absolutely certain about that. *Maybe Sally'll slug him if he grabs her.* Curt laughed at the image, and walked outside to where his bicycle was waiting.

The library is always warm, Curt thought as he pushed his way through the brass-framed glass doors. He headed toward the reading room, hoping to find

Mrs. Prutzman. He looked around the reading room. Over by the newspapers, an old man slept in his chair.

Across from the sleeping old man sat another man. Curt couldn't see his face, but he sat upright in the chair, like he was expecting to rise at any moment. To Curt, it seemed a very uncomfortable way to sit. Though the man's back was turned, Curt could see he was deeply tanned. His hair was straight and long, tied back in a ponytail. His hair showed only traces of greying. He was dressed in a denim work shirt, and black leather motorcycle pants. The primary thing that caught Curt's attention was that the man seemed to be reading an unabridged dictionary!

Curt turned away from the man. People can read whatever they want, and who knows, maybe he was trying to find an obscure word that wasn't in other dictionaries. It was none of his business. He walked toward the front of the room. Mrs. Prutzman was at her desk looking at paperwork when Curt walked up. She had a notebook next to her, and she was writing in it. His footsteps echoed slightly in the deep silence of the room, and the man who'd been reading the dictionary straightened up in his chair, his head rising. He was listening.

"Mrs. Prutzman?" She looked up, and Curt said, "Hello, Mrs. Prutzman, I brought the pictures for you." He fumbled inside his backpack, retrieving his English book. He flipped it open, and pulled the two Polaroids from the book. She studied them, checking that they were clear and focused.

"I think these will be just fine, Curt, I'll write the letter and get it off to Prescott, and we'll see what we can find out."

"I put it back in the Stack, Mrs. Prutzman. That funny stone crystal or pyramid or whatever it was. Somebody tried to snatch my backpack for it yesterday, so I thought that would be the best thing to do with it. And besides, we have the photos now." He smiled at the old librarian.

Muriel considered that for a moment, and then she gave him a firm nod. "Good. I think it's best that way, don't you?"

Curt agreed. He thanked Mrs. Prutzman and turned to go. The old man was still sleeping by the newspapers. The man who'd been reading the dictionary was gone, and the dictionary was closed, lying carelessly atop a newspaper. It had creased the newspaper page when it was set there. Curt rode home slowly. He was certainly glad this day was over. Now he could go back to thinking about normal things. Things like Cheryl, and Tommy's '55 Chevy, and college. He sighed. The lights seemed to be with him this evening, and not one car came close to him all the way to his house.

Muriel Prutzman was running a little late Tuesday afternoon, so she wrote the promised letter, placed it and one of the photos in an envelope, and put it in the out-box for the library mail. If it didn't go out tonight, it would certainly go out in the morning. And Prescott wasn't all that far from Hobbs. Her friend would have it in the next couple of days. She thought she was probably just as interested as Curt as to what that strange thing might be, and why it might have been hidden in such an unusual place. It surely was a funny thing to find in a lumber mill. She waited patiently for the last people to leave.

She closed the library at six and drove home, passing by the post office on her way. A dark green car that had been traveling behind her, unnoticed by the librarian, turned right at the next intersection past the post office. Muriel pulled into the drive, parking by the closed garage door. She left the car there, and used her key to open the front door. Harold Prutzman was waiting at home for his wife as usual. Harold had already prepared dinner—he was like that.

22

Cal Johnson coughed as he raked the sand, scratching random lines back and forth over each other. He'd been inside there for almost thirty minutes now, and so far he had nothing to show for it, except the cloud of dust he now stood inside of. The air was still, and the dust just hung there in the air, moved only by his movement, and his breathing. He took a break, leaning on the rake handle, coughing and hacking. He inhaled deeply, trying to catch his breath, and immediately wished he hadn't as the fine dust was drawn up into his nostrils and down through his mouth into his lungs. He went into another coughing fit.

Don Bristow remained outside the Stack. He'd gone inside the incinerator chimney first to look for the elusive crystal pyramid. It didn't take him very long to find and examine the opening behind the discarded brick, which still lay in the sand. If that damn boy had brought the thing back, he'd not put it where he'd found it. As soon as Don had determined that the crystal wasn't there, he walked outside, leaving the rest of the search to Cal. Wordlessly he'd handed the other man the garden rake, and grunted, "Get goin'. We ain't got all day, Cal."

He leaned back against the fender of the Jeep, and watched with amusement as Cal hacked and coughed. As far as he was concerned, this was just the type of work Cal was cut out for. He shook back his long ponytail as dust billowed out the doorway of the incinerator's chimney. He moved a little farther away; he wasn't planning on breathing any of that dust. He was becoming impatient, and glanced at his watch. He shouted, "Found anything yet?"

"Naw," Cal responded between coughs, "there's nothin' in this goddamn place. I think that Paxton boy lied. That's what I think."

Don smiled. "Rake it one more time, Cal, just to be sure. We don't need Vic breathing down our necks."

Cal mumbled his acquiescence. "Alright, Don. I do it one more time an' then I'm comin' out if I found anything or not."

Don smiled again. He could barely see Cal in the cloud of dust that hung inside the Stack. From the outside, the late afternoon sun illuminated the cloud into golden phosphorescence. Don thought it quite beautiful—especially since Cal had to stand right in the middle of it and breathe it. "Let's step it up, Cal," he taunted, "we don't have all day, ya know." Cal mumbled something, and in a short while, he'd thoroughly raked the sand inside the Stack a second time.

"Okay," Don called. "Wrap it up, Cal, it's getting kinda dusty out here, and I want to go into town tonight without having to change my clothes first."

Cal was glad to get out of there. Don looked at him and smiled—the man was filthy. His white tee shirt was, by this time, more like a brown tee shirt. The armpits, where he'd been sweating, looked almost like they were caked in mud. Don thought about Cal's lungs, and how they must be filled with dirt. He grinned at the thought, keeping some distance from the other man so he'd not get his clothes dirty.

Cal saw Don's grin, and smiled back at him, and Don saw he even had dirt in his mouth. Now that was even funnier! Cal removed a small bottle from his hip pocket, uncapped it, and took a long pull; then he coughed. He didn't even wipe the lip of the bottle first. Don was delighted—this jackass was the best show in town. "Get in the car, dirtbag."

Cal smiled again. He liked Don's sense of humor. The two men walked down the steep hill, and were soon back to the second road, which wound along private land and came to the chimney by the back way. Don opened the tailgate of the Jeep, and watched as Cal shoved the rakes into the back of the vehicle, and then scratched his head, staring into the Jeep as though he'd forgotten something. "Hey, Don, why'd we bring two rakes? I didn't see you doing any work."

"I did work, asshole. I had to supervise you, didn't I?"

"I can work without supervision, you know," Cal responded defensively. "You don't got to be tellin' me what to do all the time. I hear what Vic tells us just the same as you, an' you know it."

Don laughed. "If you'd worked like you should've in there, you would've been using both rakes at one time; one with each hand, you know? We would've been outa' here an hour ago."

Don slammed the tailgate shut. Cal, who was leaning against the lip of the opening with his right hand, just barely had time to jerk back before the tailgate crashed into place. Cal walked to the passenger door at the front of the Jeep, to find the door locked.

"No you don't, dirtbag. You're not riding up front with me." Don made Cal ride in the back seat with the windows open. He glanced in the mirror once at the other man; he wasn't smiling now.

The fire was almost out. Victor stared into the flames and saw his own dream dying with them. He half-heartedly poked at the fire with the iron, and then dropped it back into its rack. He returned to his leather chair. Mary sat across the small table from him, silently waiting for him to speak. She would give him time to gather his thoughts, though she already knew the bad news.

"The crystal's not in the chimney," he said evenly. Mary remained silent. The guttering fire cast a ruddy light across her face now, crawling over her features and her white dress. "That Paxton kid lied," Vic continued. "He obviously still has the crystal in his possession. Don saw him last night from outside his house. He saw him carrying a camera, and saw the flashes through his window, and then today he saw the little bastard give a photo to old lady Prutzman down at the library. She's sending it to someone, so Don says."

Mary sensed Vic's tension, and spoke quietly. She didn't want to upset or anger him further. She changed the subject. "I think I know what triggered the girl's PK abilities."

Vic glanced up, interested. He seemed pleased, and that pleased Mary. They'd been together far too long to let a mere boy and a small-town librarian cause dissension in their ranks. She went on placidly. "She's a poltergeist, Vic. Do you know what that means?" She waited. He seemed even more interested now. She smiled. "Hormone balances and puberty, the book says."

"So?" Vic didn't feel like lectures or guessing games tonight—or cryptic conversations, for that matter.

Mary decided to get to the point. "If we can manage to cause the right imbalance, I believe we can fire her just like you'd fire a rifle." She paused, waiting for Vic to appreciate what she'd said. "Basically, I see two possible approaches. The first is the most practical for our purposes and, I imagine, it will give us the fastest results. Using hypnosis as a deep psychic 'leash,' we can feed her LSD and then simply direct and control the direction of the effects."

Vic asked, "You really think you can control her trip?"

"We could at least try," she reasoned, "If that doesn't work, we can always try the second option." Vic thought about that, and nodded with a slight smile. Perhaps things would work out for the best after all. He stood and threw another log on the fire. The wood was dry and it blazed brightly, showering sparks out into the room. He crushed a few under his shoe that had made it as far as the rug.

Early the next morning, Mary was delighted with the progress they'd made; and with only one previous session too! Sarah was already mesmerized. She couldn't believe how easy the girl was. The faceted glass crystal spun slowly in her fingers. The bright sunlight flooding in through the open windows of the parlor glinted from the crystal into the young girl's eyes; then, almost immediately, her eyes closed. Mary spoke slowly, soothingly. She realized that their success probably hinged on her ability to precisely control the girl. It was a matter of life and death.

But the girl was inquisitive. She was already asking questions; she wanted to know where the rest of the young people were, complaining that she'd only seen Moondog and Bobby. Mary's mouth twisted into what might have been a

smile. Currently, there were only seven young people left in the house—*some…
attrition is always to be expected, after all*. The boy, Bobby, had proved useful;
he'd made it very easy to get the girl she'd wanted. But now he was expendable
just like the others.

Mary continued speaking, slow and commanding in her word choice. Her
voice was only a distant buzz in Sarah's consciousness, but it was a ringing
command in that part of her mind normally accessible only in dream, or deep
meditation. "You will listen now only to me. You can hear only my voice. I am
in control of your mind and your body. Do you understand this?"

Sarah nodded her agreement, the subtle movement coming with real effort.

Mary reached into her pocket and withdrew a small plastic box. This she
opened to reveal several small squares of gelatin. She removed one carefully
from the box, using a small tweezers and pressed the red lid closed with a soft
snap. She slid the little box back into her pocket.

"Eat this." She laid the gelatin against Sarah's lips. Sarah's tongue flicked
out, and the morsel dissolved almost immediately. Mary sat back, picking up a
book she'd been reading. She knew she'd have to wait perhaps thirty minutes
for the desired results to manifest themselves.

Finally, it was time. She laid her book on the table, and looked expectantly
at the motionless girl. "Now, dear…open your eyes."

Even in her deep hypnotic trance, Sarah felt the LSD. When her eyes
opened, she saw the room expand to twice its size. Then she looked at Mary
and wondered how two people could fit into a room that was so very small.
Someone was speaking. The sound exploded in her head—brilliant streamers of
color rippling through the air around her, like ribbons tied to a kite. She watched
them, fascinated by their beauty as they drifted past her, and changed into birds.
She saw Mary smiling, and she smiled back.

This time Sarah understood the words that were being spoken to her. She
looked dutifully to her right. *This is taking a really long time…* Yes, she could
see the wine glass standing on the table. She stared at it as instructed. The sun
was captured inside of the glass! She saw the brilliant radiance, and as the glass
shifted the sunlight splintered into a lovely prism of colors that danced in the
air around the glass. She looked more closely. The rainbow was also captured
inside the glass! This was a really sad thing. *No sun in the world, no rainbow
in the sky…* This wasn't right! Something had to be done. Suddenly she understood that Mary was telling her how to free the sun—how to free the rainbow.
If the glass broke…

Sarah tried to reach the glass to knock it from the table and free the sun. She
was surprised at how far away it was now. She stretched her arms twenty, then

thirty feet, but the wine glass remained just beyond her reach. She saw with sudden horror that her arms, long writhing things, were now flopping uselessly in a tangle on the floor. They looked just like snakes! *Jesus...snakes!*

Mary realized Sarah's attention had wandered. She spoke louder now, grabbing the girl's attention, bringing her mind back under her control. "Listen to me," Mary commanded, "you will hear, and you will obey! No matter what you see and feel, Sarah, I am in control of your mind and I am in control of your body. Hear my words now. There are no snakes."

Sarah watched in a detached wonder as the snakes began to dissolve into vapor, breathing a sigh of relief. Now she could concentrate again. The glass was just too far to reach with her hands, but...*Almost anything will break it... I could free the sun.* She looked once more at the wine glass. It was so thin, so very brittle.

And then it began coming apart. Sarah saw a crack forming—crawling in slow motion over the glittering surface. Tiny thread-like fingers spread eagerly, seeming to clutch at the glass, and then its very form suddenly changed. It was no longer a glass; it had been reduced to mere splinters of color, flashing briefly in the light. Sarah saw the sun, and then it was gone. She saw the rainbow, and then it was gone. She was horrified! Something bad had happened! She'd destroyed the sun and the rainbow. And the worst part was the laughing! Mary was laughing, and she stared in numb horror in the direction of that sound.

Mary stood between Sarah and the light. Her face was in shadow, and Sarah stared into The Mouth! It was a big mouth, and dark beyond understanding. The noise that issued from that cavern was terrifying. There was only one escape. Sarah looked up, and disappeared into space...

Sarah didn't know what time it was. She stared at the blank walls surrounding her. She knew something terrible had happened, but she couldn't remember what. The door opened. It was Mary—a shadow flashed through Sarah's mind, and was gone again. The woman approached the girl, her white hospital shoes making a soft susurration as they moved along the concrete floor of Sarah's bedroom. Mary was smiling. She was holding something...it was a small cage, with a mouse trapped inside. She also had the small plastic box; Sarah seemed to remember that box; she'd seen it right before...what? Then she noticed that Mary was holding something else...something glittery...Sarah didn't want to look at...something glittery...she knew she had to look at it...

Later, Victor Lewis listened to Mary's story with extreme interest. Sarah had actually broken the glass in the first session, but she'd not been able to control the mouse's movements later. They'd tried very hard, she and the young girl, she reassured her husband. It almost seemed the girl's abilities ended there, with broken glass and nothing more. She informed Vic that the girl was sleeping now.

"Don told me he thinks Prutzman is going to mail the photo tomorrow," Vic commented calmly sipping some wine. "He said she passed the post office on her way home, but didn't stop. We need to act on that quickly."

Mary smiled. This was the kind of job at which she excelled. "Let me handle her tonight, Vic. Maybe she'll dream a solution to our problem." She laughed, as did Victor. It was a humorless sound. Victor rose, and poured his wife a glass of old wine. They were going to celebrate a little; things were starting to turn around.

Mary said, "In any case, I think it's time to pursue our second option with the girl. We should put Plan B into operation now, that way we won't be stalled if we need it later. We may not have the time then." Victor smiled. This would be fun, even if it took a couple more days. Vic rose from his chair, walked to the ornate Edwardian side table by the wall, and lifted the receiver of the telephone. He dialed.

"Uh…hello?"

"Hello, Carl…is your dad home?"

"Yes, sir. I'll get him for you."

There was a moment's pause. "Hank here, what can I do for you?"

"We need your help. Can you and Carl come over immediately?"

The room was circular in construction and perhaps thirty feet in diameter, with only one door. In the center sat a small cot. Sarah wondered why she'd awakened in this strange room. She was feeling slightly nauseated and confused. *What's happening to me?* Mary was there; she told Sarah to sit back down on the cot. She did as she was told; the bright, flashing light in Mary's hand made it impossible not to obey the woman.

The door opened—people were coming in. One was Moondog; a new, heavy gold ring flashed in the light on his index finger. Another was the man she'd seen on the porch of the house yesterday…or had it been the day before? She wasn't sure. Then Vic walked in with the last person who was by far the most important. It was Bobby. Now Mary was speaking again, flashing that hateful light into her eyes again. She wanted Sarah to eat something—it tasted sweet…

Sarah didn't understand what Mary was saying. The words exploded from her lips in what seemed to be some strange language. Sarah realized suddenly, through the haze of LSD that it was actually English after all. She was telling Sarah to look at the floor. There was a glass cage containing a small white mouse, and a simple maze constructed of transparent plastic.

Mary was speaking again. "Listen to me, Sarah, dear. I want you to control this mouse for me with your mind. Do you understand?" Sarah didn't, and numbly shook her head. Mary continued, thinking of her second plan to harness the girl's psychic ability. "We thought about bringing your boyfriend up here to stay with us as well…His name's Richie?" Sarah nodded mutely. Mary looked sad now, Sarah noticed, not comprehending. "Yes, Sarah, we were going to go down to Tucson and bring Richie up to surprise you; but this is what we found."

Now it was Mary's turn to concentrate. She pressed into Sarah's mind, taking images from the girl's memories and reshaping them for her own use. Suddenly Sarah saw Richie! It was like a dream, but she was awake. It was dark…and then the projector shutter opened, and the film began. Sarah recognized the theater, and the movie…and she recognized the girl sitting beside Richie. It was her friend, Linda Brock! She was letting Richie touch her…and she was touching him.

Sarah slumped suddenly to the floor. Not even Mary's call could wake her. She was gone back into space—Mary realized they were probably pushing her too hard. The experiment a failure, Mary glanced at her watch. She had somewhere else she needed to be tonight as well, and it was almost time to hit the road; *thirty minutes…time enough to get ready.*

Vic said, "Go take a short rest. I'll take care of things here. We'll try to waken her and try again. Maybe with the three of us concentrating, we can get her back up. And after we're done, I'll carry Sarah back to her room. Don and Cal will be waiting for you by the car when it's time."

Mary nodded gratefully. With all the responsibility, came the headaches. "Don't forget to feed the basement, dear."

Vic laughed. "I haven't yet, have I? They'll be in good health and wide awake when it's finally bath time—if we still need them, that is."

23

Later that night Muriel Prutzman finished doing the supper dishes; they'd eaten later than usual. Muriel's husband sat in the living room watching television. Muriel started the dishwasher, and turned to go. She was tired. She sat on the couch beside her husband, with a sigh of relief. She smiled at Harold.

He asked, "All finished with the dishes?"

She smiled, nodding. "I'm bushed," she said, and sighed again. She no longer had the stamina she'd had only a few years ago. Her doctor had told her to spend less time on her feet at work, but there was always so much to do. The volunteers just couldn't do some of the tasks, and the assistant librarian only worked on the weekends. That left her to do the lion's share, though she loved her work anyway, and never complained, even to Harold. Even though it wore her out, she felt what she was doing was worthwhile. She pushed herself to her feet. "I'm going to bed, Harold."

Harold glanced up and replied, "I'll be right up after M.A.S.H., dear."

She smiled at him—she knew this was his favorite program, and reruns ran late at night now. She climbed the stairs slowly, leaning heavily on the banister. She took a leisurely bath, and by the time she was ready for bed, Harold was there with her. She always had a hard time sleeping without Harold beside her. Muriel closed her eyes, and thought vaguely about the picture she'd mailed. *Very strange goings on for a peaceful town like Hobbs...*

Muriel sat up suddenly. She looked at Harold in the darkened bedroom, sleeping peacefully beside her. She quietly swung her legs out of the bed, putting on her slippers and robe. She'd suddenly remembered something important. *That photograph...it's in the kitchen. I should move it. I need to move it to a more secure location...what if it fell in the sink and got wet? The Paxton boy would never forgive me.* As she turned from the bed to leave the bedroom, she saw the second photo Curt had given her atop her dresser. She walked from the bedroom softly shutting the door behind her. She moved silently down the stairs, through the short hallway and into the kitchen. *Now where did I leave that picture?* It was still in her hand, but she didn't seem to notice. She walked slowly, carefully. It was dark. *I should turn on a light...*

She knew the photo was here, somewhere in the darkness. She walked to the sink, dropping the picture. In the pale moonlight, she saw the white border of the photograph, glowing faintly. She sighed in relief. *Good thing I checked.*

The photo was lying in the sink, very near the drain. *The Paxton boy will be really disappointed if I ruin his picture.* Light, she needed light. Her left hand groped along the wall above the sink, feeling for the switch she knew was there. She turned on the light. Now she could get the picture. She looked into the sink in surprise and dismay. *How on earth could it've slid that far down into the drain?* Well, she'd just have to reach in after it. She rolled up her right sleeve, and groped for the picture.

Harold Prutzman was not a heavy sleeper. He awoke just as soon as he'd heard the sound. He sat up, still half asleep, looking at the vacant spot in the bed beside him. Muriel wasn't there. He got to his feet, head tilted slightly as he listened. *What the hell's that noise?* It was coming from downstairs somewhere. Harold put on his robe and slippers, and walked the path Muriel had walked minutes earlier. He followed the sound into the kitchen. There he found Muriel, standing by the sink in the dark. At first his still half-sleeping mind suggested she was finishing some dishes she'd forgotten, but no, she wouldn't do them now, and certainly not in the dark. None of this was making any sense. He saw Muriel, leaning over the sink, her right shoulder hunched up, her left hand gripping the edge of the sink. *Why is she pushing so hard?* He ran his hand along the wall, and found the switch.

The white radiance of the fluorescent light was merciless. Harold stared in horror. Then he began to scream. Muriel turned toward him, eyes vacant. She held her mangled right hand before her. The blood! The blood had turned her baby blue fleece robe into a mad jigsaw design of blue and red splashes and slashes. Red streams pulsed from what had once been her hand. *My God!* He could hear the blood splashing to the linoleum, making bright starbursts wherever it struck—and it seemed to be striking everywhere.

For a moment, Harold thought he'd pass out. His head was pounding, his heart racing. His mouth was as dry as that flannel should've been. His vision was greying, closing in… But fortunately Harold was able to pull himself back together. He knew he had to do something, and do it right now. Muriel collapsed into a widening pool of her own blood, and that did it. Harold shouted, running to her side.

He snatched the fabric belt from his own robe, wrapping it around her wrist. Then he clawed at the dishwasher, finally managing to open it. He reached inside, grabbing a dinner knife from the tray, and shoved it though the belt, and began twisting it. The blood flow slowed. He wound it one more time, tying it in place with the ends of the belt. The flow was mostly stopped, reduced to a small trickle. His head was still pounding. *That goddam noise…*

Harold rose, still in shock, and turned off the switch over the sink that controlled the garbage disposal. The machine ground to a stop, flinging a few more drops of blood and bits of flesh defiantly up into the sink. Harold vomited, turned and reached for the kitchen phone. Numbly he snatched the receiver to his ear. He couldn't take his eyes off of all that red stainless steel; that red stainless steel…

Cal jumped when he heard the scream that tore out into the night from the darkened house. He'd been watching the street and hadn't seen the lights come on in the house. He was trembling. Don watched him with cold amusement. He'd been startled by the sudden shout from the house too, but he'd expected it, and hadn't jumped and squealed like some goosed schoolgirl. He snorted his derisive laughter. He glanced into the mirror from behind the steering wheel. Mary was in the back seat, doubled over, head invisible behind the back of the driver's seat. It looked like she was reaching for something she might have dropped on the floor. But Don turned, his curiosity getting the better of him. He looked over the seat, and saw her pushing hard against the automobile's carpeting. He watched, fascinated, as she ground her fist into the floorboard.

He glanced toward Cal next, and saw the wino looking into his eyes. Those eyes were wide with fright. Don just couldn't resist. As Cal stared at him in blank fear, Don suddenly raised both of his hands, hooking his fingers into claws. Making his eyes bug out, he hissed, pulling his lips back into a toothy snarl.

Cal shrieked at the unexpected gesture. Mary was also startled, and her trance broke—as did the dream-spell she'd cast over Muriel Prutzman. Don gunned the engine and the Mercury roared to life, pulling from the curb in a short squeal of burning rubber. Mary sat back in the seat, shaking her head. Perspiration flowed down her face in rivulets. To Don, looking quickly into the rearview mirror, she looked like a woman who'd just surfaced after a dive into a swimming pool. Mary felt dizzy—that headache was back, and this time it was a corker!

Then she felt anger. "What the hell just happened? The bitch is still alive, you know," she hissed. Don could see in the mirror that Mary was furious. He needed an explanation, and he needed one quickly. Naturally, he lied. He gave an exaggerated shrug, and said, "Cal's got the jitters, I guess—he just shouted all of a sudden for no reason at all."

Cal couldn't respond at the moment, because a large bottle of wine was tipped high in front of his face, and his mouth was full of the bittersweet taste of the grape of forgetfulness. The lip of the bottle chattered against Cal's teeth. Don watched Mary in the mirror as he careened around a corner to avoid an oncoming emergency vehicle. He grinned. Cal was in the shithouse for sure this time!

Sarah opened her eyes. She surveyed the room, wondering if she'd imagined the whole thing...*what whole thing?* She just couldn't remember. Instinctively, she felt that Mary had something to do with her loss of memory, but she didn't really know that for certain. She took a deep breath.

The latch clacked softly. Sarah slowly turned over on the bed. Moondog was standing in the open door, smiling at her. That ring caught the light, and she looked away. "You like my new ring? Got it from my Dad just a couple of days ago. By the way, Sarah, do remember anything about what just happened?"

Sarah thought about that for a minute, and then said, "N...not really...did something happen?"

Moondog was smiling. "You can go back to your own room after you meet Brutus." He walked to her, and touched her lips. There was something on his fingers, something sweet. Something she feared, though she didn't know why. She tasted that taste again as Moondog taunted her with a large ring of keys that he was spinning around his index finger. He put the little plastic box into his shirt pocket. It didn't take very long for the LSD to begin its work this time—she still had a good deal of the former dose running in her system. She sat up, then stood.

"Can I go now?"

He dropped the keys to the floor. "Ah, ah, ah..." he whispered, wagging his index finger back and forth, "after you meet Brutus."

Sarah began crying. That taste always came just before something bad happened. Moondog spoke with authority. "Stop that crying. After you've met Brutus, you can go back to your room, pack up your stuff, and leave if you want."

Sarah stared in mistrustful disbelief. Had she heard right? Moondog repeated what he'd just said, more slowly now as if he was speaking to someone very slow to comprehend. She suddenly realized that she really did want to leave this strange place of glass, anger, and rats. She was wondering what that meant when the acid gripped her brain. *What's happening to me?*

Moondog asked her gently, "Are you getting off on the acid?" So that was it! But he was still speaking. "Sarah, I'd like you to meet Brutus. He's a very good friend of mine." Sarah looked around in bafflement. When she spoke, it sounded like her voice was coming from someone else. "I don't see anyone, Moondog. Is Brutus like, invisible?" She heard the boy laughing.

A face suddenly materialized. It was a dark face, and long. Brutus had deep brown eyes. She stared in confusion at the big Doberman. Moondog was still laughing. To Sarah, it looked like a black cave from which ribbons of color flew; but these colors weren't bright and cheerful—they were dark, smarmy browns and dirty greens, and deep blood red.

"I like girls," she heard Moondog say. "I like girls a lot. And Brutus, he likes it when I get what I like, because then he gets a treat." He looked down, affectionately patting the dog on his head. The big Doberman looked up at him adoringly.

She pulled back from Moondog, tripped over her own feet, and fell heavily into the chair that was behind her. Brutus rumbled deep in his chest, showing white teeth in a grin that was anything but adoring. The boy moved forward again, reaching eagerly for the girl. She flinched, and the dog jumped up onto the chair, and was now eye to eye with the frightened girl.

Moondog reached out to her. The light caught again on that damn ring. She saw it clearly now; it was inscribed with two big, blocky initials: CL. He touched her cheek, and a tear flowed silently down her cheek, and at Moondog's touch another image came into her mind. Richie…making time with Linda in *their* theater! *If that girl was here right now, I'd strangle her,* she threatened in her mind.

Then the door opened again, and Carl Larsen turned quickly, guiltily. He hadn't expected Vic to walk in on him!

"What the hell are you doing in here, Carl?" Victor's stare was neither one of surprise, nor of good will. It didn't take an imagination to know the meaning of the glowering countenance.

The boy looked at the ground sheepishly. "I, uh…was just lookin' for a little fun is all."

Carl, the girl thought. *The ring; Carl…something…*

Victor pointed to the clothes on the floor. "What are these here for?"

"I, uh…said she could have them. I told her she could take all her stuff and leave if she'd put out for me."

"Yeah? Well, we can't afford another incident like the one last year."

Carl smiled, as though reviewing a cherished memory. "She ran. It wasn't my fault," he explained. "I was—excited, you know? She fell in front of that truck."

Victor glared at Carl, and he said, "Okay, okay, I, uh…pushed her a little. I was too turned on to think."

"Alright. But you will leave this particular girl alone. We need her—you have no idea how important she is to Mary and I. And this should be adequate warning, even for the likes of you." Victor paused, letting the warning sink in. Then he added, "Besides, I doubt we could cover for you a second time." Carl nodded, properly contrite. But Victor was not yet done with him. He ushered Carl and his dog to the garage. "Go home, Carl. Don't come back unless I call for you. Under absolutely no circumstances are you to approach this girl again for any reason; do you understand me, boy?"

Carl couldn't mistake the threatening note in Victor's voice. He just nodded in silence, and walked to his car, opening the right door for Brutus, and then climbed behind the wheel and drove off into the very early morning darkness.

Victor picked up Sarah's clothes that Carl had taunted her with, then led Sarah to her room, and gently tucked her in bed. A moment later, she was deeply asleep...or passed out again. He went to the dresser and quietly collected the rest of her clothes. Carl had scared her. Vic was certain she'd remember that fear, and that was a very bad thing. What if she decided to run away? He smiled in the semi-darkness, shut off the light and left the room, Sarah's clothes in hand, locking the door once more. He didn't notice her shoes, which he'd kicked under the bed by accident.

That night, Sarah dreamed of birds, lots of birds, flying free through a dream-summer sky. And in the circular ritual room where she'd been rescued from Moondog, now dark, there was nobody there to see the small gray mouse that was still sitting obediently in the left hand corner of the cage, where Mary had instructed Sarah to direct it through the maze earlier. It waited there, not knowing why.

Mary Lewis slept deeply. It was unusual for her to sleep without dreaming. She hardly stirred when the man got into bed with her. Vic lay there a long time before sleep finally took him. An odd thing, sleep...even after all this time, he still wasn't used to it. Time was running out, and now they were going to have trouble controlling Carl. Vic knew he'd arrived just in time to save the girl from Carl. Vic knew they couldn't afford another murder, not now when they were so close to completing the project. The last one had been a close call; if that auto mechanic hadn't taken the money, they might all be in jail right now. Vic was angry. They needed the girl far more than Hank or Carl ever dreamed. They thought she was a toy...a toy! Well, Carl better not interfere again, if he knew what was good for him.

The other boy, Sarah's brother, was important too. If anything happened to either of them at this late date, it would be very bad for he and Mary, especially if they didn't procure the crystal soon, or more children. *Fragile things, children,* he mused. Victor Lewis sighed. In all his years, it had never been this difficult—or this close.

He looked at his wife. Something needed to be done about those headaches. Perhaps the girl would cure her. In any event, both of the last two 'dreamings' had been unsuccessful. The crystal was still in the Paxton boy's hands, and the slut from the library was still alive. Vic snorted in merriment. *From now on though, they'll be callin' her lefty!* He snorted again. At least the photo had been destroyed; of that Mary had been certain.

24

When Curt arrived at school Wednesday, Cheryl was angry; *no,* Curt thought, *seething.* At first she didn't want to say why. Finally Curt convinced her that he'd help her if he could. She leaned in closely and whispered, "That bastard Tommy Driscoll tried to rape Sally last night."

Curt recalled his conversation with Tommy the day before, but he'd never imagined this might happen; Tommy was always just bragging about his supposed 'conquests,' and everyone pretty much knew it. But this—this sounded real. Cheryl continued, glancing both ways suspiciously, clearly worried about being overheard by other students.

"Tell me what happened," Curt said, keeping his voice low to match Cheryl's tone.

Cheryl closed her locker with a bit more force than necessary, and Curt winced.

"Sally said he took her to a spot up on Hobbs Hill Road, and told her that if she didn't put out, he'd put *her* out." Curt tried to speak, but Cheryl wouldn't allow that. "He told her that they were where the 'werewolf killing' had taken place almost a year ago. She said he was grinning when he said that. He said Carl told him a large animal was seen in the area by the police the night before, and that Carl would certainly be one to know, being as his dad's the police chief."

Curt stared in disbelief. Could this possibly be his friend she was talking about? He'd known Tommy for a while now; long enough to know he was all talk and no action when it came to making out. He'd heard the stories from Tommy himself—and had overheard some girls as well. He let Cheryl continue. "He ripped her blouse trying to undress her. She said she begged him to stop, but that he refused. Then she said he tried to force her to get drunk, wanting her to drink some whiskey he had in a stupid little thermos. He said he was going to 'get some,' as he put it, or he'd give her to the wolf."

Curt was almost numb with shock and surprise. "Did she tell her parents or call the police?"

Cheryl looked at him in disgust. "Her parents? Ha! That's a laugh—they don't care anything about her." Curt remembered his surprise that they would let their daughter go on a date on a school night. They probably didn't care, after all.

"So…did he…do it?"

"She got out and ran into the woods. Tommy just left her out there all by herself in the dark. She said that after he'd left, she walked back to the road. She hitched a ride into town." By this time Cheryl was almost shouting.

"Hey, hey, Cher, take it easy on me…I didn't do anything."

Cheryl paused, taking a calming breath, and said in an even voice, "Yeah, I know, Curt. I'm just mad is all."

Curt put his arm around her, after checking the hall for any teachers. He thought for a moment and said, "I'll tell Tommy that I know about this, and that he'd better watch his step. I'll tell him Sally's parents are thinking about calling the police. That should calm him down some and keep him away from her. I'm not sure what's going on with him, but I know he wouldn't want to end up in jail."

Cheryl reached up, kissing him on the cheek just as the bell rang. As she turned to go, Curt said, "I'll see you later. Please relax. Things'll work out all right, I'm sure of it." Cheryl smiled and walked away. Curt spent most of the first period thinking about what he'd say to Tommy when he saw him in gym class next period. In the end, he decided to let Tommy do the talking.

At long last, the bell rang. Curt scooped up his books and hurried out the door. Just as he was walking past the journalism classroom, the door opened and there was Tommy right in front of him!

"Hey, Curt…how's things?" He grinned. As the door closed part way, Curt got a glimpse of Mrs. Blackwell. She was standing near the door inside the darkened room. He knew this was her planning period. Curt also noticed that her brow was beaded with perspiration. She smiled faintly at him, as she closed the door.

"Tommy, I didn't know you were into journalism."

"Oh, I'm not. Um…Carl asked me to drop off an envelope for him."

On their way toward the gym, Curt asked his friend, "Hey, Tommy. Did Mrs. Blackwell seem sick to you?"

The corner of Tommy's mouth turned up. "I dunno. She looked fine to me, but I don't really know her. You could ask Sally Gibson, she told me she takes a class from her. Heck, Curt, you can go ask her yourself, can't you?" He grinned, and walked a little faster. Curt picked up his pace to keep even with his friend.

Tommy pushed open the door to the gym and both boys entered. The locker room was already filled with boys. Amid the noise and confusion of shouted obscenities and slamming lockers, Curt asked Tommy about the night before with Sally. Tommy said Sally went with him willingly out to Hobbs Hill Road. He said she knew it was a make-out spot and that she'd said she'd like to go there with him.

"So we get there, and she won't even give me a kiss; can you imagine that? Finally she kissed me a couple of times, but wouldn't go any further." He confided to Curt that he'd used the werewolf story to try to intimidate the girl. Tommy grinned sheepishly at Curt. "I guess I got a little carried away."

"Sally's really upset about this you know. She told Cheryl all about it, and Cheryl told me that you tried to get Sally drunk."

"C'mon, Curt, Sally was half-pickled already. She drank most of the stuff in my thermos all by herself. Look, the next time I see Sally, I'll apologize, okay?" Curt was unconvinced any of this was the truth, and for the first time since he'd known Tommy, he didn't trust his friend.

"I think it'd be best for you if you just stayed away from her entirely. Her parents are thinking about calling the cops. If they decide to press charges, you could end up in jail, you know." Tommy's face paled, and he nodded.

"Never thought about that," he said. "I just got a little carried away. I'll leave her alone. I don't even have any classes with her this semester, so that'll be easy." Curt was satisfied he'd be true to his word—at least in this instance.

When gym class was finally over, and they'd showered and dressed, they walked out together. Tommy glanced around furtively and pulled Curt over by one wall.

"Hey, Curt, look at this!"

Curt looked down. Tommy was holding a group of Polaroid photos in his hand. He shuffled through them rapidly. The photos showed a young girl with three men and a woman. They were all much older than the girl, and only the woman was looking at the girl. The men were all staring down at the floor. There was something on the floor at their feet. The last three photos revealed the object to be some kind of transparent maze, inside of which a small mouse cowered. He looked up at his friend, not understanding. "What the hell's this?"

Tommy snickered, ignoring his friend's question. "Boy! I'd like to meet her."

Curt thought the girl looked young…maybe fifteen, or less. He said, "Uh, Tommy, don't you think she's a little young?"

Tommy laughed as he slipped the photos back into his bag. "Eight to eighty, that's my motto." He started to saunter away.

Curt shouted after him. "Hey, Tommy, where'd you get the photos? And what's up with the mouse?"

Tommy just shrugged. "Dunno," he said. "Carl loaned 'em to me. He said I should show them to you, and see if you wanted to be in on it."

"In on what, Tommy? You're not makin' any sense."

"Well, if you must know, Carl took the photos—says the girl's got some kind of special talent, and the next time he parties with her, he'll let me have some." He walked back to Curt, and whispered conspiratorially, "If you want, I can ask him if he'll let you come with me. He said to tell you that together is safer than apart." He shrugged once more, and added, "He said you'd know what he was talking about." Then he laughed uproariously. Curt said nothing. Tommy added, "Curt, if your honey ever says no, let me know, all right? What're friends for, eh?"

"Hey, Tommy, what kind of special talent does the girl have? What are you babbling on about anyway?"

"I can imagine what her talents are, Curt." He grinned again.

Curt watched as Tommy walked away, casually swinging that ever-present thermos. He wondered what was happening to his friend. All he talked about these days was sex. Curt wondered how the '55 Chevy was coming along—Tommy hadn't even mentioned it.

After class, Curt stopped by Mrs. Blackwell's room to see if she had anything for him. She was with another student at the moment, but if she'd been sick that morning, it surely had passed by now. While he waited, he glanced at the Hobbs newspaper lying on her desk.

He suddenly felt as though he'd been run over by a truck. Muriel Prutzman had amputated her hand in a garbage disposal! He stared numbly at the paper, his vision greying. He leaned against the journalism instructor's desk. The article said she'd mumbled something to an ambulance attendant about getting a picture out of the drain. Investigators, the article continued, found no photos amid the carnage.

He sat down heavily in Mrs. Blackwell's chair. *That damned crystal!* Whoever wanted it was willing to assault him, and had somehow mangled Mrs. Prutzman—*no way she'd do that to herself.* He thought back to the assembly— *Carl and the police chief; Carl and Tommy; Tommy and the pictures…Tommy and Sally. The odd things that Tommy had just said to him about together being safer. That had been a threat,* he suddenly realized. Then he thought of his only vaguely remembered dream of Cheryl. Somehow all of this had to be connected…the same names kept cropping up. He knew he needed help, but he didn't know which way to turn. He rose quickly and left the room. Mrs. Blackwell heard the door close, turned, and saw her chair empty once more. She smiled. *Curt must've read the story about ol' lefty…*

Wayne Simms pushed the wide broom across the tile floor. *Why can't the damn kids throw their scraps of paper and other crap in the trash barrel instead of all over the damn floor?* He scowled. Kids were sure messy these days. He reached for the large ring of keys attached with a chrome hook to his belt. He heard the jingle as he sifted through them. If classes hadn't been out for the day, he'd not have been able to hear that sound. He started humming a song from his long ago youth. The song was titled, "Silence is Golden." He couldn't remember who did it originally.

He slipped the key into the lock and turned. Pushing the door open, he walked into the darkened room. That was when he heard the other sound. He decided not to turn on the lights. Wayne heard a muffled groan and voices. He crept up to the swinging door separating the classroom from the 'production' room where the school paper was pasted up and printed.

He heard another groan and a whimpering cry. He recognized one of the voices as that of Jennifer Blackwell, the instructor. The other voice sounded odd and was unfamiliar to him. He stared through the small window in the swinging door. Jennifer Blackwell sat behind her desk. Even though the room was dark, Wayne could see well enough. Jennifer's hands were tightly gripping the arms of her old oak office chair. Her face glistened in the dim light. She was conversing with someone. But there didn't seem to be anyone else there, and this room had no telephone.

Wayne couldn't see exactly what was happening to Jennifer, but it was certainly spooky. She strained forward, as though listening to a whispered voice. Then she spoke again, but much to Wayne's surprise, it sounded like a different woman speaking. It looked like the woman was having a conversation with herself! He shook his head in wonder, and suddenly, Mrs. Blackwell went silent.

She rose slowly to her feet. She smiled, and then she laughed. She glanced up suddenly, almost like she'd seen him, and Wayne ducked smoothly back into the darkness. He knew he hadn't been seen. He quietly left the way he'd come in.

The custodian smiled, but he was a little concerned as well. Was Blackwell going nuts? But in the end, he knew it wasn't his responsibility; he left the room to recommence sweeping the halls. He shook his head in wonder. There was no telling what one might see while sweeping floors! After Mrs. Blackwell had left, he went back in to the journalism classroom. He was expected to empty the trashcans, after all. He walked up to Mrs. Blackwell's desk, and as he picked up the trashcan, he saw scratches in the varnish on the arms of the old oak swivel chair. He stared in wonder; the woman had mangled the hard varnish with her fingernails. Whatever happened just now, he realized, had happened before. He made a mental note to spend more time cleaning around the journalism classroom.

Curt called the Prutzman residence as soon as he got home from school. He really hadn't expected an answer.

"Hello?" It was a very tired voice that answered.

"Mr. Prutzman, this is Curt Paxton. Your wife was to have mailed a picture for me."

His answer surprised Curt. "She told me she'd mailed it from work yesterday. What the hell's going on, young man? She raved about that picture in the hospital until she was sedated and taken into emergency surgery. I think she must've shoved the other print down the…when she…" Curt heard Mr. Prutzman sob. He felt this was all his fault. He never should've taken the crystal in the first place. Why had he been so damn curious? Why couldn't he have left well enough alone? He thought about that enigmatic stone, and the strange marks incised upon it. It was currently buried safely under the oleanders in his back yard. Nobody would find it there.

Curt said, "I'm sorry about what happened, Mr. Prutzman. This is real important. Can you give me the name and telephone number of the man in Prescott she sent the photograph to?" There was a short pause as the old man riffled through a card file. A moment later, he'd found the card and passed the information along to Curt.

"What's going on, young man? I have a right to know."

Curt answered the question quietly and truthfully. "I don't know. I do think that our only help can come from this…George Luedke. I have to go now. I'll stop by the hospital to see your wife tomorrow." There was only silence on the line. Mr. Prutzman had hung up. Curt couldn't blame him. Curt hung up, and then dialed the number the old man had given him. The phone rang three times. Curt was about to hang up, when he heard the click of the receiver being picked up on the other end.

"Hello, this is the Luedke residence."

Curt liked the man's voice. Mr. Luedke sounded strong and sure of himself. Curt asked, "Did you see the newspaper this morning?" George Luedke said he had. "I'm Curt Paxton. I need your help." Curt didn't talk to his dad that evening. Instead, he went to bed early. Tomorrow was going to be a busy day.

*The sun hung motionless in the morning sky, and the air was extremely clear…*and Curt Paxton dreamed his terrible dream of morning become night.

25

In her bedroom, Sarah slept, and dreamed of a mouse huddled in the corner of its cage…she awoke in darkness. The dream returned to consciousness gradually, and with that one dream, came fragments of another, darker dream involving Moondog—or was his name Carl? And there was something about a dog, too, wasn't there? The LSD had distorted her perspective enough that she couldn't really remember what had happened. All she knew was that Moondog had become someone she feared. And what about the rest of them…Vic and Mary…for some reason they wanted to make her angry, had worked at that really hard. Why?

She had a brief flash, an image. Richie and Linda kissing in the darkness of the movie theater. Was that real? It seemed so, almost as if she'd seen a movie of the event. Richie was in Tucson. Linda was in Tucson. Suddenly, she felt the anger growing. And there was a mouse connected somehow to her, and to that anger. *Mary.* But that was a stupid thought, Sarah realized. One person can't control the thoughts of another. Still, there was one thing very obvious to her: she was in danger.

She shuddered; she had to get out of there. She didn't exactly know why, but the urgency was there nevertheless. She sat up. Her mouth was dry, her tongue felt swollen. She recalled that Moondog had told her she could leave right after he…well, anyway, he'd said she could leave, and that was good enough for her.

She swung her legs over the side of the bed and stood. Getting down on her hands and knees in the dark, she felt around the bed, and then fumbled for the wall, which she followed to the light switch. In the brightness, she opened the drawers of the small metal chest, planning to dress and be ready should the opportunity of escape present itself. Then she sat down on the floor beside the bed, and began crying—her clothes were gone, all of them. As she wept, her right foot moved, passing beneath the bed, and struck something.

She stopped crying, turned, and groped under the bed. She'd found her shoes—at least she could run.

She ran…

She heard that in her mind, but it wasn't her thought. *Moondog!* She shuddered, suddenly feeling very cold. She jammed her right foot into her sneaker, tightened the laces, and tied it rapidly. She was now tugging the lace of her left shoe.

She heard the door at the end of the corridor thud heavily. *Someone's coming!* Sarah prayed it wasn't Moondog.

Brutus.

The lace broke. She sobbed, struggling to tie the shoe. Outside the door, she heard the measured tread of heavy shoes. *Mary.* She heard the key go into the lock. And then the lace was tied! She turned off the light, and scuttled back to the bed in the dark, pulling the blanket up to her chin.

She remained motionless for a moment after the light came on, feigning sleep. She yawned, and then turned sleepily toward the woman. The woman was smiling again, but Sarah no longer knew if that was a good sign, or bad.

"Well, now," Mary said cheerily, "how are we feeling this morning?" Mary felt good—the headache was gone, at least for now. The men were all still sleeping. Now it was time for the girls to play. She set the stainless steel tray on the bed between them, still smiling at Sarah.

Mary's the enemy.

The thought suddenly struck Sarah. She couldn't pinpoint exactly when she'd reached that conclusion, but she was absolutely convinced of its truth. She looked back at the woman, somehow knowing that to show any fear now would be her undoing. "I'm okay," she lied, forcing a smile. Her eyes flicked toward the still covered tray. With the realization that Mary was the enemy, came a loathing for the old woman so intense she felt ill. She glanced over Mary's shoulder—the door hadn't shut all the way.

"I'm certainly glad to hear that, dear," Mary responded. "We'll have breakfast in a little while." The woman's smile now seemed a leer. "First though, you have to take your medicine." Sarah was terrified, but Mary seemed oblivious, certain of her absolute control over the girl.

The old woman lifted the linen that covered the tray sitting between them. Upon the tray were three items—a saucer with a tiny red pill, a large and very tasty-looking glazed doughnut…and a small glass cage, holding a frightened mouse. She looked up at Mary, confused.

Mary picked up the old bone china saucer with the pill. She carefully reached for it, lifting the red thing with her fingers. "This is a bit different from the last, sweetie," she said, "I seem to have misplaced the other box."

Moondog… The woman smiled again, and Sarah saw it as a spider's smile. Sarah stared at 'The Mouth,' and remembered something else—they'd given her acid! They were drugging her, but why? Mary was touching her lips, forcing them apart. She opened her mouth, and Mary placed the little red pill on the tip of Sarah's tongue. The Mouth smiled its spider's smile.

"Swallow it now like a good girl," Mary crooned.

Sarah pushed the pill with the tip of her tongue, tucking it between her teeth and lower lip. She pretended to swallow.

"Now let's have a look like a good girl," Mary almost whispered.

Dutifully, Sarah opened her mouth wide, allowed Mary to peer in. She raised her tongue as well, so the woman could see it wasn't hidden under it. She closed her mouth. She could still feel the pill, a hard knot between gum and lip. Pills didn't dissolve as quickly as gelatin, but she'd have to work fast.

Mary, still smiling, said, "I found the mouse this morning, dear, huddled in the corner of its cage." Sarah looked at her blankly. "You did it, dearie! The mouse in the ritual chamber? The one you were instructed to control with your mind? You did it! I'm so very proud of you. Now before you can eat this delicious doughnut, I want you to do it again, just for me. Can you do that?"

Sarah knelt up on the bed facing Mary, holding the bed sheet over her nakedness, her feet carefully tucked beneath her so the old woman wouldn't feel them. The old woman smiled expectantly at the girl, her attention drawn now to the mouse. Sarah seemed to be looking down at the mouse as well—at least that was where Mary thought her gaze was directed. Sarah was, in reality, looking at the stainless steel tray the small cage rested upon, along with the doughnut. It looked heavy—and solid.

Mary put her hands in her lap expectantly, lacing her fingers together like a small child. She was looking directly at Sarah now, and somewhere in Sarah's mind, Sarah felt the initial probing, like a single finger touching her mind and her thoughts, and divined its source. She had to act. *Now!* She grasped the tray in both hands, lifting it over her shoulder. Doughnut and mouse went flying. She swung the tray in a shining arc, striking Mary directly in the face. There was a brief splash of red, and a '*boooiing*' that lingered in the still air around them. She raised her arms once more and with a snarl of fear and rage, she struck down again, this time using the rim, slamming it with both hands and all of her strength into Mary's forehead.

Mary's vision went suddenly dark; the blackness was filled with brilliant pinpoints of light, each stabbing into her brain like the sun-glittered lance heads of heavy cavalry. The hoofs of those lancer's chargers thundered in Mary's brain—that headache was back! The little bitch had hurt her. It was hard to breathe. She opened her eyes. Her vision was blurred, her sight doubled. She squinted, shaking her head like a dog attempting to remove water from its coat. The pain!

Her focus was returning now. She looked around the room frantically, looking for the bitch who'd hurt her. Then she saw the object of her wrath. Sarah was outside, pulling the door closed. Mary lunged forward, dizzy almost to nausea. She stumbled against the now closed door. She heard the automatic lock snick into place.

"I'll kill you, bitch!" She was shrieking now. "Let me out or you'll be sorry!" She hammered futilely on the heavy steel door.

Outside, Sarah backed slowly away. She was panting in fear, and yes, exaltation! It was almost beyond comprehension; she was out, and Mary was in. She looked down at the key in her hand. Mary had carelessly left it in the lock. *What if they have another?* Then an idea struck her; something she'd seen done in an old movie on television a few weeks earlier. She went back to the door, put the key in the keyway, turned it just enough to prevent its removal, and rocked it back and forth...back and forth.

The old iron key finally snapped. Sarah stooped, looking at the lock. The keyway was completely jammed. They'd need a torch and a locksmith to get the old woman out of there now! And she knew also there was no telephone in the room; Mary was completely cut off. Until someone came looking for her, in that room she'd stay. Sarah felt proud of herself, as she hurried naked down the cement corridor, seeing the garage she knew was at the end of it—seeking freedom.

Mary gradually calmed down, using the controlled breathing techniques she'd learned over the long years of her life. She stopped shouting, realizing the futility of shouts and screams. There'd been enough of that in these rooms over the years that no one had heard either. She sat on the bed, head pounding. *It probably doesn't matter anyway,* she thought, *when that LSD comes on, the little bitch will be reduced to a quivering mass of meat and bone...and blood.* She looked down absently at the bed sheet, splashed with her blood. She looked closer. There, in a congealing drop of deep crimson, was a little red pill, almost invisible in the clot of blood. *The bitch spit it out!*

Then another thought. *Everyone's probably still asleep upstairs.* That would be her way out; that would be the bitch's doom! The headache was intense; Mary was beginning to worry that perhaps she'd been somehow damaged in the attack. She pushed the thought aside. *Later.* Right now, she had to get her act together. She needed to be freed from this room; then they'd take care of the little running bitch.

The headache was an intense throbbing pain behind her eyes, and in her face. She consciously calmed her breathing again. If she was going to stop Sarah, she had to gain control of the pain. She closed her eyes, and slowed her breathing even further, calming herself. She knew pain was just an illusion of the biological body—a body she'd learned to dominate a long time ago. She started slowly at first, gently pushing the pain back further into her thoughts. It wasn't needed. It wasn't wanted. She pushed it back. Further, further…almost gone…

If she was to rouse the men to free herself and get after the bitch, she'd have to do it with telepathy, and she wasn't about to let a little physical pain, now almost a forgotten thing, stop her. She sat on the floor in the center of the room. She further slowed her breathing, and her heart slowed with it. In moments, she was extremely relaxed. Entering her own trance state, she numbed her body, the pain completely shunted aside for the time being. She concentrated…

Sarah ran to the end of the corridor, and paused a moment, ear to the door. No sound. She turned the knob; it was unlocked. She wondered briefly if her luck would hold. *No time for that now,* something in her mind warned sternly, *just go.* She opened the door, and stepped into the garage. Blackness engulfed her as the door closed behind her. She snatched at the knob, catching it before it could slam back into the frame. She eased it closed, hearing the faint click of the latch sliding into place. She realized she'd have to block it somehow—block a possible pursuit. She fumbled along the wall, searching for a light switch with her hands and splayed fingers. There had to be a switch!

Blinding white light. Sarah glanced around in the bright light radiating from the two banks of six foot fluorescent tubes mounted on the ceiling. She squinted momentarily, allowing her eyes to become accustomed to the light, and then saw what she needed. The rolling toolbox stood against the back wall of the garage, only about eight feet from the door. She shoved against it; it was almost too heavy for her to move—but that would be a good thing once it was blocking the door.

She shoved again, leaning her shoulder into the effort, and grunting. She put one foot against the grill of the big green Mercury and, using the car for leverage, shoved again. She pushed with her legs and felt the toolbox roll a little. She shoved again, feeling the bright chrome grill of the car give a little beneath her foot. She pushed again, and the toolbox rolled a little further. It took her five tries to get the damn thing to move a mere eight feet so that now it stood in front of the door. She stood back, panting. *That'll slow them down, at least for a little while.*

The door would only open about three inches now before it struck the tool chest. With only three inches, they'd not be able to reach in far, not be able to gain the handhold and leverage they'd need to push it out of the way, no matter how strong they were. They'd have to go all the way back into the house, and come out some other exit, probably the front door. At least she'd have a head start on them, and she was a fast runner. She glanced around the garage rapidly and grabbed a rubberized rain slicker hanging from a hook beside the door, and as she backed away from the tool chest, she had another thought. She lifted the lid and grabbed a large Phillips-head screwdriver from a snap hook inside the top of it. *Just in case...*

Now all she had to do was get out of there. The big steel garage door was closed, of course. *How the hell does the damn thing work, anyway?* She saw the chain along the left side, following it up with her eyes. At the top it ran around a large sprocket. Then it returned to join its other end. There was a sliding bolt to lock it in place, which she easily shoved aside. She'd have to open the door by hand, pulling on the chain. Sarah tugged. After a few inches of taken up slack, the upper sprocket seized up; it wouldn't budge, not a millimeter further. *Is it still locked?* She looked frantically, but saw no other lock. She tugged harder this time, with all her strength; it still didn't move. She sobbed. She wasn't strong enough.

They'd catch her. *Moondog'll come with...Brutus...* In desperation born of that thought, she jumped, grabbing the chain. She hung there, suspended a foot and a half off the floor. She held on, and suddenly the sprocket turned with a metallic grunt, and the door was rising. But once her feet hit the floor, the chain stopped, and with it the movement of the garage door.

Now that her feet were firmly on the floor once more, she still hung on to the chain. She realized that if she let the chain go, the door would just close again, and she'd have to begin all over again. She leaped up once more, climbing the chain. She pulled herself hand over desperate hand...and the chain again slowly turned the sprocket. She climbed the chain, using her weight to pull the door slowly up...up.

When it was finally almost four feet up, Sarah was exhausted. Her feet were once more on the cement, and her breathing was ragged. The muscles in her arms and legs burned; her stomach muscles felt as though they might cramp at any moment. She sighed. She'd just have to release the chain, and try to roll out under the door before it came all the way down again. *If I don't move very fast, I could get caught under that door...then they'd have me. I can do this...*

26

The small room glowed a very pale blue light in Mary's mental image of the place. With perfect recall of anything she'd once seen, in her mind's eye, the room was absolutely identical to the room in which she now sat, eyes closed tightly. She was very tired; far more tired than she thought she should be. Again that odd, disturbing thought. *Is there something really wrong with me? Something more than what the girl just did to my face? I wonder…*

She dismissed that thought; right at the moment, it was counter productive. She needed help; that was the priority. The aches and pains perpetrated upon her by the little bitch-girl were beginning to make themselves felt once again. She could shut those pains down, she knew, but right now she didn't have the time. That other headache was also returning; the one that had nothing to do with the damage inflicted by Sarah. That one would be much harder to suppress; and she'd not be able to do it sitting on a cold concrete floor. More than anything, she wanted to be in her warm bed beside Victor, blissfully unaware of the pain and the fatigue. But there were priorities; there were always other priorities, it seemed, especially these last few years. It was starting to be like before; starting to be like the last time. She sent that thought away. First, she'd have to awaken the men—that was primary.

Mary shifted her concentration now, imagining herself rising, and simply walking through that pale blue doorway, and up the glowing stairs of her home. Now there was another door before her on the carpeted landing. It also glowed with that flickering blue light that was not really light. She passed through this door as easily as she had the other, and now she was visualizing her bedroom.

She could see her husband, lying on his back, in the huge, antique four-poster bed, the top blanket and spread tossed aside, only the lighter bed sheet covering him. The fire was out now in the fireplace, but the room, she knew, would still be warm. She stared at Vic in the pale blue light, and saw his chest rise and fall, slowly and calmly. He was snoring.

She knew that in the Astral Light, she'd not be able to effect physical contact; she'd never be able to simply shake him awake. But she was quite adept at manipulating dreams. She walked to the side of the bed, her thick legs partly merging unnoticed with the glowing mattress, and then she dropped her psyche into her husband, rapidly seeking and finding his sleeping mind. *"Wake up, Vic,"* she shouted urgently, *"I need you right now, Vic."*

Victor Lewis stirred. He made a soft animal-like growl, smacked his lips twice, and rolled over, now facing away from Mary. But he was coming into wakefulness; he could feel his body reanimating itself, and so could Mary. She withdrew her mind from her husband's body. He would know now, and staying inside would only slow and confuse him.

Awake now, Vic lay still, considering. Something had disturbed him. He opened his eyes sleepily, sitting up in the darkness of the bedroom, and then came to a sudden revelation. *Mary's in trouble!* Vic leaped from the bed, throwing on his robe. *Where could she be?* The answer slashed across his mind in sudden fury. *With Sarah? Yes! That was the answer.* And suddenly he realized why he could know such a thing. *Mary's here, giving me the warning! This is bad.*

Frightened now, and fully awake, he grabbed his robe instinctively from the foot of the bed as he strode past in the dark. He didn't slow his pace as he shoved his arms into the sleeves, and tugged the cord tightly about his waist. He stalked to the intercom switch near the door, and punched the button. There was a faint electronic buzz. He let the button go, and hit it again with his fist, his anger mounting.

"This's Don," a sleepy voice mumbled, "What's up, Vic?"

"Get your asses out of bed," he shouted. "I need both of you here, goddamn it, and I need you here right now!"

Cal awoke a moment after Don. Through the fading stupefaction of the wine he'd drunk, he could hear his door practically being knocked off its hinges. Don was pounding on Cal's door before he'd even gotten his pants on. He stood outside Cal's door, struggling to get his left leg into his jeans with his shoe already on his foot. He'd managed the right one, and now he gave the jeans a savage tug, and his foot was free again. He zipped the jeans with his left hand, still hammering on the door with his right. "Let's go, booze-hound! I hear our master's voice calling. You want me to tell Vic you were too drunk to get up?"

That comment made Cal jump to it. He shouted back, "Gettin' dressed Don, don't have a hemorrhage, alright? I'll be right there. He returned his attention to his clothing, and dressed rapidly. He struggled with his zipper; the damn thing wouldn't cooperate. It was corroded, and difficult to move. He gave it a tug, and finally he was dressed. He ran to the door, flinging it open.

Don and Cal watched Vic warily. He was ranting. Something was wrong, and they were trying hard to deduce what it might be. Victor Lewis paced the room, his fists balled at his side. He was screaming at them. Then it all clicked into place as Vic shouted for the third time, "Find Mary and do it fast!"

Cal stared blankly. "Find Mary?"

Victor raged. "Check the lower levels, you imbecile. Check Sarah's room. You better find her before I'm dressed, or you'll be joining the children in the basement!" The two stood a moment longer, and Vic shouted, "Move, goddamn it, get your asses in gear!" The men blinked in the face of Vic's rage, turned, and left his bedroom. They ran down the hallway, heading for the entrance to the stairs.

Sarah dropped the chain, rolled to her knees and then her belly. She tucked her arms tightly around her body. She rolled quickly to her left, and saw the door descending. *Not gonna make it,* her mind babbled, but the door banged into the concrete just as she'd cleared it. She was outside!

"Move, goddamn it, get your asses in gear!" Sarah heard Vic's shout coming to her faintly from an open window somewhere above her and knew the pursuit had already begun. She ran. The adrenalin pumped, and she headed away from the house, beyond the faint light given by the lamps on both sides of the front door of the ancient house, and into the black night and the scrub brush. She had a vague idea where the road lay in relation to the house, but she'd have to get there first. She figured that once she got to the road, she'd just follow it into town, remaining unseen by staying inside the concealment of the dense foliage. She ran on into the early pre-dawn blackness.

In the basement, Mary knew she'd succeeded. She heard footsteps approaching at a fast pace. She smiled; now it was her turn. She heard the hall door as it crashed closed behind the pair of footsteps coming to her at a run. *Now the bitch'll pay...* She reached up to her face, gingerly touching her nose. It was quite swollen, and hard to breathe through. *Probably broken.* She looked down at herself. Her dress was scarlet with her own blood. There was a banging on the door now.

Cal's voice. "Hey! You in there?"

"Forget the door for now," she shouted back. "The girl's escaped through the garage—get after her, and bring her back. She's already outside; go get her right now. But mark my words; I want her brought to me alive. Alive, and undamaged; do I make myself clear?"

Cal and Don glanced at each other. They hesitated a moment in indecision. Leave Mary here? Vic had told them in no uncertain terms to find her, and help her. Neither of them wanted to cross Vic...or Mary either, for that matter. Finally, they decided that Mary was probably the most dangerous to cross. After another moment of indecision, they turned down the hallway. Light shone under the far door.

Upstairs, Vic hurried to the phone on the bedside table. He pulled the chain that turned on the table lamp. Only Hank and the boy would be close enough to help in time. He snatched the receiver, as his fingers stabbed the buttons, and then the phone was ringing. Suddenly Victor heard the muffled wailing of an alarm. The sound drifted up from the small room off the parlor that he called his office. He recognized the distinctive sound; the perimeter alarm on the security fence had been tripped! *The girl!* The phone rang four times in his white-knuckled grip.

"Uh, hello," the young voice of the boy said. "What is it?"

"Go wake up your dad. This is an emergency! The girl's escaped."

Vic heard the boy put the phone on the table. An instant later, it was lifted once more. "Hank here, what's up?"

"The girl's gone. She's on the run. She—somehow she got away from Mary. At the moment, I don't even know where Mary is yet, but the girl got out through the garage. I just heard the fence alarm go off."

"She's on foot, isn't she?"

"Of course she's on foot," Vic snarled in red-faced anger, "d'you think she stole a damn car?"

"Alright, alright," Hank soothed. "Calm down, Vic. We'll come right up. Only be a couple of minutes."

"Hurry it up. She's seen too much to let her get to town."

"We'll find her Vic," Hank soothed, "we'll get her."

Sarah stayed in the brush as she ran. The wrought iron fence had been easier to scale than she'd originally thought it would be. As it happened, the cast iron spear points on the top were not sharp at all; she'd barely scraped her side going over it. She knew she was making noise, but she wanted some distance between herself and that house. She hadn't heard the garage door, so she figured her impromptu barricade had worked. She was proud of herself, but she was cold and exhausted.

She paused for just a moment, using the precious time to button the rain slicker over her chilled body. She cinched the belt tightly about her waist, and shoved the long shank of the screwdriver through it as though it was a sword. And though she was pleased with herself, she knew she'd have to concentrate on running right now, and hopefully live to pat herself on the back another day. She shivered, wishing she'd grabbed a jacket as well as the slicker.

The ground was uneven and in the dark she'd fallen only a few hundred yards from the fence. She'd skinned her knee on a large fallen tree trunk, but she got back on her feet immediately, crashing headlong through the brush once more. She was thankful that whoever had taken all her clothes had missed her shoes. The grade was getting steeper now, and she had to slow her pace. In the dark she could break something if she fell again, and they'd find her—*Moondog would find me.* She sobbed, hurrying on as fast as the thick underbrush would allow. Low hanging branches whipped at her face and arms. She knew she was being bruised, but that was preferable to what lay behind her. The road, her mind told her repeatedly, was just ahead.

27

Cal and Don both hit the garage door together, like a couple of football line-backers. They grunted in surprise when the door moved a couple of inches, and then stopped. Cal wormed his bony hand through the small gap, touching the tool chest, groping to identify the blockading object. He tried to push it, but of course it didn't budge. He withdrew his arm, and informed Don as to the nature of the barricade.

"Can you get it?"

Cal grunted, shoving his arm through the small gap again, and pulled at the tool chest. With an extreme effort he was able make the tool chest rock slightly on the uneven concrete, but he couldn't move it.

Don said, "Let me try."

"I s'pose you think you're stronger'n me, huh?"

Don glared blackly at Cal. The cold look in his eyes made Cal back down as Don hissed, "Damn straight. And you do realize our heads'll roll if ol' Vic Lewis catches us foolin' around down here. Well, at least your head will roll." Reluctantly, Cal moved back, and Don replaced him at the opening. He reached in and pushed, pulled, and cursed mightily, but he couldn't budge the barrier either. The box was just too damn heavy, and they couldn't get sufficient lever-age. He pulled back. "C'mon, Cal, let's get back to Vic. We gotta tell him about this."

As the two men ran down the hall, Cal was chuckling. He said, "Only thing stronger about you's your smell!"

Don put out his leg, tripping Cal. He uttered a short bark of a laugh, and then snarled, "Get up, you clumsy jackass! Get back up on your stupid feet!" As Cal struggled to his feet, Don stood back, offering no assistance. Don grinned at him, and Cal grinned back. Don was such a joker! Cal had taken only a handful of steps, and Don tripped him once more. This time his head struck the cement wall with a resounding *thunk*. Once more, Cal got back on his feet, as Don berated him. Don could see the dark red mark already forming on Cal's face. By daylight he'd have a real doozie of a black eye. And to Don's delight, there was a little bit of blood seeping down from Cal's scalp. He made a silent, come-on gesture with his head, and strode off, leaving Cal to follow.

They paused briefly at the door to the cell where Mary was still incarcer-ated. Inside, muffled by the metal and cement, they could hear Mary muttering. They looked at each other nervously, and Cal absently wiped the trickle of blood from his forehead, and then wiped his hand on his dirty jeans.

Cal whispered, "C'mon, Don…let's get back to Vic. Mary told us to do the garage and we did. It's not our fault we can't get in."

Don nodded in agreement. It wouldn't do to get Mary mad—she could do things they didn't understand, and that frightened them. Cal shoved Don's shoulder, and they ran back to the stairs, and up into the house. Cal panted as he ran. "Let's not screw this up, good buddy. We get paid a fair amount of money to do pretty much nothing but watch Mary and Vic play their spooky games. We do a bit of gardening, but we mostly have lots of free time."

Don agreed. "Let's get going. Working here is much better than sleeping in some alley by a dumpster." Cal nodded in agreement. "Or, in your case, Cal," Don added, once again grinning, "sleeping *in* the dumpster." Cal laughed again, and they turned and ran the rest of the way to where Victor was waiting for them.

They burst into the room just as Vic was hanging up the phone. "Well?" Vic shouted, "Speak to me!"

Cal and Don both spoke at once. They paused as Cal was cowed by a withering scowl from Don. "Shut up, stupid," Don hissed.

As Don told the story of what they'd discovered, Vic listened intently, then said, "Get the car. Cruise the road. See if you can pick her up. She's over the fence, and we can't allow her to get to town, not with what she knows." Vic put his hand on Cal's shoulder, squeezing very hard. Cal winced in pain, but said nothing. Vic stared into Cal's eyes and said in a steady, menacing voice, "Don't blow this, guys. You get paid plenty for doing very little around here. Now's the time for you to earn your keep. And when you find the girl, and you'd better, I want her brought back here alive and as undamaged as possible. That means nothing funny in the back seat on the way back, Cal. You get my drift?" Cal nodded. He wished Vic would let go; the man was squeezing much harder than need be. Finally, Vic released the man.

They turned and ran from the room, into the foyer, out the front door, and into the darkness. Cal stumbled; Don grabbed him roughly by the shoulder— the same one Vic had been squeezing, and hauled the man to his feet. "C'mon, dipstick, get movin'." They ran around the front of the house to the garage. Shoving up on the outside metal handles, the door slid up almost silently on chain and gears. The light flooded out into the night as they hurried forward.

He smiled a friendly smile. "You wait here, Cal. I'll get the keys." Cal just nodded, gingerly rubbing his injured shoulder. Don ran to the back wall, taking a second to survey the blocked door. He put his shoulder against the tool case, leaned into it, and it rolled far enough that the door could be opened. That was good enough for now; he could make Cal put it back where it belonged later.

He went to the workbench and lifted the keys from a nail. When he turned, he saw the grill of the big auto, and the large dent. Not knowing the cause of the damage, he'd just explain to Vic that Cal had done it while drunk. He grinned as he opened the driver's door, sliding into the seat. Life was good when you had a patsy to take the blame for everything. He backed the car out, feeling as well as hearing the throbbing of the supercharged engine under the hood.

Sarah stopped; she was winded. Crouching by a large bush, she tried to be invisible as she panted and gasped for air. The wind carried shouting voices; she knew they were chasing her. In the wind, she heard a car engine come to life. She ran on.

Don barely waited long enough for Cal to get himself settled into the seat before he slammed the Hurst shifter into drive, turned on the headlights, and started with a jerk into the still-black predawn night. Cal flailed for the door handle as it was pulled from his grasp by the sudden movement. But he got hold of it again, and was finally able to get his door closed. He sat back in his seat, and smiled over at Don. "We almost lost the door that time, Don."

"Woulda' been your fault, Cal, my friend, it's your door, remember? This one beside the steering wheel is my door." Cal simply nodded, sitting back and relaxing. If Don wanted to drive, let him.

As they left the property, he drove slowly, playing the spotlight mounted near the driver's door along the shrubbery and low trees near the driveway. Beside him on the other side, Cal was also moving the spotlight on his side of the Mercury. Vic had opened the gate with his remote. There was no sign of the girl.

Don shot a quick look over at Cal, and smiled. Reaching into his duster pocket, he produced a bottle of wine. He'd grabbed it from the garage when he snagged the keys; having something like this around when he was with Cal was always good insurance. He handed it without comment to Cal. *If things do go badly,* Don thought, *I'll need an excuse...a...fall guy! And ol' Cal sure is that.* He laughed at his cleverness, and Cal glanced him, the screw top already removed from the bottle of cheap wine. But Don didn't say anything.

Cal shrugged, tipping the bottle to his lips. The joke, apparently, was not going to be shared; and that was all right, as long as the wine was shared. He laughed at his joke, and managed to get some of the wine up his nose. He pulled the bottle from his lips, coughing and snorting dark red wine all over the front of his shirt. Don laughed, slapping Cal on the shoulders as he leaned forward. "Don't die on me, buddy," he said, "I still got things to blame on you." Cal stopped coughing long enough to laugh.

Mary was still sitting in the center of the floor. Her head hurt terribly, but it wasn't as bad as it had been a few minutes ago. She allowed her mind to wander. She imagined herself walking toward the garage down the concrete hallway, feeling the cold cement beneath her unshod feet. That would be how it had happened, she knew, since Vic had taken the girl's clothing. She paused, almost to the door now, imagining...

Suddenly she had Sarah's scent. Mary felt the familiar pulling sensation inside of herself, and suddenly she wasn't inside her body any longer. She was in the Astral Light once more. She inhaled deeply. She could smell the fear trailing out behind the girl very distinctly now. Her consciousness pulled once more against the restraint of her physical body and then shot through, out of the house, and into the trees at the speed of thought, like a heat-seeking missile.

The forest seemed to glow in an eerie green radiance. Each tree and branch stood in minute detail as she traveled past. There would be no blurring of details, regardless of her apparent speed, for she was not seeing with physical eyes. Something was just ahead of her. She slowed now, drifting almost to a stop. She couldn't feel the ground beneath her feet, of course, and it would be impossible to stumble. But the girl could. Mary smiled. *The girl will stumble, has already. She's hurt herself, the poor dear...* Mary knew that Sarah was close, very close. She sniffed. The young girl's scent was very strong here. Mary moved forward slowly, knowing the girl would not be able to see her...or to know she was there until it was too late. She saw the girl. Sarah was crouching by a large bush, resting, as though any unaware living being could hide from Mary in this twilight world that was half imagination and half reality. The girl's panicky-bright electromagnetic field stood out sharply in contrast to the lower, calmer light emanating from the uncaring plant life she was attempting to hide within. Mary smiled, circling like a shark. *Foolish child,* she thought gleefully, *I have you now.*

Sarah turned, suddenly feeling sure she'd been discovered. She put one hand over her mouth to muffle her panting breath. Her eyes moved frantically, but she could see no one in the darkness. Sarah lowered her hand from her mouth, almost laughing in relief. Mary knew she was invisible to the girl's eyes. She drifted silently down around the girl's head and shoulders like a cloak. She knew Sarah was feeling confusion now...and the pain. Mary smiled. She knew how to make Sarah's pain and fear worse, much worse. *Human imagination,* she thought, *is truly a remarkable thing. It's so easy to make people believe anything at all. Just put something in their heads, and they think it's the truth. And I know just what images to use...*

She whispered inside of Sarah's mind. *"You will remember, Sarah,"* she crooned. *"You will remember...EVERYTHING!"*

Sarah glanced up; she'd thought she'd heard something. She tried to think. She felt as though she was remembering something...but what? She gasped, looking around nervously. She'd thought something had touched her. There were no sounds now, except the buzzing of crickets. She was alone. Maybe she was safe after all...

The men? Sarah saw! *All of those men looking at her.* She gasped in shock, glancing around once more. *Where did that thought come from?* Now she remembered the pushing and the taunting laughter. She recalled Moondog standing there, holding a Polaroid camera, the flash repeatedly firing. She looked at the small gathering standing around her. She recognized several. Mary was there, as was Vic...and Bobby. One of the men whom she didn't recognize was ugly and old...he had bad teeth and sores on his body. Then she saw Richie...her Richie! He was in a theater fooling around with a girl; it was her friend Linda! They were there now, fooling around, and glad that Sarah was gone. Sarah was certain of that in a way she couldn't understand. Suddenly she vomited, covered her eyes, and wept.

She tried to staunch the flow of memories hemorrhaging into her consciousness. She felt like her brain had ruptured. As she sat, sobbing, she became aware of another sensation—pain. Her eyes ached...and her nose! How her nose ached. *Why would my nose ache,* she wondered, the images fading slightly as she shifted her concentration, *my nose isn't hurt.* She was crying loudly now. *The pictures...*another thought. *They'll sell them. Around town, around the world.*

But suddenly Sarah knew that wasn't the case; that was just what she was being told. She was much too important to Mary and the others for them to do such a thing! And suddenly she realized, *They need me. They have to get me back for some reason, and it's not to sell me—it's much more important than money to them. But what...?*

The pain returned. Through her misery, Sarah suddenly made a connection. The pain wasn't hers; it was Mary's! The intruding thoughts were Mary's, not hers. Sarah remembered a few horror movies she'd seen. *What's the name they used? Psychic attack?* And then she realized something else. If Mary could touch her mind, maybe she could touch Mary's. The pain increased. Now Sarah was feeling around inside of Mary's mind. Something was wrong. The pain was very, very deep. This was no ordinary headache; it was something else.

Moondog...

Sarah felt Mary pushing back, retaliating. She leapt to her feet, and stumbled off into the darkness. The memory flow had ceased abruptly; she'd somehow managed to break away from Mary's mental grasp. She suspected that Mary would find her again, but now she knew she could fight back. And in that time, and in that place, as she ran, stumbling through brambles and scrub oak, in spite of her fear, she'd never felt more powerful, more in charge of her own destiny.

28

Victor Lewis sat by the phone, drumming his fingers on the tabletop as he waited for it to ring and bring him the good news he needed to hear. "Damn," he uttered, for the sixth time that morning already. Time was short—it would be daylight soon; they couldn't afford the exposure, especially in their current state of weakness and unpreparedness. They were cutting things way too closely; they should have had that crystal right from the start, with no outside intervention or interference.

Partly, he realized, it was Carl's fault. He'd not tried hard enough to stop that Paxton boy and his friend from even attempting to enter the chimney. Vic sighed. Yes, it was partly Carl's fault; he should have known better. Still, he had no idea what the thing was, and up until the Paxton boy found it, he'd not even been aware of its existence.

Sarah Wells simply had to be recaptured, and at any cost to anyone else, except for Mary and himself, of course. He rose to his feet and hurried back down the hall to the stairs. He was puffing and red-faced by the time he reached the door at the bottom of the steps. It was propped open with an improvised wooden wedge, and he proceeded into the cement cellblock in his basement. Stopping before Sarah's cell, he fumbled with his keys, eventually finding the correct one, and tried to push it into the keyway. It wouldn't go. He squatted, squinting into the lock. *The little bitch broke the key, but I can still get in there.* Retrieving the penknife from his pocket, he put the smallest blade into the lock, and in just a moment, the broken key was aligned with the keyway.

A quick trip to the garage produced a tiny magnet, around which he deftly twisted some very thin copper wire. He carefully slid the magnet into the keyway. He felt the sudden pull as the magnet contacted the remains of the old iron key. He gently slid the wire and the magnet from the lock. The broken end of the key came with it. Then he put in his key and turned it. The spring latch moved, and he tugged the door open.

He took one step into the room, and stopped. He saw Mary, and realized she was working. Moving slowly now, and quietly, Vic circled his wife until he was on the opposite side of the room. Vic sat on the floor facing the woman, and looked into his wife's face. He paled with shock at what he saw. Mary's face was deathly pale, and was stained with blood, much of it dried by this time. Her nose was squashed to one side, purple and swollen. A great splash of drying blood covered the front of her blouse.

Mary's eyes were closed, Vic saw, and her lips were moving as though she was speaking, though no sound came from her. He watched the blood dripping slowly from her left nostril, pooling in the dried blood in her lap. *Plip. Plip.* He heard the sound of the blood, and longed to hold a tissue or handkerchief to her nose, but he didn't dare. Whatever might be happening, he dared not break her concentration. That might be fatal, for all Victor knew. He had no idea what his wife was doing, so he'd just have to bide his time, and hope she'd finish quickly so he could speak with her. He'd just have to wait. With Hank and the boy on foot, and Don and Cal in the car, he felt confident that they'd soon have the girl.

Carl crept through the brush as quietly as he could. He had to move slowly in the dark to prevent a fall. The ground here was uneven and treacherous even in the daylight. He paused, listening. He could hear Brutus up ahead, panting and snuffling his way along the girl's trail. He smiled—Brutus would find her for sure, well before anyone else might. Across the road, Carl heard his father moving steadily forward, also on foot. Though his father had a powerful flashlight, he didn't have it turned on. He'd wait until he heard the girl so he'd not give his position away, should the little bitch be armed. Who knew what she might have taken from the garage on her way out here. Hank was taking no chances. In his jacket pocket he could feel the comforting weight of his old Colt Detective Special revolver. He didn't really think he'd need it, but it was good to have along just in case. Carl jumped for cover as a car came down the road. The headlights illuminated the brush. Taking advantage of the light, Carl scanned the roadside, looking for signs of the girl's passing.

He didn't see Sarah, but he did see Brutus standing on the shoulder. The car slowed as it approached the animal. Carl whispered hoarsely, "Brutus. Here, boy." The big dog turned, trotting into the overgrowth. The car passed Carl, accelerating. He was certain they'd only seen the dog. He broke cover, moving uphill toward the house. He thought they'd have the girl in a half hour or less. Why, he'd still be able to go to school! He stalked back into the brush, following Brutus and his snuffling nose.

Sarah tripped over a branch and went sprawling in the dirt. She gasped, but didn't make any loud sound beyond that of falling into the weeds. She looked up, and smiled. She could see the asphalt of the road glittering dimly under the stars. The ground was cold, and Sarah was damp and chilled. She shivered, feeling nevertheless a feeling of renewed hope. The road was only thirty yards away now; she knew she'd make it there. As she got to her knees, she heard a sound. A car was coming. She knew this wasn't the Mercury—it sounded like a small car. It sounded like salvation.

She rose to her feet. She was dizzy and she thought she could feel the LSD coming on again. She'd only ingested a small amount before she'd spit out the horrible little red pill, but whatever small portion she'd ingested, was starting to work on her. Suddenly, the trees and shrubs were glowing with a soft incandescence. It was amazing how clearly she could see now. She smiled. She could actually see in the dark! And then she stumbled. Rising, she ran on toward the road, which for some reason seemed to be receding from her as she ran, rather than getting closer. *That's not possible. It's only twenty yards now.* But she was moving so slowly…

She saw a small clearing in the faint green glow—only weeds and light scrub stood between her and the road. An auto was approaching, picking up speed. She saw the brilliance of the headlights before she saw the car.

As she stepped into the roadside clearing, something struck her from behind, knocking the wind out of her. She grunted in shock and surprise, and then she staggered, and fell once more. Her body felt suddenly so heavy, and that headache! She pressed both hands against the sides of her head in a futile attempt to stop the throbbing pain. It was to no avail. She looked toward the road in time to see the small white car fly past her, and around the turn. She tried to scream, to lift herself up. Her voice froze in her throat as she realized she wasn't alone in the clearing any longer.

A man was standing before her now, facing away from her. She saw that he was wearing some kind of white robe. The man turned, and she stepped backward, falling again over a large tuft of weeds, tumbling again to the earth in a seated position. The wind knocked out of her, she looked up into the man's face. At first she didn't recognize the face. At first she thought it was Victor's face… no, Moondog…and then it blurred with her own memories, and became… *Daddy!*

Sarah's father walked toward her, smiling in an odd way. *"I saw your pictures, Sarah,"* he said quietly as he took another step forward, the strange white robe now suddenly her father's work clothes. He was holding something in his hand—a photograph. *"You're really talented, and I'm so very ashamed of you, Sarah."* The girl pushed herself back across the ground. She couldn't quite seem to regain her footing.

"You ran away," her father said sadly. *"You ran all the way here, and now that you can finally make some productive use out of your miserable life, you run away again. Shame on you, Sarah, your mother and I raised a completely useless child."* He took another step toward her. *Now she could see the tears in*

his eyes. "*Your mother has died, you know. You broke her heart. The day you left she had a heart attack and now she's dead and it's all your fault.*" He was holding out a five-dollar bill in one shaking hand. "*That's all you're worth to me now, Sarah. And I'm going now to join your mother. See? I have a gun. I'm going to kill myself just like your mother did.*"

Sarah thought for just a moment about what her dad had said. There was something there that hadn't made any sense, something that called out the lie of the whole thing. Her mother had a heart attack, but then she killed herself too? Sarah suddenly laughed; she couldn't help it. The vision had been so very real; she'd almost been convinced to go back to Vic and Mary on her own! She laughed once more, and stood up.

Sarah felt the headache again, and through the shock of the sudden, intense pain, she felt Mary. This woman had been the perpetrator of that terrible vision, Sarah now realized. But she made a mistake, and Sarah knew that it had saved her. "I'll teach you to make fun of my parents, you bitch," Sarah screamed. "How do you like this?" She reached back into Mary's mind as she'd done before. Suddenly the false memory of her father was gone. *I'm gonna get you now, bitch!* Her mind screamed into Mary's. Sarah felt a change in Mary's composure, felt the bright blossom of sudden and completely unfamiliar fear.

Now she was deep in Mary's brain looking for the source of that headache. *She could feel the pulse and rush of blood through the woman's arteries and veins. Suddenly she felt something close, vice-like on the back of her neck. Mary was trying to pull her out. Sarah turned to face the woman, a snarl of anger coming from her lips.* "I'm going to rip your head off," *Mary was shouting.* "I'm going to rip your head off, and then you're going to die." *She clutched at Sarah's throat with her hands, twisting savagely.* "I'm going to pull your head off."

The suggestion reached Sarah's mind, and suddenly she felt tendons pulling, muscle tissue tearing. *Mary was grinning at her, seeming victorious. Suddenly Sarah could feel the skin on her neck stretched very tightly. Mary's grip just kept on getting stronger...stronger! Sarah's neck now felt twice as long at is should be. The tension was closing her trachea and she was having trouble breathing. Something cracked inside her neck—a tendon popped, and her head fell lolling against Mary's shoulder, her neck no longer able to support the weight of her own head. And then Sarah bit her. Hard.*

A large chunk of flesh came away in her teeth as Mary screamed and let her go. Sarah fell against the yielding, warm brain tissue of the other woman. She looked up. At first it was hard to focus; the headache was excruciating—throbbing, throbbing with the beating of Mary's heart.

As her vision cleared, Sarah realized she was looking at Mary's pituitary gland; it glowed a deep red. Behind the gland was a blood vessel. She could see the artery pulsing, sending the life-blood into her brain. But there was something wrong with that artery, Sarah suddenly knew. She watched, fascinated as the sides bulged with each thunderous beat of Mary's heart. Sarah felt like she was inside of a drum. The noise was numbing, but she kept her eyes on that artery. The bright red balloon of the bulge in the artery pulsed and pressed against Mary's pituitary gland. Sarah suddenly knew this was the source of all that pain.

Mary was suddenly gripping Sarah's head again. She was snarling like some wild animal. She wrenched it savagely left, then right. Mary was shrieking now, "I'm going to take your head!" Sarah felt her neck stretching again; but this was far worse than the last time—she could feel her vertebrae separating... the spinal cord... "Not real," she thought in sudden remembrance of her other encounter with this woman. "Not real...fake." The pulling suddenly lessened, and Sarah reached up, grabbing the pulsing artery in both of her hands. She was ignoring Mary's weakening grip around her own neck as she squeezed the hot, pulsing artery.

Mary screamed as Sarah squeezed the blood vessel in both hands. Above Sarah's fists, the red balloon expanded, pressure building. She squeezed more tightly. "This is real, though. This is real, isn't it, Mary?" The woman gasped, and screamed again. Sarah felt the older woman's fear wash over her and she exalted in it. With each pump of Mary's heart, the balloon distended further. Just as Sarah felt herself blacking out, she released her grip with her right hand, touched the bubble in the artery with her fingernail, pressed down into the hot tissue, and slit the artery. Bright blood spewed against Mary's pituitary gland. It splashed warmly over Sarah's arms...

Vic heard Mary's scream; this one came from a physical throat into the physical world. He stared in surprise and shock as he watched Mary collapse without any further word, to the cold cement floor. He distinctly heard the *thunk* as her forehead struck the concrete. He was stunned. For just a moment he sat motionless. He knew breaking her concentration was dangerous, but he decided he had no alternative. He rose to his feet, and stepped forward. He waited a moment, listening and watching. Nothing happened. He knelt beside her, rolling her onto her back.

Her eyes were open, and her lips trembling, though there were no words spoken by the woman. He grunted as he slipped his arms under hers and began dragging Mary down the short corridor, through the now unblocked door into the garage. He had to pause twice for breath—Mary was heavy. Inside the garage, he opened another door that led into one of the other storage spaces. He flipped the switch, and the room was bathed in light. He set Mary down gently, and opened the passenger side door of the new Oldsmobile. Next he opened the old, hand operated garage door before returning to Mary's side.

He dragged Mary to the car, and lifting, pushing, and shoving, finally managed to get her inside. He shut the door, ran to the driver's side, and got in. He shoved the key into the ignition and turned it. The engine started immediately, and he backed down the driveway to the road, shoved the shifter into drive, and roared off, heading toward town.

Victor was breathing heavily; he wasn't used to this kind of exertion any more. His body, like that of his wife, was aging and needed more care than even just a few years previously. He shot a glance at Mary as he careened around a turn. Then he slowed. He knew that if he were to help Mary, they'd need to get to the hospital in one piece. He stole another glance at the woman. She hadn't moved, and her eyes were still open and staring. "Mary? Can you hear me?"

He glanced over again. Her eyes had moved; she was looking at him! A brief smile crossed her lips before she slumped back once more into blankness. Vic was pleased. He loved Mary, sure, but more importantly, her psychic power was what held things together. She made it work. Vic didn't think he could run this operation without her, and they'd been together for so very long…

As he sped toward town, Vic knew he'd have to come up with a good story. *My telephone isn't working,* he decided. *When Mary collapsed, I didn't have any choice but to bring her myself in our car.* He smiled. They'd be more worried about his wife than why he'd brought her instead of calling for an ambulance.

And then he saw the bright red glow in the pre-dawn darkness. It read simply, EMERGENCY. He stepped on the gas, making the last couple of blocks in what was record time. He hit the brakes, and slid the Olds around the turn into the emergency parking lot. At the entrance, a police car was just pulling away. No other cars could be seen. Vic was glad. He looked again at Mary. She was staring up at the headliner of the Olds, but he could also see she was still breathing. He leaped from the car, running to the doors, which swooshed open almost silently.

The receiving nurse looked up from her clipboard. She saw Vic standing there in his bathrobe. She gasped, "Your Honor! What's wrong?"

"My wife," Vic panted, "I think she had a stroke."

The nurse grabbed the phone, and spoke briefly. In seconds a doctor and two orderlies were at the Olds, moving Mary to a gurney. They wheeled her into the hospital at a run. Vic heard the doctor whisper to the orderlies as they rushed Mary into a small room. "Let's move, guys! This is the mayor's wife, you know…"

29

Sarah sat dazed in the clearing. She was panting and perspiring freely, despite the cold. She shivered. She rose unsteadily to her feet; she could still feel the LSD. She knew she'd hurt Mary badly. She grinned. The woman deserved that and more! *Let her come,* she thought, *I kicked her butt once, I can do it again.* She took several halting steps toward the road. The shoulder of the road glimmered in the occasional moonlight, almost looking like a trail of coins...*or is it a yellow brick road?* She wasn't sure—it didn't matter. Wherever it might lead, to the Emerald City of Oz or to Hobbs, it would take her away from this place.

Her neck hurt, but she didn't feel too bad, all things considered. She slowly rotated her head, wondering briefly if it might fall off from the tugging she had endured in her fight with Mary. She was slowly realizing that the combat had been psychic, and that she wasn't injured physically—though she knew Mary had been severely injured. What was the difference? And then she figured it out. Mary knew her attack on Sarah was physic...but Sarah hadn't. In her dazed state, she'd actually been inside the old woman's head somehow. She also realized that if she hadn't truly believed she was *really* breaking that blood vessel, it wouldn't have happened. *The world really is what we think it is—we're creating our personal worlds one second, one thought at a time.*

She stood in the tall grass by the shoulder, trying to get her bearings. *It's so hard to concentrate when you're tripping.*

"Sarah," a voice whispered from a bush a little behind her, "help me."

She whirled in the direction of the sound. She knew that voice! Had her brother somehow escaped too? "Bobby? Is that you?"

He must have escaped at the same time she did! She laughed, saying, "Come on out, dummy. Let me get a look at you." A figure stepped from the green tinged LSD fueled glow of the bush. Then Bobby laughed, and his face melted.

Sarah stepped back. "Moondog!"

Carl laughed. "You stupid girl! You're not getting away this time. I got you fair and square. My dad and I are gonna take you back to Vic and Mary and we'll be big shots, the both of us." He laughed at her fear.

Sarah took a step back, then another, moving even closer to the road. She reached down in the darkness and grasped the handle of the long screwdriver she'd tucked into the slicker's belt, her hand tightening on the handle. Moondog, too full of his own importance at the moment, didn't see the subtle change in her hand position. She took another step back.

Carl said, "Take her, Brutus." The Doberman came out of the blackness like a rocket. He snarled, leaping up against Sarah's breast. The dog knocked her over backwards, and she felt the sudden, vice-like grip of the dog's jaws on her shoulder. She pulled the screwdriver from her belt, and drove it up into the Doberman's chest with all of her remaining strength. She felt her hand strike the dog's body and realized all eight or nine inches of that steel was inside its body. She twisted the thing, rotating it round and round, and felt a sudden, hot rush of blood come pouring down over her supine form. It was the last thing she felt. Brutus whined, and stumbled away from the now still form of the girl, limping into the brush, whimpering with each step.

Carl chuckled. "The little slut never did get my name right." Now he shouted, "I'm Carl. My name is Carl. Can you hear me?"

Brutus collapsed a short distance away, but Carl was too involved at the moment to realize his dog was seriously injured. He was excited, breathing fast. Panting just like a dog as he walked toward the silent form of the girl. He shone his flashlight over Sarah's still form. He grinned. Death was such an… intimate thing; something to be shared like this, one living to enjoy, one dead to bring that joy. It was an intimate thing; much more intimate than even sex. The bright beam of his light stopped on Sarah's shoulder and breast. There was blood everywhere—and more coming out every second! He stood transfixed by the prospect of death—by the ecstatic realization that he'd caused this. He was beginning to think he might be some kind of dark god, the taker of the dead to the underworld where he could enjoy them through eternity. He took another step toward the girl lying almost in the roadway.

The light! Carl stood a moment transfixed in the brilliance of the twin beams. His thoughts had been far away in that dark place he liked so very much. But the dark place was gone now. The blackness in front of him exploded in dazzling greens—and red. And then he saw his shadow fall, dark as the night, across Sarah's body—like a finger pointing accusingly… *There he is! He's the one! Get him!* The car was braking. Carl turned, running into the brush. *Damn! It's happening again!* He turned off his flashlight, running right past Brutus, not seeing him in his panic, and in the intense darkness of the underbrush. The dog stood, whined as he watched his master run away from him, and stumbled off toward the hills alone.

Well into the cover of the foliage, Carl stopped, and dropped to the ground beside a large boulder. He looked back toward the road, wondering where his father might be. He recalled seeing his dad last a few miles back. He probably saw something, and went off to check it out, Carl reasoned. He was the police chief; if he were here, he'd just take over.

The car, nothing but a black silhouette behind the brightness of its head-lights, slid to a stop. The door opened, and a man stepped out, running to the inert form lying nearly in the road. A luminous cloud of the fine dust he'd kicked up when he'd slid to a stop now surrounded the driver. Carl watched as the man set his flashlight on the ground, gently moved the girl, feeling for a pulse.

In the concealing darkness, Carl laughed, pleased and certain the girl was dead. He stopped giggling when, to his dismay, the man kneeling beside her pulled off his shirt and used it to stanch the flow of blood. The man rose, and picked Sarah up. He ran back to his car, and held her in just one arm as he opened the passenger side of his car and placed her on the seat. He ran around to the other side, leapt behind the steering wheel. The engine thundered to life, and a bright red light was suddenly revolving on the dash. Carl watched as the yellow Dodge Challenger roared back onto the road with a snarl that sent gravel into the brush like a shotgun blast.

"Damn. The pigs got her!"

Detective Peter Davis threw the Challenger down the narrow road. The girl was in bad shape, but he thought she might just have a chance if he could get her to the hospital in time. He glanced at the girl slumped in the seat next to him. Her shoulder was still bleeding, and she'd obviously already lost a lot of blood. He wondered about her strange attire—a rain slicker, sneakers with one broken lace, and nothing else…and the blood. Where had this strange little girl come from? Where might she have been going? Who, or what, had attacked her. His mind returned to that other time…

The Challenger slid smoothly around the turns in the road, its custom built and finely tuned suspension was strong and held the road well with little sway or leaning in the turns. Peter glanced at the speedometer—he was hitting seventy. Finally he saw the red sign ahead, and for a second time that morning, a vehicle slid into that curve and shot down the drive to the emergency room.

Dr. Karen Wilson saw the young girl as she was brought in for emergency surgery. She'd been going off duty, but decided to stay to assist the girl. She examined the wounds with a practiced eye, and knew immediately they were the result of an animal bite. Whoever had used his shirt to stop the bleeding had probably saved the girl's life, she realized. The ER nurses stripped the shirt and slicker from the unconscious form with a practiced fluidity. They were also surprised to find the slicker was her only garment. But they had no time to think about that now. They were focused on prepping the young, nameless girl for surgery. The slicker and its belt were laid aside for the police, who'd undoubt-edly need it as evidence.

This was a strange week! The day before yesterday the town librarian had been brought in with only one hand, and so far this morning, the mayor's wife and now this girl had been admitted! Both were in critical condition. It wasn't even daylight yet. Dr. Wilson guessed that the girl was about thirteen or so.

One of the nurses nudged her. "Look here. I think this poor girl's been drugged as well."

Dr. Wilson examined the girl. Her pupils were extremely dilated, and though unconscious, she was salivating. She was drenched in perspiration. "We need a complete blood workup," Karen announced. "We need to know what she's on. The police will want that evidence as well."

The nurse nodded. "This could be a kidnapping."

Karen just nodded. The door to the surgery opened.

"Alright, we're ready here," the surgeon said, "let's get to it." Sarah was rolled into the adjoining emergency surgery, and was carefully lifted from the gurney up onto the table. The big overhead light came on…

Dr. Wilson sighed; it was time to go home. She walked through the auto-matic door that led to the waiting room, dropping her gloves into the trash receptacle. She walked briskly toward the door, when the desk nurse called out to her. "Hey, Karen, I guess Peter's a hero, eh?" The woman gave Karen a smile and nod of affirmation. Dr. Wilson looked at the nurse blankly. The nurse said, "Didn't you know? It was Peter who found the girl lying out on Hobbs Hill Road."

"Hobbs Hill Road?"

"Yep," the nurse responded, "about where the other one happened."

Karen sighed. "I didn't know. Where is he?"

The nurse grimaced. "He's outside in the parking lot trying to get the blood off the upholstery in his car." Dr. Wilson thanked the nurse, and walked out into the parking lot, looking for her boyfriend. The sky to the east was pink and peach above the dark silhouette of the mountains. It was dawn. The sky was leaden overhead, and the air carried a chill. The doctor shivered as she walked toward the yellow Challenger.

As she approached, she could see Peter Davis bent over as he worked on the upholstery. She smiled. She always liked that view of him. She studied his tight jeans.

"Hey, Peter, love…I hear you saved the girl."

The woman's voice startled him, and he struck his head on the edge of the doorframe. She heard a muffled expletive, and grinned. He turned, smiling ruefully, rubbing his head. She stepped up to him, and kissed him. "I love you," she whispered.

"I love you too."

She put her arm around his waist, hugging him. "So, are you ready to go home?"

"I am," he replied. He glanced back into the car. "Good thing I have vinyl upholstery," he said, "I think I got all the blood off."

Karen nodded. "I'll see you at home." Peter smiled, strode around to the driver's side and stepped in. He turned the key and the big engine came to life.

Hobbs Hill Road ended in Aztec. Peter turned left, following Karen. He eased the Challenger into his parking space beside Karen's in the apartment complex parking lot. They got out and walked toward their apartment. They were both tired.

While Karen showered, Peter put on the coffee. There was a steaming cup waiting for her when she returned, wearing a short terrycloth robe. Peter liked how she looked in that robe. A towel encircled her hair. He smiled as he handed her a steaming cup of his very best brew, as he liked to call it. She sat on the sofa to drink her coffee while Peter showered. Peter returned to the living room, sat beside Karen, and told her the story of how and where he'd found the girl. He said he saw a man in the flash of his headlights when he made the turn, but he was already moving away into the brush. He hadn't recognized the male, seen only as a blur as he'd run, but he was obviously her assailant. But then was not the time to hunt him; the girl was badly hurt and needed immediate attention. He explained how he'd been coming into town from the north when he happened upon the assault in progress. He told her where he'd found her.

Karen caught her breath. "Well, I'll be damned! That's out near the mayor's house, isn't it?"

"Just down the hill a ways," Peter answered.

Now it was time for Karen to tell her part of the story. She first told Peter about the mayor and his wife. The woman was still unconscious after apparently having a stroke. The doctor who worked on her said he thought she'd live, but couldn't vouch for her mental condition afterward. Then she told him her opinion that an animal, most likely a big dog, had attacked the girl—and that she'd apparently been drugged. By the symptoms, Karen said, she surmised it was some sort of hallucinogen.

Just then, the phone rang. Karen grabbed the phone, and answered it on the second ring. She listened a moment, and then tossed the phone to Peter. "It's Lieutenant Jackson," she said by way of explanation. She sipped her coffee, watching Peter intently.

"Yeah, Ken, what's up?"

Karen watched Peter's face with concern as he listened. She didn't like the way he looked when he hung up. "What is it, love?"

"Ken just talked with a woman who said she saw a large dog near where I found the girl this morning. Apparently she was a few minutes ahead of me, traveling in the same direction. Anyway, she saw this dog, but no people. I've already called in to report the fleeing person I saw…do you remember last year?"

Karen nodded. How could anyone forget that night? The newspapers had had a field day. A young girl had been struck and killed by a tow-truck in almost exactly the same spot where Peter had found the girl this morning. At the scene, the driver said he'd seen someone push the girl into the road. Later he changed that story. In his revised edition, it had been a large dog that had been chasing the girl. Another driver, had been just minutes ahead of the tow-truck. He'd also seen the animal. The tow-truck driver had been very vocal, and very public about what he saw. The newspapers had run with the story for days. The police, unfortunately, never found much solid evidence.

The forensics people had found several footprints in the area. One set obviously belonging to the girl who'd been killed, and another set belonging to an adult male, whom they failed to identify. There'd also been a set of animal tracks—identified as those of a very large dog.

After two weeks with no progress, the chief called a halt to the investigation. Peter was reassigned, and that was the end of it. The newspapers, seeking circulation at any cost, labeled the girl's death, 'The Werewolf Killing.' The police called it an unfortunate accident. It had created quite a sensation for a while, but when no new evidence materialized, the papers found other headlines. Now it was happening again. What if the papers got wind of the fact that the person who found the animal-ravaged girl today was the detective who'd investigated the tow-truck slaying last year?

Karen saw the worried frown on Peter's face. She decided she needed to distract him from his gloomy thoughts. "Let's wait and see what the medical and forensics people have to say this time, Peter." She smiled at him, and leaned over to give him a kiss. He returned her kiss, but first he set down his coffee.

30

The phone was ringing. Peter groped around the night table, eventually finding the offending object. "Yeah, what is it?" He stifled a yawn, and then became suddenly more attentive. He sat up in the bed, and listened, making an occasional comment, asking an occasional question.

Karen, who'd also been awakened by the ringing phone, sat up next to Peter and was watching him.

"Look. I think talking to the press about this right now would be a big mistake; you remember what happened the last time?" More silence, and then Peter sighed. "Yeah, I know. This kind of decision is up to the chief."

Karen silently mouthed, "Who is it?"

Peter responded in kind, "Ken."

Karen tossed back the covers, and padded to the bathroom. By the time she'd returned, Peter was just hanging up the phone. She looked at the clock; it was barely six in the morning. She climbed back into bed, and pulled the blankets up. The apartment was a little chilly this early in the morning. "So what's going on, Peter?" She snuggled up against him, putting an arm over his chest.

"I'm sorry, babe," he said, "I gotta get going."

"Hey! This is supposed to be our day off together." The tone of her voice bespoke her disappointment.

He looked longingly at her and said with a sigh, "Yeah, I know. It's this thing with the girl. The preliminary lab results are in."

"Really? That was fast."

Peter nodded. "Ken said that the initial medical report from the hospital seems to indicate the girl has not been sexually assaulted. They did a rape kit, just to be sure, and sent it off. But that'll take days to get back. They also agree with your assessment of her being on a hallucinogen. They're thinking LSD, since they found nothing in either the blood test, or urinalysis. Also, her pupils and the related symptoms faded very rapidly."

This surprised Karen; if this were a case of human trafficking, the girl would surely show signs of abuse. "So what else?"

"She's still in a coma, though the doctors aren't sure why. Sure, she suffered a large amount of blood loss, but still…"

"What did Ken have to say? Was the girl just out with friends, and did some acid and they dropped her off when she got weird?"

Peter gave her a rueful expression. "Don't know the answer to that one.

Kids sometimes drive up Hobbs Hill Road to party and make out, so who can say?"

"Still odd about the dog attacking her though," Karen said thoughtfully.

Peter nodded. "I agree. Ken says the hospital's going to have a psychologist see the girl this morning. Her physical injuries, beyond the dog bites, are bruises, scrapes and contusions, all fairly fresh too. They think all of it happened while she was out running around in the woods last night."

"Psychologist's probably not a bad idea. This coma could be from the LSD perhaps, or some other trauma. It would almost have to be psychological, if what you say about her physical condition is true."

Peter nodded, and then said, "And by the way, Chief Larsen's going to do one of his press conferences later this morning. Apparently the local newspaper got wind of the attack somewhere and called the station. They asked if we had a comment on the girl who was raped by the werewolf."

Karen sighed disgustedly. "I seriously doubt that came from the hospital," Karen said with certainty. "I think they know better, considering last year."

"Well, anyway," Peter responded, "somebody told a reporter. Probably got ten dollars for the tip, too." Peter was already up and getting dressed. "The chief wants me there since I was the one who found the girl."

"What will you say to the reporters?"

Peter grinned. "I'll tell them this is an ongoing investigation, and that I'm not at liberty to say anything about it to anybody."

"Will that anger your chief?"

"I don't care," Peter responded. "We're not a public relations business. And even if we were, it's too early in the investigation to know anything much." He shrugged into his shoulder holster, and slipped his department issue .38 Special Smith and Wesson into it, and snapped the safety strap. He dropped two speed-loaders for the revolver into his right pants pocket, and put on his jacket. By now Karen had risen, and went to the kitchen in her robe. "Lemme at least make some coffee before you go."

Peter glanced at his watch. "One fast cup, and then I'm outta here."

"One cup of coffee coming right up," she answered with a grin.

As they sat together at the table, waiting for the coffee to perk, they discussed last year's case, and the strange similarities it shared with this one. When the coffee was ready, Karen rose and poured them a cup each. Peter quickly finished his coffee, rose, leaned over the table, kissing Karen, and headed toward the door.

"Be careful," she called after him. He smiled over his shoulder, and went out to meet the reporters at headquarters.

There were three reporters waiting for him when he arrived at the police station at seven-thirty. Peter tried to avoid them, but it was useless. Instead, when they approached him, small cassette recorders in hand, he dismissed them curtly. "I just got here. At the moment, there's nothing I can tell you beyond the fact that this is an ongoing investigation. If you want something else, see the department information officer."

"You were the man who found the girl, right?" Peter ignored the question.

"You found the werewolf victim last time, too, didn't you?" another reporter asked. "You're not the werewolf, are you?"

"If I were," Peter said with a smile, "I'd be going after reporters, not young girls." He shoved past the last of the three, and strode into the lieutenant's office and shut the door behind him, nearly clipping the nose of a Phoenix Gazette reporter with the door.

"Boy, am I glad you're here." Ken looked up from his desk, giving Peter a rueful smile as he nodded to the office door, and what waited on the other side. Lieutenant Kenneth Jackson was forty-three and prematurely bald. He wore no 'fake hair' as he referred to it.

Peter walked to the window, peeking back into the station between the tightly closed blinds. He saw Officer Hernandez surrounded by reporters. She was trying to be as polite as possible, answering each of their questions with finely crafted non-answers. Peter grinned. He pulled his finger out of the blind, and it snapped back into its fully closed position. He turned back toward Ken. "I'm sure she'll keep them busy for a while," he commented.

Ken smiled. He didn't know what he'd do without Christina. "Well, let's get down to it," he said with no fanfare. "Have a seat and let's see where this all goes. The chief is doing his conference at ten. He's instructed me to have something ready for him to say when the time comes." He tossed a sheaf of papers to Peter, who snagged them just as they were sliding off the desk toward his lap.

Peter read the preliminary report. As he read, Ken filled him in on the latest. "Doctors are almost positive the girl has not been sexually abused. As the report states, all of her injuries occurred last night out in the forest. They can find no signs of restraints having been used on her, no bruising on her ankles or legs, or wrists. They're sure she's not been gagged either."

"So," Peter said, "either this was all willing participation on her part, with the exception of the dog, of course, or she was confined in some kind of cell that didn't require her to be bound up."

Ken nodded in agreement. "There are two current theories. One is that the girl was partying and things got out of hand." Peter shook his head in disagreement, and Ken smiled. "I knew you'd not go for that one. The second theory is that she was brought here from somewhere else; though why, remains a mystery. And if someone dragged her all the way up to Hobbs from somewhere else, why turn her loose like that?"

"Unless she escaped, and they set a dog out to find her."

Ken nodded. "But who? Why? Certainly not sex trafficking. At the present time, the girl's still in a coma, but the doctors are confident it won't last. She was badly bruised, but the only serious wound was the bite on her shoulder. The animal missed her throat by inches."

"She was naked, and in a rain slicker? Not a standard garment unless it's raining, and it wasn't. I think she grabbed it from wherever she was being held. Maybe they took her clothes, thinking her nudity would hinder her escape."

"But from where—the mayor's house?" Ken laughed at the joke.

Peter returned his attention to the written report. Forensics in Phoenix had the slicker she'd been wearing; they'd driven it down as soon as they'd gotten it from the hospital. It was an inexpensive slicker, the type found in discount department stores all across the country. Interestingly, there were two types of blood on her clothing. One was hers obviously, and the other was canine. Peter looked up in surprise, and Ken nodded. "It looks like she was able to injure the dog, quite severely too, considering the quantity of the animal's blood found on the slicker. I want you to go back out there, and see if the animal is still in the area. I have an officer out there now protecting the crime scene. Forensics is there as well."

Peter nodded. "Is that all?"

Ken looked up from his folded hands and said, "Find out what happened to that girl. We need to nail this down fast. The reporters won't give up this time, you can bet your ass on that."

Peter snuck out the back way. None of the reporters noticed him slip out. Now, the rumble of the 426 Street Hemi in his classic 1971 Dodge Challenger soothed him as he headed back up Hobbs Hill Road. Still, he felt nervous. There wasn't much violent crime in Hobbs, beyond the occasional barroom fight. Mostly he'd been investigating thefts, and the occasional tourist mugging. Peter liked it here; liked the quiet routine. Homicide was not his cup of tea. Hell, if he'd wanted that type of work, he could've gone to work for the Phoenix PD; they'd certainly tried. He sighed. He'd do this job, and then get back to the usual work. Up ahead he could see the black and white unit parked on the shoulder. He slowed. There was a yellow plastic ribbon stretched between the trees and the road's guardrail at the turn. It surrounded the crime scene.

Officer Grant nodded to him as he approached. "Nothing much to report here, yet, Detective. The forensics people are still up in the woods."

Peter nodded and began the climb. As he moved, he scrutinized the ground. He saw nothing out of the ordinary.

"Hey, Peter! I thought today was your day off."

Peter saw Frank Bastian walking down the slope. He grinned, responding, "Yeah. Well…you know how it is."

Sergeant Bastian nodded. "We've been over this area three times this morning so far. This is what we have up to this point." He pointed downhill, toward the road. "There's a fair amount of blood down there where you found the girl. We expected that. About half way up, though, there's some more blood, not much, just a large drop or two here and there. We've already taken samples. There're signs all over the place that people have been walking around up here, but with the grass and bush, and mud…well…you know."

Peter did know. He'd experienced the same thing last year. They both turned. Someone was approaching through the brush. Peter smiled. "Hey, Dave, I thought for a second there that you were a werewolf."

Sergeant David Haskell grinned. Sweat droplets stood out on his brow. He was breathing heavily. "Boy! This exercise stuff isn't all it's cracked up to be."

Peter laughed, "Maybe fewer enchiladas and a little more walking would help with that problem."

Sergeant Haskell said, "Look what I found." He held up a large plastic bag. Inside was a Phillips head screwdriver with a ten-inch shank. "There's blood all over the shank, and the handle. There's what look like smudged fingerprints in the blood—small fingers, like a young girl might have."

Peter took the bag, turning it this way and that, examining the contents. "We'll get this to Phoenix today for the lab boys to evaluate."

"I also found this." Bastian held up another, smaller plastic bag. It held a key. "No telling what it was doing up here, but you can see the fancy part that opens the lock is broken off. Also, it's iron and shows absolutely no sign of rust—not even the side that was in contact with the ground is rusty. Considering our weather the last week or so, it's been here only a very short while."

The three men started back down the hill.

"We're not gonna find much else up here, I think," Bastian said, "We'll get this stuff to the lab and let them work their magic." Peter watched Dave Haskell as he huffed and puffed his way down the slope like an off-the-rails steam engine. He concluded that Dave was not really cut out for this kind of work.

Officer Grant was leaning against the side of his cruiser when they arrived at the bottom of the hill. "Find anything?"

"Just more blood…and a screwdriver."

"A screwdriver?" Grant was as puzzled by this as was the officer who'd found the thing.

"You stay up here for now," Peter instructed, "I want this area protected a little while longer. Let's find out what we have here first."

Grant nodded. He didn't mind. No part of this job could be easier than watching a crime scene. He sat back in his patrol unit, picking up the paperback he'd been reading.

The forensics van left the scene first, followed by Peter. He drove slowly back toward town. There wasn't much to go on. Hopefully, the girl would wake up and supply some evidence that would fill in the blanks in this story. Hell, they didn't even have a name for the little girl. In the meantime, there wasn't a whole hell of a lot he could do.

31

Curt Paxton didn't go to school on Thursday; instead, he waited at home to meet Mr. Luedke. After his dad left for work, he'd gone to the garden to dig up the small pyramid. He'd looked around first, suspicious of someone watching. He used a small trowel to unearth it. He hated touching it now, and as soon as it was out of the ground, he wrapped it in an old tee shirt. *I wish I'd never found it.* He rose, carefully checking his surroundings once more, and walked into the house through the back door. He put the pyramid on the table, and sat down to wait for Mr. Luedke.

A short time later Curt heard a car pull into the drive. Peeking out the window, he saw a grey, four-door Mercedes Benz. The driver's door opened and an older man stepped out into the sunlight, glancing about him in a very casual way. The man walked to the front door, and before he could knock, Curt opened the door and greeted him. "Hi. I'm Curt Paxton."

The man smiled and introduced himself. "And my name is George Luedke. I believe we've talked on the telephone." Curt nodded, and invited him in. His visitor noted his rapid visual check of the street before he closed the door. The boy was clearly frightened; he had reason to be. Once inside, with the door shut and locked, George Luedke's first request was to see the 'object,' as he put it. Curt brought the pyramid, still wrapped in the tee shirt, into the living room and handed it to him without comment. He was glad to have it in someone else's hands!

The man studied the crystal for several minutes. Curt watched him intently. He already knew from Mrs. Prutzman's description that Luedke was sixty-eight years of age. He had sparse grey hair and wore old-fashioned, round, metal-rimmed glasses. Curt watched as his visitor turned the crystal slowly, studying each side in turn.

At length he spoke. "This is natural crystal; it has not been cut into this pyramidal shape, but grew this way through eons of time. It's a kind of talisman, designed and charged with energy to make something happen."

Curt was clearly disappointed; he'd hoped for more information than that. "So that's the story? It's just a stupid, magic talisman? I kinda figured that out all by myself in the library with Mrs. Prutzman's help."

George looked at the boy and laughed. "I can see you've already done some research on the subject." Curt nodded.

"Alright then, let me take a few minutes to explain some things." Curt smiled encouragingly. Now they were getting somewhere. They sat side by side on the sofa, and George Luedke started explaining the subject of magic. He only talked of the basics; they'd hardly have the time to go into much depth— and that was something he preferred not to do anyway, since this object actually had nothing whatsoever to do with magic.

George went on to explain the arcane markings on the sides of the crystal. "This device you see here is really quite ancient. Based on appearances, I'd say that it was originally carved in the twelfth or thirteenth centuries," he lied. Curt let out a low whistle. *He believes me,* George thought with relief. "Thus, the so-called 'words of power' inscribed upon its surfaces are in ancient languages, which is why you couldn't figure out what they said." He turned the piece over, looking now at its bottom, if indeed it had a top or a bottom. He glanced up at Curt; he had the boy's rapt attention. "I see some markings here…and more strange symbolisms." George hated deceiving the sincere boy, but for right now, it seemed the wisest approach.

He explained that words of power were specific words, usually the names of angels, demons, or gods who could be called upon for specific purposes related to whatever power they might hold. For the most part, he explained, this entailed the development and use of an elaborate and difficult secret language that might take a student of magic many years to learn. Curt looked up at George, consternation clearly expressed on his features.

Mr. Luedke saw the expression on Curt's face, and said, "Magic is much more than mumbling a few incantations, and up pops a demon. The idea of 'easy magic' was a myth originally devised by mediocre men who were out to make a fast buck—and by mediocre preachers who warned how easily 'the devil' could come into the midst of a town or village. Perpetuating their fears encouraged their support of the church, which would 'protect' them." Curt nodded in understanding.

"Real magic is, in reality, a type of…active meditation, with the goal of improving one's spiritual understanding of the natural world, and oneself— much like the goals of Eastern forms of meditation. But the church couldn't have that. If people thought they could improve themselves, rather than relying on the church, the church would lose its wealth and massive political power. So they branded any method of enlightenment except their own to be satanic magic.

"It worked like this. If a priest healed someone, it was called a miracle. If a magician healed someone, it was by the hand of the devil. So-called witches and healers were killed by the thousands by the church, who preached, 'Judge not, lest ye be judged.'"

Curt nodded. This all made sense to him. "But what about all the Satanists we read about in the newspapers and hear about on television and in the movies? You know, rock and roll songs played backwards and all that?"

George laughed again, and replied, "Backwards song lyrics or reading the Lord's Prayer backwards generates absolutely no power whatsoever, magical or otherwise. It may frighten a teenager's parents, but it does nothing else, other than enrich the churches that make millions of dollars playing on the fears of their very gullible congregations. Look at it this way, Curt. If magic were that easy, thousands of people would be reading the Lord's Prayer backwards, and Las Vegas would be bankrupt!" Curt laughed.

"Anyway, true black magicians are few and far between. Hedonists and money-mongers are, by definition, people interested in immediate gratification and power. Such shallow mentalities are seldom willing, or probably not even able, to dedicate the long, hard years required to really master something as tenuous, complex, and non-material as magic."

"So how did you get interested in all of this?" At this question, George paused before continuing. What he'd told the boy up to this point about the art and history of ceremonial magic was true, even if that art and that history had nothing to do with the present situation. The boy had to be protected from the truth, if at all possible.

"For me it's been a sort of hobby; something that attracted my attention a vast number of years ago. It's part of history, after all, is it not?"

Curt had to admit that this made sense. He thought for a moment, looked at Luedke and said, "All right, then tell me, Mr. Luedke, how does all of this magic stuff relate to Hobbs and what's going on around here right now? Why would someone place an ancient and supposedly powerful, and therefore quite valuable, artifact in the Stack? I'm afraid I seem to be missing something."

George nodded in approval. The boy was tenacious in his search for truth, George noticed. He had a sharp mind, and knew what questions to ask. This was something to be admired in one so young. He decided to reveal just a small amount of further information in order to answer the boy's questions.

"I moved to Prescott two years ago to research the history of Hobbs. You no doubt have heard the name Zachary Louben?"

"Yep. We studied him in school."

"What your history text didn't tell you, and what most people don't know, is that Hobbs wasn't the first place the Loubens set up shop."

"Set up shop?"

"My research clearly and irrefutably shows that they lived for a time in Louisiana, in the eighteenth century."

"What? The eighteenth century? How can that be possible! That would've made him and his wife over a hundred years old even before they got here and opened the lumber mill. That's not possible."

"Hold on, let me explain," George said patiently. He realized that this was not the kind of thing that people just…accepted. It went against all their senses of right and wrong, and even of time. He continued slowly. "They opened up a roadside inn near New Orleans, and the food they served became quite famous. They had a special way of cooking meat that gave it a flavor not found in other inns and taverns. Travelers were encouraged to eat there by friends and local businesses. The place became what we might refer to as a tourist attraction.

"Then the disappearances began to be noticed. Not all at once, you understand. The eighteenth century didn't have the law enforcement tools we have today; it took a while…several years. Undoubtedly they'd been happening for quite a while, but went unnoticed. In a transient city like New Orleans was, with the shipping and all, people came and went all the time. What finally got the investigation going, was the disappearance of seven children at the same time.

"One of the local churches hosted a picnic for its parishioners, and when the adults were called in to prayer, the children were permitted to remain outside under the watchful eye of a chaperone. When the prayer meeting was over, the chaperone was gone, and so were all seven children. That would have been hard to conceal at any time in history.

"The chaperone was discovered the next day in a small grove of trees with her throat slit. But what the Loubens hadn't counted on, was an eighth child. He was shy, and had been hiding from the others, who'd apparently been teasing him. He saw what happened. Once the people realized the Loubens were responsible, they formed a posse—what we'd call a mob in this day and age.

"They held a town meeting in the same church, and gathered up torches and an assortment of firearms. Then they moved as a group and surrounded the inn. But by the time they arrived, their quarry had fled. Somehow they'd heard about the meeting; the preacher insisted it was the Devil himself who told them. It wasn't important how they found out. What mattered was that they'd gotten away.

"What they left behind so shocked the posse that little of it was recorded, and most accounts have been deliberately destroyed—as was the inn, which was burned to the ground the same day of the raid. Only a few contemporary letters now in my possession tell that story." Curt felt the hair on his arms and neck rise.

Mr. Luedke sighed, and then continued. "What they found inside the inn was a cannibal restaurant. The customers had been eating the flesh of kidnapped and slaughtered children. Behind the public part of the inn, in the kitchens and storage rooms lay true horror, Curt. Human limbs hung from meat hooks, carefully cured; body parts littered the back rooms. It was further discovered that the entrails had been sold to farmers for their hogs.

"They also found a bathtub filled with blood inside the Louben's living quarters. It was noted that the blood was still fresh. Scattered about the room were the bodies of eleven children and babies. And there were footprints, bare footprints leading from the tub into the bedroom. It appeared the Loubens had been bathing in the blood of children.

"Needless to say, the posse pursued them as best they could. No one knew what direction they'd taken, or if they were even still in the area. But mobs have their own dynamics and logic, if one may call it that. The mob came upon a local man of 'slow wit,' as the document I read referred to him. He was splashed with blood, and found sleeping conveniently beside the road the posse was traveling along. Quite a coincidence, wouldn't you say? I mean, considering the number of ways out of New Orleans. But mobs have their own dynamics and logic.

"This unfortunate was…sacrificed; set up to take the blame so Zachary and his wife would have time to escape. They painted him with blood and most likely hypnotized him; they were very good at that, from what I've been able to learn over the years. Anyway, the posse skinned the man alive, but the Loubens got away. This horrific violence by the ordinary folks of the town was another reason they suppressed any documentation of what happened.

"Everyone in the region was questioned, of course. Magistrates strutted around in their black suits, and the town marshal or perhaps it was a sheriff, was very diligent in the search for these two satanic demon worshippers, as they'd come to be called as the investigation ground on to its inevitable conclusion. Of all those questioned, nobody identified the Loubens, or, in fact, any man and woman in their fifties traveling the roads out of the city that day."

Luedke waited for Curt to process what he'd just heard. Curt listened to the ticking of the old Seth Thomas mantle clock. He felt cold, but it wasn't a physical coldness he was experiencing.

Suddenly George stood up. "C'mon. We need to see Muriel." Curt got up, legs shaky. He was glad they were going somewhere. He grabbed his jacket from the hall tree by the front door, and they walked outside, both of them looking for watching eyes. The street was quiet. They walked to George's sedan and got in. George turned on the radio—elevator music. Curt didn't mind; he still felt numb and oddly frightened from the stories he'd just heard.

As the Mercedes traveled toward the hospital, George said, "The Loubens, you may have surmised, are vampires of a kind. The reason nobody reported seeing them on the road that day in Louisiana, was that everyone had been look-ing for an older couple instead of a young couple perhaps in their twenties."

"What? You mean bathing in blood makes a vampire young again? I thought they had to drink the blood, or something."

George laughed. "Not exactly. They used some kind of power to make this transformation. It is very likely that this pyramid crystal played some vital role in the whole sordid operation."

They rode in silence for a bit, and then George finished the story. "The Zachary Louben who moved to Hobbs in 1881, that you've learned about in school, was the same Zachary Louben who'd fled New Orleans almost a hun-dred years earlier. I have bills of lading and store receipts he'd signed; receipts both from New Orleans and from Hobbs in the late nineteenth century. I had them analyzed by two of the country's very best handwriting experts. The con-clusion both of them reached independently was that both signatures were in the same hand—except of course that the later signatures appeared to be those of the younger Louben."

The gray Mercedes pulled into a parking space in the visitor's lot. Before he shut off the engine, George turned to Curt. "I believe Zachary Louben is still in Hobbs. I have to find him before it's too late."

32

It'd been a long drive. Don Bristow had wanted to take the Mercury, but Vic had insisted he take the old Plymouth Valiant instead. He hadn't liked the idea, but he knew better than to argue with Vic. And the Plymouth wasn't really all that bad; it had the so-called 'police package.' That included a strong 220 horsepower engine as well as various suspension additions. It could be fast, if speed was essential, and most of all, it was inconspicuous—rust deliberately left on fenders and wheel wells to make the vehicle look as old as it really was. But looks could be deceiving, and Don appreciated the anonymity of the car after being on the road with it for a while.

But now the job was done, and he could get back up to Hobbs. He popped the two pills into his mouth, and chased them with a glass of water he'd drawn from the kitchen sink. The speed would keep him awake on the trip back home—it was a four-hour drive, and he'd already been up ten hours. He carefully wiped the glass with a paper towel, which he pocketed. He walked back into the bedroom and looked in the closet, grinning.

The young man's head was looking down into his lap, and his long blonde hair hung down, covering his face. He sat—or almost sat, technically, with his rear end slightly above the floor, legs splayed in front of him. The rope was still tight around his neck, holding him in that position. Don snorted; the kid would be there until someone found him. By now his face was purple, and his swollen tongue protruded as though he was giving a final, if quite humorous, opinion of Don and what he'd done to him. Don laughed again, thinking of the pleasure he'd have explaining to Vic and Mary the excellent job he'd done for them.

In his lap lay a number of Polaroid photos. Even in the low quality of the Polaroid images, Sarah Wells was easy to identify. Along with the photos was a handkerchief with a brown stain covering half of it. He grinned again. *Thank God Carl likes trophies of his conquests!* The boy had dipped his snot-rag in the blood pool left on the ground after that meddling cop had taken the girl away. Along with the photos and the rag was a piece of notebook paper taken from the desk in his small apartment. Upon this paper, Don had scrawled two sentences in big block letters: 'I did it. I'm sorry.'

Don had surprised the Owens boy when he'd walked in. It was an easy ambush, as things like that went. Owens had casually met Carl briefly two days ago when he'd driven up to Prescott, and then Hobbs, looking for work. They'd met in a quite accidental but fortuitous way. Owens had been in the arcade at the shopping mall, where he'd been asking around in the various shops about finding work. Carl had been walking by, and heard the boy mention his name.

Carl, with a cunning one would expect from the son of the chief of police, had recognized this young man's name, having heard it previously from Bobby, in conversation. He befriended the young man, challenging him to a game at the arcade, there questioning him to determine if this was the same Thomas Owens Bobby had spoken of. Amazingly, it was. Carl realized he might be useful. Vic and his father always told him to be on constant watch for either young recruits for 'The House,' or as possible patsies for crimes they might have to commit; and with what Carl already knew about this guy, he was perfect.

Thomas Owens was without a job and was looking for one. He'd been seen around Prescott and Hobbs on several occasions prior to this one. His movements, because he lived alone, would be impossible to trace beyond that. Carl was quick to befriend Thomas, even paying for the video games they played together. Later, as they shared a pizza that Carl had also paid for, Carl told Thomas that his father owned a car dealership, and he was looking for someone to train as a mechanic. By the time Thomas left the mall that day, he was convinced he and Carl were the very best of friends. And Carl had a new patsy in his back pocket.

Now, with the debacle involving the Wells girl, he'd come in handy much sooner than they'd thought. He'd discussed this chance opportunity with Vic. They'd originally planned to lure him to Hobbs, but now...well...

Don didn't know how long it would take people to find the Owens kid, but that didn't matter. He was now clearly the assailant the police would be looking for in the death of the Well's girl; the evidence was very clear, and every investigator liked a nice simple solution to things like assault and murder.

Why Thomas Owens might want to attack the girl was up to the police to figure out. Don thought they'd brand him a psycho loner. The various photos of the girl would convince them that he'd been stalking his younger brother's girlfriend. Now he congratulated himself on his cleverness. *I oughta get a bonus outta this one,* he thought with considerable glee.

Sitting in the driver's seat of the Valiant in the apartment parking lot, he could relax—as much as the speed he'd just swallowed would allow, that is. It was early afternoon, and this apartment building was a small, one-level affair with only eight units. The parking lot was devoid of cars, with the exception of his, and that of Thomas Owens. Everybody else was probably at work, he figured.

As he started the Plymouth, he wondered idly if Thomas Owens's family would actually be able to sell a dead man's car and how much the old 1971 Ford Pinto might bring. The paint must have originally been some shade of green; but it was now a very faded, vaguely lime color. He laughed. *Not nearly as much as if it didn't belong to a possible rapist and attempted murderer.* He laughed again, sure that Vic would find a way to silence the Wells girl before she could talk.

He pulled from the complex, turning west on Speedway, heading toward I-10—and out of Tucson. He hummed contentedly, thought briefly about stopping at one of the topless taverns that dotted Speedway in this part of town, but then he thought better of it. There was no point in pressing his luck. He was virtually invisible in this rust-bucket car, and he'd talked to no one. He'd wait until Orange Grove to pull off for gas, nice and far from the scene of the 'suicide.'

Muriel Prutzman sat in the hospital bed, the top raised so she could see her visitors. Curt tried not to stare at the shockingly white bandage that swathed her right arm. She was pale, and an IV was still hooked to her arm, supplying fluids to speed her recovery. He shuddered trying to imagine the pain she must've endured as she pushed her hand into the disposal.

George and Muriel had hurriedly exchanged greetings and polite inquiries. George knew that time was running out, and the painkillers the nurse had just given Muriel would be kicking in soon. She'd heard most of what George had told Curt. She listened as George finished the story.

"All those familiar with the history of Hobbs and the Louben lumber mill disaster, know Marshal Jake Thompson died in an auto accident in Phoenix in 1921. But there is something else many do not know, not even the most dedicated students of Arizona history: Before his death, Jake Thompson had been writing his story of those events.

"I managed to procure his diary in an auction almost twenty years ago, along with some other artifacts that had belonged to him. After his death, his relatives donated some of his things to a museum in Kansas City, where he'd been born. The museum never got around to cataloguing the collection, and it was finally auctioned as one lot back in 1970. It is very fortunate indeed that I managed to acquire those documents.

"It seems that the marshal had an informant who'd contacted him about the Loubens sometime in late 1920. That informant was an East Coast mystic who'd also been hunting the Loubens. He'd told the marshal that Zachary and his wife had apparently escaped the mill explosion—it is a fact that no bodies were ever discovered, and no older couples were seen on the roads leading from Hobbs in the days immediately following the explosion. Familiar story, eh?

"The explosion at the Louben mill caused no fires directly; fire reports as well as a number of reliable personal accounts of the time, and later the former marshal's diary, show clearly that Hobbs burned as the result of overturned kerosene lamps and candles from the resulting concussion. I can't be certain as to just what caused that explosion, but if my suspicions are correct, and each new discovery I make says that they are, we're facing a danger the likes of which this planet has never experienced." He looked from Muriel to Curt.

"Worse than the asteroid that killed the dinosaurs?" Curt grinned. He knew this was serious, but a danger this planet had never experienced? Of that he was doubtful.

George looked at Curt. "Yes, young man. I mean what I said. In any event, Jake insisted in his diary that he'd seen Zachary Louben and his wife on a downtown street in Phoenix in 1920. He wrote that they appeared much younger than they should have been, though he didn't have the information about them we have today."

Now it was Muriel's turn to speak. "A girl was brought into the hospital early this morning. I overheard the nurses discussing her condition. They thought I was still asleep." She smiled tiredly. "She'd been attacked by an animal up on Hobbs Hill Road and nearly killed. From what I was able to gather, she's currently in a coma." Muriel looked at George and Curt, and then continued. "She was found in the same general place as the girl who was killed last year. George, you must remember? The papers all called it the werewolf murder."

George said, "The police gave up on that case awfully fast in my opinion. Another oddity for the town."

"That's what everyone else thought too," Muriel added. "Even the local paper, that had been supportive of the chief up to that point, had voiced concern that the dead girl was not being given her just due. But our police chief said that since there was no evidence of foul play, or even any evidence of the large dog or wolf a few reported seeing, that it was nothing more than an unfortunate automobile accident. He actually blamed the girl for being out there at night."

"As I recall," George said, "the detective in charge of the case was almost fired because of his complaints about inadequate investigative time. He was reassigned, as I recall, to do paperwork for a few months as a disciplinary measure."

Muriel nodded. "I told Harry you were coming. After I heard about the girl today, I thought you might want to look into that story as well. He's at the library right now making photocopies of the newspaper articles of the time."

George laughed. "Even in the hospital, you're still a librarian."

Muriel smiled. "I'm getting sleepy now. Why don't you stop back later; Harry should be here by then."

George leaned over, kissing Muriel on the forehead. She was already asleep.

He turned to the boy, saying, "C'mon, Curt, we've got to see that policeman. We have no time to lose."

Curt stood, glancing at his watch. It was only one-thirty. Normally he'd have been hungry by now, but the events of the morning had gone a long way to suppress his appetite. As they walked out of the hospital, George stopped for a moment and bought a copy of the day's newspaper from a stand in the lobby. It was an extra edition of the morning's paper. The headline read gleefully, WEREWOLF STRIKES AGAIN. YOUNG GIRL CRITICAL.

As George backed the Mercedes out of the parking lot, Curt read aloud the account of the crime. Once again, the police chief was attempting to defuse the event before it even got going. Suddenly Curt stopped in mid-sentence. He looked at George in amazement. "Damn! I've seen this girl!"

George slowed the big sedan, glancing over at the paper. Curt turned it so he could see it better. He saw the photograph of the girl, lying with eyes closed and bed clothing covering her almost to her neck. Apparently the reporter had taken the photo in the hospital. George wondered how he'd gotten away with that. George glanced up at Curt, accelerating again. The boy looked ill, pale. He stammered, "I…I saw a Polaroid of this girl yesterday. M…my friend Tommy Driscoll had it. He got it from his friend Carl. It showed this girl standing in the center of a circle of adults, several men and a woman. All the men were looking at something on the floor that looked like a maze or something. I think there was a rat inside it."

"Who's Carl?"

Curt felt sick. It took a moment for him to respond. "Carl Larsen—he's the police chief's son!" Realization of what he'd just said, struck him. He looked over at George, wide eyed. "Goddamn, this could be bigger than I imagined. That involves Carl somehow in what happened to the girl, and where she was being held."

George spoke calmly as he changed lanes smoothly, blending with the early afternoon traffic. "Don't lose control now, boy. We have some very important work to do, and I'll need your assistance. Believe me when I say to you that time is running out, in a way you cannot yet comprehend. We've got to see this Detective Davis just as soon as we can. He found the girl, and he was the same police detective who discovered the other girl a year ago. He may be the only policeman we can trust. There's no way of telling how pervasive this situation could've become, or how far the police department might've been corrupted."

"Corrupted? You think the whole department is involved in some kind of massive crime conspiracy?"

He looked over at Curt. "No, certainly not the entire force—but how can we, as outsiders, know who we can trust? This is extremely serious. We're in this really deep Curt. I'm not just saying this to frighten you, but you should realize that wherever Zachary Louben is, he'll try to kill us the instant he knows we're onto him."

Curt didn't want to think about that. Instead, changing the subject, he said, "I like your Mercedes, it's a cool car."

George smiled. "It's not my car. I drive a three-year-old Ford. I rented the Mercedes after I talked to you. If anyone's looking for me, they'll most likely be looking for the Ford."

Curt laughed nervously. "Do you really think this…Louben guy will try to kill us?"

"There's no doubt in my mind, Curt. From what you've said, I think it's possible that Zachary Louben is the police chief."

33

Detective Davis was just about to leave the station. It was already almost two o'clock on what was supposed to have been his day off. He'd made it all the way to the door of his office, grabbing up his jacket from the rack. His telephone rang. He thought briefly about turning the call over to the other detective on duty, but then took the call. He sighed, picking up the receiver. "Hobbs Police. Detective Davis here, what can I do for you?" He listened for a moment, the expression on his face going from disgusted, to interested, to skeptical. He hung up.

Ken looked up at him. "What's up Peter? I thought you were outta here." He looked more closely and said, "You look worried, Peter. Is there a problem?"

"Huh? Oh, it's nothing, Ken. I just forgot an appointment." As he headed down the hallway to the back door of the station and the parking lot, he thought about the strange telephone conversation. The person on the phone had told him to tell no one where he was going. If he came alone, the caller had reassured him, he'd get help on the so-called 'werewolf case.'

Peter left the station by the back door, a frown on his brow. Walking to his car, he looked around, eyes narrowed, searching for someone possibly watching him. He saw no one except a uniformed officer he knew, just exiting his unit. He smiled and nodded at the officer, and kept walking. There was no time for idle chatter; the strange voice on the phone said to come immediately. He arrived at his Challenger, and he opened the trunk. He lifted out a pistol case, unzipping it.

From the case he extracted a customized Colt National Match M1911 .45 caliber pistol. From another case he removed a loaded magazine, which he deftly slipped into the butt of the big automatic. He racked the slide, keeping the muzzle directed toward the rear of his car, chambering a round. He pushed up the specially enlarged thumb safety, and shoved the pistol into his waistband.

He dropped an extra loaded magazine into his left pants pocket. He was off duty, technically, so having his personal firearm wouldn't be against any of the department's regulations. If he was knowingly going into a potentially hostile situation—and who could say where this odd telephone call might lead him— he wanted a bit more firepower than the .38 Smith and Wesson model 10 loaded with department-issue ammunition could afford.

He got into the yellow Dodge, left the station parking lot, and headed toward the Hobbs Motel on Oak Street, where he'd meet with this mysterious person who claimed to have information about the 'Jane Doe' currently in a coma at the hospital. He turned the call over in his mind. *Not much to go on.*

When he arrived at the motel, he made a slow pass along Oak Street, looking both at the motel and the surrounding area. He spotted a couple of potential ambush locations. There was a steel dumpster on the east side, which he ruled out. The room where he was told to meet his informant could not be seen from the dumpster. There were several trees, but he could see no movement near them. He turned the Challenger around, and drove into the parking lot, turning the corner to where room 14 would be located. There were only three other vehicles there at this time of day. All of them sat empty. Finally he turned the Challenger, and backed into the parking space beside a grey Mercedes sedan that was parked in front of room 14.

Now, sitting at the cheap Formica dining room table inside the room, he looked over his informants. There was an older, reasonably well-dressed man, and a teenage boy. The boy kept silent as the older man spoke. Detective Davis listened patiently. Obviously he was dealing with a deranged man. At first, the conversation seemed to revolve around werewolves, and now the old man was going on about vampires! Finally he raised his hand, stopping George, and said, "I thought vampires only came out at night. Daylight's supposed to kill them."

George replied, "We're not talking about movie vampires here, Detective; we're dealing with living persons, not some imaginary demonically reanimated cadavers." The old man turned to the boy and said, "Curt, why don't you tell the policeman what you know about all of this?"

And Curt did. When his story was finished, Peter understood the reason he'd been asked by this George Luedke to bring the official police report filed on Curt's hit and run case just outside the library. Now he opened the folder, and read through it rapidly. When he'd finished, he looked up, and said, "Well, I'll be damned!" Curt and George looked at him expectantly, and he continued. "The report states that the automobile involved in the accident was a rather worn out, lime green '67 Plymouth Satellite, not a dark green '65 Mercury hot rod."

Curt rose to his feet, almost knocking his chair over backwards in astonishment and anger. "That's impossible," Curt said indignantly, "I distinctly told Officer Grant what kind of car it was, and the color too. My dad was sitting right there with us. He heard the whole thing. You can ask him if you don't believe me. I also told Officer Grant that I couldn't read the license plate, but I know it was one of those old, orange colored Arizona plates." Curt looked from Peter to George, his surprise releasing and allowing him to once again take his seat.

Peter opened the file once more. "I don't know about any of your vampire comments, but something funny is obviously going on here—the report also says the car in question had Utah plates." The boy and the older man looked at each other, and Peter said, "I think I may have seen your Mercury a couple of days ago, now that I think back. It was next to me at a traffic light. Loud engine."

Curt then told the detective about the Polaroid pictures he'd seen of the girl in the hospital...in the company of those men, and under what circumstances he'd seen them.

George spread his hands before him, and said, "As a police detective, I ask only this of you. Just look at the evidence. We have the police chief's son showing around photos of the girl you found out on Hobbs Hill Road with adults, doing what? A mouse in a cage? That's what it looked like, Curt tells me." The boy nodded in agreement. "You have to admit that something odd is going on here.

"And is it merely coincidence that you found the girl in the same spot, more or less, where the other young victim was found last year?" George gave the detective a hard stare. "As you well know, Detective, the chief ended the investigation of that case pretty quickly, as I recall from reading the story in the Prescott paper. You were even disciplined for filing a complaint about how the investigation had been run. And now you have another almost dead girl, a hit and run at the library involving a falsified police report. You said it yourself: Something funny is going on here."

Peter said nothing for a moment. He was interested once more in what the man and the boy were telling him. Beyond the werewolf and vampire nonsense, the actual story seemed to paint a grim picture of affairs in Hobbs. He'd originally come to Hobbs to avoid really dangerous police work. Here, in this sleepy, largely retiree community, he'd figured he could do a good job, have the time to actually help people, and not feel like a walking target every time he stepped out of his car. He felt the weight of the automatic in his waistband.

Peter had made up his mind. He was going to take all of this seriously, and begin his own, quiet investigation. He looked from George to Curt. "I'm going to do a little checking around. If what you say is true, we don't want to tip our hand right now." He looked hard at George. "I don't mind telling you that I don't believe in vampires. I'll tell you that right off. However, something strange is clearly going on around here. I'll call you if I hear anything." He glanced at the motel phone, seeking the number to write in his notepad. He clicked the button on his ballpoint.

George said, "Forget this number. We're leaving here right after you. I'll get in touch with you—tomorrow perhaps?"

Peter nodded. He didn't like it, but he'd dealt with informants on several occasions, and this ploy was nothing new to him. The guy was moving around from hotel to hotel in a rented car. Obviously he was taking the threat seriously. Regardless of the monster talk, what he and the boy had said had merit. It was worth at least a couple days of quiet looking and listening.

At that same time, Harry Prutzman had just finished making the photocopies of the articles Muriel had sent him to get at the public library. While he was there, he also decided, almost on a whim, to make some copies of various transcripts of city council meetings. When he was finished, he carefully locked the library with the key he'd picked up at his house, and walked to his car. Since the terrible accident, the library would only open on Saturday, when the assistant could be there. If Muriel could return to her duties, things would return to normal. If not, a new head librarian would have to be hired. Harry smiled to himself; he knew in his soul that this wasn't going to keep Muriel out of her beloved library. As he drove down Apache toward Hobbs Hill Road, he didn't notice the white Ford Taurus that had followed him from the library, always maintaining a discreet distance behind him.

Officer Grant kept his distance, allowing sometimes two cars between himself and the librarian's husband. He'd been instructed to watch the old man's movements, and that was all. He was not to interfere in the old man's affairs under any circumstances. He didn't know the reason behind these orders, and he was certainly a little bit curious, but when Chief Larsen told him to do something, he did it. With everything the chief knew, Grant figured he'd be in prison for sure, and he'd be there a long time! He thought back to those days just before he'd come to Hobbs.

The Phoenix Police Department had been getting ready to indict him for taking payoffs. He'd gotten wind of the investigation by accident—a dropped piece of paper with his name at the top. He'd retrieved the paper, taken it with him to the restroom where he'd read it. Afterward, he dropped the paper, away from his desk, where another detective discovered it. He must have been in on the investigation because Grant saw the look of relief on his face when he found it, face down on the floor.

Grant knew he'd have to act quickly, if he was going to avoid prosecution. He tendered his resignation that very same day. When he resigned, the charges were dropped. For the Phoenix Police Department, accepting his resignation streamlined things, and achieved the same results: Grant was off the force.

The Phoenix PD had almost had him. Fortunately, they didn't know he'd been dealing confiscated coke back out onto the street. He knew they'd never have dropped the charges if they'd known that!

Now, here in Hobbs, he was a real policeman again. Rick Grant liked being a policeman. He liked the badge and the gun. Yep, he knew how to use authority, alright! He wasn't a detective, but he didn't really care about that. He'd stashed enough cash from his former second business as a drug dealer that if push came to shove, he could light out for parts unknown, and live happily if somewhat frugally for six or eight years.

He braked, slowing to stay far enough behind the old man so as not to arouse suspicion, although he probably needn't have worried. The old fool in front of him might just as well have been blind for all the care he was taking to see if he was being followed. The old man started up again, and Grant slid his foot back to the accelerator.

He looked at his reflection in the mirror as he sat two cars behind Prutzman at a traffic light. How had Hank Larsen, a hick police chief many miles from Phoenix, found out about the drugs when the Phoenix Police Department hadn't caught on? *Don't matter, really. When I'm ready to hit the road, I can take care of ol' Chief Larsen...* He patted the department issued .38 Special revolver in the shiny black leather holster at his hip.

He pulled into the hospital parking lot, and watched the old man walk up the short flight of steps and through the front door. Now came the waiting. He slouched down in his seat, pulling the collar of his jacket up around his neck. With the engine off, the Taurus was already getting cold. He sat up with interest when he saw the Paxton boy leaving with someone moments later. *Who the hell's that with him?* Rick jotted a note in his book. It read simply, *'Old man. 60s. Grey Mercedes. With Paxton boy.'* He waited patiently, watching. The Paxton boy and the mystery man got into the Mercedes, and they left the parking lot. Grant stayed put. He'd been instructed to watch Prutzman, and regardless of Paxton and the stranger, here is where he was staying, at least for a while.

In the hospital, Victor Lewis sat by his wife, gently holding her hand. The doctor had said she was improving, but Vic couldn't see much change. She was semi-conscious only part of the time, and even then, not at all coherent; when her eyes were open, she hadn't recognized Vic. That had been the most disturbing part of this whole affair. What if her mind stayed away? The human brain is a very delicate instrument, and Mary's brain was vital. He sighed, patted Mary's hand, rose, and walked slowly to the door. He glanced at his watch—it was already 2:00 p.m. He had urgent business to attend to at home—Don was probably back from Tucson by this time, and Vic was eager to hear his report. Vic turned, and said to Mary that he was leaving, but that he'd return shortly. She gave no response in answer. Vic walked out.

Vic knew Don was in a good mood as soon as he saw him. He walked to the eighteenth century settee in the parlor and sat with a glass of very old wine in his hand. He deserved it, he figured, with everything going on right now and their deadline so close. Don sat in the wingchair Vic gestured to, also holding a wine glass in his hand. Vic smiled at him. "Well? How'd it go?"

Don laughed quietly as he explained, in detail, how Thomas Owens, brother of Sarah's boyfriend, had committed suicide after feeling remorse for having tried to kill his younger brother's girlfriend up in Hobbs. He told him of the 'suicide note' and the photos he'd left with the boy's body. The photographs, taken from time to time during her short stay in The House, were only close-up shots of the girl. In one she was wide-awake and smiling. In a couple of others, she was obviously sleeping. Don confided in Vic that he thought those were the better ones.

Victor was a happy man. Don had done an excellent job on just a moment's notice, and he'd done it without Cal. He knew the Owens boy's parents would want the investigation over as soon as possible—and so would Hank Larsen, of course. If things went according to plan, none of this would ever touch any of them. Vic quietly considered Don for a long moment. He took a sip of wine, placing the glass on the side table, and said, "You know, you're a very valuable employee. I'm going to reward that value in kind." He handed Don a stack of twenty-dollar bills. "That's five grand. A bonus, if you like, for a job well done."

Don was stunned. That was a lot of money! "Hey, thanks, man," he said in awe, "I can use the money to buy me a new motorcycle."

Vic smiled. "Just don't go and get in any trouble, okay? I didn't get you out of Florence for your health."

Don grinned, thinking back. His conviction for killing that whore should've kept him in prison for a minimum of fifteen years. Somehow Vic had gotten him out—someone had obviously been bribed somewhere, with a lot of money; or, he'd thought at the time, with a threat. Either way, he'd gotten out of prison the easy way. His parole papers were genuine, and he dutifully reported to Hank every month right here in Hobbs. All in all, a pretty sweet deal.

Vic had gotten him sprung for his talents in breaking and entering, and in staging 'accidents'—the fatal kind. Before he'd been jailed, he'd been an enforcer for a now-defunct motorcycle gang that'd called itself 'Satan's Own.'

He'd been arrested three times on suspicion of murder, but the district attorney had never managed to make the charges stick.

One time he'd killed a grand jury witness who was about to testify against Satan's Own in a very heavy drug investigation. It seems the key witness OD'd in his motel room. Don had dressed as a cop, and had just walked into the motel past a uniformed police officer, to 'check out' the room before the arrival of the witness. He'd placed some cocaine in the bathroom where he knew 'Hog' Jenkins would find it. Hog liked coke, and he wasn't real bright. He thought his friends had smuggled it to him. In a way, he was right about that, except they were former friends. He'd done a couple lines right before his court appearance. He never made it to court; the coke had been very pure. The press, of course, roundly criticized the police, but that didn't restart Hog's heart. Charges were dropped. He'd killed the whore a year later.

As Don rose to leave, he paused and said, "I'll do whatever you require, Vic. You know that."

"I do know that. And, if you complete your upcoming tasks over the next few days as well as you've accomplished this one, there'll be a hundred grand in it for you; all in cash, of course, unless you'd like some other form…gold perhaps?" He grinned at Don. "And I have another little job for you right now. He reached into his jacket pocket, and removed something. "I want you to put this in Curt Paxton's house." He handed Don a Polaroid photo of Sarah, similar in nature to the one they'd put in Thomas Owens's apartment. "And this as well." He handed Don a small plastic bag. Don knew crack cocaine when he saw it.

Don whistled. "I'll get it all done for you, Vic. For that kind of money, I'd kill my own mother…but there's one problem."

What's that?"

"It's Cal. He gets in the way. And I can tell you that if he gets into trouble, he'll rat us all out, for sure! He'd spill his guts for a bottle of wine."

Vic was silent a moment, considering what Don had just said. Finally he responded, "I know you're right. I'll keep him close to home for now. We might need him for something in the future. But from now on, you operate on your own. The time is getting short, and I'll call you very soon." Don rose, satisfied, and left the house. The speed was no longer in his system, and he was crashing.

34

Don Bristow sat in his car, watching the Paxton residence for several minutes. It was only three that afternoon, and in this working class neighborhood, adults were still at work, and kids just now leaving school. He'd have to work fast, but he still had time. He thought about what he could do with a hundred grand, and grinned. He exited the Valiant, making one more visual sweep of the street and surrounding homes, just to be sure. Don liked being sure. He saw neither person nor vehicle moving, so he walked boldly to the Paxton's front door, carrying a wrapped box. If someone answered, he'd simply be delivering a package, and when he found that this was the wrong address, he'd apologize and leave. Easy.

But nobody answered his knock, and so, with another furtive glance around to see if anyone was about, he walked to the east side of the house. He found a sliding window that had not been properly latched. A little manipulation with a penknife, and he was in. He donned his supple leather gloves, and climbed over the sill, moving rapidly from room to room.

It didn't take long to find the Paxton boy's bedroom. He pushed the door all the way open, and walked in. He looked around, grinning. This was something at which he was really good. He opened the dresser drawers one at a time. In the bottom drawer were a number of long-john style underwear for the winter months. *Perfect!* Here he stashed the rock cocaine and the photo of the girl. *He won't be looking in this drawer until it gets really cold, and the cops'll have him long before then...*

He left the way he came in, touching nothing, taking nothing. He'd been meticulous about not moving any object or leaving prints in the light layer of dust on the tops of the boy's furniture. He'd been a ghost in there, and he was proud, as usual, of his craftsmanship. Back outside, he shut the window and again used his knife to push the lock back in place—well, almost in place. The knife didn't give him the leverage he needed, but it looked pretty much as it had when he'd found it. He dropped behind a shrub as a kid sailed past on his bike. *School's out...gotta go.*

Curt and George arrived at Curt's home at four o'clock. Curt invited George in. It seemed obvious to George that Curt was troubled and puzzled by something. Inside, George sat on the sofa, and Curt asked him if he'd like something to drink, a beer perhaps. The old man declined the beer, saying he'd like water instead. Curt went to the kitchen and returned with two glasses of water. He handed one to George, and then sat in a nearby chair, resting his glass on his knee. George waited patiently; when the boy was ready, he'd speak.

"Remember when we talked about Carl Larsen, and the young girl in the photograph he showed me?"

"Go on," George urged.

"And remember what you said about vampires and magic?"

George smiled. "Yes, I remember. I said it after all!"

Curt laughed nervously, nodding. He took a sip of water and set the glass on the coffee table. He leaned forward, facing George. "There's something else I'd like to ask you about, if you don't mind. I don't know if it has anything to do with all this, but I think…I feel…that it might somehow."

George waited, not speaking.

"You obviously know a lot about magic, and stuff like that." George nodded. Encouraged, Curt went on. "There's this dream I have once in a while," the boy began. "I first had it years ago as a very young child—I can't really remember the first time, I might have been six maybe. After that, I had the same dream from time to time over several years, and then it suddenly stopped. I haven't had that dream in years. I was wondering if you know anything about dreams?"

"Why don't you tell me about the dream, Curt. If I can help in some way, I'll be glad to." The old man smiled at Curt.

Curt proceeded to tell his story. "The dream starts with the sky, and the sun…" He then told his dream. It poured from him in a hot river of molten, poisonous words. Rapid, short sentences interspersed with sharp inhalations. It was a volcanic eruption of fear, loathing and, at the end of it all, such a deep pity that even in the telling, tears streamed down his cheeks.

George listened without interrupting, reading the fear, the anger—and the anguish. Black morning sky. The end of a life…the end of all life. The end of the dream. Self-consciously, Curt wiped the tears away, and smiled. But it was a sad smile; the kind of smile one sees on a person relating some anecdote about a recently departed loved one.

"Alright," George said, "what do you think it means?"

Curt considered the question for a moment. "I don't think 'means' is the right word, exactly. I checked out some books on dreams from the library. Some were about interpreting dreams, and some were of a more psychological nature—you know, books by Carl Jung and Freud and the like."

"Go on," George encouraged.

"Like I said, I don't think this dream 'means' something in the way the psychologists say, I think it IS something. It's something that really happened…

somewhere else, or maybe sometime else."

Now it was time for George to pause and consider. He asked, very carefully, "You feel it's showing you something from the far past? Maybe before there was any written history?"

"Mr. Luedke, I looked up Erieuxta. There's no such place, and unless it's someplace not yet rediscovered, it doesn't exist. And even if it did, how could a morning sky turn to blackness?"

"Perhaps a volcanic eruption? An explosion such as the detonation of Krakatau in 1883 could produce such an effect, I imagine."

"But if a cloud of volcanic ash was at fault, why could I see stars? And the sun was funny too…it was red…and way too big."

"So what do you make of all this?"

"The dream is of a real place, Mr. Luedke. That place…Erieuxta, it existed. All those strange people really lived there…and all those people died that day. They all died the day their planet died—the day something flew up from the pyramid-temple or whatever it was, and…disappeared inside of itself, all… angles and lines." *Origami.* Curt shook his head, angry with himself once again for making such a stupid comparison.

"You're speaking of another planet then?"

"It has to be," Curt whispered, wiping his eyes again. "Look up, Mr. Luedke. We still have a sky. We still have air. That's why the sky turned black, wasn't it? Something made the air go away."

George sighed. "Alright. We'll speak of this again soon. In the meantime, tell no one about this dream."

"Why?"

"We'll discuss this tomorrow. First there are some things I need to check on…things I need to find out."

Curt nodded. "Do you think Erieuxta was a real place?"

"Yes, Curt, I do. But for now that's all I'll say. Stay in tonight and watch your step, alright? If you go talking about this dream, Carl's dad might have you picked up for mental evaluation. I don't want to come by tomorrow and find you've been sent away somewhere. Stay in tonight, alright?"

"I understand," the boy said, nodding. "All of this is so weird, I just can't believe it. The real world shouldn't be like this."

"Believe it, boy. Watch your step at school tomorrow. I need you alive. And before you ask, yes, you need to go to school tomorrow, right on schedule too. You already missed one day, and we don't want anyone getting any more suspicious than they already are. We have no idea who else could be involved in this thing. We have to be very cautious. Very cautious indeed."

Curt shivered as they parted company. He watched from the front window as George walked from the front door to his automobile. George had asked him not to turn on the porch light, even though it was getting dark. There was no point in shining a light on what they were doing, he'd told Curt. George got into the Mercedes without even a backwards glance, and drove back to the Hobbs Motel.

He glanced several times in the rearview mirror. The white Taurus he'd noticed earlier was still behind him. He'd seen that same Taurus parked at the hospital earlier in the day with a single occupant behind the wheel when he and Curt had left. He smiled grimly. So they were already on to him; it would make things a bit harder, but he knew that at least for now, they were only going to watch and wait, probably hoping for a chance to discover the location of the crystal stone. When he arrived at the motel, he parked under a floodlight near the office, and went to his room without a backwards glance. The Taurus was across the street, sitting at the side of the road with its engine off and one occupant behind the steering wheel.

Inside, George sat a little away from the window, watching the car from behind the drapes. He waited for a while, then rose and turned out the light. He lay on his bed fully clothed and ready for a fast escape should one be necessary.

He lay there, hands behind his head, thinking. Should he tell the Paxton boy everything? Could he handle it? He shook his head. There really wasn't much of a choice anymore, was there? *The boy has had that dream. He's actually seen Erieuxta—and even knows the correct pronunciation of that strange word.* George knew he'd have to tell the boy at least something tomorrow. He was convinced the boy would help him. After all, if Zachary Louben really was planning what he feared he was planning, there would be nowhere to run.

Officer Grant sat for a while longer, watching the front of the old man's room. *Wish ta' hell the old man would make up his mind; follow the library guy, follow this guy...who next?* The pale green door hadn't opened again, and the drapes were pulled. He saw the lights go out inside the room. *Good enough.* He started the engine and pulled away from the curb. The old man was clearly in for the night. It was time to hit a few bars.

Thirty minutes after the Taurus sped away, George Luedke opened the door of his room, and walked through the darkness to the grey Mercedes. He opened the hood, and yanked some wires loose, then returned to his room. No one had seen him.

Back in his room, he called an all night garage and towing service. When the phone was answered, George said, "My car's been vandalized. Could you come and tow it in? It's a rental, and I'll call the company in the morning." The man said he'd take care of it. Thirty minutes later, the big red and yellow tow truck had hauled the Mercedes away. George smiled. *They'll have a hell of a time finding me now.* He went back to his room and packed his belongings. Then he called a cab.

35

On Friday Curt rode his old bike to school. The police hadn't yet returned his new one. He wondered idly if they ever would, considering the police report Officer Grant had filed. At least now he had someone on his side. George Luedke seemed to be a man who knew what he was doing, and right now Curt needed that. He was convinced his dad knew nothing of what was going on. At least his dad might be safe; there'd be no reason to harm him if he knew nothing.

Seeing no Mercury on his journey, he was heartened. No other autos came near him, and he meticulously followed the legal rules of the road today—no point in making another 'accident' easy for whoever was trying to kill him. *And all for a stupid piece of stone. I just don't get that...*

Dismounting, he chained his bike to the school rack, and walked rapidly toward the doors. As he pushed his way through the old oak and brass doors, he saw Tommy Driscoll. He was involved in an animated conversation with Carl. Curt looked away from them, hoping to pass by without drawing attention. Once past, he glanced back. The two boys were not interested in anything beyond their conversation. *So far, so good...*

Cheryl was waiting by her locker. Sally Gibson was standing with her. Curt smiled a greeting as he walked toward them. Cheryl gave him a hug. Glancing around rapidly, she determined there were no teachers in the vicinity. She leaned over and kissed Curt. He put his arm around her; she felt good this morning.

Cheryl said, "Tom-the-bastard called Sally last night and apologized."

He looked at Sally. She was studying the floor. She raised her eyes to his, and said, "Thanks for talking to him for me." She blushed.

"Nothing to it, Sally," Curt said, hoping he sounded casual. "He was way out of line, and I think he knows it."

"He lied about where we were going. I just can't trust him anymore." She paused, adding, "He drinks an awful lot too, don't you think?"

Curt said, "There's lots of guys you can date, and lots of other girls he can date. I don't think he'll bother you again, and yes, I think he drinks an awful lot."

The bell. Sally scooped up her books from her open locker, slammed and locked the door, and said, "I gotta go." She smiled warmly at Curt. "Thanks again."

As Sally walked away, Cheryl commented, "It was nice of you to intervene on her behalf with that bastard. Maybe he'll learn to keep his hands to himself after this." Curt glowed in the praise. He felt good about helping Sally. Tommy was getting way too aggressive lately. He fetched his first period books, shut his locker, and headed toward the classroom.

Curt passed the first hour in a kind of daze. There was just so much to think about. People were trying to kill him, his girl didn't want him to go to college, and his best friend was becoming a real sleazebag. He wondered idly if Carl could be a vampire too. With that thought came an image unbidden. Carl and his father in a hot tub together, filled with boiling blood. He shook that image from his head.

Second period gym class was the usual strenuous bore. At one point Curt asked Tommy where the photo of the girl was. At first Tommy pretended not to know what Curt was talking about, but finally he relented. As they toweled off at the end of class, he said, "Carl took the picture back. He said he had to give it to his father. He made me promise not to tell. I hope you can keep a secret."

Curt grinned, nodding. *If only you knew what secrets I'm keeping...* He asked, "Did you see the newspaper yesterday?"

Tommy shook his head, saying he'd been working on his '55 after school until dark, and then he'd done homework.

Curt said, "That girl…the one in your picture. She's in the hospital right now. She was attacked by a big dog."

Tommy grinned. "The werewolf? I saw that on TV last night just before I went to bed."

"She almost bled to death, Tommy."

Tommy responded quickly—too quickly, in Curt's opinion. "She's probably a junkie or something, Curt. I wouldn't be surprised if she was cut up in some drug deal gone bad."

"The cops think she's like thirteen or fourteen, Tommy. And who would be dealing drugs in the middle of the night on that lonely stretch of road? If that were my business, I'd want to be where there were people to sell to."

They dressed in silence after that exchange. Tommy had shown no compassion or even interest in the girl. He glanced several times at Curt, but said nothing further. As they left the gym, Tommy shouted in an overly jovial voice, "See ya' later, Curt!" Curt watched his former friend swagger away. *Something's wrong with him, alright.* He felt certain that Carl was behind this change in Tommy's behavior. *Carl's behind all of this…but who's behind Carl?*

That same morning, Detective Peter Davis sat at his desk. He listened to the old ceiling fan chugging around in eternal circles—much like this case, he mused. He was looking at the latest lab reports on their Jane Doe. This was indeed a grim case. The little girl had dog blood on her hands and right wrist. Apparently she'd stabbed the dog with a screwdriver to defend herself.

Several questions came immediately to mind. The dog had lost a lot of blood and was probably dead, so where the hell was the damn thing? Where had the girl gotten the slicker he'd found her wearing, and where was the lock that enigmatic, broken key was intended to open? Where were her real clothes... where did she acquire the screwdriver? *Round and round...just like that damn squeaking fan...* He was already getting a headache, and it was only ten o'clock. *It's gonna be a long day...*

He turned back to the report. The girl had obviously been drugged. They were certain it was a hallucinogen, most likely LSD. That, coupled with the blood loss and psychological trauma, surely contributed to her unresponsive state. Karen had said they thought the girl would awaken in several days. *That odd duck George Luedke said a few days was all any of us have.* He shook his head once more.

The lieutenant opened his door. "Peter. Get in here right now."

Peter rose, hurrying into Ken Jackson's office. Lieutenant Jackson closed the door. "We've gotten an anonymous tip about the case you're working on. A boy called here a few minutes ago. He said he saw a picture of your Jane Doe in the possession of another kid at school."

Peter was surprised. *Why'd Curt call? I already knew about Carl and the photo.*

Ken continued, "We're working on getting a search warrant right now for the Paxton residence."

Peter glanced up sharply. "The Paxton residence?"

"Yeah. Our informant says this Curt Paxton had the picture, and that he was probably one of the girl's assailants."

Peter felt numb. What the hell was going on? He made a decision. "Ken, I have to tell you something. I talked with the Paxton boy yesterday..." he told the lieutenant most of what George Luedke and Curt had told him.

Ken looked at him in disbelief. "The chief's son?"

"And probably the chief too," Peter confirmed.

"Jesus, man...do you have any evidence?"

Peter showed the lieutenant one copy of the police report detailing Curt's 'accident.' Then he showed him two other documents he'd found in the 'to be burned' file. Both were reports of eyewitnesses who confirmed Curt's story about a green Mercury, not a Plymouth Satellite.

Ken let out a low whistle. "Christ! We better watch our step on this one."

Peter nodded. "And our backs."

Lieutenant Jackson went to the file cabinet in his office. Hobbs had yet to be computerized. He withdrew the personnel file of Richard Grant. He read a moment, before speaking. "The chief hired this man himself about a year ago for the patrol unit. There's not much information about him in the file. I'll tell you what, I'll run his name past DPS and see what they turn up. In the meantime, I want you to drive down to Prescott and see that truck driver who witnessed last year's 'werewolf' attack. It'll be a few hours before we get that warrant. We've got to see if we can get to the truth before then."

Peter took the back road to Prescott. Instead of heading directly down Coronado, he went west, then north on Hobbs Hill Road. He wanted to see the crime scene once more, in the daylight. The extra drive would take only twenty minutes. Peter slowed, studying the crime scene again as he drove past. He glanced up the heavily wooded hillside. The mayor's Victorian mansion was just visible through the trees. He thought briefly about the mayor's wife. *A lot of people were ending up in the hospital all of a sudden.*

He turned, heading back to the south and Prescott. As he punched the accelerator, he saw something else. A short distance down the road, and below the hilltops, three buzzards were circling lazily in the high thermals. He grabbed his radio and called Lieutenant Jackson. Jackson said he'd dispatch the forensics team immediately—and forget to notify the chief. Peter replaced the mic. Now he had an ally.

Peter found the garage easily. It was situated on Gurley, one of Prescott's main drags. He turned into the parking lot, and shut down the engine. As he stepped out, he saw a man approaching, wiping his hands on an oily rag. He was four steps away when he recognized Peter.

"What do you want?" His tone was belligerent.

Peter smiled coolly. "Well, I'll tell you, Joe, I still don't believe you saw a dog that night last year."

Joe Lindhart stared back sullenly. "I saw what I saw and you can't prove nothin' else."

Peter took a menacing step toward Lindhart. "We've had another attack on a little girl, Joe. Only this girl's still alive. When she talks, and I know she will, I'll nail whoever got to you, and offer them a nice, sweet deal for what they know about you. Then I'm coming back for your head…unless they beat me to it, that is. You're still a loose end, you know."

Joe took a step back. Peter moved another step forward, not allowing the man distance. "If by chance you remember something before the girl tells me her story, give me a call." He held out a business card.

Lindhart slapped it from Peter's hand, shouting, "I had nothin' to do with either girl. I was just drivin', that's all."

Peter grinned. "I wouldn't drive too far, if I were you."

Joe said nothing, and Peter got back into his car and drove off. Joe stared after him a moment, then returned to his office and picked up his phone.

Peter was angry. He was convinced Lindhart knew more than he would admit—proving it, however, was going to be the problem. He pushed the Challenger around the turns as he wound his way back to Hobbs.

Ken Jackson looked up as Peter walked into his office. He was grinning. Peter shut the door. Ken said, "Hank found the judge—apparently this is his day off. He was pissed about being interrupted. Guess who was sent to find him?"

Peter grinned. "I'll bet it was Rick Grant."

Ken laughed quietly. "Damn, Peter, you oughta' be a detective! Anyway, the judge is concerned with probable cause—an anonymous call from a kid's pretty flimsy. He refused the warrant."

Peter visibly relaxed into the chair. Good news, finally! Perhaps they'd have a little time after all.

Ken said, "Karen called while you were gone. She said she needed to talk to you. I doubt anything more will come down here today. Why don't you go to the hospital and see what she wanted. Then go home. If I need to get in touch with you, I'll call."

"What about the buzzards?"

A crooked smile crossed Ken's lips. "The forensic team was called back. Apparently they called in and the chief took the call. He informed them that the taxpayers didn't want to waste money on buzzard chases, and that from now on they can't go out without his prior approval."

"Interesting," Peter said. "Well, I'll see you later, Ken. Watch your back." Ken nodded.

Peter met Karen at the hospital. As they headed home, Karen told of her day. "Boy, has this been a weird day," she said. "The mayor's wife is getting freaky." Peter looked at her. "She's not conscious yet, but she's talking about strange things." Peter thought about his conversation with Luedke and the Paxton boy. Karen smiled nervously, continuing. "She's giving everyone the creeps around the ward. She talks about the past like it's happening right now."

Peter shrugged, asking, "Don't brain injured people sometimes do that?"

"Well, sure," she responded. "But she's rambling on about living in New Orleans." Karen paused for effect. "In the year 1794!"

Peter almost missed the red light at Avalon. He was dumbfounded. "What's she saying?"

"It's all kind of disjointed, but it has to do with blood and maybe some kind of religion."

"Jesus Christ! George may have been telling the truth."

"Who's George?"

Peter then told her the story in rapid, staccato words. It was the story of vampires. He grinned when he saw the look on her face. He said, "Hey…I don't write 'em!" Karen laughed, but not with much humor.

They ate an early dinner at home. She could see he was starting to take this vampire talk seriously. He was nervous; he couldn't sit still. She put her arms around him and kissed him. It was the kind of kiss guaranteed to get his attention. She smiled. "Wanna play doctor?"

And some distance away, Victor Lewis listened intently. He didn't like what he was hearing. He hadn't heard from Joe Lindhart in almost a year. Now he'd left a message for Vic, and the mayor had actually had to return his call! It was infuriating. On top of everything else, Joe said that Detective Davis was still snooping around, and that a little more money would help keep his mouth shut.

Vic hung up the phone. Joe was right; a little money would help keep his mouth shut. He rose from his chair and walked to the intercom. "Don. I want to talk to you…"

36

Curt answered the phone on the third ring. It was George Luedke. Since Curt's dad was working late, Curt told George to come over. Curt hung up the phone nervously, the handset clattering against the phone. All this 'vampire' business wasn't doing him any good at all! He'd even broken his date with Cheryl for tonight, feigning illness. He was afraid he'd drag her into this mess.

An hour later, at four-thirty, Curt heard the soft sound of a car coming up the gravel drive. He parted the curtain just a crack, peering out into the afternoon gloom. The car was a new Volkswagen Fox. The driver's door opened, and he saw George step out. He was carrying a satchel over his shoulder that displayed a large advertising logo. In his other hand he carried a clipboard. He looked like a door-to-door salesman or a survey taker. He scanned the neighborhood, and Curt grinned, opening the door.

George spoke without preamble. "Can you come with me right now?"

"Sure. My dad won't be home for a couple hours yet. I'll leave a note telling him I'm with Tom Driscoll working on his car."

"That's fine, Curt, but hurry." George looked around once more, and stepped inside, closing the door. Curt scribbled a note to his dad and taped it to the refrigerator. He knew his dad was meeting Katy Higgins later, so he'd not be missed until very late…or perhaps not even until tomorrow morning.

"So why the VW?"

George smiled as he drove into the late afternoon light. Clouds were rolling in, and sooner or later, a storm would break. "I was being followed. White Ford Taurus. I vandalized my Mercedes, had it towed, moved, and rented another auto."

Curt whistled. "You've been busy."

"I think the person following me is a cop. He knew how to tail someone, almost expertly." He turned and smiled knowingly at Curt.

Curt laughed. "You'd have made a good spy!"

George turned a corner and pulled into the deepening shadows behind a small bungalow apartment. They exited the vehicle, moving quickly through the back door into the dark interior. George flicked the light switch, and the gloom retreated from the room, which turned out to be the kitchen. George pulled two cans of Coke from the refrigerator and they sat at the cheap, green Formica table. George took a sip of his Coke.

"Curt, the time has come to tell you the rest of this story. And if you don't think I'm crazy now, you will by the time I'm finished." Curt nodded as though in agreement. Crazy now or crazy later, it was too late to back out. "First I want to tell you about the dream. A number of psychics over the years have seen visions of a civilization alien to this planet. Most of those visions are very similar in nature to your dream. Whether more or less detailed, they all end the same way—a beautiful morning sky turning dark as stellar space."

"You're telling me other people have had the same dream I've had?"

George held up his hand. "Wait. It gets crazier. The first record I've been able to find dates to 1637. An anonymous French woman was burned at the stake in her village for speaking of a war between demons and angels. The demons won by her account, so she was burned. The Church couldn't have demons winning battles, you see. Now, in more modern times, a few psychics have also explored their own visions of this world and what transpired there."

"Psychics?"

"...And...others. Never mind that for now. This vision is old, Curt, as old as time. The events you saw in that dream of the destruction of a city named Erieuxta—that pronunciation, incidentally, is in proper 20th century Earth English—occurred a bit more than five thousand years ago, and it wasn't on Earth. The point of origin of these images is a planet yet unknown on Earth. This epic disaster—the instantaneous loss, in what on Earth is called an hour, of a bit over ninety million sentient lives—has left an indelible energy-record in what psychics and others on Earth call the 'Astral Plane.' It caused a men- tal-psychic tidal wave that crashed through the heavens, eventually reaching into the farther reaches of this galaxy. Can you guess what caused this mass extinction?"

Curt thought back to the dream. "I still think it was the atmosphere! I remember I couldn't breathe. Something destroyed the atmosphere." He looked at George, to see if he was on the right track. George nodded.

"That's very good reasoning, Curt. Now here's the first part of the story. There's a certain planet named Eribus circling a star known on Earth as Alpha Scorpii, or Antares. That's where this disaster occurred. Antares is at the center of the constellation Scorpius. The name comes from ancient Greece, meaning 'equivalent to Ares,' due to its red color. The star is seven hundred times the diameter of our sun and over six hundred light years away. The destruction of that planet was done to cover the escape of a number of murderous beings from... outside, that'd infested this world, and had been feeding on its inhabitants for years. Eventually 'detectives'—I suppose the word would be—discovered this location, and when they closed in to apprehend these beings...well, you saw what happened. The battle fleet attempted to follow, but the invaders of Eribus had called for reinforcements of their own, and a short, bitter engagement was fought over the corpse of Eribus. The destroyers suddenly broke off, all folding simultaneously, and were gone."

"So they got away?"

"For a time, yes. But the…detectives didn't give up that easily, and they began a dragnet of literally astronomical proportions to find this darkness and contain it. Though it was not known for some time, they had come here, to this planet—and why not? This planet is ripe and abundant with the things they feed on—vivid imagination, fear, hatred, the agony of tortured death, and hopeless resignation. During this time the searchers were far from this quadrant of the galaxy, but gradually heading in this direction with a battle fleet.

"This entity and its legions made planet fall approximately five thousand years ago, with their fleet mostly intact. Its travel from Alpha Scorpii was almost instantaneous. They chose the most advanced civilization they could find, and settled in what would come to be known as ancient Egypt, spreading gradually to other lands. By the time the pursuing fleet arrived, the invaders were well entrenched.

"Interestingly, at this time, there's an Egyptian goddess named Serket, the scorpion goddess. She reigned over fertility, nature, animals, magic, and healing venomous stings. An alternate reading suggests her ability to 'tighten the throats' of her enemies. So she would help her followers, and destroy the unfaithful. She apparently had many priests, but no temples, and is portrayed with a scorpion atop her head.

"It seems she had a close association with the early proto-dynastic kings, implying she was their protector. And in fact two rulers are known as 'Scorpion Kings.' Scorpion I lived in Thinis, the capital in the first dynasty. The location of this city is still a mystery, for it was razed utterly in the battle that followed.

When the pursuing fleet arrived, most of these entities returned to their ships here, and from a hidden outpost on a small planet located between Mars and Jupiter, they gave battle. For ten years the great fleets of Light and Darkness made war through the solar system and in the skies over North Africa and the Middle East, each contender being reinforced from time to time. Fire and thunder shook the earth, though most of the warfare occurred in space around this planet. Their outpost planetoid was blasted into oblivion, as it had no indigenous life. What remains of this world is now called the asteroid belt.

"Scorpion II lived one or two centuries later, and was called the King Scorpion of Nekhen. There are several possible historical figures this person may have been. But both, we know, were masks of the darkness that had fallen through space from Alpha Scorpii. By this time, the invader's fleet had been long destroyed, and there were few of them still planet-bound on Earth. Those remaining were hunted down and either captured or destroyed as time passed. It was assumed finally, that all of them were gone, and the victorious fleet departed. But they were wrong."

Curt was mesmerized. He didn't know if he believed all of this, but...

"The two survivors' trail goes cold at that point, and they don't manifest again until the mid-1400s. Vlad Tepis, named 'Dracula,' meaning 'son of a dragon,' is suspected of torturing and killing forty to one hundred thousand human beings. He was supposedly killed in 1476, but there are some who know that, like many dictatorial monarchs, he had body doubles he'd use for public appearances in case of assassination attempts. The entity was not slain in 1476, but his body double was.

"Tell me, Curt, have you ever heard of the Countess of Bathory?" When Curt shook his head, George explained. "She lived between 1560 and 1614. She was reputed to be a vampire of sorts. Supposedly she killed village children and bathed in their blood. It allegedly kept her young. She was tried and found guilty, primarily by the Church at the instigation of other landholders who wanted her estate. She died in confinement in her own castle."

"You said she 'supposedly' killed the children?"

"Yes, I did. It's now believed the charges were trumped up by the jealous barons, bishops, and cardinals of the time. It was easy to convict someone on charges of witchcraft; if the Church accused you, you were guilty. But there's more to the story than that. The Church was eager to convict; she was a witch and a vampire after all. The other landowners were eager also, for if convicted of heresy and communing with Satan, she'd lose all her holdings to them. Needless to say, she was convicted—it galled the Church and the male landowners to see a mere woman in possession of such wealth and power.

"But in that household was a person of some influence. The document with his name is now lost, unfortunately, in a fire set during the communist purges in that part of the world. In that document was a name, written in faded, and smudged ink. The name appeared to be 'Louben.'

"Oh my God," Curt exclaimed.

"Yes. And of course that individual inherited a substantial amount of land, and was never suspected as the real killer of all those children. Louben needed the blood, as he and his counterpart need to revitalize the physical bodies they reside in from time to time. They restored themselves with both the DNA and the terror and pain they inflicted on the children—for that blood was taken from them as they died. "

"They're the thread that runs through all these stories?"

"Yes, my boy. The track is lost once more until the eighteenth century. This is the story of the roadhouse outside of New Orleans I already told you about. That was when they decided to 'go west' as the parlance described it in those days. And that brings us to Prescott, Hobbs…and the story of the sawmill—and the Stack."

"So these…things are immortal? How can these detectives, as you call them, kill them?"

"If they fight, they can be killed if necessary. Those pursuing them do not kill for vengeance or anger, but only in the defense of their own existence, or that of the lives on the worlds they protect. No one really knows from where or when this darkness came. It's only speculation, but it's believed they entered this space-time continuum through some kind of multi-dimensional event, perhaps even that which caused this universe to come into existence."

"They've been here since time and space began?"

"It is the best theory currently available. Now listen carefully," George continued. "Remember our little talk about magic? Well, there's more to tell. Magic uses forces and energies described as being of mystical origin in the ancient books. As science progresses, much of what was once called magic takes on the respectable cloak of academia, and with a few changes in word choice, it becomes 'science.'

"The governments of a number of Earth's nations have, for years now, been studying what they sometimes refer to as 'remote viewing'—what mystics and magicians call 'astral travel.' Physicists of this world know that the outcome of some of their experiments with subatomic particles can be changed by their … outlook on the subject—their thoughts change results on the subatomic level. Mind over matter, if you will. Perhaps, on some level the energy that makes matter is the same energy that is thought; it's all connected.

"In considering this…connectedness of everything, consider this. There was a primal god of early Greece. This divinity, who has little mention in the mythology, was often conceived as a primordial deity, representing the personification of darkness. He is associated with the underworld, and the places where the newly dead wait. Reflections of this deity can also be found in ancient Norse, Sanskrit, and Semitic writing. Can you guess the name of this divinity?" Curt shook his head. "The Greeks named him Erebus." Curt's eyes widened. "Phonetically similar, wouldn't you say? That electromagnetic disturbance six hundred light years distant is reflected in the mythology of Earth's culture. And all of this comes together in these entities' desperate need for the crystal pyramid, as I shall explain.

"Their time is running out. They know they've been discovered, and are preparing to flee once more. They will destroy this planet just as they destroyed Eribus—as they've destroyed other worlds even before they came to the Alpha Scorpii system."

...give it back. I know what you want. Do you know what I want?

Curt jumped with the memory. *A dream...Cheryl.* It was suddenly and entirely back in his mind. He quickly gave George an edited version.

"I have changed my mind," George said after some thought. "I no longer believe this entity is hiding as your police chief. It's your mayor...and his wife! Of course, how could I be so blind? Him and his counterpart. The girl in the hospital; the mayor's wife in the hospital..." He paused thoughtfully.

Curt pleaded with open arms, "How long does this go on? I'm no magician—how can I stop someone...something as powerful as this?"

"Oh, but you already have. If you hadn't found the pyramid, and they still had it, we would not be having this conversation, for words cannot travel through the vacuum surrounding a planet with no atmosphere. But time is running out. Stars, planets...they all attach to and give off energy. Everything is part of everything else, as Earth's physicists are just starting to find out. The positions of the stars as they are relevant to this planet, are now in correct alignment. If these beings don't fold in the next few days, they won't be able to—they'll be trapped here. They're all dressed up with no place to go."

"Tell me one thing," Curt said. "How is it you know all of these things? How can you know about a planet circling Antares that nobody else knows about? What do you mean these...things, as you put it, come from outside? Outside what...space and time? And what do you mean when you say they won't be able to 'fold'?" *Origami.*

George held up one hand. He continued, "I know these things because I'm one of those detectives, Curt...I'm not from this world. I made planet-fall a thousand years ago as part of the search for these...agents of chaos, this darkness from outside. Now, there's no time for me to call for reinforcements. If this thing is to end, it falls to us to do it."

"And?"

George smiled. Curt wasn't letting him off the hook just yet. "Alright, Curt. Folding is a method of movement that incorporates both technology and natural energy, to fold space-time, and allow instantaneous travel from one location to another. It can be accomplished only at certain times to certain locations, and this entity doesn't have the time to wait until next year, when the energy streams align once more.

"They have a ship—one stolen from Eribus—it's not one of their own.

Because of this, they need that crystal. It's part of the operating system of the Eribus ship. The ship is hidden; I cannot find it. But we have the 'fold-crystal.' Without that little stone pyramid, its fold-drive won't work—it's stuck here. This means we're safe. On Eribus they folded inside the atmosphere, and sucked it away from the planet to further the chaos of battle being engaged in the skies overhead."

George glanced at his watch. "Hey, Curt, it's late—almost eleven. I'll take you home. I imagine you're pretty safe now. Zachary probably believes you've given me the pyramid; he'll be hunting me now, not you." Curt felt relief and guilt. He was safe, but at the expense of someone else.

The ride home was quiet. Curt sat back in the seat. He'd heard enough today to break his mind! Alien invaders were really here, on Earth. The very idea was astounding—and he knew some of them! As they rounded the bend on Avalon, they saw the lights.

"Look," Curt hissed. "Cops all over the place."

There were three police cars in front of the Paxton residence. Three cops in one place was a lot for a small town like Hobbs.

George said, "Duck your head, Curt. We're not stopping."

The Volkswagen passed slowly, only the driver staring, as would be expected of any passerby. Officer Grant gave the car only a cursory glance.

37

Peter Davis lay in bed beside Karen. She was asleep next to him. He watched the gentle rise and fall of the sheet that covered her. He sighed, glancing at his watch. It was only eleven-thirty…the night was young. He turned, softly kissing her on her lips. She moved in her sleep, and he kissed her again. He was stroking her cheek when she awoke. She smiled sleepily.

The sudden ringing of the telephone disrupted the mood. Peter whispered, "Damn," pushed himself up on one elbow and reached across Karen for the telephone. He caught the cord in his fingers, and dragged the receiver across the bed toward himself. "Too many phone calls," he grumbled.

Karen smiled at him. "That's the price of greatness, my love." Peter grumbled something unintelligible, and put the phone to his ear.

The voice on the other end of the line was Ken's, and he sounded worried. "Peter! You'd better get your ass in here right now…this Jane Doe and Curt Paxton thing has just hit the fan!"

Peter sat up in bed. "I'll be there in twenty minutes."

"Make it fifteen."

Peter handed the phone to Karen, who placed it back in the cradle. "What the heck's going on, Peter?"

"Work," was all he said, and began to dress. Karen knew better than to try for more information. Police matters were police matters, and she knew from past experience that Peter would explain what he could, when he could. She'd resigned herself to that fact long ago. She watched him slip his big Colt automatic into the holster on his belt, and shrug into his sports jacket.

"Be careful, Peter," she said.

Peter walked to her, bending over to kiss her. "I will. Don't worry, honey, this'll all blow over in a bit and I'll be back home in a jiffy." But the look on Peter's face told Karen an entirely different story.

Peter sat in the chair opposite Lieutenant Jackson. He couldn't believe what he'd just been told. A teacher at the high school, a Mrs. Blackwell by name, had apparently been cleaning some of the lockers in the journalism classroom. In Curt Paxton's locker, amid some drawings he'd done for the school paper, she'd found a Polaroid snapshot of the comatose girl in the hospital. She said she'd recognized her from having seen the girl's picture in the newspaper. She'd called the police chief immediately, of course, just as any concerned citizen might. This time Hank Larsen himself went to the judge with the request for a warrant. The judge had taken one look at the report the chief had shown him, and signed the warrant immediately.

Larsen himself had led the raid. Curt wasn't home when they'd arrived, but his father was now in protective custody, along with some woman named Higgins—apparently Kent Paxton's girlfriend. The house was searched, and in Curt's room they'd found yet another photograph of Jane Doe, a small amount of marijuana, and a rock of cocaine. All of this was carefully hidden in a drawer under some clothing, the chief had put in the report. There was currently an all-points out for Curt's arrest. He was to be considered armed and dangerous.

Peter exhaled heavily. "I don't get it. Curt told me about the photos on Thursday. This smells like a frame-up to me."

Ken nodded. "All things considered, that's what I think too. Can you contact either Curt or this George Luedke?"

Peter looked at the lieutenant glumly. "He said he'd contact me; he's moving around."

Ken said, "There are still three units at the Paxton residence. It's being treated as a crime scene. The DPS forensics people are going over the boy's room, and the rest of the house as well, with a fine-tooth comb." Ken looked at Peter appraisingly, and said, "Peter, it's possible he's guilty, you know."

Peter shook his head. "No, it's not. Tell me, has Curt's father or the Higgins woman made any statements?"

"Yeah. Curt's father gave Curt an alibi for the night the girl was attacked. Hank says that doesn't matter. He told me just a few minutes ago that it would be natural for the father to lie to protect his son. He also said it's possible the father might be involved with his son in some devil-worship cult. He says the pictures of the girl and the mouse in the cage proves that the girl was involved with Satanists or witches. He actually told me that this teacher finding the photo was by the hand of God to punish the evildoers working in Lucifer's name."

Peter found his voice, and said, "I'm calling BS on that, Ken. Where could the Paxtons have hidden her? The girl would have been held for several days in that area. Where did they keep her? Hobbs Hill Road isn't exactly the boondocks with abandoned shacks or unexplored mineshafts. Hell, the mayor's house is right there. Does the chief think that perhaps Curt and his dad hid the girl in the mayor's basement? And how exactly does the chief know anything at all about the girl, or what happened to her? She's not regained consciousness yet, and he's no doctor!"

Ken smiled. "I've got some good news too, if you can call it that. DPS called me earlier. Did you know that Rick Grant used to be a detective in Phoenix?

He was about to be arrested for accepting bribes when he abruptly resigned. Charges were dropped to save money, and Rick disappeared. DPS thought he'd left the state; in reality he moved to Hobbs and was immediately hired by Hank Larsen."

"Is there anything we can do about that?"

"DPS informed me that Phoenix has new evidence that Richard Grant was stealing narcotics from drug busts, and selling them back to drug dealers. They'd love to get their hands on him."

"So when do we bust him?"

"Imminently," Ken said, "he's been told to report back to the station—should be here any time now."

Peter was relieved. Perhaps they'd be able to get to the bottom of this after all. "Maybe we're gonna get lucky on this one."

"We need some luck," Ken responded, "we have to get this figured out before someone else gets hurt." They sat, watching the clock.

The squad room door opened, and two officers entered. One of them was Richard Grant. He saw Ken and Peter. He sensed something was up. Those two should've been home already. *Why are they looking at me like that?*

Ken spoke. "Officer Grant, I want to see you in my office immediately." Grant hesitated a moment, then took a step forward. Why should he worry? He felt he had things pretty much under control around here. Hell, he even had the chief on his side! He smiled, and strode confidently into the office.

Without preamble, Jackson said, "Officer Richard Grant, you're under arrest."

Grant stood motionless for a moment. He smiled. "Hey, man, what's this all about? I don't understand; is this some kind of joke?" He felt his palms dampen, and his lips suddenly felt very dry. He took a step back, then another, and only then realized he'd backed himself into a corner.

"Phoenix PD wants to talk to you about narcotics." Jackson stared at Grant, unblinking.

A previously unremembered thought flashed suddenly to Grant's mind. He smiled, glancing at the two detectives, and then he yanked his service revolver from its holster. Jackson froze for an instant. Peter Davis actually took a step back! Rick smiled. These morons were never going to put him in prison. He knew what happened to dirty cops in the slam. He was having none of it.

As he raised the .38, Rick Grant marveled at how slowly Ken seemed to be moving as he reached for his own piece. In reality, the sudden surge of adrenalin racing through his bloodstream had distorted his sense of time. His eyes shifted wildly to the other detective. Peter Davis was only just now grabbing the butt of his gun; the thing was still in his belt. *My God! He's really slow!* Rick Grant's smile turned into a leering grin. He knew he had the edge over these…turtles, these…snails, knew he'd fire first, and for some reason he didn't care.

His .38, already free of its holster, swept passed Jackson. The lieutenant grimaced, beginning only now to raise his own revolver. Davis was still pulling the pistol from his waist, the muzzle just clearing his belt. *He's one slow gunfighter…* Grant's grin bubbled over into a high, squealing laugh; his revolver was already right on target. Then he squeezed the trigger.

The report of the .38 in the confines of the office was deafening. Peter's ears sang, his pistol hanging by his side, safety still engaged. He looked over to where Officer Grant lay, seeming to huddle between a file cabinet and the wall. The bullet from Grant's revolver had not exited the back of his head, but blood was flooding in hard, rhythmic susurrations from under his chin where the bullet had entered. In only a moment, as the heart became deprived of blood, the blood ceased to spew, and was now only flowing down the front of the dead officer's uniform shirt.

Ken ran to Officer Grant, squatted down and felt for a pulse in his throat, more out of instinct than any real hope that life remained. As he stood, he slipped and almost fell in the spreading pool of blood. He staggered back two steps, marveling at how red his footprints appeared on the sand colored tile. Then he was sick.

The next morning, after only fitful sleep, Peter Davis and Karen Wilson were watching their television over coffee. The six o'clock news was about to start. The station they were watching was broadcasting from Phoenix. The news was mostly talk of the tension in the Middle East, the ending of the so-called 'Cold War' with the overthrow of various Communist regimes in Eastern Europe, and at least four more crisis situations. How journalists loved that word. Crisis! It made even the most mundane and poorly reported incident into something of import, and therefore worth watching by the television audience.

"I still can't believe he just shot himself like that," Peter said. "We'll probably never know the reason why, exactly, beyond his determination not to go to prison." Peter broke off suddenly. Right before going to a commercial, an odd and disturbing story aired.

In Tucson, a young man named Thomas Owens was found dead of an apparent suicide in his apartment by his mother and younger brother, Richard. The young man had been unemployed for a short time, and had been seeking work.

He was found with several Polaroid photos that appeared to show his younger brother's girlfriend. A terse note left at the scene said simply, "I'm sorry."

The police were investigating. And then a photo of the girl, missing and presumed kidnapped was shown. Her name was reported as Sarah Wells, and the police in Tucson were looking for her. Her parents had identified her, after the police had connected Thomas Owens with Richard, the girl's boyfriend. The television news anchor, now feigning great concern for the missing girl, said soberly, "It is believed that the Wells girl has been kidnapped and is in extreme danger. Anyone with information should call the Tucson Police department, or this station."

Both Peter and Karen suddenly sat bolt upright.

"Oh my God," Karen whispered.

38

Mary Lewis opened her eyes. There was whiteness. At first, it was so dazzling that she had to shut her eyes again against the pain. Gradually, she opened her eyes once more, looking up in confusion. She stared at the ceiling, trying to figure out where she was. Was she still in the girl's room in the basement? Had her husband not found her yet? Was something that preposterous even believable?

Her head buzzed, but the horrible headache was gone. She turned her eyes and slowly surveyed the room, realizing finally that she was in a hospital. She shut her eyes again, thinking. Slowly her memory was returning. *The girl! The little bitch hurt me...ME! Almost killed me...how is that even possible?* This was an entirely new thought, something she'd never even dreamed of in...forever, perhaps. Damn she felt old. She thought back through the events of the past few days.

The brother had been luck, more than anything else, and Don had quietly and expertly acquired the others. Vic had spread rumors around the high schools in Tucson about the 'commune.' Bobby Wells turned out to be much more than the others; they were merely natural resources. But Bobby Wells...his sister had power. And right now her power was vital. Where was the girl, she wondered? Had she been captured? Surely that was the case. Nobody could escape from them; never had, never would.

The mistake they'd made in Hobbs the last time had been taking local children. Back then, though, there hadn't been much choice. In that time and place, transport was difficult, and they'd thought that since the towns of Hobbs and Prescott had such a transient population, nobody would miss a few local children. They'd found out they were wrong. These people had an inordinate attachment to their young. It probably had something to do with their vivid imaginations and nourishing fears.

This time they'd chosen Tucson. Tucson was far enough away that a connection between Hobbs and Tucson was unlikely, and the roads were rapidly traveled. Unlike the captives being held in the basement who were merely destined for slaughter, the girl was important. For the first time since they'd come here, they needed help controlling a mind. It was unthinkable.

She sighed. She'd really wanted Sarah. After all these years she'd finally discovered someone here on this fertile planet with the ability to affect matter with her mind; it was a rare thing, not to be wasted. Psychokenesis was not a trait that was at all common in these parts of the galaxy. She grimaced; the headache was coming back. *And then that meddling Paxton boy found the fold-crystal, and I've been unable to retrieve it.* Mary clenched her fists against the headache, and in anger with her inability to control the minds of mere children. It was almost beyond comprehension that anyone around here, especially children, could stand up to her.

Her dream interference had done nothing, nothing at all except perhaps attract unwanted attention; especially with the current urgency of things. Without it, she knew, they were stranded here. She'd hoped to train the girl to use her psychic gifts to control the Paxton boy, and force him to return the crystal. She'd tried and failed. Now the girl was gone, and who could say who had the crystal now? *One of them. They found us, and have been stalking us since who knows when? They're getting better at this. It's time we move on.*

Mary didn't even know what day it was. *How long have I been here? Is it already too late?* That thought brought back that completely alien feeling of fear, so she shifted her thoughts out from herself, trying to listen in on the thoughts of those nearby—there were nurses she could hear just outside her door. She tried to touch their minds, one after the other, but to her confusion and growing dismay, nothing came. "Worry about that later," she whispered to herself angrily. *I can still hear—if I listen.* She listened carefully with her ears, discovering that the girl was also in the hospital. She'd survived. *How is that possible?*

Thinking back, she recalled the sudden, and astonishing pain that flared suddenly inside her head—the groping hand squeezing something in her brain… how it hurt! And then suddenly, there was only nothingness. She needed to get out of here. She needed to see Vic, but try as she might, her attempts at mental communication with her husband ended only in a sharp rise of pain from somewhere inside her skull. *This body has been damaged,* she thought. *But there's a way to take care of that problem.* As for getting out of this place, she'd just have to wait for Victor to come to her. *I know he'll be here soon he'll come for me. He has to.* She felt old…

Victor Lewis received a call that morning from Chief Larsen. Though the police were still holding Curt Paxton's father and his girlfriend in protective custody, the boy had yet to be found. He also reported the unexpected death of Officer Richard Grant. It looked unrelated to this case, he'd been told, as the arrest warrant had come through the Department of Public Safety from the Phoenix P.D. After the chief hung up, Vic sat back in his leather chair, sipping his coffee, and running over the problem in his mind.

Though Grant's death was probably just what the chief had said it was, it could also be related somehow to the events transpiring here in Hobbs. He was glad Mary had programmed Grant to kill himself should he be captured by the police for any reason. That had been good thinking on her part, he realized with a grin. He sipped his still too hot to drink coffee. Still, he needed better information, and he knew from where that would come. He dressed hurriedly and called Don. "I need to get to the hospital right now. I need to see Mary."

"Yes, sir," Don replied, "I'll be there in less than ten minutes."

George Luedke awoke before Curt. He dressed quietly, and walked to the motel office to buy a newspaper from the desk clerk, which he carried back to the room. Inside, he sat at the table reading. He inhaled sharply when he found the account of the suicide of Officer Grant. There was also a report on the Paxton arrests, and a photograph of Curt, describing him as a dangerous fugitive. He folded the newspaper, and tossed it onto the table. It was time to call that detective again.

Curt came out of the bedroom just as George was hanging up the phone. He looked at George. "We gotta do something," he shouted.

George held up one hand, speaking softly. "Not so loud, Curt, you'll let everyone in the motel know our business." Curt opened his mouth, and then shut it again.

More quietly, he said, "I can't just leave my dad and Katy in jail like this. Who knows what they'll do to them in there. There must be something we can do to help them."

"Listen," George said, "I just finished talking with Detective Davis. He's coming over right now. We'll have better information after we talk with him." Curt nodded, sat, and read the newspaper stories himself.

It was twenty minutes later when they heard the muffled rumble of the big engine in Detective Davis's auto. George opened the door, letting the policeman in. He shut the door, carefully scanning outside first to see if the policeman had been followed.

"Nobody followed me," Peter said, guessing his thought. He added, "By the way, the man who drives the white Taurus you mentioned is…was, Officer Grant." Peter looked over at Curt. "I see you have a newspaper, so you already know that story."

Curt stood now, despair in his eyes. "Can you add any information? Is my dad still in custody? Has anything happened to him or Katy?"

"Yes, Curt, your dad's in custody—but he's going to be released in an hour or so, and so is his girlfriend." Curt heaved a sigh of relief. Peter continued.

"There are a couple things that aren't in the paper. I think you should both know that it appears Grant was into some pretty heavy stuff. Turns out he was a cop in Phoenix, once upon a time, and he just barely escaped prosecution for taking bribes. He resigned, and the charges were dropped to save money. The thing was swept under the rug, you might say. And then our illustrious police chief immediately hired him. We were just informed that he was going to be indicted and prosecuted on new charges. It looks like while he was a cop in Phoenix, he was taking drugs from busts and reselling them. We'd just informed him he was under arrest when he shot himself."

George asked, "What about the investigation? That's going to continue, I hope? Time is running out."

Peter smiled, nodding. "DPS is requiring Chief Larsen take a leave of absence during the investigation. The investigation is theirs now, so it's out of our hands. But don't worry; this is actually better. With what we already know, and suspect, it's better letting the State boys do the looking. This way it takes the local politics and corruption completely out of the picture. If Chief Larsen's guilty, they'll have a better chance of proving it than we would."

"I believe you, Detective Davis," George commented.

"By the way, a county judge is being petitioned by DPS to have the arrest warrants against you and your dad dismissed. It seems the forensics people found a fingerprint on the baggie containing the drugs they found in your room. The print on it isn't yours—but there's a record of that print in the prison system. We're looking for that man now, though we don't know if he's living here or somewhere else. Either way, the drugs are clearly a plant, and so too are the photos."

"What about Carl Larsen?"

Peter looked at Curt. "So far, we've got nothing on him. It's looking more and more like his dad's a crook, but nothing has turned up yet to implicate him. There's one more thing related to the attacks on the girl last year and the recent attack. After his suicide, DPS forensics went through Grant's automobile. They found blood in the trunk, and preliminary tests show it's almost certainly dog blood. We know the girl in the hospital stabbed the dog that attacked her. With the amount of its blood on her and at the scene, it was a mortal wound. Grant obviously picked up the carcass and disposed of it. I suspect Grant was one of the girl's kidnappers, and probably the owner of the dog. Unfortunately, we may never find out any more than that now that Grant's dead."

George nodded, and quietly asked Curt to quit pacing. The boy sat.

Finally, Peter broke the silence. "Look guys, I've gotta get going. I'm supposed to be at the hospital right now interviewing the parents of the kidnapped girl. They came up late last night. She's still comatose, but at least now we know who she is, and the doctors think she'll regain consciousness soon.

"A couple of odd things you can think about while you stay here, well hidden, until I can call and tell you the arrest warrant has been voided. We just heard that the girl had a boyfriend in Tucson. The boyfriend had a brother who was found dead, hanging in his closet with a note that said simply, 'I'm sorry.' Several photos of the girl were found in his apartment too. We're not sure what's going on with this, but Tucson PD's currently calling this a guilt-inspired suicide. They think her boyfriend's brother was involved for some reason; maybe he wanted Sarah for himself and she said no. Not sure about that. Also, the same day the girl was brought in, the mayor's wife came in as well, also unconscious—they're saying it was a stroke."

"This thing with the boy—it's too...coincidental," George said evenly. "This has the hand of Zachary Louben upon it."

"It's still early in the investigation," Peter said. "Let's see how all this pans out before we panic." With that, Peter rose and left the motel room. He was expected at the hospital and was already going to be a little late.

Curt turned to George. "So what about the teacher, Mrs. Blackwell? She had some of those damn photos too. Is she in on this with the Loubens?"

"No more than Chief Larsen or the others," George responded. "They're all flunkies, being used as eyes and hands where Louben can't use his. When they're no longer useful, they'll be disposed of...like Richard Grant."

39

The ambulance was waiting by the entrance to the emergency room, its engine running by the time Peter got there. He drove a little farther, and parked away from the emergency entrance. He went quickly to the girl's room. There, he spoke with Sarah's parents. They insisted on taking her back to Tucson. Bob Wells was calm; he stood with an arm around Lydia.

She sobbed, saying, "It's been such a long time since we really did anything for her. We have to do this."

Bob nodded, adding, "I've been so busy hustling for the future that the present just passed me by…passed us by." He sighed, continuing, "We almost lost our family. I mean, Jesus! Without our children, without our marriage, what is there? Work? I've been way too hard on the kids. I got…physical a couple of times…" He trailed off, looking away for a moment. He turned back to the detective. "We've gotten a second chance, though I don't know why. Bobby's gone, but we've found Sarah. The doctors say she'll most likely need therapy after she wakes. I know a psychiatrist in Tucson. He'll help us become a family again. Lydia and I are already seeing him."

Lydia put her arm around her husband. She glanced up at him, smiling. It had been a long time since she'd felt this close to her husband. She said, "The last few days've been the worst we've ever experienced. I'm convinced Bobby's still alive. I've always been convinced. Sarah thought I was…uncaring. I just couldn't seem to express my feelings to her in a way she could understand. I feel like I drove her away, like I drove Bobby away, by trying too hard to keep them safe." Bob nodded silently. "I realize now that being overly protective doesn't translate as love, even though that was our intent. Kids need to be safe, but they need to feel loved as well, or there's no family at all."

Her husband kissed her gently and glanced at Peter. "I suppose it's possible that Bobby could be wherever Sarah was being held. Please don't stop looking for him. We've got to know—one way or the other. And believe me, when Sarah comes back from wherever she is now, you'll be notified immediately, and any information she has will be passed along."

"One last question, if I may?"

"Certainly, Detective."

"Tell me something about Sarah's boyfriend Richie Owens and his brother."

Bob sighed, looking chagrined. "The Owens boy. Frankly, I didn't even know they'd been seeing each other until one night he called, asking to speak with Sarah and I told him to go to hell."

"Okay, thank you. I was hoping to find out something more about the boy's brother."

"I read that in the paper," Bob said with a nod. "I'm afraid I can't help you there." He extended his hand, and Peter shook it.

Peter nodded, and Bob turned to the ambulance attendant.

Lydia said, "Please find Bobby, I just know he's still alive."

"I'll do my best." Peter stepped back, and the ambulance attendant moved to the bed. Two orderlies who'd been waiting out in the hall came into the room to help. Peter walked out of the room. *Maybe I should have another conversation with Joe Lindhart. There was more than one way to get at the truth.*

The automatic door swung open and Peter stepped into the cool October morning. He felt like he was making at least some progress. The cool air bit into his lungs as he inhaled. He zipped up his jacket as he walked to his car. Inside, he picked up the mic and called the station. "This is Peter," he said, "I need to speak to Ken."

"Got it, Peter," the voice crackled back over the speaker. There was a moment's silence. Back in the forest a crow called, and was answered by another. Windows down, he let the cool air wash over him.

"Peter," Ken's voice called him back.

"Yeah, Ken. Listen, can you call the Prescott PD for me? I want Joe Lindhart taken into custody for questioning. We've got to solve this case; it's been open way too long. And he's another loose end. Grant's gone now, whatever his involvement in this dog attack thing. If nothing else, we need him in custody to protect him in case whoever's running this horror show decides he has to go."

"Gotcha, Peter." Peter replaced the mic, and watched the ambulance pull out of the parking lot, and head to Tucson. A minute later, as he was leaving the parking lot, he saw the mayor's car drive in—Vic coming to visit his wife.

The police cruiser pulled into the parking lot next to the service station. Officer Norton was surprised that the station was closed. Joe was usually open on Saturday. He slowly drove past the front of the garage. There was nothing to see, beyond the closed sign hanging in the window of the front door. He parked his cruiser, and stepped out. He walked slowly toward the front of the garage and peered in through the greasy window. It appeared nobody was inside. The door was locked and the lights were off.

He turned next to the service bay. There was only one sliding door, and it too was locked. Officer Norton stood silently for a moment, then keyed his portable radio. "This is Unit Three. I'm at the station, but it's all locked up."

"Roger, Unit Three," the dispatcher said. "Make a complete check of the area, and then call back in."

"Unit Three, ten-four." Officer Norton walked to the back of the station. He saw Joe's car parked against the back wall where Joe always parked it. It was unlocked. He walked to the back door of the garage. This was getting puzzling. He jiggled the back door. Locked. He moved closer, squinting through the dirty pane that passed for a window.

Inside, Norton saw a pickup truck on the lift. At first, everything looked normal. Then he noticed the wheels. The truck was sitting on its wheels; there were no tires on the vehicle. *Joe wouldn't leave somebody's truck just sittin' on 'er wheels like that...no mechanic would do something stupid like that.*

He walked back to the door, and struck the window with the end of his baton. The pane of glass shattered as the wood around it, rotten from neglect, came loose. The entire window fell into the garage. Norton reached through the opening and turned the lock. The door swung open.

Norton entered, revolver drawn. He moved cautiously, listening. There were no sounds beyond his breathing, but there was an unmistakable odor. He walked rapidly to the front of the pickup. Then he almost dropped his revolver.

Joe lay in a thick pool of coagulated blood. The left front wheel of the truck was sitting on his groin. The weight of the truck had crushed his pelvis. His eyes were open, staring vacantly. His tongue was blackening, and protruding from his bluish lips. Norton was no pathologist, but he could tell Joe had lain there for at least a day. He shook his head slowly. What a grim way to go. He holstered his revolver and walked out into the fresh air. He took several big breaths, and then went to his cruiser to call it in.

Victor Lewis quietly opened the door to Mary's room. He smiled. "You're awake."

"I became conscious very early this morning. Nobody knows yet."

Vic sat in the bedside chair. Mary smiled weakly. "I have to get out of here, Vic. Soon. I know the time is now. But, Vic, I can't see into the people anymore."

"Are you fit to move?"

"I've got to be, don't I? Vic...it's starting to happen again. Can't you feel it?"

Vic looked closely at his wife. Her face was drawn and pale, and she looked very tired—and old. "You look tired, is all," he lied. "And this'll all be a thing of the past by tomorrow night."

"How can you get me out of here?"

"Can you wait here a minute?"

She smiled again. "Where else would I be?"

"I have an idea." With that, he rose and walked out into the hallway. At that moment, no nurses were in sight. He went into the next room. The patient there was recovering from a broken leg, and was currently on pain medication. He'd learned this by eavesdropping on the nurse's conversations the last time he'd visited Mary. The man was asleep, so Vic borrowed his wheelchair. He pushed it back into Mary's room, and closed the door. Vic helped her stand, none too steadily at first, and guided her to the chair. She sat, and he draped a blanket around her shoulders. He rolled her to the door, and said, "I'll be right back."

He slipped back into the room of the man with the broken leg. The man was still asleep, so it wasn't too difficult for Vic to pour some alcohol from a small flask he carried inside his jacket. Technically, it was vodka; but whatever the name, it was nevertheless an accelerant. He poured some on the sleeping man's sheets, and set them ablaze with a cigarette lighter. He left the room, and back in the hall, he pulled the fire alarm. He hurried back to Mary's room and waited. The wait was not a long one. The man with the broken leg awoke, and began shrieking for help. The ceiling fire sprinklers came on instantly; the fire alarm siren was already blaring. Victor listened at the door, waiting to hear running footsteps. That was Vic's signal.

He shoved the door open, pushing his wife down the hall toward the elevator. They were already inside by the time the nurses and doctors came running down the hall from all directions. The elevator opened on the first floor, and by then Vic had donned his hat, and the blanket was draped over Mary's head, partially hiding her face. In the confusion, nobody gave them more than a passing glance as he rolled her out to the parking lot. Don saw them come out, and gunned the engine of the Oldsmobile, screeching to a stop in front of them. He leaped out to help Vic get Mary into the back seat, and they were away.

"The Wells girl is in the hospital," Mary informed Vic.

"Not any more," he responded, "one of the nurses told me an ambulance arrived and took her back to Tucson. Her parents were here. They talked with that detective."

"We have to get out of here. We've no more time."

"Believe me, I realize this."

Don drove the Olds out of the hospital parking lot and into the street. Mary looked at Vic and smiled. He realized, much to his shock, that she'd nearly bought it! He wondered if that was even possible; and if she could die, what about him? Mary, for her part, found she was glad to be alive and she wondered, for the second time in forever, if she might actually be able to die. She rolled down the window, letting the cool morning air wash over her. She was feeling better already.

"Tell me what happened," Vic said.

Mary whispered, not wanting Don to hear, even though he was wearing the required earphones that poured loud music into his ears. "The girl did something unprecedented. She followed me back into my own mind, and somehow did something inside the biological part, inside my brain. She almost killed me. How can that be?"

Vic shrugged. "It doesn't matter. In no more than a day or two we'll be gone from this planet forever."

"Vic? We're being hunted again. I just know it."

Vic nodded. "I think it's that Luedke. The librarian had that photo we thought we destroyed. She must've mailed one and kept another. We were too late. Now I think Luedke has the stone. He must've suspected we'd try to get it back from the Paxton boy. But he hasn't found everything yet." Vic smiled. "And we're closing in on him. We have a warrant out for the Paxton boy, and his father's already in custody. We'll have the fold-crystal soon enough."

"If the boy doesn't have it, then Luedke does. He wouldn't give it up just to save the boy, would he?"

"We have to think like him in this case. And yes, I think if it came to the boy dying, or letting us get away, he'll choose to save the boy—they seem to have grown fond of each other." He laughed.

"How very nice."

"And we can always promise not to...damage this world." That caused both of them to laugh.

"We have some other loose ends to tie up as well. Grant's dead. Your mental suggestion he kill himself if he got caught worked like a...well, like a charm." He laughed, tapping Don's shoulder. The man removed the earphones, allowing the rock music to blare out into the car. "Lindhart's history as well. Don took care of that little job yesterday. Isn't that right, Don?"

Don grinned into the rearview mirror, nodding.

"Don's gonna take care of Hank and Carl too, aren't you?" Again Don nodded. Then he replaced the earphones. Private conversations were private as far as he was concerned. Vic settled back into his seat. "All we need to do now is find Luedke and the Paxton boy and get that crystal."

"That might not be as easy as you think," Mary cautioned.

"Nonsense," Vic responded. "It won't be any harder than it was on Eribus."

"On Eribus we barely escaped."

"Nonsense. They can't touch us, and they can't kill us. They'd be murderers. But them having the crystal worries me. I don't like any being having power over us—it isn't part of the natural order of things."

Mary asked, "What about the children? We'll need them if the crystal cannot be found. We should have more…"

"I've got that taken care of. As soon as we're straightened away up here, Don's taking Cal down to Prescott, to do some…shopping. The Prescott newspaper had an article about a small private school in Phoenix that's coming up to Prescott on a state history field trip. At eleven on Sunday they're supposed to be at the Courthouse Square downtown—a van full of children, ages nine to twelve, will be ours to do with as we will."

"You can't just take the bus and drive off."

"Nope. We're stopping it on the road to Prescott, and commandeering it." Vic glanced into the front seat, making certain Don was still wearing the headset. "If it goes bad, Don and Cal will be taken care of for us. We still have seven children in the basement we can use, if push comes to shove."

"Only seven won't regress our age very much."

"If it comes to that, they'll have to do. They'll take us back to our forties at any rate. Nobody will recognize us. We can just walk away, and start over somewhere else—maybe Denver. It'll give us another year to find and kill Luedke and the Paxton boy, and recover the crystal. The transport is well hidden; there's no chance they'll find it."

"I…we've never had to run before Eribus…why is that? For a very long time we've just taken what we needed and moved on."

"I think it may have something to do with taking the flesh of this Universe to live inside of. I'm not certain—it's all new to me as well. In any case, we'll most likely find the crystal before the energy lines separate."

Mary questioned, "And what might the boy and this…Luedke know?"

"My talents are not mind reading, but I'll find out what the Paxton boy knows; I'm good enough to do that."

"How will we accomplish that?"

"As soon as we're home, I'm calling the chief and telling him I want that arrest warrant negated. And further, I want to offer Curt Paxton my personal apology for this travesty of justice."

40

Peter Davis was two blocks from City Hall when he got the call about Lindhart. He slammed his fist against the steering wheel. "Damn!" Sitting at the light, he thought, *we're always one step behind this killer. We gotta get in front of this somehow.* When the light turned green, Peter punched it. The Challenger lurched forward as white smoke boiled up from the screaming rear tires. He lifted his foot. No point in getting a ticket. Then he laughed.

At the station, Ken Jackson was waiting for him. "Hey, Peter. Looks like your favorite mechanic bit the big one, eh?"

Peter tossed his jacket onto the back of his chair, and sat down heavily. "This is getting frustrating, Ken. This case has been on my books for over a year now, and we're still nowhere near an answer. I don't get it. All we keep finding are injured or dead children and dead witnesses, and no real leads."

Ken nodded. "Lindhart had a truck dropped on him. Musta been painful. The preliminary report says he probably lived a couple hours with one of the truck's steel wheels standing on his crotch. Right now they're saying he probably bled to death internally. Prescott PD thinks he was tortured to see what information he might've leaked to you on your last trip down to see him. They're not very happy that you didn't have one of their officers with you when you questioned him."

Peter waved a hand dismissively. "They'll get over it. But you know, Ken...I can't help but feel we've only dealt with the little guys on this so far. Someone is orchestrating things, but for what purpose I can't imagine. I believe this business with Lindhart, the Wells girl, that young man in Tucson, those photos showing up at convenient times and places are all part of one...thing..."

Ken shrugged. "You're the detective, go detect."

"You're a big help. Now I know why they promoted you to a desk."

Ken laughed and said, "Oh, by the way, Karen called for you a few minutes ago. She said she had to go the hospital—some kinda' emergency, and that you should call her there right away."

Peter looked inquiringly at Ken, who responded, "Hey, I'm just delivering the message. If you want the details, call your girlfriend." He grinned.

Karen sounded worried. "Peter, Mary Lewis is missing. There was a fire in one of the rooms; a patient was burned—not severely, thank God. But in the confusion, someone got Mrs. Lewis out of the hospital in a wheelchair that was stolen from the room where the fire started."

Peter listened incredulously. "How does the mayor's wife just disappear? She didn't wander off on her own, did she?"

"Unlikely. But we need to find her. I just saw her last lab reports, Peter. Something strange is happening—something unprecedented is happening with her blood. She's dying, Peter! Her blood cells are falling apart for some reason. Disintegrating. I've never seen anything like it, and neither has anyone else. At this rate she'll be dead in two or three days at the most."

"You stay at the hospital. Ask everyone, even the other patients, if anyone saw anything. She had to get down to the ground level; she didn't fly out the window, so that means the elevator, considering that she needed a wheelchair." Karen agreed, and Peter continued, "She had to be picked up in some kind of conveyance. Ask the receptionists; maybe they saw something."

"Alright. Hey, Peter? Be careful."

"I will," he said and hung up. He sat for a moment, gathering his thoughts. *What the hell's going on? Is the whole damn town going berserk?* Strange as it sounded to him, it was beginning to look like the only person who had the real story was that lunatic mystic and psychic, George Luedke.

Peter picked up the phone again and dialed their motel. The phone was ringing, but nobody answered. He slammed the receiver. "Ken, listen, I'm going to see that Blackwell woman. She's the only living lead we've got left, except the chief."

"You stay away from Larsen," Ken admonished. "That's DPS business." But Peter was already out the door.

Jennifer Blackwell had just gotten up. She glanced at the clock; it was already afternoon. She lit a cigarette, drawing the smoke deeply. She was remembering something…almost like listening to someone speaking inside her head, just like before. *Just like before,* she wondered, *before when?* She tried to recall, but the voice was too demanding; too insistent for her to do anything else but listen.

It seemed to be the voice of Mary Lewis, but that wasn't possible. The woman was unconscious and in the hospital. No, this wasn't something she was hearing now; it was something important she'd been told in the past at some time, but repeated just now, in a man's voice. *Vic… What? "Things are falling apart. The group is disbanding. You know what you have to do."*

Now Jennifer spoke aloud to that strange, internal voice. "I've done all you asked of me. I got to that Driscoll boy right in the school so you could link to him through me. You made me a promise then, do you remember? Well, I remember. You promised to give me immortality."

And as if in answer to those words, the voice in her head continued. *"Immortality will be yours, but you have to do just one more thing."*

Jennifer listened intently, eyes closed, a vague smile spreading across her lips. Suddenly she rose, and stumbled to the door of her apartment and flung it open. She stepped into a hallway that seemed now to go on forever. At the far end, she saw the walls, floor and ceiling illuminated in the soft white light that came from...*where is that light coming from?* And the voice continued, telling Jennifer to become one with the light. If she was to become truly immortal, she had to get inside that mystical light at the end of the long, beautiful hallway. The voice stopped; she knew what she had to do. She took a step forward, and then another. She knew her path; it was already laid out before her. She smiled serenely.

It was like a dream, she seemed to float down the hallway. Now she was running...running down that glorious tunnel that steadily grew brighter... brighter...she was thrilled and in awe of her speed, and knew she was experiencing a cosmic mystery. The white radiance exploded around her, united with her. She smiled, and broke into a joyful laugh. *So this is what immortality feels like...*

Peter Davis pulled his Challenger to the curb in front of the apartment building. He released the seatbelt, opened the door, and stepped out into the bright afternoon sunlight. The breeze blew gently over him, promising the colder weather ahead. He was taking his second step toward the stairs leading into the building when he heard the crash.

The sun was almost directly overhead, and the glare made him squint and shade his eyes with one hand. Looking up between almost closed eyelids, he saw the sun suddenly burst into thousands of brilliant fragments. It reminded him of Fourth of July sparklers. But he suddenly realized that there was a dark shape in the center of the light display, a dark shape falling to the unyielding concrete of the sidewalk below. He realized the dark shape had arms and legs.

He stood numbly, unable to move. He watched as the black silhouette plunged toward the sidewalk. He could hear the laughter—then came the impact. Jennifer Blackwell didn't bounce when she struck the sidewalk. She was still wildly running and laughing hysterically when she hit feet first.

Peter saw her body shorten. The leg bones fractured, then telescoped. Now she was down. Her head hit the sidewalk with a *thunk*. She lay on her back, one ruined leg twisted and pointing toward her head.

By the time Peter was able to reach her, Jennifer's blood had spread in a thick pool around her. He knelt by her head; her eyes were beginning to glaze. Peter knew she couldn't see—her eyes were looking in two different directions. Her last words were drowned out by the roar of an automobile engine.

Peter whirled in time to see a big green Mercury Grand Marquis cruise past him, engine growling like a wild creature. He'd seen that car before. He leaped up, trying to see inside. He ripped his sunglasses from his face, but it did no good. The windows were so heavily tinted, not even the outline of the vehicle's occupants could be seen. He ran to his car, and as he fired up the engine, he called in the report of Blackwell's suicide jump. Then he stood on the accelerator.

In seconds the tach was redlined. Peter shifted quickly into second gear. The rear of the Challenger was vibrating as the tires bit in, and churned up angry billows of white smoke. The Positraction rear end held him steadily in the burnout.

"Damn, he's already following us." Don Bristow had hoped he'd gotten away—the mayor was in the back seat for chrissake!

"Around the next corner," Vic ordered. "Stop and let me out. Then lose him. You can come back for me. Be certain you've lost him."

Bristow glanced into the mirror. There was no way that Challenger could catch this car. He took the corner, almost rolling the Mercury, and slammed on the brakes. Vic jumped out, and Don hit it again, beginning to move just as the rear door slammed shut. The tires were already spinning up a white smoke-screen that hid Vic from the Challenger as it rounded the turn. Vic grinned and walked the half block to the bistro. He liked this place. He'd have a nice meal and drink, and sit back for a few minutes and relive those last few moments. Activating Blackwell had been easy, even without Mary's special talents—that teacher-woman had had a weak mind.

Don took his eyes from the rearview mirror. The Challenger was right behind him! Then he gasped. The light ahead had just changed from green to red! He laid on the horn, and ran the light at ninety miles an hour. He drove straight through, barely missing the rear end of a dump truck. A big Lincoln was skidding, turning sideways and heading toward him. The grill of the Lincoln just missed Don's rear bumper. Don watched the vehicle in his mirror as it slid behind him, brakes locked.

The Lincoln slid into oncoming traffic, striking a Ford station wagon head on. Peter saw the hoods rise, buckling on impact. He hit the brakes, downshifting. Ahead he saw the Mercury crest the hill, and disappear on the other side. He saw the tachometer redline again, and pulled the Hurst shifter into second gear. Hitting the accelerator, he shoved the gearshift into third. *Those bastards aren't going to get away with this.*

The V-8 roared as the Challenger's wheels briefly left the road as it topped the hill. Peter glimpsed the Mercury as it slid into the intersection ahead. He gunned it, red light flashing and siren calling. Now was his chance to catch them. Ahead, the Mercury had barely missed colliding with an eighteen-wheeler making a left turn and had to come to a stop. Peter grinned. The driver had killed the engine!

Just as he made this observation, the green car lunged forward onto Avalon.

Peter shouted, "Damn!" He downshifted to second, and took the turn. Now he was right behind the Merc.

"This is Unit Seven. I'm in pursuit of a green Mercury Grand Marquis, license number Alpha, Charlie, Delta, two, three, three. I'm heading south on Avalon approaching Hennessy, need assistance."

Peter dropped the mic, and heard dispatch acknowledge his call. Seconds later, the dispatcher was back. "Peter, that car was confiscated last year in a drug bust. It's supposed to be in the impound lot, but Chief Larsen signed it out for special police use—with the mayor's consent."

Peter smiled grimly, as he grabbed the mic. "I guess we'll have to ask him about that."

"DPS is trying, Peter. Larsen's gone, disappeared. DPS has a warrant for his arrest. We can't seem to contact the mayor either." The radio returned to silence.

Don watched the yellow Dodge as it drifted smoothly around the corner and rapidly closed the distance. *Shotgun.* The thought inspired Don. He reached over to the passenger seat and picked up the old Winchester 97. Putting the butt on the floor, he racked the slide, forcing a round into the chamber. He smiled. This would be ironic—that old Hobbs lawman's gun, lifted from the museum archives would serve another purpose now. He slowed, moving to the right. As he'd hoped, the Dodge was pulling up next to him. He started rolling down the window.

Peter was running flat out in third, and had just shifted to fourth, when he saw the green car slowing. He moved left, and began his approach. He saw the window being cranked down. As the idea of being shot passed through his mind, Peter saw the yawning muzzle of the gun.

The two cars were neck and neck now, traveling at sixty miles an hour. The shotgun muzzle was huge, and it seemed very close. Then before he could react, he saw the driver move. He'd pulled the trigger.

Don was shocked by the silence. His mind screamed at him—*nothing happened! That should have been loud! What's wrong?*

Peter stood on the brakes. The gun hadn't discharged. He took a deep breath to clear his head, glancing back at the road. The telephone pole was approaching rapidly. At sixty, a car covers a lot of distance very quickly. With barely time to react, Peter jerked the wheel left. Though his foot was off the accelerator, Peter was still traveling at fifty when he struck the pole.

He felt himself being lifted out of the seat and propelled forward. The seatbelt held, though, and as the right fender was crushed by the pole, he remained in the seat. The firewall buckled as the big V8 moved rearward. The car spun crazily into the intersection, hurling fragments of itself in all directions. And for the first time in his life, Peter came to a true realization of just how fast fifty miles an hour really was.

The driver's door was flung open, and had not the seatbelt held him in place, he'd have been hurled to the street and promptly crushed by his own vehicle. The car threatened to roll, but it kept to its wheels and came to a sudden stop.

Peter, now reclining on the seat, upper body hanging precariously from the open door, watched in numb fascination as wisps of glowing white steam drifted up from the broken radiator and engine, turning, forming…and then spinning off into nothingness…

41

Don Bristow witnessed the crash in his rearview mirror. He grinned a mirthless grin, slapping the Mercury's steering wheel with his left hand. He immediately slowed his speed to a very respectable and inconspicuous thirty miles an hour. He turned right at the next light, then another right. It took him almost thirty minutes to complete the circle around to the bistro where the mayor waited. By now he knew that there was nobody else tailing him. He passed the bistro, slowing so if by chance Vic was looking out the window, he'd see him and be ready to leave.

He parked the Mercury in the lot beside the business, carefully staying inside the white lines. In the near distance, he heard sirens—police and fire department. *Maybe the bastard's burning.* That thought encouraged him again, and he started laughing as he opened the door to step out. He looked up, and there was a young couple walking past, looking inquiringly at him, wondering at his laughter. But they turned, and continued on their way. Don sighed in relief. He'd had no qualms about killing the young couple; but it would have made the mayor's escape a bit more difficult. That made him laugh again, in spite of himself.

Vic must have taken a table near the front, because he stepped out the door just as Don approached. With no words exchanged, they walked rapidly back to the auto, and stepped in. Don pulled from the parking lot, carefully watching for oncoming traffic, and turned in the opposite direction he'd been traveling earlier. He knew the street would be blocked farther up.

"Where to, sir?"

"Take me home. I want this car back in the garage, just as soon as it's feasible, just in case. We'll take the Olds to City Hall. I'm going to call City Hall before we leave the house so they'll have things ready for us. I want to be on the radio this afternoon. I have an announcement to make."

"Yes, sir."

Don pulled the garage door shut with a crash. Vic was already out, striding into the house to change his clothing and check on Mary. In the meantime, Don lifted the old shotgun from under the seat where it had fallen and carried it to the workbench. There, he stripped it for cleaning, and carefully examined it. A moment later, he swore under his breath—not so much at the shotgun, but at his own stupid mistake.

When he'd lifted the gun, he'd hid it for possible use, but never test fired it. Now, under the bright fluorescents at the worktable, he could plainly see the opening in the bolt that should have been occupied by a firing pin. He took a paper clip, bent it straight, and probed the opening, just to be certain. It slid smoothly all the way through. He'd been correct in his assessment; the firing pin had been removed. Apparently, the historical society had removed it, making the gun safe for display and for use in lectures where others might have access to it. It was so obvious—something that's done all the time by museums and the like. At the moment, Don felt very lucky indeed; he'd stupidly tried to kill a cop with an inoperable firearm! Fortunately nobody else knew about this little fiasco. He could imagine what Cal might have to say about that.

He heard Vic coming back down the hall toward the garage, so he slid the gun into a golf bag standing beside a metal storage cabinet. It dropped inside, completely invisible in the bag. A moment later, the door opened and Vic stepped in, dressed in an expensive suit, and carrying a handful of papers. He glanced at Don, standing by worktable, and almost asked him what he was doing. But there was no time. "Let's get going," was his only comment.

The Oldsmobile cruised down the road on the way to City Hall. Don, always looking for ways to ingratiate himself, asked, "How's Mary?"

"She's doing better. Thanks for asking. She doesn't have her powers back yet, so I'll have to do this up close and personal."

"I'm not sure I know what you mean."

"You don't need to."

Karen was working when Peter was brought into the hospital. Though he was brought in on a gurney, he didn't appear to be very badly hurt—mostly bruises, cuts, and scrapes. The worst of it, a cut along his brow where he struck the door in the Challenger's final spin, was closed with four sutures. Nevertheless, he was admitted for tests and observation.

While another doctor examined Peter—hospital policy prohibited doctors from treating relatives and close friends in the emergency room—Karen paced nervously. About an hour later, after x-rays and blood tests had been completed, she was finally allowed to see him.

"Peter! Thank God you weren't killed!"

Peter laughed, wincing with pain. "Funny…I always thought car chases worked like in the movies."

"Don't make fun of this! This is very serious."

"I know…that car will cost a fortune to replace."

In spite of herself, she laughed. "Men and their silly toys." Then she sat in the chair by his side, and they talked.

A short time later, another doctor came into the room. "Well, Peter, your blood tests are normal. And your X-rays show no fractured limbs, but you have a couple of cracked ribs, so you're gonna be wrapped up for a while. There's also a hell of a bruise on your back from where you slammed down on your pistol. I'd recommend carrying it somewhere else on your body, at least until you heal. Small price to pay, though, all things considered."

Peter looked at the doctor straight faced, and said, "Small price? Have you seen my car?"

The doctor laughed. "I know all about your car. Since you seem to favor Dodges, I guess now you'll have to go out and buy a nice new Omni or something."

"An...Omni?"

"Okay, maybe you want a change. How about a Ford Tempo?"

"Ah...no."

"You clearly need something with a small motor. Maybe you're getting too old for hotrods."

"How long will I have to be in here?"

"Well...if you don't mind a little pain from the ribs, you can check out tomorrow morning."

"Excellent," Karen commented. "I can be here to take you home. I'm off tomorrow."

"Nope," Peter responded, "I can sign myself out now if I like."

The doctor shrugged. "It's your body."

Karen sighed; there was no point in arguing the point. "It's late anyway, I'll just sign out early."

Curt and George heard the radio news broadcast about a high-speed car chase through Hobbs. An undercover police officer had been injured when his car hit a telephone pole. Both of them raised their heads when they heard the name of the injured detective. They stared at each other, dumbfounded.

The news then took a stranger turn, with the report of the odd suicide death of Hobbs High School's journalism instructor, Jennifer Blackwell. George saw Curt pale with the news.

"Looks like they're tying up loose ends, doesn't it?"

Curt nodded in agreement, as another bit of news came over the airwaves. An auto mechanic in Prescott had been killed in a tragic accident. A truck he'd been working on, fell on him when the lift collapsed. When Curt heard the man's name, he looked up at George and asked, "Isn't that the fellow who suddenly didn't see a thing last year when that girl was killed up on Hobbs Hill Road?"

"One and the same," George responded. "Another loose end."

And then, right before the weather, the mayor was on the air, imploring Curtis Paxton to come to City Hall. They listened intently.

"Once I realized there'd been a warrant issued for the Paxton boy, I knew there was some kind of mistake. From everything I've been told, these so-called 'incriminating pictures' have been showing up in a number of locations. This, of course, leads me to believe that they've been planted in desperation by the real perpetrators of this heinous crime in an attempt to frame others for this crime. I received a report from Tucson that the girl's boyfriend's brother is part of the conspiracy. He obviously has no connection with either the Paxton family or the Higgins family.

"I hold here, in my hand, a pardon and a voidance of warrant signed by a judge, and by myself as well. I'd like to personally hand these to Mr. Curtis Paxton and issue my personal apology for the way he and his father have been treated. What happened here is inexcusable. I've asked the Arizona Department of Public Safety to look into the alleged crime, and the seemingly interconnected deaths. Curtis Paxton, I await your attendance."

"Well," George said, rising, "what are we waiting for?"

"You actually think we should go?"

"Not we. You. I'll drop you off at City Hall. It's important you present yourself and gather those documents." He showed Curt the key to the VW. "Let's get going. We both have things to do, and very little time to do them in." With that said, they left the motel, got into George's Volkswagen, and headed toward downtown Hobbs.

"You're not going in with me?"

"Nope. I have some other things to attend to. I'll call you at home later this evening. Once you're all safely at home, stay there until I call, alright?"

"You think it's safe?"

"Absolutely. The mayor isn't going to attempt to strangle you in front of television cameras and the entire city council, you know."

"I suppose that's true," Curt admitted, though reluctantly. George pulled to the curb in front of the Hobbs City Hall.

This building, unlike most of the buildings around it, was new. It had been built only twenty years before, and the presiding mayor for the last eighteen of those twenty years had been Victor Lewis. It was odd if one looked closely at it, but nobody seemed to wonder about it. Over the years, one or two people who opposed his constant re-elections seemed to move away. And everyone who'd run against him in the last four elections had suddenly decided to drop out of the race at the last minute, leaving Victor running unopposed.

As mayor, he got things done. Roads that had been dirt were now paved and well maintained. And the historical society was much better organized than it had ever been. The mayor's wife had helped a lot with that, generously donating her time and expertise. Working in the tangle of artifacts, documents, and blueprints in the basement and attic of the society museum, she'd been able to find interesting and valuable papers, photographs, and other objects that nobody else even realized were there. Her discoveries had prompted several major exhibits over the last few years.

It was like she had a sixth sense for finding these things, and though relative newcomers to Hobbs, she and her husband had a vast storehouse of knowledge regarding the history of the town and the surrounding area. From time to time, people had commented that it was like they'd actually lived in Hobbs way back in the 1800s. And then they'd laugh at the silliness of such an idea.

Curt stepped out of the Volkswagen, and George pulled quickly back out into traffic. Curt crossed the open square and climbed the steps. Inside, he looked around. He'd never been in City Hall before. The lobby was modern, and well lit. A number of rooms led off the main area, and at the far end was a bank of elevators. Straight ahead was the information desk. He walked to the desk and told the young woman who he was.

"Oh yes, Mr. Paxton. The mayor's been waiting for you." She smiled warmly at the boy. She picked up the telephone, and spoke briefly. "The mayor's assistant will be right down to show you the way."

"Thank you." She smiled, and went back to her paperwork. By the time Curt had walked to the elevators, the one to his left dinged and opened. A serious young man in a nice suit and wire-rimmed glasses introduced himself, and then escorted Curt into the elevator. "There are cameramen and news reporters up there, Curt. Don't be surprised. The mayor feels very strongly about this terrible injustice, and he's determined to get all of this straightened out."

I bet he is, thought Curt.

The man, who'd introduced himself on the way back to the elevator as Colin Pratt, now led Curt through the door into the second floor conference room. Three video cameras were set up, and a number of reporters with recorders, notepads, and still cameras were also present. All the cameras suddenly turned in his direction, strobes flashing. At the far end, Victor Lewis stood behind a fine, antique walnut table, a huge smile on his face. "And here he is. Thank you so much, Curt for coming here so quickly. Please, come up and sit beside me."

Curt did as he was asked, and upon reaching the front of the room, the mayor extended his hand, and took Curt's in his, shaking for the cameras. He was still smiling, looking around for the cameras, making the most of the event. He finally released Curt's hand, and gestured to a chair beside him with an open palm. "Please, sit." Vic remained on his feet, and addressed the audience.

"When I heard of this travesty of justice, I couldn't just stand by and let it happen. That is not the reason I became mayor of this fine municipality. That is not the reason the fine citizens of Hobbs keep returning me to this office." The crowd snickered politely, and Curt thought to himself, I *wonder how many opponents you've killed along the way.* And then he noticed that the mayor was looking at him again, that smile fixed to his face like a clown's.

Victor continued with his speech. "There was no real evidence against this boy except that which was planted deliberately in his house. How do we know this? As of this moment, there are at least two other locations, here and in Tucson, where photographs and other alleged evidence have been found, supposedly linking others to this crime involving the young girl, Sarah Wells.

"We'll get to the bottom of this. We're not resting until we capture whatever monster lurking among us did these things. But in the meantime, we can fix another problem." He picked up several papers and handed them to Curt with a considerable flourish. Curt took them without comment, quietly looking them over.

"These papers that I have just handed to Curtis Paxton are official documents, signed by a judge and by myself, and then properly notarized. They completely exonerate both he and his father from any connection whatsoever with the crimes we are here discussing.

"Any arrests at this time are premature and ill advised. I would also like to take this time to suggest to the people of Hobbs that they keep their eyes and ears open. Listen to what your children want to tell you. Somewhere in this town, a monster walks among us. We must find this creature and bring him, or them, to justice, as the case may be. I would like to add that Mr. Paxton—Curt's father—and Miss Higgins are in the process of being released from police custody right now, as we're speaking."

Curt was asked to speak. Once more Vic shook his hand, holding on a lot longer than Curt thought necessary. Vic's eyes seemed far away; it almost seemed to Curt that he was listening to some faint sound in the crowd.

42

While the mayor was at City Hall occupied with his charade of Curt's pardon and the subsequent press interviews, George drove slowly up Hobbs Hill Road, thinking about the events that had recently transpired. Everything meant something—even seemingly disconnected events were really connected. That was how this thing worked, how it had always worked. He looked out his side window, passing the now deserted police chief's home, and turned the Volkswagen off the road at a curve near the mayor's house. He reckoned this was about the same spot where Detective Davis had discovered the Wells girl— it was just about halfway between the mayor's house and that of the missing police chief. George thought, *That's a real coincidence, now isn't it?*

He drove a short distance into the forest growth on the east side of the road where he knew he'd be concealed from prying eyes. He shut off the engine, and sat listening for several minutes. He listened to the insects and the birds. If anything disturbed the forest quiet, the birds and insects would know first, and he'd know immediately after that. He quietly stepped out of the auto and closed the door so gently not even the birds stopped their songs. An old pair of binoculars clad in black leather hung from his neck by a worn leather strap with rusted chromium buckles; a relic from the time he'd lived in Prussia toward the end of the 19th century. In his pocket he carried the fold-crystal.

He moved cautiously through the brush until he could see the mayor's mansion atop its hill. He raised the Zeiss binoculars, studying the edifice. It was clearly of late 19th century design as were most of the buildings in Hobbs. But he wasn't examining or admiring the various attributes of late Victorian stonework that the old building displayed so magnificently. He was scrutinizing the windows. Moving slowly, examining each in turn, he could clearly see that all the second floor windows were tightly draped.

He moved forward, listening for approaching traffic. Hearing nothing, he rapidly crossed the road at a low crouch and moved silently up the hill on the other side. He stopped periodically to listen and observe. No sounds greeted him except the wild sounds of the forest life all around him. The bird and insect sounds were reassuring, and they began again almost as soon as he stopped walking. If someone else were moving in the area, they'd be silent and watchful when he was still. He moved on.

He topped a small ridge, and froze. Now he could see the whole building and the open grounds immediately surrounding it. The metal fence that surrounded the property was newer, and from past exploration, he knew it was alarmed. There was a man working in the yard, tending a small garden near the left rear of the place. George cursed under his breath. He'd have to take the long way around to get behind the house and further up the hill. He didn't want to be seen by anyone, not even a gardener.

He moved even more cautiously now, stopping periodically to peer through the binoculars at the man in the garden. He seemed an unlikely gardener, having more the look of a drug addict, or perhaps an alcoholic, skid-row bum. A cigarette dangled carelessly from his lips, which were moving, as though he was talking to himself. George listened, but whatever the man was saying, it was too quiet to hear.

But whatever the man's addiction, it didn't really matter to George, as long as he kept on hoeing weeds, and didn't decide to go for a stroll in the countryside. Once out of sight of the house, he pulled a small device from his pocket that resembled an old-style transistor radio. It had two antennas that George pulled to their full extension. He placed the device on the ground, with an antenna on each side of the fence and pushed a small button.

With the alarm circuit shunted through his device, he climbed the fence. He picked up the small device, and returning the antennae to their storage slots, he put it back into his jacket pocket. Now he withdrew another electronic device from his other pocket, and held the crystal next to it, watching it for a moment. He moved forward, shifting the device from side to side very slowly as though it were a metal detector. In another fifteen minutes George had determined that what he was seeking was not in or near the house. There was only one other place to look.

Strobes flashed, and reporters shoved microphones into Curt's face. He pulled back instinctively, repelled by the feral, predatory eagerness of the reporters. "I'm glad this is finally taken care of," he said, "I heard about the journalism teacher's suicide, and I wonder at the cause? Did she claim she found the pictures in my locker to frame me for this crime? And if so, why would she do that? Why would she do such a thing? We worked together on the school paper for two years, and she was always friendly toward me, and eager to help.

"I wonder if there's someone else in this room who should be investigated." He turned, staring levelly at the mayor. "What would someone gain by doing all of this? A school teacher? An automobile mechanic in Prescott?" He stared at Vic and said, "Why yes, I know about that too." He turned again to the crowd of reporters. "Are you reporters going to actually look for the real reason this is happening, and who might benefit, or are you simply satisfied just to tell about how people are dying, and that I'm not the guilty person, and let it go at that?"

Put suddenly on the defensive, the reporters proclaimed loudly that they weren't going to rest until they'd ferreted out the truth of the matter. More flashes winked, and Curt held up his hand for silence. Suddenly, he seemed to be in charge of this gathering. *Might as well take advantage of it, as long as they're all still listening to me.*

Curt said, "I think all of you should stay in town for a while and talk to our mayor. He's been our mayor for eighteen years, you know. I'm sure he'll be glad to take all the time you might need, and to answer all of your questions. He can talk with each and every one of you to help clear this all up." Curt paused. "After all," he continued, mimicking Victor, "that's the reason the fine citizens of Hobbs keep returning Victor Lewis to this office." He grinned, and some of the reporters laughed.

Curt looked at Vic, and smiled. Under the lights and the cameras, Vic smiled gregariously, but Curt saw that his smile didn't reach his eyes. His eyes were cold—calculating. Curt thought, *What'd they used to call this? Bear baiting?* He added, "If anyone can help you, it'll be His Honor, Victor Lewis, our fine mayor. He's been more in touch with the police chief than anyone in town, and that makes me wonder why the chief isn't here for this interview?"

"Didn't you hear?" One of the reporters from Phoenix shouted in wonder, "Chief Larsen's disappeared, apparently. The State Police are looking for him right now."

"All I can do is urge you to work with our mayor; nobody knows more about what's going on in town than he does. We all have complete confidence in his ability to help both the police and the media to understand what's going on in Hobbs."

Suddenly Victor Lewis found himself to be the story this afternoon. Mentally he cursed Curt; now he'd have to spend all afternoon dealing with these moronic humans in a silly game of rhetorical thrust and parry. He would much prefer to kill them all, especially the boy. He glared at Curt, who smiled benevolently at the mayor and the reporters, and walked from the room. As the door closed behind him, he heard the questioning begin.

"Mr. Mayor! Mr. Mayor! What's being done to solve this horrible crime?"

"What steps are you implementing to keep people safe in town while a gang of murdering Satanists runs wild?"

"Where's your police chief? I heard something about the State Police wanting to arrest him?"

By the time he reached the elevator, Curt was laughing softly under his breath. *That'll show 'em,* he thought in amusement as he pushed the button for the first floor.

Upstairs, the mayor endured the questions and accusations. He'd regained his equilibrium now, and best of all, he'd gotten the information from Curt he'd been seeking. When he'd shaken the boy's hand, he'd done a rudimentary mind-sweep. The stupid human never even realized it.

That Luedke character had told him that he had no idea where the ship was hidden, that he couldn't find it. That was heartening news. They were departing this region of space-time Monday after dark. Everything was in readiness. He was certain they'd have the crystal shortly; there was only one person to find, and he'd have it. And then they'd have him as well. Luedke couldn't hide forever. The ship was prepped, and checked over. All systems were functional, and all energy cells were fully charged. Even Luedke wouldn't be able to find the ship before they were ready. He turned to the aggressive reporter, and smiled for the camera as he began…

Curt walked from City Hall, into the cool autumn air. It was close to five, and he was getting hungry. He got lucky, and caught the city bus just as it was pulling up to the stop in front of the building. He showed his bus pass to the driver. The driver nodded, and Curt moved to the last seat in the bus. That way he could keep an eye on the door, and the passengers. He was determined that nobody would be able to take him by surprise. He remembered how books said the Old West gunslingers would sit in saloons facing the door so they couldn't be ambushed. He grinned, but didn't let down his guard until he was safely home, and behind locked doors.

About ten minutes later, a State Patrol cruiser pulled up in front, and Curt's dad and Katy Higgins stepped out. Curt was waiting for them at the door, and once they were all inside with the door closed, they hugged each other, and Katy cried a little. Curt's dad suggested they all have dinner at the Paxton home. This was fine with Curt; he'd had enough of Hobbs for one day.

Peter Davis walked out of the hospital at 4:50 that afternoon; he was in no mood for a wheelchair. He'd called the garage earlier, and they confirmed what he'd already suspected; his Challenger was beyond repairing. The chief mechanic suggested letting the insurance company scrap it. Then he could buy it back for the same price, have still-serviceable parts that could be taken off and resold. The mechanic told him that if he wanted a new car, the parts for the old one would probably pay for half of it. Peter said he'd think about it. Right now he had other cars on his mind—a green Mercury, for example.

Karen wanted to take him home, but Peter insisted on going to the station. Karen sighed, turning toward the downtown area of Hobbs. As she drew up to the curb, she began admonishing him. "No more car chases, alright?"

Peter snorted. "Got nothing to chase with now…remember?"

"Oh, I remember. I'll probably have bad dreams about that one for the next ten years or so."

"You planning on staying with me for the next ten years?"

She playfully slapped his arm. "Of course, silly!"

"Well, in that case…" Peter reached into his pocket, and withdrew a small black box. "I'd like you to consider marrying me."

Karen opened the box. Inside, a small diamond ring winked in the light. The stone wasn't large, but to Karen it was the very finest diamond the world had ever seen. "I bought it a few days ago, waiting for the right time," Peter explained. "I thought I'd lost it in the crash, but as it turned out, it was still inside my jacket pocket. I'm hoping this is the right time." Karen wiped away her tears, and smiled. Peter slipped the ring on Karen's finger.

They both laughed, and embraced. Several people walking down the side-walk watched them as they passed. In one case, a man walking beside a woman reached over, and took her hand in his. She smiled up at him, and they turned the corner and were gone from sight.

Peter stepped out of Karen's car, wincing with pain.

"You alright?"

He smiled. "I'm marrying a doctor. I've got nothing to worry about."

"I love the ring," she shouted to him as he strode off toward the station-house, "and I love you."

Peter turned and waved. "I love you too." Then he turned back, and Karen pulled from the curb and drove off.

Inside, Peter was greeted first by the desk clerk, and then by several of the uniform officers. He moved rapidly, acknowledging each comment; the worried ones from the women, and the admiring ones from the men—most of whom probably still thought car chases were like the ones in the movies. He walked into his office to be greeted by Chief Ken Jackson, former lieutenant of the Hobbs police force. He'd been promoted to chief, at least temporarily, to fill the sudden vacancy left by Chief Larsen.

Peter's first questions were all business. He was anxious to put the talk of his chase and accident behind him and get on with the important things. "Any word on Larsen? Or how about the people who kidnapped the girl?"

"Not yet," Ken said.

"It's so strange. Why wasn't there any ransom demand? And I want to know if her brother had anything to do with her ending up here."

"You think he lured her?"

Peter shrugged. "We have absolutely nothing to go on."

Jackson then added, "Oh, by the way, we haven't found the mayor's wife yet either. Funny, isn't it?"

Peter responded, "Doesn't it strike you as odd that the mayor hasn't been down here demanding results? If my wife was suddenly taken from a hospital, I'd be all over you, and every police agency in the state."

"As a matter of fact," Ken answered, "I have thought about that. And I have a rather disturbing thought on the subject."

"Like perhaps that the mayor took her?"

Ken nodded. "Makes me wonder what she might know. Somebody may have been worried about what she might blab while semi-conscious…I mean, other than that nonsense about Louisiana, that is."

Peter nodded, thinking of what George Luedke had told him. "I might decide to do a snoop-job around the mayor's house. A follow-up on the girl's assault would make a good cover story."

Ken grinned. "Just be careful, Peter. Oh, and I'm led to believe that you might need a new car."

Peter looked at him ruefully. "Yeah. Mine got too short to drive. Congratulations on the promotion to chief, by the way."

Ken waved the comment away. "It's temporary, I'm sure. But, I have some good news for you."

"Yeah?"

"As acting chief, I pulled a car out of state impound for you to drive. C'mon, I'll show you."

Ken led Peter out the back door into the department's private lot. There were two patrol units, Ken's personal car, several others belonging to civilian employees, and an older black Camaro. The Camaro immediately drew Peter's attention, and his admiration.

Ken said, "That's now your official police car. The sheriff's department confiscated it from a drug dealer passing through Hobbs last year, heading for parts north. They had a hell of a time catching it, but the driver blew a tire, and spun out on Coronado coming in from Prescott by the back road. It's an IROC, but the badging was removed to make the car less conspicuous."

Ken tossed the keys to Peter, who caught them deftly. Ken continued. "We put in a radio, and the usual magnetic light set-up. Drive it in good health, Peter, and try to avoid lamp posts this time." Peter laughed, and thanked Ken again as he climbed behind the wheel. The car had a custom seat and racecar-like double shoulder harness. If he crashed this one, there was no danger he'd fall out. He put the key in the ignition and started the car. He gunned the engine, already liking the vehicle. He waved to Ken, pulled from the parking lot, and headed for home—he'd more or less gotten permission to investigate the mayor, and he was anxious to begin.

In the deepening twilight, George moved silently through the last of the concealing brush. He'd bypassed the alarm on the fence surrounding the Stack as he'd done the one protecting the mayor's house. The cave stood before him, its entrance carefully hidden behind a large, holographic image of a hillside. In front of that, an additional barrier of dry and quite thorny Mesquite branches lay heaped. He moved to the far right side, and found an opening. He slipped behind the hologram.

Here there were obvious signs of recent digging. The cave mouth had only been excavated in the last day or two, judging by the condition of the soil— that was the reason for the hologram. He moved through the darkness into a larger cavern, and there was the ship. *So the old stories were true. Something valuable was buried here—not gold, but instead the Eribus ship.* He dropped the fold-crystal back into his pocket. With the fold-crystal out of the ship, its energy signature couldn't be detectable—but it had been stored conveniently close by…until Curt found it. He shook his head; it was a very lucky find that just might save the planet.

The spacecraft was small, angular. Planes and angles met at seemingly odd junctions, melding together into smooth, elegantly streamlined curves. The Eribus ship was a thing of unearthly beauty, built to a geometry different from that of this planet. He briefly turned on his flashlight, examining the earth. Not a mark, not even a lizard's tracks were in the soft sand. He made a mental note to smooth it out when he left.

He passed a small device over the lock and looked at the read-out. The hatchway was unsealed—a clear tribute to the megalomania of the Lewises. *Loubens.* He grinned—nothing like easy access. He glanced at his watch. He'd not have time to try to get into the house, but this was by far the most important thing he had to do today.

He put the small device back into his jacket pocket, and removed a pair of thin metallic gloves that seemed to glitter in the wan light inside the cave. In thickness and fit, they were much like the latex gloves used by the doctors and scientists of this world. They were quite different in composition, however, and with them on his hands, he was able to open the hatch without leaving prints, scents, or energy signatures. The hatch hummed open beneath his touch, and lights flickered to life. He stepped into the spaceship.

43

When Victor arrived home, it was almost six-thirty. The reporters had been incessant in their interrogations, but he'd regained his composure quickly, with the practiced tongue of a politician with five thousand years of earthly experience behind him. And though the questioning had been relentless, he was nevertheless jubilant. He hadn't become angry; he'd remained calm and collected. Some questions he answered, others he'd carefully deflected, citing ongoing investigations. He'd learned one very important fact. Neither the Paxton boy, nor the man knew where the foldship was hidden or if, in fact, it even still existed. And now they'd not have enough time to find out.

Only one thing needed to be done, and then they could disappear into the vastness of the black once more. The pyramid crystal had to be found immediately. Once he had that in his possession, the galaxy, and this entire Universe itself, would continue to be a fertile feeding ground. This small galaxy was surprisingly rich with stars and worlds without number, much more than some of the others he'd seen in their travels. Life seemed to be everywhere, and while he had no illusions that he might have it all, he'd be able to make a good try at it!

Now, walking through the front door of his home, he recalled his brief contact with the boy. It had been nothing more than an extended handshake, but the physical connection was what he'd needed to make contact with the boy's mind. He snorted a laugh. The ignorant creature hadn't even known he'd been mentally probed. He could hardly wait to tell Mary the good news. He hurried up the stairs to her bedroom. He was whistling a happy tune by the time he reached the landing. He walked down the hall, no longer feeling this body's fatigue, to the ornately carved door. He turned the latch, and opened the door. Mary was actually sitting up!

"Mary, my dear, I have good news for you."

The woman smiled at him from the upholstered chair by the window. "I know. I felt it when you touched the boy. I don't have all of my abilities back yet, but my connection with you is very strong."

"I want to use Don and Cal tonight. I want to get my hands on that pyramid. I'm no longer willing to wait."

"Are we being pressed so closely?"

"Physical biology is pressing us. An…informer who works at the hospital told me that your blood work-up had come in, and that everyone's in a spin about it. It would seem your blood cells are disintegrating—supposedly this is something completely beyond their feeble mental capabilities. They're actually worried about you. They've stepped up the search for you, and I was asked to comment on it several times today. So far no one suspects that it was I who came and took you home, but I can't believe that sooner or later someone won't make that suggestion. Right now I'd rather not kill anyone else. It'll attract too much attention.

"But, Victor, we don't have the fold-crystal. How can you be so sure we'll get it in time? Have you a plan then?"

"I do have a plan, Mary. But we have a slight problem with regard to those children and their field trip. That bus full of young school children we were going to take tomorrow won't be coming up here any time soon. I heard some news about that this very afternoon at my press conference with the Paxton boy. One of the reporters asked me to comment on the fact that the bus trip in question had been cancelled by the school because of the negative news reports about the Wells girl."

"What? But...we need those children."

"Not if we fold tomorrow, we don't."

"But...can we be ready by then? My mental abilities are coming back on-line slowly, but without the energy replacement I need from the feeding, it's going to continue to be a very slow process."

"I have a plan for that," Vic said with a mirthless grin. "I just remembered something Carl Larsen said once in passing. And here's the best part of it. This plan won't require any more mental exertion than that which might be needed for the two human emotions of empathy and love."

Mary smiled crookedly. "Why, Victor! I'm afraid I don't know anything about either one of those things." Vic laughed. "Neither do I."

Cheryl Hanson was beside herself with happiness when she'd discovered the phone call was from Curt. "Where the hell have you been? I've been so worried...you said you were sick on Friday, and couldn't take me out, and then I couldn't get ahold of you at all the next day. AND THEN, I find out from the RADIO that you're wanted by the police for something to do with that poor girl's attack!"

Curt spoke calmly. "Cher...all that arrest stuff was false. I was being framed. I even have a letter from the judge and the mayor saying so. I had my very own press conference today, and they released me—it was on the radio and TV earlier today. They let my dad and Katy go too. Now they're looking for Chief Larsen to do some explaining, but they can't seem to find him. Looks like he's flown the coop. I don't know if Carl's around yet or if he left with his dad."

"So all of this was just some kind of big misunderstanding?" She sounded doubtful.

"Looks that way. I've had a busy day, and we've just gotten home and eaten. How about I take a short nap, and I'll call you again a little later when I'm not so tired." His voice dropped to a whisper. "My dad'll be in bed by then, and we can talk without... supervision."

Cheryl giggled in spite of herself, her anger and fear now a thing of the past. "Okay, Curtis Paxton...but you better!"

"I promise," he responded, and gently put the phone back in the cradle. *That was harder and easier than I thought it would be.* Curt had told her some of the truth, of course, but he couldn't tell her all of it...she'd think he'd gone off his rocker with the rest of the town! Even now, with what he knew, he wondered just how secure his rocker might be! He wondered idly what project George had been working on while the mayor was tied up at the press conference. Curt walked into his bedroom, and today he didn't shut the door. *George'll tell me when it's time for me to know.*

Cheryl told her dad and mom that she was going to go lay down for an hour, then get up and finish her homework. They both agreed that might not be a bad idea. She walked into her bedroom, closing the door behind her.

"And that's what I want you to do." Vic looked sternly at Don, and especially at Cal. "If you even think about getting drunk tonight and you screw this up, I will personally kill you with my bare hands, Cal—you got that? Look me right in the eye and tell me you get it."

Before Cal could respond, Don asked, "If that happens, can I watch?"

"Watch? Oh, I can do much better than that, Don—I'll let you hold him down while I choke the life right out of him." Vic didn't smile as he said that, a fact that was noted by both Don and Cal.

"I'm gonna be okay," Cal protested, pouting.

Victor hissed, "This has to go off without a hitch. Got it?"

"Y...Yes, sir," Cal stammered.

Victor turned to Don and said, "And you know what's at stake here too, don't you?" And he winked.

"Yes, sir," Don reassured, thinking of the hundred thousand dollars that just might be his by later this evening. He winked back at Vic, but Cal hadn't been paying any attention to the men as they talked.

Vic said, "Good. Now you both need time to prepare. Here's the address and phone number." Don nodded, taking the slip of paper. "Are there any questions about what you're supposed to do?"

"No questions, sir," Don replied with surety.

"Excellent. Now get moving."

The mayor strode from the parlor. "Guess we need to get going," Cal said. "No wine in the car tonight."

"Aw, Don...we can wait and just use a little bit of it to celebrate when the job's done, can't we? It's good for my nerves, you know."

"No wine in the car—Vic's rules, alright? Don't complain to me about it. If you don't like it, take it up with the old man. Or better yet, ask Mary what she thinks of that idea." The thought of even talking about the weather with Mary frightened Cal badly, so he nodded meekly, and turned with Don as the other man headed down the hall toward the garage entrance.

Inside the garage, Don started giving the Mercury a quick once-over. His thoughts turned briefly to the shotgun with no firing pin. He wasn't about to make that kind of mistake with the car tonight; that was certain. He checked the air pressure in the tires, and found one of the back ones a bit low. He filled it to the recommended pressure, then opened the hood and checked the oil, brake fluid, and belts. He was very thorough. Considering what they were about to do, he wouldn't want to have a mechanical failure when they were on the job.

While Don checked the car over, Cal busied himself at the workbench. He had a small leather satchel similar to the type doctors used to use when they'd make house calls. Into this bag he dropped a roll of duct tape, three large black bandannas, a short crowbar, a heavy screwdriver with a flat point, and the zippered vinyl syringe kit Vic had already prepared for them.

He glanced over at Don. His head was still under the hood, so Cal used the opportunity to slip a pint liquor bottle into his inside jacket pocket. The bottle had been hidden behind some old rags, and was covered in dust. Cal didn't mind the dust; after all, this was his emergency survival ration. The liquor was by this time long gone, and he'd since replaced it with wine. He grinned at his cleverness. *God will provide,* he thought, *and if God don't, I will.*

And then they were ready. Don glanced at the piece of paper giving him the directions. He shoved it into his jeans pocket, already memorized, and got behind the wheel of the big green automobile. He looked at Cal, loafing by the worktable. He shouted, "You comin', you waste of skin?"

"I wish you wouldn't always be callin' me mean names, Don," Cal said, a hurt look in his eyes.

Don started the engine, and the rumbling almost drowned out his answer. "How else would you know I care?"

"But you don't care."

"No, but if I did, how else would you know?"

By now Cal was confused, and he longed for the taste of that sweet wine. Don knew about Cal's secret survival stash of wine. He didn't care; if anything at all went wrong with this little caper, Cal's drunken body would pay the price. And Don figured that was just how things were supposed to work out.

Don parked at the curb, and they both sat in the darkened auto for a few minutes. Don scanned the windows of the houses near them, and he watched the street. Parents were keeping their kids in for now—even the mayor said there were monsters out in the dark! "Okay, Cal, let's do it."

Both men tied bandannas over their lower faces, and opened their doors, pushing them closed so they'd not make any undue sound. Nevertheless, Don was reassured by the weight of the Smith and Wesson .357 Magnum he'd stuck into his waistband at the last minute. *I'm prepared...coulda' been a Boy Scout.* He snickered softly as they approached the house.

Fortunately, the shrubbery that shielded them from observation from the street didn't extend in front of the window. Getting in would be easier than he'd hoped it would be. First, he examined the edges of the glass for any sign there might be an alarm. There was none. Then he gently shoved on the window. It was locked. Don cursed under his breath; he'd have to do it the hard way.

He tapped Cal's shoulder, and the wino jumped. For a moment, Don thought he might yell out, but he didn't. Don whispered, "Gimme the crowbar."

Cal handed the instrument to Don. He put the wide, flat end under the window frame, and put his weight on it. The latch, not completely turned, slipped a little bit, and then grudgingly released its hold on the window. There'd hardly been a sound. Don grinned. Those old turn-latches were frequently not properly latched. He noiselessly lifted the window, carefully parting the drapes. He withdrew his head, and motioned for Cal to give him the syringe and the duct tape.

Cal handed the items to Don, who immediately climbed through the window, and into the darkened bedroom. Cal, watching through the window, licked his lips, wondering if the girl would be naked.

Cheryl awoke with a gloved hand pressed firmly over her mouth. She tasted the leather. There was a sharp pressure on her upper arm, then a sharper pain. She could feel herself relaxing into the arms of the strange man in the mask. Though she felt unspeakable fear, she couldn't seem to shout very loudly. She couldn't move her arms either. She was drifting now, falling into a terrifying numbness. The strange man released her, but she no longer cared.

Don quickly wrapped the girl's ankles with duct tape, and then he did the same to her wrists, binding them securely. The gag, made from the third bandanna, was twisted and tied tightly into the girl's mouth. Satisfied that Vic's drug concoction had rendered the girl senseless, he lifted her, and walked to the window, handing her out to Cal. As soon as Cal got out of the way, Don climbed out, took the girl, and headed for the car with Cal following. Behind him, through the window he'd just forced open, Don heard a telephone ringing. *Better move.*

Don ran the last three yards to the Mercury, and as soon as Cal had the back door open, he tossed the girl unceremoniously onto the back seat. Cal climbed into the back, as Don ran around to the driver's side, got behind the wheel and drove away into the night.

Don watched Cal in the rearview mirror. He was staring at the unconscious girl, with an almost dazed look on his face. "Don't even think about it, Cal. Vic wants her completely unharmed."

"I'm not gonna hurt her," Cal said softly, "I'm just makin' sure nothin' got broke when we were gettin' her outta the house."

"Well stop it, or I'll tell Vic...and Mary." That was enough to make Cal keep his hands to himself.

A short time later, Kent rapped on his son's bedroom door. Curt, still dressed, rose sleepily from his bed. He opened the door, and looked at his dad. Kent said, "There's some guy on the phone. Says he needs to talk to you right now."

"I'm coming," Curt said as he half-stumbled, still groggy into the hallway.

"You Curt Paxton?" The voice was rough, menacing.

"Yes, this is Curt."

"I got something you might be interested in trading for."

"What's that?"

"Curt?" Cheryl's voice carried terror inside of it. "They want me to tell you to bring that crystal to where they say or they'll chop me up."

44

Cheryl sat, a musty canvas bag tied over her head. She was secured to a chair, but she had no idea where she was—it was in this chair, and under this bag that she'd regained consciousness. She remembered being grabbed up from her bed—the sharp poke…and then nothing until she'd awakened, bound like this. She surmised she'd been drugged, though her captors so far had been uncommunicative. After the brief telephone conversation with Curt, which took place through the canvas, the man had snatched back the phone, pushed a button on it, and said, "He's waiting for your call, sir."

But someone else was there in the room as well—another man. He made a vile snorting noise when he breathed that reminded Cheryl of a pig. Now the two men were whispering, and the pig uttered a frightening giggle, to which the other man responded with a definitive, "No!" The pig was grumbling when the phone rang once more. The pig kept up his grumbling until the other man told him to shut up. Apparently, the pig wasn't in charge. Cheryl thought that was probably a good thing for her.

"Yeah?" It was the pig's friend. "Alright, sir, I'll be right up."

Up, Cheryl thought. *I must be in a basement, then, if the pig's friend had to go 'up' to see the man in charge.* Her hope faded. She'd seen enough movies about bound women, basements, and strange men. She felt terror returning, filling the space that hope had recently vacated.

She heard the door close, and a moment later the pig was at her side, that horrible snuffling sound very close to her cheek. She pulled away, disgusted. She could smell his odors even through the musty canvas that encircled her head. She felt her nausea rising. He smelled of unwashed clothing, and stale… something.

Death.

The word came unbidden and wild into her thoughts, carried there by the rushing black waters of terror. *This is what death smells like.*

And then the pig touched her.

Curt sat for a moment, bound by indecision. Then he got up. He had to contact George; he'd know what to do. In fact, he'd probably be the only person in Hobbs who would know what to do. He was the only one who really knew what was going on in this town. And, as if in some mental connection, the telephone rang. Curt jumped up, snatching the receiver to his ear.

"Curt, are you free?" George's voice sounded calm.

"Yes. And we have a problem."

George listened calmly as Curt told him about the two phone calls that had followed in rapid succession. "George…they want the pyramid. They'll kill Cheryl if we don't return it at midnight tonight."

"Where do they want to meet us?"

"In Prescott, at a garage that's closed. The man said there was a big sign on a metal pole right next to the building that says Lindhart Gas and Mechanical Service; it's on Gurley Street."

George sighed. "Alright, I know of the place, Curt. That's the same Lindhart who lied about last year's werewolf killing. He was found dead early this morning. Somebody dropped a truck on him and crushed him." George paused, then added, "This is a message as well, Curt."

"So what do we do?"

"We have no choice. We will surrender the crystal."

"What? After all this?" Curt was indignant. There had to be something else they could do. "What if we call that detective? The police are good at finding kidnappers and things like that."

"If they get wind of the police being present, all is lost," George responded calmly. It's better to give them the crystal, get your girlfriend back safely, and then we can regroup."

"How do we do this?"

"Just as they say we should. I'm coming right now to pick you up. Stay inside your house until I get there."

"Yes, sir," Curt responded, and immediately began pacing the floor nervously looking at his watch, as though he could speed up the time he had to wait.

After what seemed an age, George pulled up in front of Curt's home, still driving the Volkswagen. Curt quickly locked his house, and ran down to where George was waiting. He jumped into the vehicle, slamming the door behind him. "Let's go," he urged. George stepped on the accelerator, and the car pulled smoothly from the curb. They drove for a time in silence.

It was Curt who eventually broke that silence. "I didn't tell my dad."

"That's for the best."

"I hate lying to him."

"You're probably saving his life, you know."

Curt sighed. "I suspect you're right, but it still feels funny."

"This will all be finished, one way or another, sometime in the next twenty-four hours, Curt. Then you can go back to your normal life."

Curt snorted a laugh, as though George had told him a joke. "What kind of life could possibly be normal after all this?"

"Are you planning to go to college?"

The sudden change in subject caught Curt by surprise. He nodded. "Yes.

"Are you going to major in art?"

"Yes…I think that the human spirit and the Universe are connected in some way; each is not a separate thing. You've said as much yourself when you told me about Eribus. Seeing and reaching for beauty in art is part of what makes us…it's part of what keeps us human. The other part is our daring to look into the dark, unknown places; the possibly dangerous places just to see what's there. And to sometimes be startled by the sudden flash of beauty like the unfolding of butterfly wings."

"You have a saying in this world—'curiosity killed the cat.'"

"Yes. I know now that saying is wrong. It should be 'curiosity defines the cat.'" George nodded in agreement. They pulled behind the motel and parked. They waited in George's room until it was time for the meeting.

Cheryl sat silently in the back seat of the Mercury. She was beyond emotion by now, numbly sitting passively next to the pig in the back seat. The bag over her head was still tightly tied, and she vaguely felt the pig pressing himself against her. It was getting progressively harder to breathe. She was tiring— tiring of everything. She didn't move when the pig touched her arm. She was beyond movement. All of this was happening to someone else. This wasn't Cheryl's life anymore…it was someone else's…it had to be, it just…had to be.

Cal spoke, impatience evident in his voice. "How much longer, Don? I'm gettin' hungry back here."

Don didn't respond immediately, calmly surveying the darkness that enveloped the closed garage. In the moonlight he could vaguely make out the strips of yellow police tape that stretched across each window and door of Lindhart's business. Finally he spoke. He taunted Cal. "If you didn't go an' break your watch, you'd know what time it is."

Cal huffed, and Don grinned. "It's five to twelve, moron, get ready."

Just then they saw the headlights of a car as it came around the turn and pulled into the parking lot. It stopped, thirty feet from the Mercury. The driver left the engine running, headlights on. The passenger door opened, and a dark shape stepped out. It was the boy. He was holding something in his hand; it was a metal box. He clutched it tightly against his chest. Don knew instinctively it was whatever that thing was that Vic and Mary were so hot to take back. All he cared about was his hundred thousand.

Don watched as Curt set the box on the ground between them, and stepped back two paces. He turned to the back seat. "Go get it."

"I thought you were gonna get it," Cal whined.

"I am…eventually. You're gonna go get it now, and make sure it's real. And then I'll show the girl."

Cal grumbled, but he stepped from the car, and walked forward into the bright pool of light between the two autos. He stopped two paces from the box. He heard the Merc's door open behind him, and then the heavy crunching of Don's footsteps accompanying the scuffling, stumbling footsteps of the girl. He held his breath.

Don shouted, "I let you see the girl, and he gets to open the box to check what's inside." The boy said nothing; he was only a black silhouette in the high beams of the Volkswagen. Don roughly pulled the hood from Cheryl's head. She squinted and turned from the lights, raising her bound arms defensively.

"Cal, bring the box to me, now." A different voice; it seemed deliberately disguised—someone was standing in the darkness behind the Mercury. Cal complied, carrying the box into the darkness. Vic opened the lid, and smiled. "Alright, he said. We're done here. Wait ten minutes." There was the sound of a car engine being started, and the chirp and clatter of gravel being spun up by wheels in the dark. The car drove away, headlights off until it was well away from the garage.

"Go back to your car, and I'll bring the girl," Don said quietly. Curt complied, and when he was standing by the passenger side door, Don grinned and pulled a revolver from under his jacket. He turned, and fired four rounds through the windshield into the driver's seat of the Volkswagen. Before Curt could respond, the big revolver was pointed in his direction. "We…that would be Cal and I, decided that we'd keep the girl for a while yet."

Curt took a step closer. "I wouldn't do that," Don warned, waving the revolver. "You'll get her back in a few days. Cal and I want to take her for a test drive first, if you know what I mean." He laughed, and turned the gun to Cheryl's head. "Now you be a good boy, and get back in that car and think about where you're going to bury your friend." He laughed as he dragged Cheryl back to the waiting Mercury, tossed her into the back seat with Cal, and thundered away back up the road to Hobbs.

"George!" Curt shouted as he leaped into the VW. He looked over, expecting to see a riddled corpse. Instead, George sat there calmly looking at him. "How…" Curt began.

George opened his shirt, and Curt caught a glimpse of something metallic; or was it just flickering light that looked like metal? The old man closed his shirt again. Curt said, "You wore a bulletproof vest."

"Something like that," he responded. "Though I'm glad he only used a ballistic weapon." With that enigmatic comment hanging in the air, he turned the VW and also headed back toward Hobbs. "Let's go get Cheryl, shall we?"

The IROC Z28 was standing, engine idling in the darkness, lights extinguished along the road leading from Prescott. Peter Davis recalled the words of the mysterious caller. "You want the green Mercury? Here's where you'll find it." So, here he was, waiting. A few minutes later, a Plymouth Valiant drove by. He ignored it. A moment later, there was the Merc, just as the caller had said.

Peter pulled smoothly from the side of the road, picking up his radio. "They're coming. Be ready." Then he turned on his flashers and siren, and rocketed down the road behind the Merc.

"Cops are behind us, Don."

"Nobody can catch this car, he said with confidence as he floored the accelerator. He glanced in the mirror. Those headlights were gaining on him. "Damn," he said, shoving the shifter into fourth gear.

45

Cheryl sat in the back seat of the Mercury. In their hurry, they'd forgotten to replace the canvas bag over her head. She could breath once more. Someone was chasing them; she could hear a siren wailing a distance behind them. The pig, whom she now knew was a disgusting little man called Cal, was clearly worried…he'd taken his hands off of her. He was swilling something that smelled bad from a dirty glass bottle. *Oh, Curt. Did they shoot you? Did you have to die for me?* The Mercury lurched forward, gaining speed, and suddenly Cheryl came to a realization. *A person with nothing left to lose, and everything to lose, is a very dangerous person…*

Peter Davis saw the car ahead suddenly swerve. He grabbed the mic. "Unit seven, we need paramedics and uniforms at my location. NOW!"

Cheryl, forgotten for the moment, lifted her arms, and brought them down over Don's head. She leaned back hard, grunting with effort. She strained backward, putting both feet against the back of the driver's seat. Taken by surprise, Don momentarily released the steering wheel, and the car lurched crazily to the right. Don gagged—he couldn't catch his breath, and he knew the duct tape would never break. He was clawing frantically at his throat. The girl was saying something.

"How does that feel? You can't have me; I choose not to let you." She leaned back even harder. By now the pig had seen what was happening, and he was struggling with the girl—but her bound wrists were under Don's chin, and the harder he struggled with her, the harder it became for Don to breathe.

Peter watched in fascinated horror as the Mercury suddenly swerved to the right again, almost sideswiping a cottonwood tree, then left, across the dividing line on the road. And then the car went into a spin, striking a dirt embankment. The engine coughed, sputtered, and shut down. Quantities of steam were coming from under the hood. The two undamaged doors, both on the driver's side, opened as Peter skidded to a stop.

Don staggered out. The girl's arms had released their grip on impact. Now Cal was pushing her out the back door. Don could hear sirens approaching. He grinned, grabbing the girl, pushing the muzzle of the revolver against her temple. Cal was beside them now, holding an open switchblade that glittered in the Camaro's headlamps. They looked into the glare and could see only the silhouette of a man.

"Drop the piece," the faceless man said.

"No, you drop yours, or I drop the babe."

"Last warning. I'm counting to three."

Don barked out a laugh, and that was when there was a sound of thunder, and a .45 caliber slug whistled past Cheryl's ear, impacting Don just under his nose. The round traveled through his mouth, almost unimpeded, and into the base of his brain. For an instant, though already dead, he stood as his grip released. Cheryl fell away, and Peter fired three more rounds in rapid succession into Don's chest. Then he turned the Colt pistol toward Cal.

In the bright glare of the headlamps, Cal could see the finest wisp of gun smoke drifting up from the faceless man's pistol. The smoke glowed in the light, and seemed to Cal to be a living thing, a dragon, perhaps. "Don't shoot me! Don't shoot me!" the man squealed. Peter thought he sounded like a frightened pig. And then the pig's bladder let go. He dropped his knife, and dropped to his knees. "You said you'd count to three!"

"You take your cinema way too seriously," Peter responded, keeping the Colt pistol trained on the cowering man.

As Cal was begging for his life and promising to tell all, four Yavapai County sheriff cars closed in from both directions. Behind them were two ambulances from Prescott. They blocked the road as the medics examined the girl, and the recently deceased Donald Bristow. Peter's head came up. A car was approaching. He turned.

Behind him, a Volkswagen Fox had just stopped at the roadblock. Peter walked up. He was only mildly surprised when he saw George and Curt step from the vehicle. "Now why am I not surprised to see you two?"

George ignored the question. "Is the girl safe?"

"Yes," Peter answered. "They're prepping her for the ambulance right now." He pointed behind him, and Curt took off at a run. "So, George, how have you been?"

"I'm fine, thank you. We negotiated a trade for the girl's life, but they reneged on the deal."

"Why would they kidnap Curt's girlfriend?"

"He had something they wanted."

"And what might that have been, and who, exactly, are 'they'?"

"Cheryl!"

The girl sat up on the gurney, grinning. "Curt! I thought they killed you."

They hugged, as the ambulance attendants waited, giving the young lovers some time.

"Nope. Not me. They killed my friend though."

"But…"

Curt laughed. "He has a bullet proof vest. Cher…when I got that phone call, I was willing to do anything…anything, to get you safely home."

"And I am, Curt. Whatever you gave them in that box saved my life. They'd have killed me right away otherwise." She lowered her head. "They did…other things, Curt." She looked up. "Do you still love me? Can you?"

"I'll love you forever, Cheryl. When they called, I thought my life was at an end. I couldn't bear the idea of living without you."

"But…"

"No buts. The future begins now." They embraced again, and an ambulance medic coughed. Curt and Cheryl laughed. She said, "They have a job to do." She looked into Curt's eyes, sensing more than seeing the steely resolve. "You have a job to do too, don't you?"

"Yes. And tomorrow all this will be behind us."

"You're coming home…aren't you?"

"No power on this planet…or any other will prevent that." He kissed her one more time, and then the paramedics rolled the gurney to the rear of the ambulance, and lifted it inside. The doors closed, and Curt watched as they drove off in an aura of red and blue, heading back toward Prescott.

When Curt got back to the VW, he heard George and the detective having a conversation. He interrupted them. "Cheryl's going to be okay, I think. She wasn't hurt in the crash. She saved herself, really."

Peter nodded. "That's one brave girl you've got there, Curtis Paxton. Can you live up to her example?" He grinned.

"I…I," Curt stammered.

Peter laughed. "George told me you fellows have something to do that would be best done alone."

"And?"

Peter stared at Curt, hard eyed. "It's against my better judgment, but I'm going to let you two go. Do what needs to be done to end this."

George said, "Thank you, Detective Davis. Though you may not believe me, you are saving your world from extinction."

Peter looked at the older man skeptically. "You better get going, before I change my mind and just go back to thinking you're crazy."

George nodded. "I concur."

A uniformed Yavapai County deputy approached. "Detective Davis. We need some kind of statement from you."

"Nope," Peter replied resolutely, "I have nothing to say at this time. You'll get a full report after I speak to my superiors and an attorney."

"Very well," the deputy said, "we'll be in touch with your organization."

Peter smiled at the young deputy. "Thanks. And, could you fellows move your units? These two have nothing to do with this investigation, so they should be allowed to go on their way."

The deputy looked suspiciously at George and Curt. Finally he said, "I don't see why not." He waved, and the sheriff's cruiser was backed up to make room for the Volkswagen Fox.

George glanced at Curt. "Get in—now."

Curt complied with George's order, and as they passed the roadblock, the deputy noticed the bullet holes in the windshield. "Hey, wait a minute…"

Peter said calmly. "I didn't want to say anything, deputy. That man is a Special Agent with the FBI. He's on an entirely different case; he was in Prescott investigating the strange death of that garage owner neither the Prescott police…nor your department has been able to solve."

"Why does a killing in Prescott interest the FBI? Why's there a boy with him?"

"He didn't say. He liaised with us, because of the connection with the girl killed last year. Whatever he's working on, it's vital, he tells me, that it remain a secret. Telling you is a courtesy—please don't make me regret it."

The deputy's superior came up just then and asked him to search the Mercury. The supervisor, an old friend of Peter's smiled. "Sorry about that. He's been on the job a few months, and he's still learning his way around."

"Not a problem, Bill. With the questions he asked, I'd say he's going to be a good man."

"What do we do now?" Curt asked. "They got the little pyramid. Looks to me like we're screwed."

George laughed. "Not at all. But, I do have a small confession to make. I didn't tell you the entire truth."

So as they wound their way back through the darkness toward Hobbs, George explained. "I told you we had no idea where their ship was hidden. I lied."

"Why?"

"Tell me, Curt. When you were at that big to-do with the mayor, did he touch you? Maybe shake your hand?"

"Of course he did. What's that got to do with anything?"

"He's not like Mary, but he would've linked consciousness with you at that point. He read your mind. He has no idea that I do know exactly where their ship is hidden, and that I've been inside it."

Curt stared in amazement. "But that doesn't matter, since we gave him the crystal."

"Yes," George agreed. "But we have more surprises for him as well."

46

Victor Lewis turned into the driveway of the mansion on the hill. Time was short, and they needed to get moving. It was time to shed this world. He hit the brakes hard, and the Valiant slid to a stop before the closed garage door. He pounded up the steps, rapidly fumbling the key into the lock. He opened the door, and headed up the steps to Mary's room. He flung open the door, and stopped in his tracks. Mary looked bad. She'd aged significantly since he last saw her only this morning. He ran to her, helping her to her feet.

"Are we taking a bath?"

"No," Vic responded. "We don't have time for that. I have the crystal. We're leaving, right now. Come on." He helped her walk to the door, and by a sort of osmosis, he transferred some of his biological life energy to Mary. She stood straighter, and smiled. "I guess then, we'd best be going."

Vic grinned, and they moved down the stairs side by side. Vic was glad in a way that they were leaving. They'd had a good run here on this planet—much longer than they'd been able to stay on Eribus. And, the imaginations of the human biological specimens were much more…vivid than they'd been on Eribus. Through their long span of time in this Universe, they'd found that imaginative intensity to be a rare commodity.

To be sure, many worlds had highly developed life forms that supplied a rich stew of fear and terror; but on this world—the feeding had been inordinately rich, as though every energy meal was what the young creatures of this world might call, 'a yummy dessert.'

But there was also the disadvantage of having to take on a biological form. The first time was in Erieuxta. Later, in the place now called Egypt, that hadn't been necessary. They were considered to be divine beings right from the time of their arrival. But that pleasure and freedom had been short-lived.

And so they'd taken on the biology of the planet. And they'd done that before, but it locked them into that form until they were ready to leave the planet. It was…limiting, and after the metamorphosis, they were required to supply their biological forms with the sustenance of this world.

The blood baths had been a stroke of genius on Mary's part. Each time they did this, they could absorb not only the life force, fear, and terror, but also the very building blocks of a physical body—the DNA structures of the dead. This proved to have two advantages, they'd discovered. The first was the obvious one; they could indefinitely prolong the lives of their biological forms. The other was not so obvious. By using the DNA of their food they could adapt their shapes to some extent, changing eye colors, shapes of facial features, and the like.

Given a relatively short period of time, they could transform themselves into completely different looking beings. This was a real advantage when one needed to flee a region in a hurry. But now that was all at an end. It was time to close down this feeding ground—and like all their others, if they couldn't have it, they'd make certain that nobody else would either. Vic grinned as he helped Mary into the jeep he'd pulled from the garage.

Once he'd cleared the driveway and turned toward the Stack, he opened a compartment on the console beside him and lifted out a small box, handing it to Mary. He sighed. It was most annoying to have to do all these things with physical exertion—but biological beings didn't make ships that would respond to the mind, at least they'd not found one yet. They raced up the road to the Stack. In four-wheel drive, Victor Lewis and his wife easily made it to the fence. He unlocked the gate, and they drove through. They stopped at the crest of the hill, next to the chimney. Mary handed him the small box he'd given her. He pushed the button on top of it, and dropped the control box into his pocket.

In the cave below the Stack, the Eribus ship lit up. Emitting a soft bluish glow from its angles and planes, it lifted from the hard ground and moved forward, floating through the hologram that then winked out. It hummed slightly as it drifted up into the night sky, turning its blunt, beveled nose toward the cyclopean darkness that was the incinerator chimney. It moved forward slowly—floating in its magnetic field.

George was driving fast. He took the turns on Hobbs Hill Road at a speed that made Curt want to shut his eyes. George glanced at him. "Don't worry, Curt...we'll get there in time."

"That's not what I'm worried about."

George laughed. "We'll be there shortly." He slammed the shifter into fourth as he accelerated out of a turn.

Ahead, barely lit by...something...the Stack rose, almost a black silhouette against the storm clouds that were gathering. Lightning flashed.

"He's activated the Eribus ship," George said matter-of-factly.

"So we're too late?"

"Nope. We're going to be right on time."

The Eribus ship was coming down to the ground near the Stack. As it descended, it emitted a soft blue radiance below it. Vic turned to Mary. "I have to retrieve some things from the incinerator. I'll be right back." Mary nodded.

Vic ran into the dark interior of the Stack. While the Paxton boy had found the hidden crystal, there were other secrets behind other stones he hadn't found. Using a small flashlight, he located the opening in the interior wall where the boy had found the crystal, its cover stone still lying in the sand below the opening. He counted seven bricks to the right, and three up. Satisfied, he took a knife from his pocket, flicked it open and began cutting away the mortar holding the large stone in place.

The mortar had softened with age. It had been there since 1947 when Vic had repaired the original seal he'd put there in 1897. Now the mortar, really only plaster of Paris, gave easily beneath the sharp steel of the knife. He pulled the brick from its place, tossing it to the ground. He shone the light into the opening. Then he smiled. It was still there. He reached in, retrieving the box made of a metal not of this Earth.

"Got it," he called to Mary. He turned, and stepped from the Stack. In the end, he was surprised at how easily the prey of this world could be intimidated. Still, it hadn't been all that different on Eribus. Biological creatures were simply…inferior to their masters, especially when it came to sly trickery and sleight of hand. He laughed, relieved that soon he'd be able to shed this confining and frustrating cluster of cells and organs.

George and Curt were almost to the turn that led to the Stack. Above them, the sky was churning, lightning flashed.

Curt stared in amazement. "A storm? Now?"

"It's being caused by the Eribus ship. The electromagnetic disturbances that surround the vehicle are causing this…it's nothing to be overly concerned about. In the end, it will mean nothing."

"You seem awfully sure of yourself," Curt said, staring at George as he downshifted into the turn, tapped the brakes lightly, and stepped on the accelerator once more.

"Patience, Curt," George responded enigmatically. "You'll see everything and understand in due time."

"Do we need the police?"

"I am the police," George responded matter-of-factly, as he slid the Volkswagen through the last curve. "I'm the only police who can do anything to bring this thing to an end."

Ahead, the eerie glow of the Eribus ship lit the Stack, making the old bricks seem to glow with their own phosphorescence. And above, the lightning crackled and the thunder rumbled, as though the sky itself had been offended by the mere presence of these beings.

Vic returned quickly to where Mary waited, leaning against the side of the car. A hundred feet away, the Eribus ship hung motionless, mere inches from the earth, cushioned, it seemed, by the blue radiance below it. He smiled. "I have the drive key and the detonator. Are you ready?"

"I've been ready for a very long time." She smiled.

"Then let us be on our way." He looked up into the Milky Way. "There are many other worlds we can eat." They walked to the ship, and Vic passed the control over the hatch. It opened with a slight hum, and the radiance of the control panels flooded into the night. He helped Mary up, and was about to climb in himself, when he was bathed in the bright white of automobile headlights. He turned, cursing.

George slid the Fox to a stop, and opened his door. Curt stepped out the other side. Vic looked at them and laughed. George was very calm. He walked forward and said, "You are in my custody."

Vic laughed again, and swung up into the ship. He showed George and Curt the pyramid. "I hope you have a very unpleasant death." Then the door hummed shut behind him, and the radiance below the ship intensified.

"He's getting away!"

George turned to Curt, grinned, and walked back to the car and opened the trunk. "Come here, and have a look." Curt walked back, feeling defeated. In the trunk of the auto he saw three metal panels about six inches by ten. They had what looked to Curt to be some kind of small electronic components, but they were black and fused, as though they'd been exposed to intense heat. Curt look up at George questioningly.

"That," George explained, "is what's left of their fold-drive."

"I don't understand," Curt said.

"Without that equipment in operational order, their ship cannot fold—even with the crystal. They can't disappear to some far reach of this or some other galaxy. I didn't just find their ship; I disabled it. It matters not that they now have the crystal. By the time they realize what I've done, we'll have them in custody."

"We?"

George just smiled, and pointed. "I also told you I didn't have time to call for reinforcements. Victor Lewis…or whatever it wishes to call itself, would also have gleaned that information from your mind in its office that day. But it could only learn what was in your mind, not what was really happening."

The Eribus ship was now beginning to rise slowly into the air, dust eddying in tiny, luminous whirlwinds below it. And then Curt saw something else. A greenish-blue phosphorescent cloud had detached itself from the thunderheads, and was drifting over the Stack, and the Eribus ship. Then Curt saw what was inside that light. He stared, trying to make sense of what he was seeing.

An immense…something, hovered there, a little more than a hundred feet from the ground. The object itself reminded Curt of a butterfly, though the comparison was absurd. The thing was black, looking more like the framework of a gigantic butterfly, frozen in mid-flight, its giant wings seemingly locked at a slightly upturned angle. The object was huge, almost two hundred feet from wingtip to wingtip. And the wings, if that's what they really were, seemed merely a delicate framework constructed like the veins in that impossible butterfly's wings. And between those veins, over and around them, strange lightning flashed and coruscated over the metal in strobe-like flashes of green, purple, red, and yellow. The earth all around the Stack was lit in bright flashes of color. The thing was awe inspiring in its beauty, and in the immense power that was reflected in that otherworldly beauty.

"My reinforcements are here," George said. He turned to Curt. "Without its fold-drive, they cannot shed their biological shells. When it came here, there's one thing it didn't know about this particular Universe. Whatever laws of physics…or laws of magic that govern wherever it came from in the beginning, don't work here. By taking a biological form, it made a kind of contract, if you will, with this Universe.

"I think it came to realize this first on Eribus. That was where it learned about bathing in the blood of the young to restore its biological hosts, but at that time it had an operating fold-drive. At fold, it was able to shed its Eribus biology, returning to…whatever it is in reality.

"After planetfall here, it didn't want to make the same mistake. It tried imitating a Divine being but, eventually, it was seduced by the intensity of emotion, vision, hearing, and thinking of the peoples of Earth. It trapped itself once more in a physical form."

"And now?"

"And now it has condemned itself. Mary knew it in the hospital, I believe. She could feel herself dying…not just her body, but also her actual existence. That's something it never felt before in all its long span of existence. That was something it hadn't planned for, and came to fear. It would happily expunge the life from other entities, feeding on emotions and anguish, but to feel that same experience was so beyond its ability to comprehend, it simply denied it until it could no longer. Now it will finally come to know the meaning of entropy as its energy fades without possible restoration."

THE DEVIL'S RIFLE

"You keep calling them it…"

George paused, trying to find the explanation. "There is only one entity. It manifested in two forms because that is the way of life in this part of the galaxy, at least. It was probably unintentional, truth be told. If you remember the Egypt story, its first manifestation here was female—the goddess Serket. But that changed by the time of the first Scorpion King. It may have divided in the manner of a one-celled being here on this planet. It may have…given birth to itself, another one of this planet's many stories of virgin birth perhaps. In any event, it became weaker, each half having to rely on and safeguard the other."

"That's why it had to move around so much," Curt realized aloud. "And on some level, it must have realized the threat to its existence—if one died, both died."

George grinned. "You know, you're pretty good at this!"

Curt laughed. "Before you ask me to go with you to hunt monsters, I need to tell you I plan on going to college, and loving Cheryl."

"She is fearful that when you leave for college, you'll find someone else while she finishes up her senior year here in Hobbs. She isn't against you going to college, you know—she's afraid of losing you."

"Then I guess I'll have to convince her that won't happen."

"You risked your life to save her—I think she got that message," George laughed.

"So what happens to…it?"

"Our ship will carry the Eribus ship out of Earth's orbit, and release it into space. It will travel a trajectory that will never bring it close to any star system. Eventually, if the thing inside finds a way to survive, it'll head out at almost light speed into the Great Black, far out beyond all the stars. There, it will travel the void for eternity…or for however long this Universe may exist."

A hatch opened in the butterfly's belly. "It is time for me to leave now, Curtis Paxton. It has been a privilege and an honor to live here on your beautiful world, and to have been able to work with you." He reached into his jacket pocket, and handed Curt a white metal five-pointed star. Across the center were engraved characters that appeared to Curt to be something like Runes, or hieroglyphs, perhaps.

"That," George explained, "is my badge. You see? I really am a police officer!"

"Thank you," Curt said quietly. "Thank you for this, and especially for showing me the wonderful and terrifying possibilities of light and darkness. You've opened my eyes, and for that I could never repay you."

"There's one thing you could do for me."

"Anything."

"In ten Earth years, we'll come back to make sure everything is the way it should be. At that time, I would be honored to receive a painting done by a famous artist by the name of Curtis Paxton." He smiled. "I collect art."

"How will you find me?"

"I can find anybody. I'm a detective, remember?"

"Can I ask just one more question?"

"Certainly, Curt."

"Is this what you really look like? Are you like us? You don't…kill to have a body, do you?"

George laughed. "No, Curt, this is not my true form. But unlike that other, we use an artificial biology to give us the forms of the worlds we protect. But form is not what defines us, Curt. We are defined by what we do and how we live, not by what we look like. On your world, could there be two creatures more different yet so alike in the radiance of their love as human and canine?" Curt could only shake his head. "I rest my case, Your Honor," George said in his best courtroom voice.

They shook hands then, and George turned toward that thing of radiant, ethereal beauty that hovered over the Stack. A platform descended from inside the ship in a beam of dazzling white light, and George stepped onto it. He waved once, and was lifted into the belly of the butterfly. The next moment, it shot up into the air at an impossible speed, soaring in a majestic spiral, dragging the Eribus ship with it up…up at an ever-increasing speed. It bored a hole through the thunderheads, lighting them from within with its stunning strobes of red, purple, green, and yellow. And then a cleansing rain began to fall.

Curt walked back to the Volkswagen, and curiously looked into the still open trunk. He smiled. The alien circuitry was gone. Then he was suddenly illuminated by the bright headlights of a black Chevrolet Camaro Z28 IROC. Curt lifted his hand in greeting to detective Davis and put the extraterrestrial lawman's badge into his pocket.

47

The following day, the Arizona Department of Public Safety, along with Yavapai County Sheriff's deputies and the Hobbs police, forcibly entered the Victorian mansion just off of Hobbs Hill Road. A young, anonymous caller who sounded to Peter Davis a lot like Curt Paxton, suggested that the mayor and his wife would be found dead in the basement. During a thorough search of the premises, it was Peter Davis who discovered the entry to the sub-basement. And what was discovered there appalled the police officers.

Locked in small, lightless cells with no sanitation facilities, they found seven youngsters ranging in age from about five to sixteen. None of the younger children were able to speak, and could only stare at their rescuers with either blank, emotionless eyes, or with looks of fearful anticipation. The only one at all communicative identified himself as Bobby Wells, Sarah's brother. But he was clearly very confused and was taken to the hospital along with the others.

Another room in that concrete sub-basement contained an ancient claw-foot bathtub with chipped porcelain. The inside was stained dark brown, and what had initially been interpreted as age and dirt was shortly revealed by the beams of flashlights to be bloodstains. Disgusted and sickened, Peter walked out through the garage and into the cool October breeze. He looked around, shaking his head. Someone tapped his shoulder and he turned.

"You alright Peter?"

Peter looked at Chief Jackson and nodded. "Hard to believe, Ken," he said, "all this time right under our noses. What the hell were the Lewises into anyway? Was it a religious cult thing?" Ken could only shake his head; it was too much to consider right now. They stood silently for a moment, letting the cleansing air wash over them. But Peter Davis was a detective, and he surveyed the surrounding land. Something had caught his attention, some small movement. "What's that?"

Ken scanned the distance. "What?"

"Over there by the fence," Peter commented, starting forward. Ken followed. Fortunately, the breeze was blowing in the other direction, so the first indicator they got was the buzzing of the cloud of flies that had gathered on the corpse. When they moved forward, the flies grudgingly vacated their meal. Being careful to disturb nothing, the two police officers looked at the cadaver. The young man's face was so damaged, that visual identification would not be possible.

The hatchet that lay close by was obviously the cause of that damage. One of the boy's hands lay splayed in the grass a short distance from the rest of the body. On the middle finger was a large gold signet ring bearing the initials CL. The two men looked at each other. Now they knew why they hadn't been able to find Carl Larsen.

"He's chopped up pretty good," Ken commented. "You think his dad did this?" Peter shook his head, just as a deputy shouted and gestured for them to come back into the mansion.

"I thought you should see this," the deputy said. He was pale. They walked down into the basement. By the furnace, a number of technicians and policemen stood staring. Ken and Peter pushed their way through. In a small storage room beside the furnace there lay a disordered heap of small bones, and four skulls, obviously those of children. They walked away, both grateful that this would be a job for the techs.

"How long ago do you suppose the Larsen boy was murdered?"

Peter responded, "I'm no tech, but I'd guess several days at least."

"I'm thinking the same thing. Hank's had days to make tracks. You think we'll ever catch up to him?"

"Nobody can run forever, Ken. Sooner or later he'll pop up somewhere and we'll get him."

They were sitting in Ken's office three days later when the telephone rang. Ken answered, and then handed the receiver to Peter. "It's your girl, Peter."

"Karen! How're things at the hospital?" He listened intently, thanked her, and hung up. He turned to Ken. "Sarah Wells's doctor in Tucson called. She's awakened but can remember very little about what happened. They're certain her memory'll come back gradually, and with the help of psychologists, hopefully it won't be too traumatic.

"The Wells girl did say one interesting thing…she was violently adamant that she would not now, nor ever, allow anyone to hypnotize her. They think she was under hypnosis when she was held captive and confined in the mayor's basement. All she remembers right now is running into the woods. She says she was attacked by Mary Lewis there, and by Carl Larsen and Brutus."

Ken interrupted. "Brutus?"

"Yeah…seems the dog we were looking for belonged to the chief's son. She was pretty sure she killed it. Funny though, she insists she also killed Mary Lewis; claims to have cut a blood vein in her brain."

Ken shook his head. "She's obviously not thinking clearly. We may never know exactly what happened."

"What matters most is that it's over."

"Amen to that! Say, aren't you up for a couple weeks leave?"

"I've been busy."

"Yeah, I know…wrecking cars and proposing to pretty girls. I think you ought to spend some quality time with your bride-to-be, don't you?"

"We agreed to get married when this was over."

"Then what the hell are you waiting for?"

Peter grinned, giving an exaggerated salute. "Yes, sir!"

"Go on, get outa here." Peter grinned, and left by the back door.

Neither Ken nor Peter would be the ones to discover the elusive Hank Larsen's hiding place. He wouldn't be found until the next spring when urban hikers from Phoenix would find a skeleton a short distance from an obscure hiking path in the hills above Hobbs. A badly rusted revolver lay beside it, with one cartridge expended.

At the end of November, Curt received notice of acceptance to Arizona State University, and was studying the class schedules. He promised Cheryl he'd faithfully return to Hobbs each weekend to spend time with her until she graduated and could join him at the college in Tempe. She wasn't yet sure what she'd major in, but she was determined to continue her education, and her relationship with Curt.

Karen and Peter were wed two days before Christmas. Between the church and the limousine, a police honor guard lined both sides of the walk. When Karen threw her bouquet, it was Cheryl Hanson who caught it.

And of course, Mary and Victor Lewis were nowhere to be found. But the police would have to widen their search considerably if they had any hope of finding them. They were sitting together, now only semi-conscious, in a completely dark and disabled spaceship traveling at a speed of about 150,000 miles a second. By this time, the solar system that held the planet called Earth was no longer visible, even if they had had any operable view ports out of which to see. Their ship had been flung out from the magnetic field of the larger ship, and was now hopelessly lost in the Great Black beyond the Universe of light, soaring forever in timeless infinity.

AUTHOR'S NOTE

The first time I saw "The Stack"—yes, it's real—nobody I knew seemed to know what it was. It just stood there, mute yet demanding, near Mayer, Arizona, on the road to Prescott Valley and Prescott, pointing up into the sky. Well over a hundred feet tall, it was hard to miss against the brilliant blue of our Arizona skies! After we got the Internet, I found out it was the chimney of an unfinished early 20th century smelter. The rest of it was never built. But even with the knowing, the question remained: What is it? And more importantly: What is it…really?

This chimney became the pivot point for me, some might say fixation, when I began writing The Devil's Rifle, which in reality is my first novel. For my story, I moved its location to an imaginary town just north of Prescott, which I named Hobbs, Arizona, and made it the chimney of a late 19th century lumber mill. This story grew up from that seed.

ABOUT THE AUTHOR

Keith Mueller was born in Tucson, Arizona, and is a graduate of the University of Arizona with degrees in art and art education. He served six years in the US Air Force as a firearms instructor and competitive shooter on the Air Force pistol team at Lackland AFB, and later as an instructor at the Air Force Academy. He's had an interest in metaphysical studies, shamanism, ancient cultures and religions since the late 1960s, personally practicing some of these disciplines. Though he's had an interest in writing for many years, retirement has allowed this interest to finally manifest in this book series.

www.ingramcontent.com/pod-product-compliance
Lightning Source LLC
Chambersburg PA
CBHW062131170626
46813CB00002B/659